Helena Janeczek

THE GIRL
WITH THE LEICA

*Translated from the Italian
by Ann Goldstein*

Europa
editions

Europa Editions
8 Blackstock Mews
London N4 2BT
www.europaeditions.co.uk

Copyright © 2017 by Ugo Guanda Editore S.r.l.
Via Gherardini 10, Milano
Gruppo editoriale Mauri Spagnol
First Publication 2019 by Europa Editions

*This book has been translated with generous support from the Italian Ministry of
Foreign Affairs and International Cooperation.*

*Questo libro è stato tradotto grazie a un contributo per la traduzione assegnato dal
Ministero degli Affari Esteri e della Cooperazione Internazionale italiano.*

Translation by Ann Goldstein
Original title: *La ragazza con la Leica*
Translation copyright © 2019 by Europa Editions

A catalogue record for this title is available from the British Library
ISBN 978-1-78770-185-4

Janeczek, Helena
The Girl with the Leica

Book design by Emanuele Ragnisco
www.mekkanografici.com

Cover photo © Robert Capa
© International Center of Photography/Magnum Photos

Prepress by Grafica Punto Print – Rome

Printed in Italy at Arti Grafiche La Moderna - Rome

THE GIRL
WITH THE LEICA

CONTENTS

"She was clearly . . . the pretty girl you couldn't help following,
like destiny."
—GEORG KURITZKES
Radio interview, 1987

Despite your death and scant remains,
the hair that lay golden on your head,
your smile, soft flower in the wind
and the skip in your walk,
dodging the bullets to capture
scenes of battle,
all still give us breath, Gerda.
—LUIS PÉREZ INFANTE
From "*To Gerda Taro, Killed on the Brunete Front*"

THE GIRL
WITH THE LEICA

PROLOGUE
COUPLES, PHOTOGRAPHS, COINCIDENCES #1

E ver since you saw that photograph, you've been gazing at them, spellbound. They seem happy, very happy, and they're young, which is fitting for heroes. You couldn't say good-looking, but you couldn't deny it, whereas they don't appear at all heroic. That's because they're laughing, a laugh that closes their eyes and exposes their teeth, a laugh that's not photogenic but so frank it makes them glorious.

He has horse teeth, bared to the gums. She doesn't, but her canine protrudes into the cavity where the next tooth should be, with the charm of a small, attractive imperfection. The light spreads over the white of his striped shirt, flows onto the woman's neck. Her clear skin, the diagonal of the tendons molded by her profile against the chair back, and even the curved line of the armrests amplify the joyous energy released by that unison laugh.

They could be in a square, but, sitting in those comfortable armchairs, they give the impression of being in a park, where the background blends into a thick curtain of leafy trees. You wonder, then, if the frame they have all to themselves might be the garden of a grand bourgeois villa, whose residents fled over the border when Barcelona became a hotbed of revolution. Now that cool spot under the trees belongs to the people: to those two laughing with their eyes closed.

The revolution is an ordinary day on which you go out to stop the coup that intends to suppress it, but you pause anyway to celebrate. Wearing the *mono azul* like a summer suit, putting a tie on under the overalls, wishing to appear handsome in the eyes of the other. Of no use here the mastodon of a gun, which has passed through the hands of countless soldiers before getting to the anarchist militiaman, who now can't touch the luminous neck of his woman.

Apart from that obstacle, they're free of everything at this moment. They've already won. If they keep laughing like that, if they go on being so happy, knowing how to get a shot out of that old firearm doesn't seem too urgent. Those who are in the right will win. Now they can enjoy the sun tempered by the broadleaf trees, the presence of the beloved.

The world should know. It must see in the blink of an eye that on one side is the centuries-old war, the generals disembarking from Morocco with fierce mercenary troops, on the other people who want to defend the lives they have, who want one another.

In that early August of 1936, a lot of people are arriving in

Barcelona to join the first population in Europe to take up arms against fascism. They describe the city in chaos in the universal language of images, which leap from the pages displayed on the newsstands of half the world, hung up in party and union headquarters, waved by newsboys, reused to wrap eggs and produce—images that leap in the faces even of those who don't buy or read newspapers.

The people of Barcelona welcome as brothers the foreigners who've come to fight by their side, and are getting used to that Babel of volunteers wandering all over the place, savoring the greeting *compañero, compañera*, then getting help from gestures, onomatopoetic sounds, pocket dictionaries. The photographers, who aren't waiting for weapons and training, are part of that continual flow to the volunteer militias. They're here for us, they're like us, comrades: those who see them on the job understand and let them work.

But the two militiamen in the photograph, enthralled by their own laughter, don't notice anything. Whoever is taking the picture moves, shoots again, risks giving himself away to take a closer shot of the couple united by the broad, intimate smile.

This photograph is almost identical to the first, except that here the man and woman are obviously so enraptured that they don't care about the life around them. The scissor-like steps that cut the pavement behind them, revealing that they're not in a park but maybe even on the Ramblas, where the city, mobilizing, gathers. The neighboring chair, where another woman is sitting.

Of her head you see only a tuft of curly hair, of her body only a covered arm. You'd need her gaze, the gaze of someone who has seen up close what you can deduce from the images but can't see with your eyes.

The photographer who has captured the two comrades isn't alone. There's a man and a woman, positioned on the right side of the street, one beside the other.

Then you discover the photograph of a woman sitting in the same armchairs, and you find it hard to believe that such brazen good luck can exist. Until, in the upper right, you notice a sliver of the profile of the young militiaman who in the other photographs is smiling ecstatically at his blond girl.

This worker, holding a fashion magazine in her discordant hands and a gun between her legs, doesn't really seem the type to be seized by gossipy curiosity about a couple of photographers who, after competing to capture the noisy laughter of the comrades in love, immortalize her as well. No, you say to yourself, someone like that sees and doesn't see the things that don't concern her. She remains slightly alert, because she's been given a weapon, but mostly she wants to savor that moment of peace.

But a few days later—so you imagine—that militiawoman arrives at the beach where the training takes place and finds the two photographers. He looks almost like a Gypsy, or rough and ready anyway, she could be a model out of the magazine the woman was reading on the Ramblas, but with a cumbersome camera around her neck that hangs to her hips.

Now the woman is curious: Who are those two? Where do they come from? Are they having an affair, like the many that flourish in this climate of mobilization and high summer and freedom, or are they husband and wife?

Something like that, since, allies and colleagues, they speak to each other in a harsh language. She is smiling and quick as a cat, but more poised when she instructs the comrades on how to position their weapons. They're both working hard, they're euphoric and lighthearted, and share their Gauloises as a gesture of brotherhood and thanks.

"I've seen them before," the militiawoman intervenes, when the photographers go off and an excited exchange of comments begins, but no one listens to her. The interesting news comes from the journalist comrade who brought them here. They've just arrived from Paris and nearly got killed already when the twin-engine plane made an emergency landing on the Sierra. A big shot from the French press broke his arm, but the two of them not even a scratch, thank heavens. He—his name is Robert Capa—says that Barcelona is magnificent and reminds him of his native city, Budapest, except that he can't go back as long as it's in the hands of Admiral Horthy and his reactionary regime. Gerda Taro, his companion, must be an *alemana*, a German, one of those emancipated young women who didn't submit even to Hitler.

"Can you tell us when the photos will be published?" the militiawomen press him.

The journalist promises to find out, but not from the photographers, who are about to leave for the areas where the fighting is: first they're going to the front in Aragon and then south to Andalusia.

A year after those photographs came the first eighteen deaths in Barcelona, in the buildings gutted by artillery fire from the cruiser Eugenio di Savoia. The militias were disbanded, the militiawoman returned to the factory. Maybe she sews uniforms for the Ejército Popular, where the anarchists have to obey without protest, and women are no longer welcome. But in the factories they still listen to the radio, comment on the news, keep up their courage.

Then imagine that someone reads aloud from a daily with the date of July 27, 1937. It says that Madrid resists heroically, even though the enemy, with the criminal aid of German and Italian planes, is advancing toward Brunete, where a tragic event has occurred. A woman photographer who came from far away to immortalize the struggle of the Spanish people has fallen, such a great example of valor that General Enrique Líster bowed at her coffin and the poet Rafael Alberti dedicated solemn, heartfelt words to comrade Gerda Taro.

"Isn't she the one who photographed us on the beach?" one worker exclaims, calling to the girls who have started talking of their own affairs at the factory door. Yes, it's her: in the article it also talks about the *"ilustre fotógrafo húngaro Robert Capa que recibió en París la trágica noticia"*—"the illustrious Hungarian photographer Robert Capa who received the tragic news in Paris."

The workers in the uniform factory are astonished, touched by their memories.

Sun on their shoulders, sand in their shoes, the laughter when one of them staggers on the shore, thrown off balance by the recoil of the weapon, the roar of triumph when another hits the target. And then that foreigner who—you knew immediately—

had been a *senyoreta* with soft hands, and could have stayed in Paris photographing actresses and really elegant models, and instead came to photograph them, as they learned to shoot on the beach. She admired them, too; she even seemed to envy them a little. And now she's dead, like a soldier, while they break their backs in the factory, and then have to scrounge for food, but they're still alive. It's not right. May the fascists die in hell.

Among those struck hardest by the news is the woman who was sitting with the fashion magazine on the Ramblas. The emotion that grips her at that moment—with the relighted cigarette butt blackening her fingers, the sewing machines firing behind her—is not only the emotion of someone shaken by gratitude for the sacrifice of a little thing from a cold country. An image caught distractedly a year earlier, when she looked up from her reading, has resurfaced, clearly: a dark-haired man and a blonde with a bob are photographing a blonde with a bob and a dark-haired man who are laughing happily. The blonde's head is bent over a camera that conceals her forehead.

The dark-haired man works with a camera so small it leaves his eyebrows exposed—they're thick, like the militiaman's. Then, as soon as they've finished shooting, they laugh too, exuberant and complicit. Even the eyes of a stranger like her can see that those two recognize themselves in the other two. And are just as much in love.

By a small coincidence the photographers, arriving in Barcelona, ran into a couple they resembled. Maybe it was also chance that allowed Gerda Taro to photograph a laugh at its peak, while Robert Capa may have lost a few seconds adjusting the wide-angle lens. If she'd been working with the camera he'd taught her to take pictures with—the Leica—her negatives, too, would have had the rectangular format that lets us attribute to Capa the second photo of the couple and the one of the woman with the magazine. Gerda would not have obtained the perfect centering of the square image if she hadn't bought a cheap, medium-sized reflex, a Reflex-Korelle. But after six months their joint income was sufficient so that he could get a Contax and entrust the companion of his hungry years, the Leica, to the girl who had encouraged him to leave them behind.

They had no money when they left Paris—she at the start of her adventure as a photographer, he without a contract, although the newsmagazines were starting to ask for him—but they possessed an inexhaustible faith that they would make a name for themselves.

Living in Paris with nothing but a Leica was the art of getting by, day after day. They were even convinced that they—André Friedmann and Gerda Pohorylle—would find more work under pseudonyms. They invented the story of Robert Capa, who possessed what they lacked: wealth, success, an unlimited visa with the passport of a country that was revered thanks to a power not ravaged by wars and dictatorships. Joined in a secret society whose starting capital was an alias, they were even closer in life, with more audacious dreams to pursue in the future.

Then the fairy-tale time ended. As soon as the Spanish Republic came under attack, the only skill needed was to be in the right place at the right time, to capture a reality that was supposed to stir protest, keep it alive, force the intervention of the free world.

But if a photograph also reveals the photographer, the two snapshots of a couple in whom it was so easy to see themselves can't not reflect the authors. In Taro's photo, the man and woman share the space equally, connected by the laughter released into the air, in a composition so harmonious that that overflowing energy is heightened by contrast. Capa's photo places the woman at the center, exalts her attractive physicality, but from the perspective of her radiant gaze as she leans toward her companion.

They were walking beside each other, they caught sight of the two militiamen so similar, so happy. But it wasn't the taste for a game of mirrors that drove them to photograph the same subject, hoping that one of the two would get an image to send to the newspapers. It's the promise that comes true on the faces and bodies transfigured by that happy laugh, the utopia lived in the space of a few instants that allowed that man and that woman to be free of everything. Free, yes, and united in ideals and feelings, but not equal. Robert Capa in fact caught the desire to yield to the other without restraint, Gerda Taro a shameless joy that is sent out to conquer the world.

They were different, they were complementary, on that day in August separated forever from what would happen later. They recount it themselves, involuntarily, as candid as the immortalized laugh, through those self-portraits stolen from their comrades in arms, and in love, in the brief summer of anarchy in Barcelona.

PART I
WILLY CHARDACK
Buffalo, New York, 1960

Who is this who comes and every man admires her,
who makes the air tremble with her brightness . . .
—GUIDO CAVALCANTI

Is something this beautiful supposed to be liked by only one guy?
The sun and the stars belong to everyone, after all.
I don't know who I belong to.
I guess I belong to myself alone.

"Ich weiss nicht zu wem ich gehöre" (1930)
—FRIEDRICH HOLLAENDER and ROBERT LIEBMANN
sung by MARLENE DIETRICH

D r. Chardack woke up early. He washed and dressed, carried a cup of instant coffee and the weekend New York *Times* into his study, and leafed through the political coverage, which he intends to follow more closely now that the race for the White House is getting tight. Then he puts the newspaper facedown, takes out pen and paper, and gets to work.

Outside there's not a sound apart from the sporadic cries of swallows and crows and the distant swoosh of a car looking for a gas station or heading somewhere. Later the neighbors, too, will be getting in their cars, to go to church, to visit relatives or restaurants for "Sunday's Special Breakfast," but fortunately Dr. Chardack has no such engagements.

Just after he's drafted the beginning of an article, the telephone rings. He's not surprised, and he calls out, "It'll be for me!" to the rest of the house, more out of habit than to prevent his wife from stumbling sleepily toward the phone.

"Dr. Chardack," he answers, as always, without any greeting.

"Hold on, sir, call from Italy for you."

"Willy," says a voice muffled by intercontinental telecommunications, "I didn't wake you, did I?"

"Nein: absolut nicht!"

He realizes immediately who's calling. There were still the old friends, stamped like the mark of a nasty fall from a tree in the Rosental Park, and the ones who were still alive could turn up at any time.

"Georg: did something happen? Some problem?"

At the time when he was Willy, he had been the friend you went to for practical help: money, essentially, since he always had more than the others. That's why his interlocutor is laughing now, laughing hard, as he says he doesn't need anything, but something, no doubt about it, has happened, and it's something he did, over there in America, a thing so big that it was impossible to resist the impulse to call, rather than write a letter.

"Congratulations! It's magnificent, what you've done—one might even say epoch-making."

"Thanks," he replies, almost too automatically. Dr. Chardack isn't the type for compliments; he prefers witty remarks, but not a single one comes to mind.

Once, they were champions of laughter. No, that's an exaggeration, but they were good at animating the dead-seriousness of a debate with stabs of irony, and Willy Chardack had been just as good as his companions. His present colleagues, too, appreciated his dry humor, enhanced by the German accent (the accent of the mad scientist), and he was glad not to be too cantankerous for American standards, a character.

Dr. Chardack, listening to the distant voice of Georg Kuritzkes, sees him again *en plein air* with the whole wonderful group, not necessarily outside but in the gay, luminous world of a French film, although they weren't yet in Paris. But the Rosental didn't have to fear comparison with the Bois de Boulogne, and the *passages* of Leipzig were famous. There was industry and commerce, music and publishing, all boasting centuries-old traditions, and such bourgeois solidity attracted new arrivals from the countryside and the East who made the city more and more like a true metropolis, even in its conflicts and clashes. Until the fights and the strikes turned vicious, along with the world economic crisis that was accelerating the

German catastrophe. The tense faces that Willy found at home, when his father was exasperated by the line of people looking for a job, any job, while he was already struggling to keep on errand boys and warehouse workers, because the market for leather, which had prospered in Leipzig since the Middle Ages, or thereabouts, was tottering.

He and his friends, who didn't have to struggle with insolvent clients, were inclined to fight against everything, even if they came from respectable families. They were free to do it, free to go on outings and sleep in tents under the stars, free to laugh, free to court girls, some of whom were pretty, even spectacular (Ruth Cerf, a beanpole who'd become a majestic blonde, and then Gerda, the most enchanting, lively, and amusing person he had ever encountered in the female universe). The love of joking didn't fade even when Hitler was about to win and you had to be ready to pack your bags. No one could take away that resource that made them equal, comrades, a way of being that defied the Nazis. But truly equal they were not, and Georg provided the best example of that. Georg was brilliant, but with a kind of excess, to squander, like the supply of shirts (Egyptian cotton shirts!) that had languished in the closets of the Chardack house ever since Willy had adopted the habits of the left. Georg Kuritzkes was intelligent, handsome, athletic. Loyal and trustworthy. Great capacity for assembling, instructing, organizing. Confident dancer. Passionate connoisseur of the latest musical trends from overseas. Courageous. Determined. And also witty. How could a Willy Chardack be a girl's first choice? They called him "the Dachshund," long before the nickname— adopted immediately by the slight Stuttgart accent of Gerda Pohorylle—became hateful to him. He couldn't. But the fact that Georg was also amusing nourished an affection that went beyond those youthful hierarchies, and was evidently enduring, as the thrill of hearing him again demonstrated. The effect of a laugh rediscovered after a time that seemed an eternity.

Georg has filled him in on his brother in America who's married, and has moved to a house with a view of the Rocky Mountains. In fact it was Soma who sent him a newspaper clipping: which took forever to arrive, avoiding the dead ends of the Italian postal service—a total surprise, exciting.

"I bet they'll give you the Nobel."

"Come on. We're just an engineer who does his experiments in a garage next to a house full of kids and two doctors in a veterans' hospital. In Buffalo, not at Harvard. The medical industry arrives on a reconnaissance mission, loads us with pats on the back and promises, but so far we haven't seen any money or requests to license the patent."

"I understand. But fitting a heart with a small motor that enables someone to swim, play soccer, run for a bus—it's a revolution, for heaven's sake. They'll realize it."

"Let's hope so. When you called, I thought it was the hospital or a patient we'd discharged. 'Is there a problem?'—now I say it like the telephone operators—'I'll put the call through.' But I'm pleased, of course."

"I'd like to see. In the end you'll be the only one who made a difference. I told you: you're the one who made the revolution . . . "

This time Dr. Chardack has an answer ready. He'd like to talk about the students who are trying to turn America upside down merely by sitting at a lunch counter where Negroes aren't allowed, meaning that Woolworth's and the other commercial chains have opened their lunch counters in the racist South to colored customers. He'd like to compare their solid and pacific faith, guided by a preacher baptized in the name of Martin Luther, with the faith he encountered in the son of an English carpenter who became an electronic engineer thanks to a program that sent veterans to college. "Providence dictated the crucial mistake to me, my dear Chardack—you'll see, it'll all turn out fine," Greatbatch, the engineer, repeated when the doctor hurried to the garage with yet another problem. He'd like to say to Georg that he, the godless person, is really the one who was reborn with every electrical pulse of a sick person's heart, and that the only god he's devoted to, Aesculapius, satisfied him.

"My work is enough for me," he says.

The other laughs, a conspiratorial laugh, with that thick strong timbre, but Dr. Chardack catches a crack in Georg's voice and lets him continue.

"I'd also like to devote myself to medical research—you don't get bored and you're certainly doing something useful. In my field, unfortunately, miraculous inventions are unlikely. If only we could insert a device like yours after a stroke!"

Again Dr. Chardack catches a polished pebble, a regret. But he can remedy it with a joke: "For me the heart and for you the brain! We divide the vital organs the way the superpowers do the world and now even the cosmos."

"The important thing is to have something to divide, isn't it? And now that you'll be invited to all the continents, I insist that you get in touch if you come over here."

Now that they've arrived at the polite remarks, Dr. Chardack is more cheerful. Ultimately it's no a small thing that of their shared purposes and dreams—medicine, Gerda, antifascism—they both still have the first.

The conversation concludes with Dr. Chardack and Dr. Kuritzkes exchanging addresses; the latter is thinking of leaving the FAO[1] and the UN in general, even though he's bothered by the thought that he might no longer be welcomed everywhere. "I'll wait for you then, Willy, I'll wait for the tired muscle of old Europe to greet you in triumph . . . "

---

[1] The United Nations Food and Agriculture Organization.

Standing for a few seconds in front of the phone, which is back in its cradle, Dr. Chardack still hears his friend's last laugh, so enveloping despite the implicit sarcasm. But as soon as he realizes its source—that hinting on the telephone without speaking plainly—he stiffens.

Why had Georg gone to Rome? Did he really believe that there at the FAO they would defeat hunger? He had never been naïve or a fanatic, in fact. Maybe he wouldn't have gone to Spain if that crazy girl hadn't arrived to convince him, and to say no to Gerda, just imagine. She was seriously loony, even more so than Capa, who'd practically had a stroke when he discovered that a long Italian vacation with the famous Georg wasn't enough. No, that reckless girl had brought photos of the Republican militias into the cradle of fascism! Gerda had coolly replied that they were nothing, an excuse to make a scene, and those who were present at that squabble in the welcoming din of a Paris café could only repress an admiring smile.

Georg Kuritzkes, in any case, had joined the International Brigades and then stayed on in Marseille and joined the Résistance, while Willy sailed for the United States. But before he left for the mountains he had got his degree and, after the Liberation, had done a thesis that won him a post as a researcher at UNESCO.

Dr. Chardack stays clear of politics now, but politics sticks its foot in where he is. How could he stomach the fact that the United States doesn't want scientists with the capacities of Georg Kuritzkes because of a holy terror of anything red? And yet Georg doesn't necessarily regret it. Maybe he went back to Italy because the UN sent him, but he must like it there if he hasn't changed too much.

Dr. Chardack is relieved by that conclusion, and when he goes back to his papers the mass of clouds coming off the Atlantic has already evaporated.

He's finished the first draft of the article, and the doors

slam downstairs (they're all going out, luckily), but this is not the moment of the day when he feels how far away the world he's fallen into is. It's after lunch, when he decides to make the rounds to check on patients early and then drive to the neighborhoods in the south—Polonia, Kaisertown, Little Italy—where they sell old-fashioned sweets. Maybe he should think of doing this more often, even though no one in the family expects it. But Dr. Chardack has always rejected any effort that is not directed toward a realizable goal. He likes bringing home a cake, not the abstract task of becoming a *true American*, when what he's done and is doing is enough and more. He calls himself William, pronounces his surname in the American way, served two years in Korea, the pump for transfusions he fashioned out of a grenade won him two medals. He's proud of it, of course, because he's proud of the young men he saved, just as he's proud of the many American lives that will now be saved thanks to his implantable pacemaker. So don't ask anything more of him: America is a nation to be part of, not a religion in which to be reborn. Sometimes he misses the good things they have over in Europe. *So what?*

And then, having made sure that the patients are stable, he decides to leave the car at the Veterans Hospital and walk to Hertel Avenue, where there are a number of Italian and Jewish cafés and restaurants. Besides, when the weather permits, Dr. Chardack likes to walk, a habit that is not at all American. The fact remains that the streets he walks along—nearly the sole pedestrian, the only one in jacket and tie (but a light jacket, put on over the short-sleeve cotton-polyester shirt), on a Sunday afternoon in late summer—are the streets of North Buffalo: laid out with a ruler, marked by saplings that justify the name Avenue, lined with wooden houses, freshly painted or slightly peeling (a few), red, yellow, greenish, blue, cream, icy white, some adorned with an American flag, smaller houses and larger, houses with a generous patch of lawn (and no fence!) in front, surprisingly able to stand up to snow and hold the heat (coolness less), as he has discovered over the years.

The only annoyance is that someone might want to give him a lift. "Thanks, no!" was his customary response, since he lacked convincing explanations, until he had the flash of inspiration to explain his eccentric "just walking" as a way of preventing a heart attack. "Oh really, doctor!" the neighbors responded as they clutched the car keys, a little intimidated. But on the street now are only a couple of girls exchanging secrets, and some squirrels looking out at the sidewalk with the impudence that distinguishes them from their poor, fearful relatives in Europe.

Walking in a space that ignores you while you know it well enough sets thoughts in motion or crushes them at every step. It wasn't in Leipzig that Dr. Chardack got used to long city walks but following the boulevards of the Fifteenth, Seventh, and Sixth Arrondissements, often crossing over the border into the rich or working-class neighborhoods of the Right Bank. The metro didn't cost much, but it was the first expense avoided by Ruth and Gerda, who couldn't count on help from their families. Money thrown away, they claimed, and after all walking helped you keep your figure. The Dachshund sneered that it was the least of their problems. The girls let him buy them a coffee, but metro tickets only in extraordinary situations. What was the fun of traveling underground, packed in as if in a cage, when they were in Paris? At the word "cage" Willy gave up objecting that it was about to rain. Gerda had been in prison, she had gotten out by a miracle, and even her flight from Germany had occurred under a lucky star. "Where do you have to go?" he asked her. "Do you know how to get there?" "Thanks, Dachshund, I can manage, but if you've got nothing else to do maybe you'll come with me a little way." Maybe he had something else to do (take refuge in the library and come out at closing time), but instead he dragged his medical books well beyond the Pont Saint-Michel and back, the mark of the briefcase handle incised into his fingers.

She was tireless: after a month she seemed to have been born Parisian. There was the day when she could go and collect the money she'd earned from her small jobs, but she had to trek all the way to the Opéra and, on the way back, buy some croissants and a basket of strawberries for Ruth, who must have gone to the room by now. "She'll faint if I don't bring her some sugar, not even twenty-one and so tall." Or she had to pop over to the post office in Montparnasse to send a letter to Georg—in fact a mailbox and a tobacconist, for the stamps, would be enough, and then, since they were there, couldn't he buy her some cigarettes? Sometimes when she had already licked the stamps for Italy and he was still waiting for the change, she concluded that if dachshunds with rough coats didn't exist you'd have to invent them . . .

Then she had applied herself to getting her *baccalauréat* by studying privately. Georg had been generous with encouragement to Gerda and exhortations to Willy to help her with the scientific subjects she'd never studied. Almost as a challenge, she preferred to summon him to the École Normale Supérieure, which was more beautiful and tranquil than the Sorbonne, where the Dachshund was enrolled. When they were thrown out, they retreated to a bench in the Jardin du Luxembourg, where she pulled out of her bag the periodic table of the elements and the formulary of simple physics, the two of them supporting the dangerously worn pages along the lines of the folds. They remained in that chemical and physical intimacy made of paper until Gerda got impatient or cold. How many minutes of contact would the Dachshund's flannelled thigh be allowed, how much of a view of silk stockings emerging from under the formulas, of her small feet beating the rhythm of the repetitions?

In the morning, opening the blinds, Willy examined the clouds above the hotel courtyard. When they were dark enough to indicate that she would skip the lesson in the park, he darkened. A day that was cloudy and not too cold was fine for him, but his meteorology could never manage to guess how long before Gerda got up from the bench. Suddenly she'd stand, walk along the straight green wall of trees, enormous compared to her. She walked with a light but slightly agitated step, or maybe it was the effect of the gravel crunching under her heels, stab after stab. The Dachshund stayed behind to correct her, holding the sheet of paper. Gerda stopped and turned, she wanted to find the formula, the sequence of elements, before he reached her. "Should I slow down?" Willy wondered, unsure whether it was to give her time or to maintain that intent gaze. Doubt itself probably slowed him, since Gerda almost always managed to hurl the answer at him, which rewarded the Dachshund with a fleeting triumphant smile. But sometimes, seeing the classes just coming out of the Lycée Montaigne, Gerda kept going straight, as if their efforts to learn were mocked by the little jackets and smoothed hair that made all those childish faces, revived by the end of the school day, look the same. Her acceleration toward the entrance on Rue Auguste Comte, with the students of the ancient Paris lycée pouring through, communicated, That's enough, let's forget it. Willy lengthened his stride, preparing to tell her abruptly that those kids were not a valid reason to get annoyed and leave him there. Strangely, Gerda stopped running, too, as if she'd suddenly realized it, but Willy, following her, heard a soprano voice, getting louder and louder. "*Lutetium, Hafnium, Tantalum, Tungsten, Rhenium, Osmium, Iridium, Platinum, Goold . . .* " Gerda declaimed, as if it were a surrealist poem. The students squeezed together to let her pass, barely deigning to make faces at her. But in the eyes of some of the boys shone a light that Willy Chardack knew well.

*

Dr. Chardack will forever remember Block D of the periodic table in that imitation, theatrical French, a section that, coincidentally, includes mercury, which is what the battery of his pacemaker is made of. In reality, the mercury battery doesn't work well, and he and Greatbatch will have to solve the problem—a task the doctor can't wait to tackle. But Dr. Chardack doesn't get intimidated by challenges. Greatbatch has never asked him where he got his cold blood and fearless faith in inventions: maybe because he considers it part of the design of Providence that he found right in Buffalo a heart surgeon so capable, and willing to work into the wee hours in his garage. On those nights it was natural to talk about his past in the old world, while Dr. Chardack has had enough of cafeteria lunches and dinner parties where some colleague or complete stranger tends to ask the same eternal questions:

"So you went to university here or back in Germany?"

"Well, in Europe, but not in Germany. In Paris."

"Oh . . . in Paris!"

"Not even *in Paris* does the morgue smell of Chanel No. 5," he had once frozen a table, before the host laughed as if it were a joke among colleagues, *not bad*, but inappropriate in front of the ladies, who considered Paris *so romantic*. Thus, as soon as the ladies retreated to the kitchen, the host returned to the subject. "We had some good times, right, Bill? Nothing more democratic, after death, than the job of the doctor, and I see that they teach us in the same unpleasant way everywhere . . . All right, can I pour you another drop?"

"Cheers," Dr. Chardack answered, bringing the reply to his lips as well.

The problem, in fact, had been the living. There were certain professors with a determination to fail those who stumbled in the exams, not on the facts but on a word or a correct declension.

"It's an invasion!" the placards on the streets declared, and in the classrooms groups of students coalesced who had arrived in Paris from every place where spreading fascism and nationalism had gained the upper hand: here the Italians, up there the Hungarians and Poles, then, in smaller groups, the Romanians and the Portuguese. They were everywhere, the *judéo-boches*—the last straw—because now there really were a lot of them, feared for that reason, and because they were often among the smartest.

Learning everything by heart, rattling off, word for word, five-hundred-page textbooks. Straining their eyes until late at night in the faint light of lamps stripped of their pale-flowered shades (well, yes, in intention very romantic), trembling with weariness and the damp cold, the acidity of too many *cafés crèmes* drunk during the day so as not to collapse on the mattress of the hotel room.

"Soon a Frenchman won't be able to be treated by a French doctor," commented the students generally associated with Catholic groups but more devoted to besieged France than to Jesus Christ. They uttered the phrase like a station announcement, snorted at a classmate, furtively insolent.

You had to be the best to be sure of passing the exams. You had to respect every deadline. Hurry. Hope that the far-right leagues wouldn't repeat the terrible events of February 6, 1934, with greater success ("They can make champagne, but they still can't make a coup" had been the contemptuous, exorcising summary of a fellow-student from Berlin), that the government wouldn't yield too much to the more reactionary pressures, that the left would win the next elections. Otherwise, you could also expect, among the other restrictions, an entrance quota to restore French universities to the French, and then what else would they come up with to make life impossible for the immigrants?

Two years of uncertainty. But after the victory of the Front Populaire, celebrated until dawn on that 4th of May, 1936, the nationalist or simply anti-Semitic teachers had become even worse bastards, convinced that only their exemplary efforts could protect France: stop the invaders in the course of their studies, reject them one by one, exam after exam.

But the advantage of the mother tongue and every privilege of birth were eliminated as soon as they entered *la morgue*: not the one of defunct Grand Guignol fame but a morgue with stagnant, damp air as cold as death. There they all took on the complexion of the corpses: both the scion destined for Papa's office and the middle-class kid whose relatives had invested in him their own savings and anxieties for promotion, and including a few from the provinces who prided themselves on having broken the necks of chickens. It was basically a question of numerical probability: the macabre-scientific rite revealed nothing about the future qualities of a doctor, as Willy himself said to his classmates to encourage them.

And yet it had been a moment of validation and revenge. A moment when no teacher could deny the evidence laid out on the autopsy table. Objectively good at it. Good at it period. For Willy and his friends from Leipzig it was all they had to rely on: so as not to keep waiting for a destiny they rejected to loosen its grip. Recognizing it would have meant surrendering the palace to the fascists who had driven them out, confirming the lies about the "destiny of people and races," the phony legends of those who believed they were heirs of divinities extinct for millennia. Destiny was a false myth, a trick, a reactionary pretext. But in Paris, too, they had to take that destiny into their own hands, with everything they could display. Willy hadn't hesitated to grasp the scalpel. And the only one of them who had arrived in Paris with a trade in hand had kept herself afloat with the typewriter. Until her fingers, now slightly callused at the tips (but maybe Gerda exaggerated), embraced the compact body of a camera.

"Our Gerda plays the Remington the way Horowitz plays a
Steinway" was a remark originating in the cafés that served as
sitting rooms for those who lived in meager spaces or a dormitory bed. At the same time they were the exchange, the always
volatile black market for those who sought work or were offering it. Gerda had the advantage of an excellent knowledge of
French, acquired in a finishing school on Lake Lausanne, but
this also gave her the allure of an upper-class girl who had
never lifted a finger. In other words, she got her first jobs not
because the employers expected that she was a good typist but
out of sheer charm. So the surprise was that much greater
when she delivered, rapidly, impeccable work, and, just as rapidly, her *renommée* grew. Anyone who had given "our Gerda"
a letter to type *vite-vite* could have been the source of the
remark about the Steinway. But no, Dr. Chardack reflects, not
noticing a bicycle cutting across his path, the phrase went back
to Fred and Lilo Stein, who had welcomed Gerda and the
Remington into their apartment and had seen her at work for
that whole period.

Willy wasn't convinced that staying at the Steins' was the
best arrangement for "our Gerda." "How's it going up there in
your Montmartre exile?" he would ask her every so often.
"Well, very well," she answered, praising her new room, shared
with Lotte, a journalist friend who was the perfect roommate,
since she was also constantly chasing after jobs. And she never
failed to lavish praise on her magnificent landlords. Which the
Steins in reality were not, with that sublet which circumvented
the contract signed by a French photographer who had left
them in the lurch. But the tenants who had agreed to it delivered the rent with a punctuality unthinkable for Gerda and
Lotte. If, however, the place wasn't silent by a certain hour,
they threatened not to pay a cent. Unfortunately, if the girls
wanted to honor their delivery deadlines, they had no alter-
native: when Lotte's cacophonous hammering was over, her

journalistic stop and start, Gerda began her accelerated march, the inexorable ringing and rolling of the new line that reverberated behind the closed door. Thus, having appeased the tenants with a nightcap ("*un petit cognac c'est mieux pour dormir d'une tisane . . .* ") and the proper excuses (Fred wanted to offer a discount, but Lilo stopped him immediately), the Steins had placed the Remington as far as possible from the bedrooms, on the dining table, where only they, the land-lords, absorbed the full impact of the background of typing. They said they were used to it, they said that Gerda's rhythms evoked the unrestrained drumming of Gene Krupa in Benny Goodman's swing band, and even the vigorous revolutionary art of Shostakovich and Khachaturian. "Our Gerda plays the Remington like a Steinway," they concluded, and she laughed, perfectly in tune with the praise for her solo.

Willy had somewhat lost sight of her in that period, even though Gerda always welcomed him warmly when he appeared in Montmartre with a good bottle. The Steins, charming and friendly, invited him more often, but there hadn't been a chance to deepen the friendship.

Years later, though, he had seen Fred and Lilo again, on that fateful day, May 6, 1941, printed on the ticket for the ship that, sailing from Marseille, was taking them to the United States. Willy had arrived at the ship as tense as the ropes that tied his life to a wharf in Occupied France. He kept an eye on everything but had basically looked only at the gangplank, the moorings cast off, and, finally, the disappearance of the coastline. Fred had recognized him, as they were about to go below deck. "How nice to see you again," they greeted each other, with the incredulity, the relief, the lump in the throat contained in that polite remark. During the journey they had become intimate; the Steins wanted to talk and Willy was happy to listen to them. They were planning their new lives in America, but they talked easily about Gerda, about the good times with Gerda, which was natural. It was the medium of their friendship and, all in all, a subject immune to the worries that had to be left behind at least for that month on the open sea. Yes, the knowledge that she was dead and buried in Paris allowed him not to wonder where she was and what could still happen to her . . .

Dr. Chardack looks around and realizes how monstrous that thought seems in the quiet, deep-green frame of a suburb where the biggest worry is the raccoons that root around in the garbage at night. It seems that, more than once, a woman has found herself face to face with the intruder that climbed into the garbage can, looked at her with annoyance, and only then decided to flee. Things that a person born in Europe has trouble believing, things that are still worth a paragraph in the Buffalo *News*, and Gerda certainly would have been wild about it, despite wondering how one could live in a place where there was no one more exciting to meet than, as they would say, a *Waschbär*, a raccoon.

In any case, Gerda had been crucial for enduring the Atlantic crossing. Fred and Lilo's memories had led him to discover some things he hadn't known. For example, that Fred was so enchanted by Gerda's typing skill that he had photographed her at work: fingers soft on the keyboard, face changing from smile to grimace, to resolution, concentration, challenge, puffs of smoke suggesting an established dialogue between the two machines, typewriter and camera.

At the time of the Montmartre exile, Willy was convinced that Gerda's interest in photography was only a slight fever, the curiosity that went with a new source of entertainment. She needed amusement as she needed air, that was true, and André Friedmann, who had been hanging around her for a while, made her laugh, undoubtedly. There was no other reason to spend time with him. What ambitions or possibilities could that amiable windbag from Budapest have, with his disheveled hair and ridiculous French, a fellow who was attempting, like hundreds of others, to get some of his photos published in the newspapers? He tried to be bold, to pass off his wretched condition as a choice of style, but Gerda wasn't receptive to that message, and after a while the young man, who wasn't stupid, had stopped going after her, satisfied to stay in the friendly and mainly comic role that she assigned him. Photography and the photographer remained a pastime, a hook for widening her circle of acquaintances (for example, Cartier-Bresson, with that elegant manner that betrayed his family's wealth), until Gerda moved to the Steins'.

To Dr. Chardack it still seems inconceivable that Friedmann, that is to say Capa, could become a name known even to an Italian-American girl from New Jersey. ("Robert Capa? You never told me!" his wife had exclaimed, seeing him go pale at the wheel when the radio announced that Capa had died in Indochina.) He would have bet, rather, on Fred Stein, who in Paris had become respected and in New York hadn't done badly, but Capa's stunning success was something else.

Stein was from Dresden, had taken his degree in Leipzig, and in Paris was valued for his anti-fascist activity and as a photographer. He had managed to progress on his own, to gain the esteem of colleagues, even to run a studio in Montmartre. And Gerda admired this, admired the transformation of a jurist deprived of the right to practice, first by Hitler and then by France, which the stink of reagents in the bathroom used as a darkroom reasserted every day. On the other hand, if noble France hadn't provided for a separate toilet even in the apartments of a so-so building, the needs of the tenants and the requirements of the laboratory would have had a hard time living together. Anyway, the tub was full of prints hanging to dry on the clothes rack, something that, according to Willy, his friend couldn't have been happy about.

One day when Gerda was still living in the hotel with Ruth Cerf, she had asked him urgently for help. The situation was ridiculous and also a little indelicate, and its subject was bedbugs. After discovering the true origin of a rash taken for an allergic reaction, the girls had done everything possible to disinfect their room, beginning with the parasitic colony's fortress, the ghastly mattress. The problem seemed to be resolved. But, damn it, now they needed a hot bath, an immersion from which they'd emerge with red faces and the wrinkled fingers of newborns, cleansed of the disgusting film that seemed to remain stuck to their skin, even if they washed twice a day in the rusty sink. They didn't have money for hot water, and, besides, the bathroom was even more revolting than the entire hotel. Willy barely had time to give them a bewildered glance when Gerda launched into the proposal.

"You invent something to distract your concierge and we go up. Afterward it will be easy, we'll be careful, we'll leave one at a time. You don't have to do anything else, just the key to the bathroom, now, don't forget it."

It occurred to Willy to send them to the public baths, but the only one nearby, the Bains d'Odessa, had a terrible reputation. So he surrendered to the risk that the concierge or the maids would discover that he brought girls to his room (and two at once!), but everything had gone according to Gerda's plan. That night, though, his heart was still pounding, he was sweating, and to resolve the excitement he ended up using the most humiliating and mechanical method. The knowledge that they were naked, there across the hall, a few steps away. Then the blow (the blow to his heart) that he wasn't prepared for: Gerda returned, not to pick up her bag but to get a jar of Nivea out of it. And after telling him "If you want you can turn around" (he had immediately faced the wardrobe) she had taken off her clothes and rubbed in the lotion. "Unfortunately you have to wait until it's absorbed!" "That's all right, I'll wait!" he had replied. "O.K., but I'm sorry to have to punish you for too long . . . "

In fact when she communicated that she was ready, Gerda still had to rub the lotion on her legs, wait more minutes, put her stockings back on, pull down her skirt. Turning around, at that point, was comical. All that remained to him was the hope that he hadn't blushed already before Gerda gave him a little kiss and, with the door closing, whispered, *"Danke, Dackel,"* and immediately slipped away.

It was partly that episode that had made him bet against the overregulated life in Montmartre: and the Steins' bathroom, so often unusable, had appeared to him an emblem of that restricted freedom.

Yet Gerda, the Steins recalled, had immediately been enthusiastic about the new use. She had asked if her friend Friedmann could develop there sometimes and, most important, she had volunteered to help, so imploring that they couldn't say no. Yes, our Gerda saw a great possibility emerging along with the strips of negatives and had taken to following Fred at every free moment of the day. "I'll steal your job, can I?" She learned to do developing, retouching, and enlargements with speed and focused joy; her teacher barely had time to assign her a new task when she was already talking about projects. She assaulted everyone she met with her progress in photography, she spoke of almost nothing else. She didn't really know how to get practice, because the Steins' Leica was available only when they were home, while André's, for goodness' sake, very often ended up at the pawnbroker's. That crazy Hungarian had holes in his pockets, plus the courage to tell her that she was overdoing it with that so typically German fixation on saving. "Me, Willy, you know?" Anyway, she was now working on mastering the technical and theoretical part, and then her teachers claimed that the eye could also be trained by shooting without a camera. "Sure, but it's as if a beginner in surgery, you, for example, always had to be satisfied with cutting the air! Does it seem possible?" "No, you're right," Willy had said, but he was no longer certain about many things. Was Gerda giving up the idea of getting her degree in order to attempt a career as a photographer? Didn't she see how much competition there was, how much easier it was to support oneself with the typewriter? One day he had asked her and she had cut him off: "You think I don't know it?" She was content that she could get by with her typing work, and she even referred to herself as a *Tippmammsel* ("*chez nous, c'est une mademoiselle qui batte sur la machine,*" she explained to the French), but she felt alienated, she was bored. And above all she couldn't bear having to work off the books, at the mercy of anyone who could present exploitation as a favor and take away the work at any moment.

And while she continued to prove to him the perfect reasonableness of her dreams ("It's not something you do overnight") Willy had remembered a detail of their lessons at the École Normale, which, though already conspicuous as they sat on the bench in the Jardin du Luxembourg, at the time he had paid little attention to. Occasionally, in the neighborhood of the École Normale, or in the corridors, on the stairs, in the sheltered cloister where they stopped to smoke a last cigarette before entering some classroom, they encountered a man with the cross-eyed gait of professors of a certain age, cap pulled down over his lowered head, well-fed stomach swelling the middle buttons of the raincoat. René Spitz, who as a student of Sigmund Freud had been summoned to occupy the chair of psychoanalysis, needed a personal secretary and that secretary had been Gerda. Thus, every time she caught sight of him, she waited until he was close and squealed "*Guten Tag, Herr*

Professor!" as if seeing him made her the happiest person in the world. The professor didn't reciprocate, or responded by mumbling in the Viennese style; in any case he kept going straight, the instinct for flight prevailing over the imperative to preserve decorum before the student body. The reaction provoked in Gerda a radiant sneer, like a young tough. "Did you see? You greet him *à la boche* . . . and *pfff!*" He was only a petit-bourgeois hypocrite who, unfortunately, could find plenty of little Jewish girls willing to slave under his conditions. But she would not remain what she was now, and you didn't have to be a disciple of Freud to be sure of it . . .

Who knows what Gerda would have said seeing him walking through the peaceful emptiness around those small bright-colored houses, his sweaty face no doubt slightly red, his stomach more pronounced, but otherwise so little changed? And she, who was certain she'd see him with a chair at the Sorbonne or in an important American university, how would she have greeted the result of those expectations? After all, she hadn't been so wrong, after all, he had become something more than an ordinary *Herr Professor*, but in a place so ordinary, a place they both would have had to look for on the map. But what would Gerda have become if she hadn't met André Friedmann in a dull period, if he hadn't introduced her to a photographic agency, and, above all, if in France hiring a foreigner hadn't been forbidden by law? Wouldn't she have quickly found a job worthy of her talents and her beautiful presence? And wouldn't she have continued to use the Dachshund's lessons to finally enroll in a faculty where girls in general were rare birds and girls like her a subspecies before whom the doors of science opened wide to a suitable mind, an unsuspected persistence, and maybe even some charm? No, not necessarily . . . Maybe she would have been happier if she'd met not necessarily a Rothschild but a facsimile of her old boyfriend in Stuttgart: a man of liberal views and generous hands when it came to his wallet . . .

Getting lost in these conjectures while he walks in the sun is turning out to be a very useful pastime. Dr. Chardack is accustomed to summing up conclusions of an experiment, even one that's mental and involuntary. On the other hand, he had already thought at the time that, with a variable in the initial configuration, a small intervention of chance, Gerda Pohorylle could have been anything, in a city like Paris.

In the letters that Gerda always shared with Willy—maybe because she felt a little lost in the early days, maybe to keep their affections joined, and in the order she had established in Leipzig—Georg wrote that in Italy life wasn't such an obstacle course. He had repeated it on a mound of snow when they met him in Turin to go skiing in a well-equipped resort in the Alps. They had stopped at the top of the piste: below they could see neither the start of the cable cars nor the two giant silos, the new hotels that the owner of Fiat had had built with the solemn support of the Father of the Country. Georg had proposed a break and had taken advantage of it to speak. "Let it be clear," he had said, "there are no excuses for those who have imprisoned, beaten, sent into confinement or exile our Italian comrades, setting an example for even more criminally minded pupils." And yet in Italy you could be born a Jew and become a minister, member of the hierarchy, big shot, court artist esteemed by the gang leaders, even—looking at Gerda—chief concubine of the chief whoremaster: not an enviable role, given that male lust was acclaimed there as an important endowment of leadership. She hadn't commented, but had shaken out her short hair crushed under the beret, without pushing back the locks that had escaped onto her forehead. Maybe that instinctive gesture had nothing to do with it. Anyway Gerda, her face turned to the sun, her cheeks red, the foulard that peeked out under her scarf matching her green eyes half-closed in feline bliss, had still less to do with it. And so Georg had turned to the Dachshund: "You know that a large number of our fathers' clients are Fascists, even people with the surname Cohen, and not just so as to maintain good relations with the blackshirts. The furriers are Fascists but so are the small shopkeepers. Dazed by the military pomp, intoxicated by the Roman trinkets that make them feel Italian to the marrow." Then there were those whom Georg met on the wards: the ones who'd grown up in houses full of books dusted by the maidservant ("That's what they say around here," he clarified, disgusted) were thrilled to become clowns dressed as warriors. "Their fervor is at its peak now that the imperialist war is approaching!"

Willy would have liked just to enjoy the day on skis and not enter into those subjects. "In France they say that Mussolini's exaggerated warmongering is meant to intimidate the other nations," he had tried to get by, eyeing the fresh slalom tracks on the descent, "and solidify his popularity at home."

Georg had shaken his head, curt.

"We know perfectly well what our Führer is, but we shouldn't delude ourselves that this one is all bark and no bite. On the other hand the Fascists don't have much liking for Hitler, and for now we can take advantage of it. Stay in Paris, wear ourselves out in the war of the poor among all the émigrés, what's the point? We shouldn't give up fighting, but we don't need to cultivate moral scruples, either, because we choose to live where, for now, almost everything is simple and within reach of our pockets."

"Who are you making these speeches to, the mountains?" Gerda had retorted with a little laugh.

Georg had taken the square of chocolate that she held out to him, conciliatory, leaning forward on the skis planted slantwise in the fresh snow, and had bitten into his portion as if making a show of savoring the bittersweet.

Willy had hesitated to do likewise, embarrassed. There was no doubt that that bite signified a rejection that he could only be glad of, but it was equally clear that his friend, yet again, had unfolded his dialectic weapons to attract Gerda: bring her close, know that she was at his side. Political meetings as love meetings. It had been happening since she joined their group. Willy wasn't cut out for either one; even if later life had demonstrated that he could handle some basic compliments ("That blue shirt suits you, that hairstyle, that relaxed look"), and even articulate an "I'm glad to see you," a token and, more often, surrogate for an "I love you." But they were other women, the ones he had courted, women looking for serious intentions. Using that language with Gerda, you risked a flash of sarcasm or getting your hair mussed, physically or figuratively.

"*Ach*, Willy."

Georg Kuritzkes had a whole other repertoire: conspiratorial remarks, compliments disguised as teasing, grand discourses in which he cited Lenin, Marx, and Rosa Luxemburg, and inserted lines of Heine from memory. The moment Gerda arrived in Leipzig, he had launched into the competition with the boyfriend from Stuttgart without revealing himself by a single word, and yet courting her with all of them. Was that why, in the end, she had decided in favor of the medical student who couldn't offer her the chic things she'd become accustomed to, thanks to her dear Pieter, an importer of colonial goods and descendant of a Hanseatic mercantile dynasty? Probably not. Georg, however, lived nearby. His passionate courting mixed with his political passion—that, yes, Gerda succeeded in taking seriously. She wanted to adjust quickly to Leipzig and the new times. She had only to embrace the good fortune of having found her instructor: to ring the bell in

Friedrich-Karl-Strasse when she wanted, because she'd forgotten a book or a pair of gloves, scattering hairpins in Georg's attic, where no one batted an eye if the last to remain was a girl.

Then Georg Kuritzkes had enrolled in Berlin and Gerda went to see him often. She would return to Leipzig on Monday glowing—eyes, skin on her face, her movements softened, while to the Dachshund she sang the praises of her exciting days in Berlin. A woman gets like that when she can stay freely with a man, Willy concluded, stunned. Like a queen in her capital, everything belongs to her, and she passes through it, regal and benevolent. The walks in the Tiergarten when Georg was at the university, the American jazz orchestras, the monumental rationality of the new filmmakers, and the moving rigor of the bricks with which the great architect Mies van der Rohe, already admired for the Weissenhofsiedlung in Stuttgart, had erected a jagged wall in memory of Karl Liebknecht and Rosa Luxemburg. "Were you supposed to take me to the cemetery?" she had asked him, but she bought a rose from a poor fellow, placing it on the ones that had already withered, which was the right thing to do. Then, in the physical absence of Georg, that intense luminosity faded, the electricity ran out. But Leipzig still suited Gerda very well, here and now.

The air of North Buffalo, on that sunny Sunday, has a wonderful smell of cut grass, with streaks of gasoline, which Dr. Chardack inhales with the second or third cigarette after lunch. The taste like proof of the luxury of not having anything else to do. Around the houses now there's a lot of activity, people busy painting, hammering, repairing the gutter. They seem to be having fun (the children certainly), and he can only admire this simple way of renewing the frontier spirit, extracting it from the toolbox. In his case, it was years before he made up his mind to settle permanently, odysseys by car with the airport closed for bad weather (up there winter could fall suddenly), long searches to find the right house. And yet he's comfortable there, he's stopped missing New York.

How long since he's heard from the Steins? The last time, Fred mentioned health problems, worse, but not enough to keep him from important appointments: a session with Dietrich, charismatic despite her age; a snapshot of Khrushchev, fantastic; of Willy Brandt, who was still a friend and still had the same expression; of Senator Kennedy, who didn't excite him, neither the man nor the portrait he'd made, but he hoped he'd be elected. There was even a trip to Germany coming up, quick and painless, the plane ticket already booked . . .

"I'm glad for you that you have a desire to return," Dr. Chardack had muttered.

Inevitably, during the Atlantic crossing the Steins wanted to satisfy some of their curiosity about Gerda. Lilo asked when he had met her, and Willy answered that it was late summer of '29, when Herr Pohorylle had received an offer to start a business in Leipzig and had moved the family from Stuttgart.

He was on the tram, on the way home, and at a stop he had noticed a woman in front of a milliner's window. She was wearing lace stockings and shoes of a slightly darker color, an ivory-colored dress that ended in soft pleats above the knee; between the line of the ears and the shoulders, her brown hair left exposed an area of almost amber skin. Willy had hoped that the tram wouldn't start up before he could see the face of that woman, who had an unreal, cinematic elegance. But she had set off at a pace that seemed to mock him. She escaped him, turning her straight back, the hollow of her half-naked knees. When the tram resumed its course that had become pursuit, Willy believed he could see the profile of Elisabeth Bergner, she so much resembled his favorite actress. But on a parallel track he had realized that the diva-like woman was young, much younger than he had imagined.

A girl, whom he might meet, in fact he would want to meet at all costs.

He met her a few weeks later. She was already quite intimate with many in their circle, with Ruth Cerf and, especially, Georg Kuritzkes. The Dachshund thought that none of them would have any chance with her, because they were too young, and Georg, in particular, too devoted to the dispossession of the bourgeoisie for the tastes and demands of the elegant Miss Pohorylle. But, as on many other occasions, he was wrong.

Dr. Chardack wouldn't have remembered that woman seen from the tram for the rest of his life if that woman hadn't been Gerda. And if he hadn't perceived, maybe not at sixteen but at eighteen, that her allure and the frustrating capacity to escape him, and not only him, were related. No longer. The memory of Gerda now is only a time-wasting indulgence, a memory like the others. As he continues to walk straight down Hertel Avenue, with his jacket over his arm, because there's not the shade that even the slenderest trees manage to cast on the asphalt, he turns, at the same time, onto a lateral thought: for example, who gave Georg his telephone number. Not the brother in Colorado, whom he was no longer in touch with. His mother, maybe, but who could have given it to her? Ruth? Had Kuritzkes's mother and her second husband, Dr. Gelbke, helped the widow Cerf during the years of Nazism? It could be, and Ruth would be the type to remember it. But now she led a bourgeois life (married with children: how many?) in Switzerland. Did she, in any case, make phone calls to Dina Gelbke out of politeness? To talk about what? Health, old times in Leipzig and Zurich, children and grandchildren and former habitués of Friedrich-Karl-Strasse, but proceeding cautiously, and preferring the dead, starting with the adored Gerda, as opposed to all those who had scattered, not just by chance, to the four corners of the Western hemisphere . . . Who knows. Has the name of the street changed, are the Gelbkes still at the same address, Dr. Chardack wonders, his head beaded with sweat amid the thinning hair. Anyway, he's convinced that Georg got his number from Ruth Cerf. It was much easier to preserve old friendships in Europe.

Why had he never considered Ruth? Only because she was too tall and had a beauty that inspired awe? She had gotten along in Paris as a model until her type was considered unfashionable and too Germanic, a joke of the times. In Leipzig, though, they were still high-school students, and a girl like Ruth certainly didn't go unnoticed. But a twenty-year-old like Gerda was a sensational novelty, and then she was so sophisticated, so *glamorous*: inevitable that the boys had started buzzing around her, a little less so that he had remained more enmeshed than the others. Didn't they call him the Dachshund partly because, height apart, he always aimed at achievable goals?

But Gerda didn't dispense her favors only on the basis of appearance, and she had never been simply a girl to long for through a window. She was a thing much too serious for those who loved her, to judge from the reactions to the wild epics of André Friedmann when her companion was in Paris and Gerda in the middle of the Republican Army with her Leica. The by now slightly famous Robert Capa appeared on the boulevards of the Rive Gauche, all exuberance, all sexual ease, arm around the waist of the girl he had picked up for the evening. How long would Gerda have lasted with someone like that, a man who went to collect their fee and spent it on drinking and bimbos? Willy wondered in dismay. But then he'd run into him in the late morning, the aftereffects of carousing summed up in an exhausted smile. With a pleading expression, Capa invited the Dachshund to the café to talk about departures and plans. He swallowed cup after cup and continued to use the first person plural. He referred to Gerda as a poor *melamed* to the Only and Supreme, even if he kept naming her, Willy reflected ironically, with a thought to the Galician teacher who had prepared him for his bar mitzvah. It wasn't a valid excuse for his consolations of the preceding night, but one point needed to be recognized: Capa wasn't the only one to get overpowered by every kind of intoxication when Gerda came into it. Detoxifying one's system of a spring so fresh was almost impossible.

Willy had tried it with apparently good results, but at times he discovered he had lapsed. The most humiliating occasions were those further back in time, when Georg Kuritzkes had officially been chosen. The old boyfriend from Stuttgart had withdrawn with the class of those who are used to losing in the grand style, as after the crash of '29. Remaining "good friends," as she claimed, didn't seem natural to Willy, in fact had the odor of a tactical retreat: the boyfriend was waiting for the rival's resources to be slowly consumed, but that didn't happen.

Besides, it was clear that Gerda was very much in love with Georg and his world. And it was precisely the irrefutable reality that exposed the realistic Dachshund to the repercussions.

For example, he happened to observe her in the smoky living room of Friedrich-Karl-Strasse one night when Dina Gelbke, Georg's mother, brought up some episodes of her past, a Bolshevik adventure story. Gerda didn't miss a detail. Dina recounted how, very young and very ignorant, she had been roused by the furious winds of 1905, which kindled even proletarian Łodź, and had run away from home to escape the repression and join the comrades in Moscow. She told of prisons, false identities, final flight from the tsarist police, and then of the most memorable undertaking since she had lived in Leipzig: the escape from a clinic in Merano, where her first pregnancy was being monitored, to pay a visit to the man to whom she owed the direction of her life, Lenin. "I was well and no one could keep me from setting off: not my husband and certainly not the doctors."

Who had provided the opportunity to repeat the story on that occasion that had left such an impression? No, it hadn't been Bertold Brecht or Kurt Tucholsky but some minor celebrity who, passing through the city, came to the house. But while Dina told the story she looked at the young people, and with a certain satisfaction emphasized that, very soon after her arrival in Zurich, Georg, too, had displayed a revolutionary impatience and then an uncontainable rage—not toward the Swiss banks but toward the obstetrician and the doctor, or rather the entire surrounding world.

"You'd be better off knowing how to produce that rage again, since you're a little too fond of getting lost in speeches," she concluded, resting her gaze on the youths sitting on the carpet at her feet. Gerda hadn't turned to Georg with a tender or even a radiant smile. She had laughed in his face, open-mouthed, her head thrown back and moving side to side to resume eye contact with Dina and her fleshy lips, and Georg had withdrawn the hand resting on Gerda's knee, which vibrated with the fullness of that laugh.

Willy suffered. He was jealous of the proprietary careless-ness with which Georg touched her, and even more of the casual way in which he let go. He was envious of such innate assurance (what could you expect from someone who had had Lenin as a godfather?), and it incensed him that the other took Gerda not as a gift but as a merit. He was jealous also of Dina's attention to Gerda from the day her son introduced her to the household. So again he summoned up the woman seen from the tram, the still frame that came down off the screen. "Watch out, all of you," he said to himself. "If things go better here or she gets fed up with hanging around your revolutionary *crème*, Gerda will go back to what she was before in a heartbeat."

He didn't have much faith that things could go better in the Germany of '31 or '32. So he concentrated on the candid figure that admired berets and small hats in the window of the milliner's shop at that tram stop. A cheap trick. Anyway he was certain that Gerda hadn't forgotten Pieter. Her former boyfriend had gone back to the coffee-importing business, which she had helped to get going in a big way. And maybe, who knows, in memory of old times, she might agree to go with him on a business trip and open an office in South America.

Who knows what she might do if Pieter offered it to her? Would she prefer Georg, who was leaving again for Berlin, or seize the opportunity to get away from every looming misery and threat?

Willy was afraid to find out. Cocooned in his jealousy and in attempts to free himself of it, he had fought—clumsily, uselessly—against an accusation that, years later, many had spit in Gerda's face. Opportunist! She lighted a cigarette with Parisian nonchalance and, lifting her chin, exhaled: "If that's what you think . . . " The sulky expression was reflected in the mirrors, the smoke enveloped the person sitting opposite at the little table. Usually he apologized right away, as if taking care of a formality: better quickly and efficiently, or rather already smiling. To insist, to explain would have been counterproductive.

Yes, many had thought "opportunist," and it didn't seem exaggerated after the fact. But the anger passed, the disappointment faded, and Gerda remained. She was made like that, she was volatile and willful, a meter and a half of pride and ambition, without heels. You had to take her as she was: sincere to the point of hurtful, affectionate in her way, in the long term.

She was sincere when friendship required it, not when she could give a Hollywood touch to her ordeals. For example, she loved to make the Red Frog, Pieter's convertible Opel (entrusted to a friend who had dropped her at the station in Strasbourg and returned to Stuttgart in the morning), the co-protagonist of her break across the border. When she recalled that trip, Gerda skipped over the border controls and would never confess a moment's fear, even to close friends. She wanted only to show off, hold court, broaden the claque of admirers who came by her table. Had that brief trip really been so similar to a grand tour?

But there was no doubt that the former boyfriend had helped a lot after the flight to Paris—"MONEY ARRIVED STOP YOU'RE A TREASURE STOP"—because the Dachshund had gone with her to the post office in Montparnasse several times to pick up the money orders.

Only now, from the linear distance of Hertel Avenue, does Dr. Chardack realize that he understood the most important things too late. Even in the exact sciences, the observer modifies the facts, and he, at the time, was certainly not observing a body that moved in a neutral field. His sensors had grasped that you couldn't count on Gerda's loyalty in the strict sense (which induced flutterings of hope), but hadn't picked up the most relevant empirical fact. It was impossible to calculate what she would choose if the perfect occasion presented itself, for example the coffee business in South America, or under extreme pressure. Gerda would act according to her own advantage, yes, it's likely, but certainly she wouldn't turn back.

It must have been around the beginning of '34, Friedmann had not yet appeared, and in spite of herself Gerda had sunk back to the point of departure. She could display the money orders from Stuttgart as the proof of self-sufficiency necessary for the renewal of her residency permit, and then pay for the hotel room, but getting the sack from Dr. Spitz forced her to scrape by day to day. She would go out at dawn, walk the boulevards with a pack of newspapers that in the arms of such an attractive *colporteuse* tended to go quickly. She allowed herself a very sugary coffee, took care of the typing jobs, which were in short supply, and then went to sit in the sun in the park. She was Gerda: she had a magnificent appearance, like an idle beauty. Ruth also, with her earnings as a model or, in summer, as a gymnast demonstrating floor exercises to the members of a swimming club on the Seine, didn't outwardly betray the difficulty of making a living: she who had studied dead languages at the *Gymnasium* and so for the most part found silent jobs.

The Dachshund was aware that the girls weren't having an easy time, and yet he didn't understand how on earth, especially on weekends, Ruth and Gerda disappeared. "Did a rich admirer take you out of town?" he had finally ventured one day, meeting them on the street, with a hint of anxiety directed toward whichever one would accept the invitation without scruples.

"If only! We stayed home the whole time—you save a lot of calories if you stay under the covers."

"What do you do?" he had asked, bewildered.

What a question! They chatted, read, did their nails and eyebrows, mended their stockings with nail polish and, when their stomachs rumbled (who'd have thought, Ruth laughed, that Gerda could produce such growls), they shushed them by striking up not some light song, no, but a song of revolt, because the empty belly demanded it . . .

They rushed to see *Kuhle Wampe* in the winter of '32, drawn by the "empty stomach" of the title and the battles against censorship that had kept the film from being shown in some theaters.

Dr. Chardack remembers clearly only the beginning, which, like a slap at his conscience numbed by time, brings Germany back to him, now near the end. That river of bicycles rushing through Berlin as if racing for a medal but in reality competing for a day of work. The young cyclist who returns home defeated, swallows a bowl of soup, along with the reproaches of his parents ("Anyone who applies himself will get something"), and doesn't say a word. As soon as he's alone, he takes off the only thing of value he has, his watch, and flings himself into the courtyard. A sharp cry, one unemployed person less. The death of a contemporary in a few minutes of film.

Kuhle Wampe was much more successful than expected. The audience emerged moved by the actors, who, speaking in thick Berlin accents, didn't seem like actors. "All true!" In Dina Gelbke's salon a debate was kindled that was in some ways unpredictable. Willy hadn't asked himself who those sullen comrades were, precisely, but it was clear to him that they belonged to a sort of workers' aristocracy. Unexpectedly, the mistress of the house and her acolytes, who were full of praise for the *Proletkino* theorized and dramatized by their friend Brecht, found themselves contradicted by the real proletariat.

"Where were your Brecht and his comrades from the artistic collective when we organized strikes and pickets?" they protested. "Out for a walk with the Fräulein? Learning poems by Goethe?"

The vehemence of the reaction had left even the friends of the Kuritzkes brothers dumbstruck. Weaned on cinema, they would never have taken the most realistic of films for a mirror of the real. They sided with those who responded that a film has to generalize its message.

Among those present was a man who rumor said had been Dina Gelbke's great love. It didn't often happen that a woman got divorced from a husband like Kuritzkes, who gave her everything, to plunge into an affair with a penniless bohemian goy, without even bothering to conceal it from the children.

Her second marriage, to Dr. Gelbke, at least assured those three poor kids a roof over their heads was the comment of Willy's mother. He had ignored that gossip. And when, in high school, some of his girlfriends got curious about the story and that fascinating man, he had answered with a curt "I don't know anything." Willy knew only that the Kuritzkes brothers had always mentioned a certain Sas, who later showed up at their house. He was a friend of the family. A former worker who had become a schoolteacher and a music teacher. He liked to be in the company of young people and they returned the favor. That was it.

So it wasn't odd that Sas followed them to the attic, or even that he wanted to continue the discussions with them. But in the diatribe on *Kuhle Wampe* he had exploded. Absolutely right to believe in youth, he cried, you are the most affected by this war against the working class! But it's crazy to point a finger and give up on all the workers who can't understand their current poverty. His disagreement with the Communist Party, and the fact that he did nothing to hide it, except for a now completely obvious respect for Dina, had been a further reason for admiration. But because they sensed a double friction—on the one hand political, on the other the abrasiveness of a very private bond—once the laughter was over they no longer knew what to say. The most quick-witted was the girl who would never lose her presence of mind because of any embarrassment of feelings. Gerda had begun to describe the last time she went to see Georg. *Kuhle Wampe* had just been released, and they had to cross half Berlin way in advance, because at the Atrium-Palast di Wilmersdorf, the only theater where it was showing, there was an endless line. The pilgrimage of an audience so varied—workers and famous cultural figures, theater people and shopgirls, a few nightclub hostesses, and so forth—had made an impression on her, and then the music, the dialogue, the sensational editing! The scene on the U-Bahn that introduces the *Solidaritätslied*, a refrain impossible to get out of your head! But then there was that women's boat race, as if rowing—*eins zwei hop hop*—were the most useful and delightful method for changing the world. I said it to Georg and I'm not embarrassed to repeat it: you want to compare when they sing and waltz in *Congress Dances*?

"Stop! You shouldn't even mention that reactionary treacle beside the musical genius of Hanns Eisler," Sas had said, darkening, rising to the bait.

"What do you want," Gerda had retorted, satisfied, "if Communism in the movies is boring, the reactionaries will always win, you can see it in the reelections of Hindenburg . . . "

His thin glasses sparkling, Sas admitted that he couldn't say she was wrong. "But now tell me: would you give a dancing class at my music school, like the ones for debutantes?"

"For you, that and more! Or for the education of the masses, if you'd rather . . . "

And Gerda's reply dissolved in a crystalline laugh that infected them and drew them along, definitively clearing the air of the attic.

Better to laugh: then, as well as later, in Leipzig as well as in Paris. Better to make light of calamity than to remain trapped in discussions that, though rendered absurd by the Hitlerian suppression of the entire left, were revived everywhere: in the groups and editorial offices in exile, in the former barracks used as dormitories for refugees, in line at the *préfecture* or in the cafeterias where social democrats and Communists clutched the same chipped bowls as the first disoriented representatives of the Jewish bourgeoisie. But especially in the cafés, where time was abundant, and the persistence of the voices assaulted those sitting at the nearby tables. Certain former deputies, perched interminably before empty cups, claimed their old positions as if these were the ultimate foundations for their pride. Better not to stay and listen, better to joke about it. Better to feel privileged to have a student life, like the Dachshund, or to be thankful for the intimacy of a run-down hotel room, filling it with a song of proletarian struggle, and, humming, absorb the very recent notion of belonging to the unemployed *Weltproletariat*. Better still to go out into the open, repeat the duet for a public more grateful than bedbugs, and make it a hymn for the comrades stranded on the terraces of the Left Bank, with the added pleasure that the Parisians understood only that you were singing in German, and that it was a march.

Vorwärts und nicht vergessen, worin unsere Stärke besteht. Beim Hungern und beim Essen, vorwärts, und nie vergessen— die Solidarität! ("Onward, and let's not forget what our strength consists of. Hungry or full, onward, let's not forget— solidarity.")

Some two years after the worst hardships for Ruth and Gerda, they found themselves at an evening in support of the anti-fascist struggle in Germany. None of them had problems of pure subsistence anymore: Gerda and Ruth no longer shared a bug-infested bed, and the song about asserting solidarity whether you were hungry or full had been performed by Brecht's wife, Helene Weigel. Small and thin, she had a burning gaze and a face from Greek tragedy (and a bit monkey-like, to tell the truth), and she sang with the intensity of an actress, not with the full, bold voices of her friends. All that suggested to Willy the profound difference between life and the theater. Arriving late from his internship, he lingered at the back of the Café Mephisto, on Boulevard Saint-Germain, but immediately located the heads of friends and acquaintances: Ruth and Melchior Britschgi, the printer she had recently married, Gerda with the Steins and a small group, chattering in various languages, that André Friedmann, now a habitué of the bath-room-lab of Montmartre, had picked up. But this soirée was attended mainly by German émigrés, and while at other times all that *Heimat* had roused in him a slightly claustrophobic impatience, this time knowing so many people gave him pleasure, a simple pleasure, something like what he had caught on the faces of his parents when he went with them to a concert or the opening of a play: here we are, right here in the middle of the society that counts!

There none of them counted for much among the great names of German culture in exile, so imagine outside, in real Paris. But they recognized each other at a glance, a nod of the head, a gesture sketched by a hand. The closeness of the early years had reawakened that primary sense of orientation. They had acquired the solidarity you don't forget, because it arose out of material needs. Willy Chardack had never much believed in a new humanity produced by socialism, but that way of staying united had pushed them onward, *vorwärts*, as the *Solidaritätslied* song said, and with a force that they might not otherwise have found.

That was what he recognized, especially in Gerda and the broad agglomerate gathered around her irresistible, dear person. And suddenly he remembers that, meeting her on the street or seeing her get up after putting out the cigarette with a display of energy—"That's it, I can't stay any longer, I have to find out this or that, be in such-and-such a place"—he had nicknamed her Fräulein Vorwärts. It was only a joke with himself, an attempt to convince himself that he had emerged from Leipzig's mantle of jealousies, as oppressive as the sky covered with low clouds and industrial smoke. But not even that evening when, standing at the theater, Gerda seemed so close to him, did he have any idea of how unstoppable the propulsive force of his Miss Onward was . . .

Dr. Chardack is passing by the closed shutters of a supermarket, a women's hair salon, an emporium for household and garden tools, a laundry, an open gas station. He encounters kids in light clothing, too garish for his taste, families that seem to have just emerged from a faded photo of grandparents in their shtetl, except for the rubber-soled shoes of the wives in wigs. Can it be that by thinking about other things you wonder if this is America? Everyone comfortable, everyone practical, everyone walking in the same saddle shoes. Capitalism invites us to acquire equality, he reflects, real socialism assigns the best to the most faithful. The man who had gone to live in the family house on Gohliser Strasse: first a bureaucrat in the Nazi Party and now, you can bet, a bureaucrat in the Socialist Unity Party. Maybe it would have been better if it had been hit by the bombs that flattened the building on Springerstrasse where Gerda Pohorylle lived.

"Cold war," Dr. Chardack often says to himself, is a good phrase for a country that hasn't been destroyed by real war, even if certain alliances were conclusively ruined by the chill of peace.

Keeping the visa stuck in his passport, seeing stamped on it "Enemy Alien," hadn't been nice, but war was war and he understood it. Yet then William M. Chardack, recently naturalized American, had had to answer the question whether he had ever been enrolled in the Communist Party or in the SAP, the German Socialist Workers' Party.

"No," he had answered correctly.

But he had spent time with various members of that revolutionary Marxist group.

"Yes," he had admitted, "but for reasons of personal sympathy."

It turned out, though, that he had participated in various activities organized by that party, in Germany and in Paris.

"They were anti-fascist initiatives," he declared.

Agreed, but the sponsor was Trotskyist.

What was he supposed to say: That they were the only ones who were committed to a unified front on the left? That the SAP was critical of Stalin?

"I was studying medicine," he responded. "I spent my time in classes, interning, and preparation for exams. But if I found out that there was a demonstration against the Nazis, I didn't have too many scruples about who had organized it."

And at that point he thought: so send me to Palestine or send me back to Germany. But they had asked no more questions.

Several years later, when he returned from Korea, they had summoned him again.

"We're sure, Dr. Chardack, that you're loyal to the United States. But maybe you can do something more for your country."

They asked him if he knew any of the people friendly with a photographer, a woman, people whose closeness to the Communist Party, and to her personally, they knew about. Among the names submitted to him he recognized only Robert Capa, with whom he'd had no contact in the USA.

"No one else?" they had pressed him. "Think about it for a moment."

In that moment Dr. Chardack wondered if they really believed that someone like him could turn out to be an informer.

"Willy Brandt," he answered, "who is now president of the chamber of deputies in Berlin, West Berlin, of course."

Not that there had been any intimacy between Chardack and his namesake, but they had met several times at spur-of-the-moment dinners organized by the Steins, during which Willy Brandt had been attracted by Gerda's charm, like everyone.

When the tragic news arrived, and then Gerda's remains, he was the one who gave voice to the fear that she had not died in an accident under the tracks of a tank. That rumor, maybe spread by Fred and Lilo, had begun to ascend the Left Bank and circulate from café to café. The suspicion was horrible. Willy Brandt was the rising star whom the militants of the SAP trusted. Gerda, however, had been crushed right outside Madrid in July of '37, and Willy Brandt hadn't set foot in Spain for around a month, when he had escaped by a hair's breadth the roundups of "Trotskyists" in Barcelona. On the basis of what sources had he formulated that terrible hypothesis? Against it, there was that Canadian journalist who was seriously wounded in the collision that had killed Gerda. He had come to Paris, and Ruth had seen him. He had planted himself in Capa's hotel. He followed him around on crutches, struggling, a convict in chains. But the SAP comrades were not reassured. Injured legs didn't guarantee that the unaltered truth would come out of the mouth of that witness. It was discovered that Ted Allan had been a political adviser, a comrade bound to report on every deviation from the Moscow line. And that was enough for the conjectures about Gerda's death, the darkest hypotheses, to go on circulating for a long time.

On Gerda's last trips to Paris, her face tan and her legs pale, the friends most active in the SAP had urged her to be careful.

"Nothing happens to me!" she said curtly. "I work for the right newspapers, I know the right . . . "

No one had had the courage to reply that the "right people" were among those they were starting to fear. And so she hadn't noticed their intense unease or had chosen to ignore it, something she excelled at. With a nimble gesture she picked up the camera sitting on the table in front of her: from now on she'd work not only with the Leica but also with a movie camera that Capa had gotten from *Time-Life*, "you know, the famous American newsmagazines . . . " This had driven them to congratulate her and, in part, calmed them. Gerda held the camera in the palm of her hand and gazed at it with the tender joy of one looking at a kitten so young it's still cross-eyed. "You understand how useful to the cause my Leica is, right?" she concluded with a disarming smile.

No, they didn't feel like asking if she was completely aligned with the Communists, given that they were in Paris and she was returning to burn on the battlefields. And yet many of them would have liked to leave as volunteers; even a girl as prudent as Ruth was ready to go. For months she had been making time to take a nursing course, but when she finished the course she had been told it was too late. "Anyone who goes to Spain does so on his own. Our party doesn't vouch for anyone." Not even a Red Cross nurse? No, not even.

Willy had run into Ruth, who was furious with the heads of the SAP and the absurd logic of parties and party factions, exasperated that it was repeated, over and over, even now that the Spanish people were dying every day in bombardments. "Look," she had said to him, pulling out the latest issue of *Regards*, whose cover displayed a photo of Gerda's under the accusatory headline "Guernica! Almería! *Et démain?*" It framed men and women at the gates of the hospital in Valencia, where victims of the bombing in mid-May had been brought. The report spoke of a "dress rehearsal for total war," and Gerda's photos showed corpses dumped on the checkerboard tiles: a boy in short pants, a naked man only partly covered by the bloody sheet, an old woman in black, maybe alive maybe dead, on a stretcher jumbled in with others. "They don't need just photographers down there," Ruth had said, scowling, incapable of letting out a drop of rage or disappointment. "*Ach Scheisse!*" Willy hadn't asked if the heads of the SAP had persuaded her not to go or if she herself had reluctantly given it up.

Thoughts can suddenly make a leap that catapults them outside the track they've been running on for years. William

Chardack had often said to himself, and had repeated to his wife, that he had had undeserved luck. "You should thank comrade Stalin, dear, if the FBI can't create more than so many troubles for me!" His wife had only to shake her head to make him understand that it wasn't nice to mock her fear with that exaggerated black humor. But it was by chance that in Leipzig he had wandered into the orbit of a workers' faction included on Stalin's blacklist, a fact that the USA had also noted. All his friends had been close to the SAP, and so Willy had, too. All his friends (no: almost all), even the former leaders he had avoided naming to the investigating official, were still alive and getting by. So the SAP had been their salvation. The reasoning had the completeness of a logical demonstration. The flaw appears only now, as he thinks back to Ruth, who would have liked to save some lives and instead had feared for her own. All his friends (yes, all: including him) had thought that it was crucial to win in Spain, win at all costs, win period. But just Gerda, the only one who didn't give a damn about the dangers, the considerations or anything, except arriving in the right place at the right time, had gone in the end and had remained.

Dr. Chardack is sweating too much, he's getting too lost in memories that are no longer a pleasant accompaniment to a *Spaziergang*, and so he accelerates decisively toward his goal.

Mastman's Delicatessen is an institution frequented principally by families who want to make their children happy and enjoy being able to put them to bed already fed. The *delicious kosher hot dogs* and the *crispy potato latkes* sell fast, along with the rounded slices of *home-made Apfelstrudel* snowy with powdered sugar. To buy some pieces of that famous sweet he would have to go past the few tables on the sidewalk, where mothers are forcing children to finish their meals, feeding the smallest or thinnest, cleaning up the bits left over on the plates themselves. And there he stops. He sees the big pans of strudel in the window, but he stops. He smells the wave of familiar aromas every time the door opens, the din of voices among which he distinguishes intonations, words, single phrases. He looks at the boys with the yarmulkes on their heads, who've been in a separate group since kindergarten.

"I'm going backward," he thinks. "I'm going *rückwärts*, like a crab."

If he went into the place now and asked for *srree pieces of Apfelstrudel*, they would answer happily in what they assume is their common mother tongue.

"Sorry, my Yiddish is very poor," he would say.

"No problem, but with that accent we wouldn't have thought so," they'd respond.

"I'm from Germany," he would anticipate the question.

"But you are Jewish, right?"

Fair, he's not fair, tall, he's not tall, and he has a bulbous nose of a certain impressiveness. Dr. Chardack could even lower his underpants (hadn't it been the master proof in the Thousand-Year Reich?), but the others wouldn't understand why he's never taken a day off for the High Holy Days, and has never appeared in the synagogue.

Dr. Chardack often repeated that he was a man of science, and therefore detached from every religious practice and belief, until he understood that his imported formula, validated by centuries of enlightenment, had no purchase there in America. Science is science, they allowed, but the community you grow up in will never be a conference in California. What was he supposed to answer: that in fact yes, a community could exist without feeling that it belonged to a congregation or an original race? There was no way to be understood, never mind. But if they invited you for the Thanksgiving turkey, and then they invited you for Passover, what the hell were you supposed to do?

In Korea he had patched up a young soldier who, recovered enough to be able to speak, had explained to him with feverish eyes that the chosen people had been punished for high treason and, given the importance of the mission, the rest of the world had unfortunately had to get involved. Without Hitler, the Jews would have abandoned the laws of the Lord, would have become reds or at least atheists, and the Communists would have won overwhelmingly, so now they had to be kicked out of this country in the ass end of nowhere.

Chief Surgeon William M. Chardack was astonished to find such ideas in the head of a boy from some tiny town in the Corn Belt who, before ending up in the Army, had never encountered a Jew. But he had already discovered that there were rabbis who preached similar absurdities, when—it must have been '47 or '48—a traveling companion he'd parted from at Ellis Island had recognized him in the tumult of the garment district in Manhattan.

After asking how he was, Sussmann had assailed him with his torments. The discomforts, the solitude: he had never been observant, but he had tried to show up at the temple with the age and the concerns of his Orthodox neighbors. He had followed them on Yom Kippur and had been dumbfounded by the rabbi's speech: the elimination of Israel had failed, *baruch Ha-shem*, but what day could be more suitable for recognizing in that dreadful martyrdom a warning from on high?

Sussmann trembled, very agitated, on the sidewalk crowded with people and rolling hangers being pushed toward the trucks parked along Seventh Avenue.

"They've got an axe to grind, like all priests, Herr Sussmann, forget it . . . " Dr. Chardack had interrupted him.

"Please, let me finish!" Sussmann had begged him.

That rabbi had stated first that human intelligence would never be at the height of the Lord's designs, *but some facts are facts.* Conversions and mixed marriages had spread, in

Germany. And the uncontestable facts didn't end there. Marx was a German Jew, Freud a Jew from Vienna, and Einstein had even won the Nobel Prize for the discovery that everything is relative. "Consider how many children of our people have become their followers or disciples!" the rabbi cried breathlessly. "Everything began in the place where the abandonment of the Torah was most serious; and the catastrophe nearly assumed the dimensions of the Flood."

Sussmann had fought in Belgium until 1918, had returned alive by a miracle, had opened an artisan's workshop in Cologne, and after the racial laws were in place had divorced, by mutual consent, his wife, who later died there in the bombings, when he had just settled in America.

The man, crying in front of a fleeting acquaintance (how old must he be: about the same age as his father?), had embarrassed Dr. Chardack. So he said goodbye to Sussmann, repeating that idiots exist everywhere, and had gone into a shop, where he looked at himself in his new three-button suit, a consistent man, a free man. Religion was *not my problem*. And the problems that his new fellow-citizens created for themselves about his origins, his style of life and of thought, were laughable compared with what he had experienced in Europe. It was enough, at that moment, to give up the strudel and walk another stretch of Hertel Avenue. It wasn't worth it to waste more time there.

Dr. Chardack is beginning to realize that his life in Buffalo resembles that flat street, provided with everything, which allows him to keep going straight. No one can recognize him there, the way Sussmann did in Manhattan, to remind him of things that the Jews of the East, gathered at the tables of Mastman's, don't even dream of talking about. Besides, his history isn't reducible to the list of who has died or faded into the notions of deportation, internment, end. In many cases he doesn't even know whether they disappeared through the chimney or only from his horizon. There wasn't much hope for his father's Jewish employees, or for the fur trade in general, that universe contained in the courtyards of Leipzig's broad central avenue, the renowned Brühl. And his story wasn't the same as that of many of his traveling companions, who had been registered as "Hebrew" under "RACE" or "PEOPLE" by the immigration inspectors in the Port of New York, a hand correction that wouldn't have dismayed him so much if, emerging from the line of "alien passengers," he hadn't had the Statue of Liberty, colossal, before his eyes.

How many classmates, aunts and uncles, cousins of varying degrees had ended up in the camps? What had happened to the parents and relatives of Gerda Pohorylle? She had chosen the work and the name, and had died in a cruel and stupid accident, yet in a war that, with her images, she wanted to win for all. She had fallen among comrades who had gone to fight against fascism: it didn't matter what "RACE" or "PEOPLE" they belonged to.

How many of his Leipzig friends and acquaintances had gone to Spain? Among the habitués of Friedrich-Karl-Strasse, among the students and young workers who hung around Georg Kuritzkes? How many hadn't avoided the *Lager* and its extreme consequences? Dr. Chardack has no idea. But there's a name that slips out there on Hertel Avenue, where it seems a mangled American word: Sas.

A remorseful volunteer in the Great War, a physique toughened by work (steel mills in Saxony, naval shipyards in Hamburg), hands capable of denying anatomy and the proletarian epic to rest on a piano and set up a music school. The Dachshund had envied him only the Zündapp motorcycle that at a certain point Gerda had begun climbing onto for the illegal job of distributing leaflets. He had marveled that he wasn't jealous when he saw her hold on to Sas's back and vanish with a "Later!" on Pfaffendorfer Strasse, as if they were going on a country outing. But it was all so urgent in that period, and they got along very well, Sas and Gerda, although they were so different in appearance and past. No one would ever have imagined that that affinity would get them to the same goal.

Sas was arrested in Leipzig in '33 (as Gerda was, a little later), had ended up in Sachsenhausen for a year, then was released from the concentration camp and rearrested in Berlin. He was guillotined in the Plötzensee prison in Berlin, along with a handful of boys whom he had taught harmony, solfege, and the illegal use of the mimeograph machine. Ruth had told Willy in a letter dated May 1943. He had been an anarchist, radical socialist, member of the KPD, the German Communist Party (also for love of Dina, it seemed), expelled as a dissident from the KPD. How to explain it to the Americans? If you mentioned German resistance, they associated you, if you were lucky, with the group of aristocratic officers who, out of patriotism, had tried to bring down the Führer, but not before July 20, 1944. How could you explain that what little resistance there had been was thanks to the Communists, or people whom the Americans saw as the same?

Someone like Gelbke, for example. Called the "red doctor" but highly regarded in all Leipzig, he had used the flow of patients to and from his clinic to make it a connecting point for people who had to hide or flee abroad. He had managed, and had gotten away with it, along with Dina. Merely the decision to stay with a Jewish wife, who knows how, required a nerve that had evaporated in the majority of Germans under the first rays of the swastika sun.

No, the Americans couldn't understand that everything had started long before, when it wasn't yet a matter of life and death and the ideas opposed to the Nazi lie were not simply a defensive reaction.

For Georg Kuritzkes, with that revolutionary upbringing, it

had been easy. But Willy and his Jewish friends from bourgeois families were, with those same ideas, in opposition to their parents. Judging despicable their compliance with living quietly ("Who keeps the business going, who pays the suppliers and the salaries?"), pathetic the unrequited love for Germany, myopic and comforting the conviction that being excluded from certain spheres was only a detestable inconvenience. It was natural to feel superior to the old people, as it was to join forces with contemporaries who held the same views. And then there was her, the young woman who had had on her head a beret in the latest fashion, and had been transformed into a combatant in a very short span of time. How had she done it? Time, it's true, had been proceeding straight toward the end of the line since she arrived in Leipzig. But she walked beside it with that aerial gait, free to turn the corner and disappear like a dream, a stylish chimera. That was the girl who enchanted him. And when the spark of a more flammable substance came to the surface, Willy Chardack, after a moment of distress, preferred not to see it.

One of those uselessly revelatory moments went back to the early days, yes, it was 1930 and still cold. The fantastic girl from Stuttgart wasn't yet used to sitting cross-legged on the floor of Georg Kuritzkes's attic (those legs showed up better in the light coming from the dormers than on Dina Gelbke's dusty carpets) and Willy was glancing at her. Her slender neck extended under the perfectly tamed bob *à la garçonne*, her lips, redefined in red, were pressed into a line like an attentive pupil, her eyes emitted flashes of disdain, intermittent glimmerings that stirred up the green of the depths.

While they discussed the difficulties of organizing a National Youth Day in Leipzig, and the necessity of involving progressive students who were outside the party factions, Georg became nervous and stood up. How was it possible that they remained so blind and blocked, he said in irritation, when the majority of the workers in the third-largest industrial city were still inclined not to be divided between those who had kept their jobs and those who had lost them, were still united by the awareness that their poverty was due to capital and its servants, who were busy everywhere. In Germany the capitalists had made money on the war, profited from the hyperinflation, prospered in the golden years. But Chancellor Brüning certainly wouldn't make the steel barons pay for the damage of the crisis that had followed, still less Hindenburg and the other generals, who should have had their possessions seized and been sent to the farthest estate available to shoot exclusively at wild boar. No way! The parasites in uniform and the manufacturers of cannons concurred in making the German people bear the debt of the war that they had incited. And since Brüning was their docile tool, the vise of his draconian cuts crushed the working class, including the veterans who had been sent to the front as cannon fodder and had come out alive.

Georg looked at Gerda, Gerda looked at Georg, and, as she raised her eyes to him, her gaze softened, like someone waiting for the continuation of a story told by a great narrator who never relaxes his grip on his listeners, never lets the atavistic fear that leads to the epilogue oppress them.

Thus the wolves had arrived. They had multiplied owing to the mistake of underestimating them, of believing them fierce but primitive beasts, of confusing them with German shepherds, animals that could be tamed, exploited at one's own convenience. They wouldn't have gone near the houses if the country hadn't been so hungry. It was no longer only the lower middle class, the disabled, the *lumpen*, and the criminal underworld who were snared by the brownshirts. In every factory, warehouse, construction site, blast furnace that closed or cut production and personnel, the mass of the proletariat collapsed. Hunger was an evil counselor, and despair even worse.

Hunger and despair worked for the fascists and their no longer very secret supporters. The ladies of high society were already competing to see who could gorge Hitler, in the face of the workers reduced to poverty by their consorts.

"Let him choke! Get a fish bone stuck in his throat!" Gerda had cried.

"Everybody knows the gentle butcher doesn't eat fish or meat . . . " a high-school classmate had retorted, opening up a tumult of comments.

"That's enough!" Kuritzkes was exasperated."If gossiping weren't the only thing we're good at, the air wouldn't reek of his flatulence."

Thus, having obtained the fervid expectation on Gerda's face (but she had also straightened her knees, shifting the hem of her skirt upward), he didn't know how to continue.

"My father does business with Italy, and he goes there often. And every time he returns he says to my mother: 'Dina, doesn't what Mussolini—who was a socialist—has done there teach you anything? You think you'll do better with this poisonous Austrian gnome, in a country of reactionary anti-Semites?' And she yells that he can't berate her, given that she has brought up her three children by herself . . . "

Willy suspected that there was still a hint of bewilderment behind that unusual confidence, but Georg, standing there, had everyone's eyes on him.

"My father's right. We have to stop them soon and do it together," he continued curtly, a warning immediately picked up by Gerda, who drove her sharp nails into her fingertips, wrinkled her forehead, stiffening her chin and mouth as well, and let the fearsome energy of an obstinate, childish rage rise to the surface of her irises.

Where in the world did that rage come from? Willy wondered, frightened and fascinated.

Georg had lighted a cigarette, letting the others speak. And he didn't realize that his eyes (the famous Kuritzkes eyes!) were wandering over Gerda, with that glitter that made them droop, and the Dachshund couldn't believe it.

"This guy thinks that by getting Fräulein Pohorylle on his side we'll have half the revolution under our belts," he said to himself, "and he'll take her hand out of her capitalist boyfriend's."

Unmistakable, shame assailed him. What sort of friend am I if I turn mean for a woman?

Concentrate again on the speaker, eliminate everything.

Kuritzkes had again found his usual nonchalance, but Willy had lost the friend he admired and envied. Georg was like the others, an insect drawn by a magnet toward Gerda, the first flame that had managed to outshine him.

From each according to his abilities, to each according to his needs.

Georg would have done anything to have the girl from Stuttgart. He had not only more abilities but also more needs, Willy had intuited. Georg Kuritzkes had so great a need for Gerda Pohorylle because his goals and objectives were so great. And when Gerda was nearby, suddenly anything appeared within reach.

The man whom drivers see proceeding slowly along Hertel Avenue has the appearance of someone who wasn't born around there, but he looks respectable. With the white shirt and the jacket over his arm he could be a waiter, but if he's going to work why did he stop on the sidewalk? Has he forgotten something at home? Can't find the car keys?

The hypothesis is not so far from the truth. Dr. Chardack is standing still on the sidewalk because he can't find a word. Not finding the word happens to him more often than not finding the car keys. Usually it happens when he's with other people, more rarely when he's alone. As long as the memory of Leipzig ran as straight as Hertel Avenue, Dr. Chardack proceeded without obstructions in his parallel dimension. Gerda's unforgettable laughs have induced him to walk quickly, a cool gulp in the exhaust-laden air. But now Dr. Chardack has stumbled on that word that he can't find in his new language. He concentrates, he persists, but *Freiraum* doesn't exist in English. There exist only "free" and "room," words useful for asking for a room in a fluorescent MOTEL on the dark edge of a highway. Suddenly he sees himself again driving between New York and Buffalo, fighting sleep and the extremely sensible fear that if he lost control of the wheel no one would come to his aid for hours. But this Hertel Avenue, longer and wider than the Champs-Élysées, also reinforces the thought that takes shape in his sweaty head. Where there is space to lose, space going to waste, like food in restaurants, the space can't be charged with an abstract value. But in the Germany that was about to suppress freedom, *Freiraum* wasn't only Georg's free attic or the great lawn of the Rosental, that untouched tongue of woods whose every path they had all, living in the same neighborhood, known since childhood. It meant something more extensive and more complicated, but natural, because there was a word for it.

When his history and philosophy teacher caught him distracted, he would shout, "Chardack, are you dreaming?! You're not going out for recess." And it was all the same, whether Willy was pondering how to see a certain young lady (did she always take the same street?) or, on the contrary, within reach of the Kantian concept of "the human being's emergence from his self-incurred minority." There, that was the point: if you tried to emerge from the state of minority to occupy *Freiraum*, you risked not getting anywhere. If instead you grabbed it along with the others, that space of freedom took shape: the words thought or written became words uttered aloud. The useless body, bent over the school desk in a deceptive posture, was one with many different bodies (some with a very remarkable appearance). Bodies that met, moved, expanded in a common and greater space, both inner and geographic. And all together they no longer resembled the bolts driven in to keep a static construction standing; rather, they were like parts of a fine mechanism which needed play in order to function. *Spielraum*: they got us that, a concept even more untranslatable than *Freiraum*.

Dr. Chardack has dried off the sweat and resumed walking, mulling over periphrases, while immediately discarding the literal translation of the word, *room to play*, that has surfaced from a great distance. They were young, agreed, but they weren't moving in those spaces as if in the expanded precincts of an amusement park.

"Grow up, Wilhelm, stop playing revolutionary!" The paternal rebuke, somewhat out of place, made him furious. The Dachshund hadn't hesitated to leave for Paris as soon as the "game" became tremendously serious. Were Gerda's younger brothers, who had gone into hiding, playing? Was Soma, Georg's brother, playing, when, at only thirteen or fourteen, he was ferociously beaten up by the SA, the brownshirts? Was Georg playing, who had had to hide for months, or Ruth, active in the student union, or Gerda, on the motorcycle at night, headlights off, distributing leaflets in the periphery of Leipzig?

No, it wasn't a game, for any of them. But with Gerda things were, as usual, more complex.

Gerda never seemed worried. When, in Leipzig, she talked about her visits to Berlin, where the clashes were an everyday occurrence, or when in Paris she announced that she would leave for Spain alone, the others—even Capa—were profuse with warnings. "Calm down!" she sneered, benevolent. And if "Gerda, it's not a game," slipped out she got terribly angry. They should stop treating her like a child, she—who knew how to keep the books, calculated the exchange rates in an instant, remembered down to the last *Pfennig* or *centime* the shop prices—always got by.

"I have a head more solidly on my shoulders than the rest of you," she fumed. A hard head, at that.

And yet she couldn't help it: Gerda was and remained light, in all senses, even in the less flattering meanings. The illusion of lightness originated in the charm she emanated, in the paradox of an inflexible grace, in an appearance that was a gift, at times a limitation, and not the result of an effort of will or of constant interior work.

"*Ach*, Willy, life is too serious to take seriously."

He wasn't the sole recipient of that sentence whose origin he had discovered in America, finding it on a cross-stitched sampler. *Life is far too important ever to talk seriously about. Oscar Wilde.* Or was it a cushion placed on a chair?

That witticism fit her like a magic slipper: Gerda was doing things seriously even when it didn't seem that way. Maybe she fell into her own trap.

She had immediately placed the Hungarian with the Leica ("Friedmann? Pleasant blowhard"), jokingly she had started teasing him ("Shave your beard, the *maudit* type isn't much appreciated these days"), and soon found herself in the role of the friend with experience of the world and a head on her shoulders. That André Friedmann had been weaned by the only metropolis able to vie with Paris, had been born in a fashion atelier in the chic heart of Budapest, had been brought up in its gambling clubs and streets of ill repute and had then sailed in every water of *savoir vivre*, clear or muddy, didn't impress a young lady like Gerda, educated in Switzerland and refined in the revolutionary salons of Leipzig. But to have over him that Pygmalion-like authority (he called her *arbitra elegantiae* and sometimes mistress of ceremonies) made her proud. In other words, Gerda played, so to speak, at "cleaning up the Balkan gypsy," André was suited to that game, and the *copains* and *camarades* observed the spectacle of a surrealist installation masked by bourgeois customs. The cafés of Saint-Michel and Montparnasse became theaters for the play. *Spielraum* made concrete.

There you could have as many dreams of glory as you wanted, not rationed like the sugar cubes, which, when no *garçon* was keeping an eye on the silver bowl on the table, ended up in Friedmann's sleeves. Now he did it more for exercise than to stay on his feet, but the waiters at La Coupole, the Capoulade, and the Dôme knew him, and for them it made no difference if the pockets into which the energizing loot was made to disappear belonged to a greasy leather jacket or a beige bourgeois raincoat bought according to the dictates of Gerda Pohorylle. It was a game, it was theater, and they enjoyed it along with the others. Often the money that Gerda and André had in their pockets wasn't enough even for the movies, and so they invented the show themselves. The friends who functioned as the audience expected to see the play end, some day or other, because sooner or later the fabulous Gerda Pohorylle would get fed up performing with André Friedmann. Instead she fell in love with him.

In the summer of '35 they had left, hitchhiking, to go camping on an almost deserted and fragrant little island in the South of France. Certain things happened more easily far from Paris, with its too many constrictions and multiple temptations, but Gerda was so obviously in love with André Friedmann that Willy, felt suddenly liberated.

One morning he had gone looking for them to propose an outing to Cannes, the ferry left in a little over an hour. He had seen them sitting on a cliff barefoot (the polish on Gerda's toes chipped, André's very dark), while they tried to augment the daily ration of canned sardines with some fresh fish. One beside the other, they were silent, watching the hook with the float. It was unusual for Friedmann to be so quiet and still, movement confined to his fingers in Gerda's thatch of reddish hair, to which she yielded with the minimal undulations of a cat.

Willy had stopped on the path and stood there, following that abandon with a sense of indiscretion much stronger than when he saw them embracing in the water, or emerging from the tent with shiny skin and veiled eyes.

"*Merde*, it stole my bait and got away!"

Gerda had raised the rod to show the empty hook to André, who had reached out his hands to help her.

"Was I supposed to pull it up quicker?"

"No, *Schatzi*, it happens. Fish are also sly, they prefer to live in the deep blue sea and make babies by the millions. How can you not understand them."

"Eggs, stupid."

"Eggs or little fish, as my chief prefers."

"I'd prefer to catch one. Possibly bigger than an anchovy and edible."

"Fishing requires extreme patience or extreme hunger. Pay attention to me, I know what I'm talking about."

"Yes, of course. You were only thirteen and you caught a twenty-kilo pike that almost pulled you into the Danube with its ferocious force."

"What do you mean? It couldn't be a pike, my little goldfish, at most it must have been a carp. Even you know that at that age it's impossible."

"O.K., it was later, and it was a catfish taken out of the Landwehrkanal after you broke the ice with a cobblestone saved in memory of the clashes of December 1932. I went through Berlin in that period, oh, I remember them . . . "

"Are you making fun of me? Look out or I'll tickle you until you drop the fishing rod in the water. And then, pricking up your pretty ears, you'll hear all the fish of the Côte d'Azure laughing."

"Stop it! I'll give you the rod and this, too. Happy?"

"I want another. Then I'll tell you how the real story . . . "

Willy had observed Gerda take the rod out of André's hands (slowly, following the twirls of the line so that the hook wouldn't get stuck in someone's skin), carefully lay it down near her lover, and finally, slow and solemn, encircle his neck and kiss him. Friedmann had hugged her tight, freeing his expert hand to move up along her dorsal spine and down the bare back again to the bottom of her striped bathing suit, then he pressed her waist and buttocks, relaxed his grip into a soft embrace, and, finally, detached his mouth from Gerda's and let his head fall on her shoulder. Maybe André had closed his eyes, but Willy couldn't see from where he was. He saw instead Gerda run her fingertips over his forehead and, after arranging a lock that had slid over his eyes, caress his hair.

Riveted to the red earth of Île Sainte-Marguerite, Willy was stunned. Not even out of pity had Gerda ever granted him such a caress. Georg yes, but he couldn't remember where or when. Maybe it was the fault of the sun on his bare head, even though there was a little wind that, luckily, carried not only the voices but also the comforting fragrance of the Mediterranean brush. He stared at his shoes and socks, but the memory of her affections that had so often appeared to torment him had vanished. Now the kisses and embraces of Gerda and Georg were evidence in an archive, whose key he must possess but had no idea where.

Meanwhile André had started talking about himself, taking an indirect approach, and Willy again stopped to listen. His fishing initiation in Budapest, where you dreamed of rocks as warm and comfortable as these, and where the fog, when it rose, entered your bones and swallowed up even your hands in front of your nose. But the old fishermen's stories made up for everything, the boredom and the poor catch, the stink of oily water and rotten fish. Legend said that after sunset, when the fishing was better, gigantic creatures appeared in the Danube, which awakened fantastic fears in the head of a boy in short pants.

"You know, here's the best part. While I was starting to wet my pants the carp bites. A kilo and a half, for a kid not bad. I bring it to my mother, and you can imagine! How could I expect that that thing fished under the Elisabeth Bridge should end up on our table in the form of gefilte fish or fish soup with paprika? End of the carp, end of the story."

"You mean your mother threw it away right before the eyes of her favorite son? I don't believe it . . . "

"Worse. She gave it to one of her dressmakers who was particularly needy. Right before my eyes, naturally."

"And at that moment you decided that if you couldn't be a great fisherman you'd become a photographer fighting against injustice and inequality. Is that it?"

"I had no idea what I wanted to be. But I knew that the life of a good bourgeois wasn't for me. Unfortunately I wasn't born a princess like you, honey."

Those stories had put Willy more at ease. He had never been present at an equally intimate moment between Gerda and Georg, even though he was very familiar with the oscillations of Gerda's *Witz*. Of course, she had hurried to meet Georg when he returned from Berlin and stepping off the train in Turin had flown into his arms, while Willy got the bags down and stood guard on the platform. Indifferent to his presence, she had kissed Georg at the top station of the cable car at Sestriere, kissed him on the lawns of the Rosental and the shores of the Saxon lakes, in front of Sas and the whole group, made out with him while they danced at their little parties in the attic. Maybe the Hippocratic principle *contraria contrariis curantur* was valid. Willy had left the unhealthy realm of desire, ever since Gerda had applied a radical, not always painless, treatment, and after a therapeutic month he said, "Enough!" "Enough," the Dachshund had repeated, so relieved, in the end, that he had stayed, waiting to carry her suitcase down to the hotel entrance and have a taxi called.

Now he could witness a scene like that almost impassively. He had let his gaze wander between the cliff and the dark green profile of the hills, and had felt free, cured.

In June, Gerda had seen him on the terrace of a university café, the semester was over, and they were talking about departures. It was Raymond, his medical-school companion, who proposed the island famous for *The Man in the Iron Mask* and *The Three Musketeers*, so bound up with that novelistic fame that it never occurred to French youths as a vacation spot. The Dachshund wasn't surprised that Gerda was enthusiastic about it ("I read it as a girl: so the fortress really exists?") and had proposed that she come with them. He wanted to demonstrate that they were still good friends, but didn't think that she would join two ordinary medical students. She would leave with her photographer friends or even with Georg, who maybe in a letter had urged her to consider the episode a mistake, an interlude to wash away with a dive into the sea on the Ligurian Riviera.

For Willy, the moment of surprise had been seeing Gerda with knapsack and beret in front of her hotel, at the agreed-on hour and day. He remained certain that she had joined the two of them *faute de mieux*, until, on the side of the Nationale No. 7, it emerged that André Friedmann was in Marseille for work and would join them later on the Côte d'Azur. Gerda had let it out while they were nibbling grapes stolen in the vineyards of Bourgogne, and then stood up immediately, arm extended and finger raised toward the drivers. So Willy, who had gone back to squat in the ditch with Raymond, had understood everything: including the fact that receiving the news only in Lyon raised suspicions of a plot that had begun when she was still in her hotel, and I, what a dope, didn't even realize it.

In Cannes, where they had to wait for him, Friedmann appeared after walking up the Croisette sweaty and so creased that, were it not for the Leica, he could have been taken for a Spanish dishwasher in the grand hotels. He started to move faster, with his *"Hallo, hallo!"* that made some passersby *en promenade* turn their heads, while Gerda, coming out of the shade of a palm, smiled her boldest smile. Willy, keeping to the background, had thought, *"Gut, jetzt ist er dran,"* and set off for the beach, where Raymond was watching over their things. He had taken off his clothes and jumped into the water. He had stayed a while, floating, amazed by that "Good, now it's his turn," serene as the sky over his head.

Yes, only he, the Dachshund, had become deaf to the call of Gerda. It was proved by the detachment with which, now, he listened to André's garrulous voice recounting how not even in the hardest times in Berlin had it occurred to him to remedy things with the fishing rod ("And if a guard asked for my license? Get yourself expelled from Germany for a fish that may not even bite! Among you people everything is *verboten* . . . "), in Paris, on the other hand, he and his friend Csiki Weisz were desperate to try it.

"Better than stealing, we said to ourselves. Now the cops in half the city knew us, not to mention the shopkeepers. We go beyond Place de la République and, once we've trekked up there, hunger makes our heads spin. At that point, we notice the people fishing in the Canal Saint-Martin or the Seine. The Danube, by comparison, seemed like clear water. 'Let's forget it,' Csiki goes, and rolls out a series of objections, starting from our lack of equipment. Well, having borrowed a rod, we sit on the Quai de Tournelle and, numb to the bone, catch two small stocky fish. Small, but not so small they give us the strength to continue. If they'd been a more decent size we'd have had one each for dinner. So we go back to the strategy tested in the shops. I get the best-equipped fisherman talking and, while he's absorbed in his advice, Csiki exchanges our fish. We go back to the hotel satisfied, but discover we don't have a drop of oil left. Finally, there's this guy who looks like a dandy, so you can imagine what he came to do in a nasty hotel in the Sixth Arrondissement. He hands us his jar of brilliantine, generous. We fried the fish and ate them. They tasted of perfume and mud: impossible to distinguish which of the two was more nauseating. Moral of the story? Never again!"

"Here you are again, though, repeat offender . . . only here we can't make an exchange."

"But whatever little fish has the kindness to bite, it will be a delicacy."

Gerda responds with a smack on the lips that André maintains as long as he can, at his peril. The rod is back in his hands, tremulous, bending toward the drop. But when he separates from Gerda's mouth to take control of it again, he's still looking at her, not the sea.

"You believe me? You believe that I ate that fish in brilliantine, and not '*Ja, ja*, the mad Hungarian talks big'?"

Gerda, laughing, ruffles his hair: "What do you want from my life, André?"

"I don't know. Swear you believe it."

There's a moment of fluid silence: pounding and backflow of waves against the rocks, small squeaks, maybe lizards and insects shifting the brittle vegetation, maybe only the wind, although it's no stronger than a breeze.

"I swear," whispers Gerda and closes her eyes.

The Dachshund is astonished. Friedmann frozen, as if in a still, his gaze too wide-eyed to turn liquid in emotion.

You'll see, now she'll reopen them and burst out laughing, Willy thinks, swallowing. But no.

Little Gerda in the sailor-style bathing suit, the small

breasts that vanish between the stripes, her eyelids closed tight, her lips pursed, seems like a child who can't be touched.

André mumbles something in Hungarian, very softly.

"What?"

"Nothing."

"You know, not fair."

"*Èletem*. It's used like *mein Schatz* . . . more or less."

Gerda scrutinizes him while she repeats the word with a transparent serenity.

"Was that right?"

"Perfect."

"Easy to be Magyar. What did I say?"

"My life," Friedmann answers, and takes a breath.

A few minutes later, hearing them laughing again like lunatics, Willy stepped forward. With the outing to Cannes put off, he returned to the camp, stretching out in the shade of a twisted sapling, while the tourists left with the last ferry. There was only the sound of the boats in the distance and a strong scent of lavender. André and Gerda arrived with enough fish to reduce the ration of their canned companions to an antipasto. "I'm going to wash off," Gerda said, pulling Friedmann behind her, and while they set off on the path to the sea Raymond started picking up the leftovers, muttering that *ils s'enfichent de tout*, the lovers.

Dr. Chardack is unsure whether to be surprised by that memory, so intact. It doesn't seem to him that he's ever recalled it, much less shared it with anyone. Twenty-five years have passed since then, but it's not the number that's important. What's important is that the past should be left alone, with the dead in their place, but now that memory has appeared, so complete that he recalls even the scent of lavender. The things that you don't use, that you don't damage, that you put away for good, turn up unexpectedly, unaltered.

Robert Capa, he had revealed to his wife when, stopped in traffic on Broadway they heard the bad news on the radio, wasn't Italian but, rather, the Parisian creation of a girl he knew *back in Germany*. His name was Friedmann, in fact, André, which must have been an adaptation—the Hungarians have strange names. From the terse explanations he had added, after abruptly turning off the radio, his wife must have understood that the Jews and Hitler had something to do with it, and a childhood friend he'd lost touch with who really had lived in Italy. But confronted by his unhappy gaze fixed on the windshield, she hadn't pursued it.

That night on the island had been like all the others. When Raymond stopped snoring, the usual mosquitoes began, and when the mosquitoes' hour ended, the commotion in the neighboring tent ceased as well. All this had disturbed Willy's sleep only in the first days, when he had gotten a serious sunburn. Gerda and André weren't the main reason that he hadn't closed an eye. I hope it's Gerda's turn, this time! He had said it to himself over and over again with an almost euphoric excitement. But with whom could he share it? With Ruth, who overnight had found herself alone in the hotel, because Gerda had gone to stay with him, and crossed the street when she saw her? Or with Georg, who had been granted the rights and attentions of one who had been left? Because it seemed insignificant to everyone that Gerda Pohorylle's first relationship after Georg Kuritzkes was with him, the Dachshund.

But on that island something incredible had occurred and he was its witness: the only witness and at the same time the least worthy.

Under the tent pitched in the shadow of a fortress where a man had been imprisoned who, according to legend, was innocent, Willy felt alone with Raymond's whistling breath, with the mosquitoes and Gerda's extraordinary sharp cries (followed by smothered laughter), with the guilt of having given in to his best friend's girl. "It's her turn, this time!" he couldn't say to anyone.

But suddenly Dr. Kuritzkes has emerged from that past he thought he had buried.

And now he's almost running along Hertel Avenue, determined not to waste more time: not to finally buy a pastry, or to repeat to himself, as if before a jury that he didn't summon, that Gerda had ended things with Georg before giving him a real kiss. And this Georg must have known, otherwise he wouldn't have indulged the impulse to telephone him with the spontaneity that drew on an unaltered affection, the affection that binds old friends, even across years and continents.

The guilt lies there, also unaltered. Out of ideological consistency or out of pride, Georg hadn't asked for an account of anything, and he had never been able to tell him that he had been a coward, as well as a fool. So the friendship had died and today's phone call wasn't enough to revive it.

Now Dr. Chardack heads with mechanical haste toward the Italian restaurant that is just ahead, a recently opened place where he's never been. He comes out with a tray of cannoli and a rough paper bag that, according to American law, covers a bottle from he no longer remembers what vineyard. It doesn't matter, he'll find out at home. Clutching the brown paper at the base of the neck while the other hand is occupied is uncomfortable, another reason to hurry.

Twenty-five years to accept a guilt that doesn't hold up and forgive himself.

But he had been right, that night on Île Sainte-Marguerite, when he stared at the imperfect darkness of the tent with that euphoria colored by Schadenfreude (no, he wouldn't dream of paraphrasing the meaning of that word), until the first cries of the seagulls arrived and a slightly sad calm. This time, he would have liked to say to Georg, it was pointless to hope, wait, torment oneself without letting it show, as he had done.

He had also been right when, two years later (it was summer again but they wouldn't go on vacation), in the delirium and mounting unease about the funeral that the Communist Party was organizing for the daughter of Paris fallen in the struggle against fascism, he had grasped something that flung them all beyond the shock wave of that inconceivable loss.

They'd known for days that Gerda was dead, for three days they had waited in Paris and for three more days had remained beside her, before taking the bier to the cemetery.

Exhausted, scattered in tiny groups compared with the blocs from the factories or Party sections, they kept a slight distance from the head of the cortege—he with Raymond, friends from the SAP in two compact rows, Csiki Weisz with the circle of Hungarians, Cartier-Bresson, who towered over Chim making him disappear (or Chim wasn't there, hadn't come back from Spain?). They sought one another with their eyes, but not too intently, they looked for the back of Capa's neck, at the head of the procession, or Ruth, who was dragging Gerda's father through the streets that kept getting steeper, with the brother beside her (Karl or Oskar? He had forgotten . . .) who had brought him from the Serbian town where Gerda's family had taken refuge after leaving Germany.

They proceeded at the inexorably slow pace of giant parades, crushed by the brass that kept repeating the funeral march, crossing Place de l'Opéra, turning onto the Grands Boulevards for short stretches, passing over the canal where André Friedmann had often envied the retired fishermen, struggling toward Ménilmontant, coming to a standstill at the entrance to Père Lachaise and on the paths inside that led to the Communard's Wall.

A crowd encumbered by banners and red flags spread out around the tomb, making the speakers invisible. The masses of workers stank of sweat, but the wreaths and bouquets, already withered by hours of walking in the sun, stank even more. Solemn and bellicose orations, telegrams, verses (or were they poetic phrases?) dedicated to a lark who died in Brunete yet will never cease to make her song heard. Someone recalled that on that day, August 1, 1937, she would have been twenty-seven, "our Gerda," the courageous comrade who had given her young life for a struggle that she knew marked the future of them all. Listening was equivalent to waiting for the speeches to end, the audience dazed to the point where the flowers or handfuls of earth would fall into the grave from hands by now numb, like the rest of the people in line to say farewell. At least the funeral was over.

But two days earlier, in the morning, when they met at the Gare d'Austerlitz, there were only a hundred of the hundred thousand who would parade through Paris on the Sunday: half prominent personalities, half friendly faces, nearly the same people who had converged at the editorial offices of *Ce Soir* after seeing the paper with the black-bordered picture of Mademoiselle Taro.

It had occurred to Willy to go by the newspaper office only after hurrying to the hotel on Rue Vavin looking for Capa, finding instead Soma Kuritzkes, just arrived from Naples, so distraught that he was disoriented. Willy had brought him to Ruth, hoping she could help him come to himself. But the concierge had told him that Madame had left with that photographer who had showed up in a stupor when the whole building, and one might say the whole city, was still asleep. Gone where, Madame? To get your poor friend, according to Monsieur Melchior . . .

Seeing the time, Willy had taken Soma to lunch. He had thought carefully of avoiding Boulevard de Montparnasse, choosing a small, uncrowded place. "On me," he had said, seeing Georg's brother looking for his wallet. But Soma had pulled out a note for Gerda. *"Monsieur Capa a rappelé a 9 heures."* At the hotel they must have taken him for a relative and given him that note. Could Willy let him return alone to the hotel? So they had taken the metro to Rue du Quatre-Septembre and had headed together to the office of *Ce Soir*.

The first person they saw was one of Capa's great *copains*. He was smoking, squatting on his heels, his head resting against the wall, the friend who in that happy summer had invited them often to Cannes (on the ferry Gerda would put on her shoes and apply some lipstick) to pretend they were wealthy tourists, as he was.

Motionless, he recounted that Capa just the day before had been jubilant ("He ordered champagne brought to the room") because *Life* would send him to China with Gerda. Then he had started weeping, he wept with an agonizing Asian inertia, while the ash of the cigarette kept getting closer to his fingers, without falling. Suddenly he stood up. "Inoue Seiichi, Mainichi Press, Tokyo," he had said to Soma with a bow. And he started up Rue du Quatre-Septembre, to reappear two mornings later at the Gare d'Austerlitz, his suit and face impeccable, as always extremely punctual.

Gare d'Austerlitz at an hour that was strange for the *bohème* of refugees and for the Parisian intelligentsia used to carrying on into the night. But they were all there early that morning. And when the railway worker comrades had unloaded the coffin, covered by the flag of the Spanish Republic, they had had only to clench their left fists and their lips.

Then Gerda's father had advanced toward the bier and had begun to recite the kaddish. Someone followed him, *yitgadal v'yit-kadash sh'mei rabba'*, a sequence of words recovered in a whisper. But the back that shook before those hundred people, that liturgical rocking toward the coffin aligned beside the tracks, recalled the movements of one possessed. Herr Pohorylle had stopped suddenly, swayed forward, crumpled.

He had ended the kaddish lying on the soft red silk flag that enveloped the remains of his daughter.

Capa, too, would have collapsed at that moment, if the friend next to him hadn't realized it. Willy had seen them holding onto one another, and had seemed to see again André when he quarreled with Gerda: she sent him to the door and Seiichi had to drag him home dead drunk. In addition there were the cameras, the journalists from *Ce Soir*. The final picture had been this: Capa, disheveled, unshaved (oh, how she would have detested seeing him like that!), his complexion ashen, suspended between a Moscow muse and an extremely elegant Japanese gentleman.

Capa had been led away, the ceremony had gone forward. "It's over," Willy had thought, "*c'est fini.*" That phrase whirled continuously in his head, it whirled in a void and from the void picked up other phrases, "*c'est fini, fini, rien ne va plus, les jeux sont faits.*" Soma had asked him if they shouldn't join the Pohorylles, afterward, at the hotel. "*Schluss,*" Willy had said to himself. Starting tomorrow he would go back to doing his things: go to the university, help Soma with enrollment and a residency permit. And then really nothing was over: Madrid remained under siege, Hitler was preparing for war, China had been invaded by Japan, the Front Populaire was crumbling, the Communist Party was gaining a heroine and martyr out of a terrible loss.

But André Friedmann, he, yes, he was finished, Robert Capa from that moment on, whatever he did. The spaces that André and Gerda had stolen in the cafés and newspapers with their theatrical talent were finished, finished under the reality of a tank track that weighed more than a boulder.

Save yourself if you can.

Willy was no longer upset, but infinitely empty, lucid, and calm. Whatever the choices we make, he had said to himself, whatever reason for fighting we pursue or end up abandoning, from now on they will be only means for saving ourselves, each according to his possibilities and each according to his needs.

"I think they've almost finished," he said to Soma.

This youth who wants to study chemistry at the Sorbonne will save himself, and maybe also his brother down in Spain. And anyway neither he nor Georg was in the room waiting with a bottle of champagne for Gerda to return.

Dr. Chardack is walking along the tree-lined streets that lead home, and the shadow of his short figure has spread over the whole sidewalk. He stops to put on his jacket, an awkward operation with his hands full. He finds the concentration he needs to perform these gestures ridiculous, sees himself as the typical clumsy "Herr Professor." But he's not sorry about what he's become.

He was right. Georg, too, saved himself and landed in a life similar to his, a life devoted to scientific research. The past should be kept carefully outside the door. But if it knocks or rings, as it did this morning, you have to let it enter. So he did. As soon as he gets home he wants only to dedicate himself to the New York *Times*.

Grief fills him, now, almost overflowing, like the stuffing of the cannoli, and maybe it has an equally pasty, soft consistency.

That stupid death clashed so fiercely with Gerda's talent for life. Apart from the shock and the profound mourning, that disaster had been for all of them a very violent alarm. And they had saved themselves. Georg was in Rome, Soma in Colorado, Ruth in Switzerland . . . Even the Steins and Csiki Weisz and the others, except Capa and Chim, killed by a sniper in Egypt, were alive, were safe.

And Seiichi?

He who throughout the whole monstrous duration of the funeral had stood fast like a shadow behind Capa, and for an unforgettable moment had shared his joy at being able to photograph the Japanese war in China with Gerda—Seiichi had probably been the only one of the Paris friends who had

had to wear the uniform of his country, the most feared and hated in the Pacific.

It wasn't unlikely that Seiichi Inoue was dead.

But if this is a day for memories, Dr. Chardack says to himself as he lengthens his stride toward home, the bottle in one hand and the tray of cannoli in the other, then better to direct them toward something exhilarating to the point of absurd, to the point of feeling a detached wonder toward what remained forever on the other side of the ocean. As absurd as the night in Cannes when Willy met Seiichi, and they were wined and dined at the expense of the Rising Sun with a *plateau de coquillages* and expensive champagne, and then, parading along the Croisette to the brightly lit Palm Beach Casino, they had started shouting out an aria from a Hungarian-German operetta, with Seiichi suspended demonstratively between André and Gerda.

My mama was from Yokohama
Papa from gay Paree.
My mama wore only pajamas
Because he liked to see.[2]

The only thing to do at this moment is find a way to avoid having to get the house keys out of his pants pocket. The kitchen window is open, he can get to it by trampling the flowerbed, he moves as close as possible to the windowsill and shouts the name of his wife. After a few seconds the noise of dishes stops. Dr. Chardack heads for the door and waits for her to arrive and open it.

He had been right, but it shouldn't have happened like that.

---

[2] "*Meine Mama war aus Yokohama / Aus Paris war der Papa / Meine Mama ging nur im Pyjama / Weil Papa das gerne sah,*" from the operetta *Viktoria und ihr Husar* by Georg (Pál) Abraham (music) and Arthur Grünwald and Willy Löhner-Beda (libretto), first performance: Budapest, February 21, 1920 (author's note).

PART II
RUTH CERF
Paris, 1938

When the best girlfriend
And the best girlfriend
Traipse through the streets,
To go shopping,
To go shopping,
To shoot the breeze,
Wander through the streets . . .
"Wenn die beste Freundin" (1928)
—MISCHA SPOLIANSKY and MARCELLUS SCHIFFER
(translated by Shelley Frisch) sung by Marlene Dietrich

I am the Dark One,—the Widower,—the Unconsoled
The Prince of Aquitaine whose Tower is destroyed:
My only star is dead, and my constellated lute
Bears the black Sun of Melancholia.
—GÉRARD DE NERVAL, *El Desdichado*

T he sky is locked in an immutable gray, and Ruth, rain-soaked, sick of running, is carrying around Paris something she doesn't know how to tell Capa.

He returned at the end of November, exhausted, ill from the exertions and the cold he'd endured in Spain, and even though the fever has gone down, finally, he still isn't leaving his hotel room, his den. But his friends, old and new, flock to see him: Seiichi, with the clouds of *macarons* in expensive boxes from Place de la Madeleine (one open, two untouched on the night table when Ruth passed by the other day); Chim, every day, if he's not away on a photography job.

Ruth often meets him on the street where the Atelier Robert Capa is: Chim has also been going there since the start. The words ("How's Capa?" "Better." "Have a good day.") come out in the confidential tone of a whisper on the path that crosses the Montparnasse cemetery, where visitors are few, apart from groups that come to pay homage to some famous tomb.

Cartier-Bresson she saw only once, sitting on the sick man's bed, legs crossed, with those outsize childish fingers holding up the paper to read him an interesting article.

Just now it's Ruth who doesn't have time for visits, and she also goes much less frequently to the Atelier, on Rue Froidevaux: Capa's immobility means less work in the studio.

But Csiki Weisz stops by the hotel morning and evening, generally around dinnertime, "so I can make him eat and drink, otherwise when's he going to get better," and brings him the news. Primarily copies of the newspapers that give an increasing amount of space (and well paid) to Capa's most recent reporting on the Spanish Civil War: the series on the farewell to the International Brigades and the one on the battle of Río Segre were bought by all the important press outlets, including *Life*. But Csiki repeats to Ruth that not even that has the power to revive his friend's energy, in fact it makes him feel like an undertaker, someone making money off other people's troubles. "It'll pass," says Ruth. "Let's hope soon," says Csiki.

Ruth isn't in the studio when Capa shows up for a hello, playing the clown as usual: kissing the secretary, talking on the phone, messing about with his friend and assistant in the darkroom, spreading good cheer though his eyes are still ringed by dark shadows.

Csiki doesn't need to explain to Ruth that he has no faith in appearances, even if appearances should be respected. He responds to her *"Bonjour, c'est moi"* with a *"J'arrive tout de suite,"* like a good shop boy who can't leave a job already begun, and says nothing else.

Today, however, when he appears, his hands aren't wet, as usual. As soon as he sees her he hands her an illustrated magazine.

"Regards-ici."

"Let me take off this wet coat, hang on."

"Twelve pages in the London *Picture Post*."

"Fantastic."

They had begun that euphoric dialogue, made up of superlatives, when Capa decided to go to China. Ruth and Csiki spent a lot of time together, working on the material he sent. The images spoke clearly of the indiscriminate violence with which the Japanese devastated populous cities and massacred the inhabitants. But they felt reassured that Capa was so far away: with Joris Ivens, the director he'd met in Spain, and John Fernhout, the husband of Eva Besnyö, who had grown up in the same building in Budapest, that is to say almost a sister. The Pilvax was a very new *passage*, with the Friedmanns' dressmaking salon off the courtyard and the Besnyös' apartment on an upper floor; they were wealthy enough to give the sixteen-year-old Eva her first camera. For Csiki those ancient hierarchies were a guarantee that the troupe would take care of their friend. Maybe it wasn't right that they should worry about almost nothing but Capa's safety, in the face of those events, but they couldn't help it, after what had happened to Gerda. They couldn't even avoid the superstitious thought that if Gerda had returned from Madrid she would have been safe out in the East. But it was pointless to brood. The studio on Rue Froidevaux was "my Paris HQ"—Capa had written from the Asian front—and they clung gratefully to their own roles and tasks, which included commenting "Fantastic" on every important publication.

Then everything had changed again. Capa returned from Hankou ("Sorry, the diarrhea wouldn't go away"), and in the space of a newsreel the *shigella* bacteria could have been transmitted to his assistants. France and Germany had delivered the Sudetens to Hitler, after Vienna fell because the people had decided by a majority to hand themselves over to the Nazis. "*Scheissaustriaker!*" Ruth blurted out. Csiki talked less and less, aside from some laconic crack ("*Anschluss-Schluss*") or a word of universal comprehension ("*katasztrófa*") that suddenly came out of his mouth. Budapest, the second capital of the now dismembered Austro-Hungarian Empire, was being choked by the new Reich, and Weisz's and Friedmann's relatives were trapped inside it.

"You'll see, you won't be next on the menu," said Ruth to comfort him. "Too Magyar, too much paprika. And anyway you already have fascism!"

Csiki giggled, grateful.

It turned out to be easy for Ruth to work with Csiki Weisz, and even to understand him. They had been asked to take on the jobs that André and Gerda had done before—Capa's friend the laboratory, Taro's friend the captions—as if they were counter-figures, auxiliary troops behind the front lines. Besides, Ruth had always been Gerda's ally, only the affair with Willy had upset things. It wasn't that she couldn't pay for the hotel (for practical matters there was always a solution); it was a question of trust. "With men you do as you like," she had said to her, "I've never asked you anything, I've always covered for you and helped you—ever since you liked Georg, and a lot, and didn't know what to do about your Stuttgart boyfriend. You move to the Dachshund's without saying anything, then come here to get your things and leave me some money for the hotel. You don't act like that with a friend!"

When they started seeing each other again from time to time, and the ashtray at the café of the moment was overflowing with their cigarettes, Ruth surrendered to the evidence that Gerda really couldn't understand what had wounded her so much. Basically, she concluded, it was only the small rites of living together, with the inevitable rifts, the same that were now being repeated between Melchior and her. And that thought made it easy for her to enjoy an hour in her presence, which was always so pleasant. She had only to take in Gerda's sincere enthusiasm for her new movie jobs ("Max Ophüls? Magnificent! Be sure to get yourself a bit part!") and listen to her talk about the guests at the Steins', or the ideas of Willy Brandt and the other important comrades she hung around with, or the great progress she was making with the camera. "Cross your fingers, Ruth, I found a job—in fact, you won't believe it, but Friedmann found it for me."

"Really? Congratulations."

"Alliance Photo represents the best German photographers and I'm making myself liked, I'm learning. I don't give a damn if I don't get along too well with my boss, Maria Eisner, who's crazy about André, naturally. She was looking for an assistant who knows languages and also bookkeeping? Well, she found her. It's not my fault if I'm smarter than she thought."

Ruth didn't have to do anything but relax, scrape up with the spoon the sugar remaining at the bottom of the cup, observe the passersby with one eye and Gerda with the other. The smoke rings exhaled with gracious emphasis, her mouth that sipped the coffee without dribbling. And that story, punctuated by laughter, that was like the chatter of a girl in love. Maybe it was: even if the love object at the moment was a photographic agency. She had immediately told Eisner that she had experience and a talent for business. In Leipzig she managed her father's accounts, and in Stuttgart she had helped her boyfriend launch himself in the coffee trade after the collapse of American cotton. Selling photographs was certainly more inspiring than selling eggs wholesale or the four blends of which customers usually ordered the cheapest.

"I understand how the market works."

"Oh yes?" Ruth answered, distracted, because the theatrical pause required it.

"It's not enough to be prompt and so on. You have to have the right names, or else invent them. You think an editor in chief can distinguish the quality of an image? Rarely. The photograph is made of nothing, inflated, merchandise that's out of date in a day. It's knowing how to sell it," Gerda concluded, and raised triumphant, mischievous eyes toward the street.

Observing her, Ruth had an intuition: look at her, she thought, that small woman who attracts every gaze, that incarnation of elegance, femininity, *coquetterie*, and no one would ever suspect that she reasons, feels, and acts like a man. It was too convenient an excuse to forgive her, but perhaps a good way of understanding how anger never carried off all the affection. And when Gerda got up, kissing her with the side of her cheeks so as not to smudge her lipstick, Ruth no longer noticed the wake of displeasure scented with a drop of Mitsouko that she could have recognized with her eyes closed.

Gerda was unsettling. She wasn't like any of the girls Ruth knew in Leipzig: not the ones like her, who when they fell in love stopped noticing other men, or the girls whose sole purpose was to make the heads in the male universe spin. There was no doubt that Gerda was aware of having that effect; she reveled in it like an ornamental fish in an aquarium, but in an unusual way. Openly, without malice, almost candid. She liked being attractive and courted in principle, she liked certain boys in particular: but she didn't make any mystery or fuss about it. ("Don't you find Georg remarkable? I've never been fascinated before by someone so young. Did you think about him like that, too?" "He wouldn't even consider me . . . " "You can tell me, come on, I won't be offended." "What? That there's no comparison between Kuritzkes and the others?" "So you like him! But I'll be happy to give you Willy Chardack." "The Dachshund? Ah, thank you so much!")

They wouldn't have become friends if they hadn't very quickly begun speaking freely to each other, making Ruth's first impressions vacillate. The little doll from Stuttgart wasn't only more entertaining than a gussied-up featherbrain, like some of her high-school classmates, interested only in fashion and in famous figures or suitors (to boast of if handsome or from a good family, to mock otherwise). It was something different. What, precisely, Ruth didn't understand (did "without prejudices" coincide with "unprejudiced"? Not completely), but Gerda's persistence in hanging around with her had been enough to prove that she wasn't an arrogant stuck-up person.

And so she had let herself be invaded by that refreshing genial-
ity and brilliance.

They had met through Georg Kuritzkes in the pool at the
Bar Kochba *Sportverein* and then had seen each other in the
same group after the swimming season. They had already
exchanged the first bland confidences, when they discovered
that they went to the same school. Ruth was a student at the
Gymnasium while Gerda was taking stenography and home-
economics classes: not because she cared about the diploma
but because she'd also gone to a commercial school in
Stuttgart.

"You know, I'm someone who really can't stand having
nothing to do," she had said one day outside a classroom, book
in hand, waiting for the lesson to begin.

"I always arrive early," she had laughed, swaying on her
heels. "It's obvious that I like coming to school."

"The Gaudig-Schule is famous for an avant-garde approach
to teaching," Ruth had said, a flat observation that contrasted
with Gerda's enthusiasm. "They'd like to educate us to
develop our independent personality, cultivating spiritual
growth that transcends the subjects, as they must have
explained to you when . . . "

"All I notice is that the teachers are better than in
Stuttgart," Gerda had interrupted, "and more approachable
than in the Swiss boarding school I went to. On the other hand
there's not much to develop in the courses I take, stuff for girls
looking for a good match or a job as a business secretary."

So Ruth had said that she had several professors who were
really smart, thoughtful, very open and aware. Some even
allowed the students to organize political meetings, making the
great hall available. A few years earlier an imposing youth had
come from Berlin ("a Viking, you'd never have called him a student") who had talked about the class struggle in the scholastic
world. Soon afterward, a group of girls had established a

section of the socialist student union, which she was still involved in.

"In a girls' school! At ours it was something if they organized the Christmas market with our little crafts. Or the classical music concert, terrible. But naturally we all wanted to be the best."

"As for that, my classmates and I at the *Gymnasium* aren't all great friends, either."

Maybe their understanding had been sealed at that moment, when Gerda burst into a laugh so loud that it would have clashed with even the most advanced pedagogic concept, if the bell hadn't rung to muffle it.

But Ruth would never have imagined that, starting that day, whenever a class in cooking or Gabelsberger shorthand coincided with the high-school schedule, Gerda was waiting for her in front of the gate that opened onto Döllnitzer Strasse. She'd be leaning against the wrought-iron bars, sometimes with her umbrella open, more often hanging by an arm, almost always smoking: like a big sister or a woman who has a date with a man she knows will show up. The building cast on her its dark asymmetrical shadow, lengthened by the outline of the stepped tympana, neo-Gothic ornaments that decorated the gray mass of the institute at a pointless height. She was restless in her natural way, alone and tiny compared to the flow of high-school students: she was independence incarnate.

Ruth joined Gerda, they chatted a little in front of the gate, and then set off for their respective classrooms or, still chatting, toward home. In her most daring shoes (the ones she wore to school) her friend came up to about her shoulders. But they were two pretty and carefree girls together, illuminated by one another.

Ruth had never seen herself like that in her life as a student. The first thing she noticed as she walked toward Döllnitzer Strasse now was her own steps, or rather the large feet in the laced shoes resoled twice a year, polished with Erdal, in the original box with the red frog. And then the clothes that her mother altered for her or, when she handed down her better items, had made over by the dressmaker. Her father's trench coat (also his ties, since they were fashionable) resurrected from a box that stank of naphthalene. "It doesn't fit my brothers and anyway it's what people are wearing these days," she had rejected her mother's protests and, readjusting the belt at her waist, tightening it as much as possible, had concluded, "See, it's perfect," before going out the door, head down. Muffled up inside it, she had begun to feel more protected and special. To a benevolent or interested imagination, she and Gerda resembled a provincial Garbo and Dietrich. But basically the only thing that counted was that they had found each other.

Csiki Weisz repeats that it's a relief to see Capa in the Atelier again, at least every so often, and after handing her the *Picture Post* he disappears into the little kitchen that has been sacrificed to the laboratory. "*Ein Moment!*" Ruth knows very well how long that moment can last so she yells at him: "I'm making coffee, what do you say?" and immediately starts fussing with the pot and the Eltron immersion heater, a Berlin investment of Weisz and Friedmann, protected by their shabby old clothes when they left for Paris. Now it was encrusted like a marine fossil, and you had to be careful, for example pushing the magazine lying on the desk out of range of the spray. As soon as the water starts to drip through the filter, Ruth inspects the provisions in the cupboard. There's milk because they bring it every morning, but all that's left of the Heudebert *biscottes* is the tin box. She finds two apples, a bruised pear, the hardened end of a baguette, the sugar bowl.

"Have you had breakfast?"

She repeats the question until Csiki replies: "*Merci, pas de problem,"* so she begins to work fiercely on the crust of bread until she digs out some acceptable mouthfuls.

Csiki forgets to eat, he never has time to shop ("The shops close early"; "But the *boulangerie* behind here is open even Sunday morning!" "Oh, is it? I didn't know . . .), and Madame Garai, the Atelier's secretary, doesn't consider the matter part of her duties. So ever since Ruth stopped coming daily to Rue Froidevaux, the basis of Csiki Weisz's nutrition is dinners with his friend "Bandi" Capa ("Eating once a day is enough for me, look, I have horse teeth"), which are coming to an end. These dinners will be over as soon as the sick man gets back on his feet enough to make the leap from the bistros in the neighborhood of the hotel to the rations of the Republican units in Spain, where he has every intention of returning. And afterward? Ruth wonders, worried. Afterward Csiki will manage, or the émigrés from Budapest will take care of him—there's quite a group in Paris. It's absurd that she's still the one who worries about Csiki. Ridiculous that she goes in search of plates to wash or crumbs under the table, as if in the preceding months she hadn't realized that the floor was always clean, the dishes in order, even the bed in the loft always made with military perfection.

"The woman who gets you is lucky," she used to joke, which provoked a slight reddening of Csiki's long nose, even if the remark was as old as the remains of a baguette. She, too, is lucky, since as soon as she's poured his cup of coffee and lighted a cigarette Csiki opens the door a crack, "Sorry, I'll be there in two minutes." Otherwise, between one drag and the next, the nervousness about that thing to say to Capa would mount again: not too urgent a thing, but a thought to get rid of.

What should she do? Look for him in the cafés of Montparnasse? Lie in wait at the hotel? Better to speak to him right away, ignoring his convalescence and the friends crowding into his hotel room. When he's completely recovered, he'll be increasingly focused on impressing the new *copains* who call him Bob ("Bàab"), as if he were one of them, an American in Paris, as Gerda conceived him, who, to listen to her . . .

"*C'est l'Atelier Robert Capa,*" she had repeated into the receiver the first time she'd heard that diminutive.

"*Oui,*" the slurred accent insisted. "*J'ais un message pour Bob . . . Bob Capa.*"

"Ah, sorry, *Monsieur, dites-moi, j'annote . . .*"

From then on she got used to it, but she couldn't get rid of the sensation of unfamiliarity and annoyance. If André is the name of a *coiffeur* or a waiter, what's Bob? A witty uncle, the lanky deskmate, an ordinary decent fellow who does an ordinary job? She can't understand how a pseudonym can have its own life. "Robert Capa" entered her ears, like everyone else's, with a French accent. And that pronunciation made it easier to adopt: a name of uncertain origin, a stage name. The creators, Gerda and André, hadn't foreseen that some real Americans would swallow it as if it were real, even if they were so thrilled by their brainchild that they would announce it to anyone at the drop of a hat.

On the First of May in glorious 1936 a photographer was zigzagging his way against the current of the almost motionless parade, and Ruth, impatient with that epic slowness, stood on tiptoe and waved to summon him. They had taken Paris, they were a mass so vast that the result, proclaimed two days later— the victory of the Front Populaire—seemed only the final tally of a reality already measured in peaceful, festive bodies, smelling of lilies of the valley and carnations. Harmonious flowers for the harmonious demonstration, the red parade assembled in Place de la Bastille with the slogan "*Pour le pain, la paix et la liberté*" and the concrete, revolutionary union demand for a forty-hour work week.

"Come on, let's look for Gerda," André said, "we have some news!"

Ruth let herself be drawn by curiosity and by the hand that was pulling her by the coat.

"I'll be back soon," she cried to Melchior.

Along the section that they retraced laboriously, slipping sideways between the demonstrators, she imagined various hypotheses. The first, that they had got married, she immediately discarded: Gerda getting married and, on top of that, to Friedmann—no, it wasn't believable. "They're going to America" crossed her mind, and she was convinced that it must be that. The air was permeated by the socialist spring, but in the gridlock of marchers it was inevitable to think that a couple of provocateurs would be enough for it to end as it had in February of '34, with ten dead. If some fight should break out, Ruth had to be ready to escape, strictly speaking she shouldn't even have set foot in that crowd.

The first one they saw was the Japanese, standing still on the sidelines with Gerda.

"Here she is," André said, and then to Gerda: "You explain it to her, now let me smoke a cigarette."

Seiichi had lighted cigarettes for them all and Gerda held the lighter, as if striking the wheel could awaken a genius that would suggest a good place to start.

"No. You have to introduce yourself."

André had taken a drag on the filter held tight between his lips, and he stared at Ruth with a theatrical expression, even straightening his forelock.

"As the cursed poet said: *Je est un autre*. You must call me Robert Capa."

That's it?

Seiichi signaled applause. Friedmann was radiant. Gerda repeated "Robert Capa" in French, English, and German accents, insistently pointing out that it didn't get mangled in any language and was very catchy. No one noticed Ruth and her embarrassed smile. Half a step at a time, the metalworkers' contingent paraded by.

That was it, André had chosen a pseudonym. Gerda thought she had extracted the tricks of the trade from Maria Eisner, but if she seriously believed that a name was enough to start making a name for yourself, she remained an apprentice.

"You're basically petit-bourgeois," Ruth had concluded, but dreams were free.

"It sounds Marseillaise or something like that," she commented. "Anyway it sounds good."

"Capa means 'shark' in Hungarian," André replied, deaf to Ruth's irony.

"No, it's American, like Frank Capra," Gerda said, "American of Italian origin or whatever you want, but goes with that face . . . It's enough if the French fall for it."

Ruth was confused. The name was more attractive than the ordinary André Friedmann. But what other advantages could it have? The French preferred a fake Marseillais, or, say, American, to a *petit juif* from Budapest? Certainly. But given that they already knew the photographer, how would they fall for it?

Gerda, André, and Seiichi looked at her with the shining eyes of children in collusion.

"It's better than Frank Capra," Ruth admitted. "It has a sort of hint of nobility, like Don Diego de la Vega in the famous performance . . . "

"How does that come to mind!" André replied. "We thought of Robert Taylor, and for her Greta Garbo. No more Pohorylle. *Voilà*, starting today she'll be Gerda Taro."

"She's American, too, I suppose."

"Doesn't matter, international," Gerda replied. "Only Robert Capa has to be American."

A protest banner had appeared—"AGAINST THE EXPENSIVE LIFE," another "AGAINST GERMAN

REARMAMENT"—and meanwhile Gerda was saying things no less absurd than the comment with which Ruth tried to flush them out. Robert Capa lived at the Ritz, had a limousine and a race car, was a handsome guy, athletic, lover of the good life.

"Bachelor?" Ruth asked. "Then look out, because they'll rob you . . . "

"Bachelor of course!" André flared up, having apparently lost his sense of humor. "Otherwise how would he be in Monte Carlo one day, the next in Deauville, then at the bank in Geneva checking his investments. Not to mention those boring returns to America, when it's impossible to reach him, because he's traveling on a private plane. A guy who's always had everything, you know? His grandfather arrived in San Francisco during the Gold Rush, defended his nuggets against the worst scoundrels, but was killed by a drunk creditor. The widow retreated to cultivate flowers and read novels. Three daughters passionate about literature, a son passionate about botany. The boy, who became a great agronomist, married the daughter of the biggest canned-fruit producer in California."

"You're the one who wanted to write novels," Gerda stops him. "Come to the point!"

"Stories, *Schatzi*, have to be invented properly, otherwise they don't hold water."

"The heir to the canned fruit—that is, Robert Capa," Friedmann resumed, "is tired of California and canned peaches. He sells everything, comes to Paris, spends and squanders, but it's not enough for him. Photojournalism satisfies the adventurous vein that runs in the family, the need to defeat boredom. He doesn't work for money, of course, but like a good capitalist he wouldn't dream of giving anything to anyone. So he takes Gerda as personal agent. And she, with her charm, hires me as a factotum. And here we are."

"The work of Robert Capa," Gerda was precise, "I naturally have to offer at an exorbitant price . . . "

Ruth burst into laughter so loud that it attracted glances of dismay from their worker comrades to the right and the left. "The two of you are completely mad!"

No, not too mad. It seemed that Gerda and André intended to cast the bait with discretion.

"Ah, the Parisians who think they're so savvy! Newspaper editors, even those on our side, whom it would kill to raise your fee by two cents, you poor anti-fascist refugee. But when you talk about an American who travels in the beau monde of all Europe, they can't wait to meet him. *Très désolés*, he's gone to Venice with his latest conquest, we have no idea when he'll be back. And who's the girl, someone famous? That we certainly can't say."

Suddenly Gerda coaxed a little flame from the lighter, held it at its peak, then abruptly closed the lid and gave the silver parallelepiped back to Seiichi. The loudspeakers were scratching, the speeches were about to begin. "Bread, peace, and freedom!" some demonstrators proclaimed.

"What brand is it: American?" Gerda inquired.

"I bought it at Cartier on Place Vendôme."

"Stupendous. I know our bluff seems like a childish joke. But people believe what they want to believe. At least for a while. And a while is enough for us. Because afterward, I'm sure of it, we'll never go back to where we started."

Csiki Weisz shrugged whenever Ruth had an outburst about the new diminutive of Robert Capa ("Bob, a three-letter word, and they manage to mangle it!") after hearing it pronounced by some Americans. Thus, one day when Chim was arranging his photographic materials right on the table where now the café au lait is ready for Csiki, she asked him the question. On the basis of what criteria does one choose a pseudonym? And didn't it bother him that he wasn't called by his real name anymore?

"No. Chim is nice, don't you think? For someone with the face of an owl . . . "

Ruth had nodded and waited for the explanation that Chim was quick to provide, with that stolidity that belied the cliché of the photojournalist in mad pursuit of events. He told her that he had simply adapted the first syllable of his surname, Szymin, preposterous. Besides, even in Warsaw he had always had a nickname, a diminutive, just as Capa was Bandi and for some would remain that all his life.

"And that 'Bob' that won't come out of my mouth, can you stand it?"

Chim had smiled vaguely, looking up from his negatives.

"The Americans, of course, but not only them. *Llegó Roberto Capa, el fotógrafo, mira, tenemos suerte!* they say in the units. *The photographer Roberto Capa came, we're so lucky!* That's what they call him from Andalusia to the Basque territories."

That in Spain they saw Capa as a good-luck charm bewildered her. But, determined to oppose the gently ironic light that had appeared through the lenses of the person she was talking to, she launched into a replay of the birth of our hero. By the way, what happened in the end to the American millionaire?

"It was mainly Gerda who liked that," Chim said, in a timbre of voice that went below his usual placidity. "He was unmasked almost immediately."

Again absorbed in rearranging contact prints and negatives, he had talked about the scoop at the League of Nations a couple of months after the May 1st parade. The other reporters were photographing Haile Selassie, who was calling for sanctions, but only Capa's Leica had captured the unfortunate Spaniard arrested with the Italian journalists who were yelling like fascist thugs. Everyone wanted that photograph, at whatever price, even if they knew perfectly well that it was André

Friedmann who'd shot it. So he had been convinced that working as Robert Capa suited him.

"But then why isn't he always called Robert, instead of that inane Bob?"

The sentence had come out of her stubbornly, but Chim didn't bother to look up.

"A name is a name," he said, "in the end it belongs to others."

Ruth didn't agree: in French didn't you say *donner un nom*—give a name? And didn't a gift become the possession of the one who received it, and so he could choose another one?

Chim had agreed, continuing to rearrange.

"O.K., sorry: I'll let you work."

Chim had detained her, pointing a finger at his contact sheets.

"If we took a photo . . . not these, one that you're in. How would you identify yourself?"

After reflecting, bewildered, she had told him that Gerda, always ready to get the best out of every experience, had once summarized an article by René Spitz: when a child begins to smile, then recognizes himself in the mirror, then stamps his feet yelling no!, it's a crucial phase, like the later one in which he acquires the capacity to say "I." In practice, however, the professor couldn't tolerate that his secretary was an independent girl. "A failing that is, unfortunately, very common."

Chim possessed a quality that you wouldn't have guessed: a gallant version of his courtesy, a shy politeness that put any woman at ease.

So Ruth had confessed that in her modeling photographs she barely recognized herself, and it wasn't false modesty or, worse, hypocrisy.

"I see that I'm beautiful, yes, but it's advertising, I'm a commodity . . . In my family there are too many actors, maybe that's why I prefer to do without makeup and posing."

"In your case there's no need."

As if to accompany the compliment Chim offered her a cigarette.

"Anyway," Ruth resumed, "Capa even believed a little in that story of the great American bon vivant, didn't he? And if now he accepts that silly three-letter nickname, maybe it's partly because it confirms that he's succeeded in making himself believable in that role."

"Because *they* succeeded," Chim corrected her, and Ruth was silenced immediately.

And while Chim consoled her with time that smooths out everything (but he touched his eyeglasses), she told herself that that Bob would never have existed without Gerda. At the beginning of the fairy tale she was playing with André as if changing the clothes on a paper doll, and he didn't stamp his feet, in fact he let her do it—*ein braves Kind*. In the end, with Gerda, he had brought into the world nothing but himself: Robert Capa.

It's very light now in the Atelier on Rue Froidevaux, a milky, flat light, thanks to that gray sky: perfect light for an artist, not for a photography studio. Csiki doesn't complain about being confined to the kitchenette, or even about having to "hang out the laundry" in the toilet, going up and down the spiral staircase with the basin of prints, which he clears out before morning. It's not right to make Madame Garai pee under the eyes of Spanish or Chinese armies, and if a client asks for the bathroom, you can't offer him all that intimacy with still fresh photographs, Csiki maintains.

He's not all wrong, nor was it fanciful to think that Capa had chosen that Atelier because it reminded him of the golden years of the Pilvax Passage in Budapest, which was obviously something different: just two steps from Váci Utca, where the fine ladies went to shop, plus it was home to a café famous as the haunt of the revolutionary patriots of '48. The Pilvax had hosted the historic *Kaffeehaus* in the busy elegance of the twenties, but it didn't have the big windows onto Rue Froidevaux, made even more prominent by the furniture Gerda had obtained: no bric-a-brac, just a few pieces but good ones. The linear, lightweight black armchair, the two comfortable boxy chairs surround the narrow table on upholstery sawhorses in rationalist harmony.

Ruth should sit there leafing through the *Picture Post*, but, waiting for Csiki, she gets lost looking out the windows, anxious about the thing she has to tell Capa, tired of waiting for both of them, until the door of the kitchenette opens.

"So, did you see the magazine story?" Csiki says to her, and starts dipping the bread in his café au lait.

Ruth looks at him, leaning on the edge of the table, sipping coffee and smoking, more relaxed.

"Is the bread all right? I don't think there're any traces of mold."

"It's very good, in Budapest there was even that . . . "

Ruth is about to pick up the magazine when she stops, observing Csiki's slow chewing, his elbow on the table, his head bent. Maybe she should have been for Gerda what Weisz was for Friedmann: the companion always grateful for having been chosen, the companion-shadow.

It's not the first time she's thought it, going back to the early days, when André would sit at their table at the Dôme, bumming a cigarette or, if he had a pack, offering them one, but to Gerda first. At a certain point, after the usual coffee, he'd start pulling out the adventures of his adolescence, "a gang of hoodlums like Molnar's Paul Street boys, that's what we were: but we'd be more than happy to admit girls, too . . . " Ruth guessed that those stories were tailor-made for her friend, and in fact Gerda, sensitive to the Magyar-epic touches to that serial plotted in her honor, found them entertaining. "What do I care!"

she retorted when Ruth, before turning out the light at night, said that those tales were novelistic elaborations, not to say half invented. Now she has to admit that she wronged him.

It isn't so much Capa who proved this as his right arm, that thin arm that is now protecting his breakfast bowl. Csiki Weisz, who says nothing about his own childhood, except to narrate it with his gestures of every day, those of the war orphan adopted by an imaginative contemporary.

Ruth had heard the story of Csiki when Gerda was still around. It would have been too maudlin for André's tastes if he hadn't spiked it with a little humor: Weisz-père, who had fallen for Emperor Franz Joseph, but from a horse, in other words he was killed by a Hapsburgian hoof; the firstborn sent to an orphanage, welcomed home again during his *Gymnasium* years, the mother's house quickly treated like a hostel, because a certain Bandi Friedmann, hauling Csiki behind him like a trailer, extended the perimeter of their jaunts far beyond the area between the Elisabeth Bridge and the school just outside the Jewish quarter. And then there were the girlfriends, so pretty and smart—Eva, the lawyer's daughter, and Kati, the banker's daughter—who had taught the boys how to use the first tools of their trade, "and I won't tell you what else . . . " In Berlin, as photographers already well connected in the right circles, they had served as supports and models for Csiki and Bandi. You can always count on people you've done certain stupid things with at a certain point in time, no matter what.

Yes, friends show up in times of trouble. The letter of condolence that Kati Horna had sent arrived in Rue Froidevaux from Spain where she was photographing for the anarchist press. Eva Besnyö's telegram arrived from Amsterdam (BANDI IS HERE STOP DON'T WORRY STOP) when Capa had disappeared into thin air after the funeral, and reassured Csiki and then Ruth, who had quickly informed all the worried friends.

In times of trouble true friends recognize one another. Thanks to Csiki Weisz, Ruth had discovered Bandi, when he engaged her in the studio shortly after the funeral.

It had taken a lot to treat him seriously, at least the bit that he deserved. After all, what had Gerda done at first?

"He's twenty!" she said scornfully.

"And Georg Kuritzkes? Don't tell me you're going to be fussy about the difference of a year . . . "

"But he still has pimples."

Then, toward the end of '34, Gerda had started going with the Dachshund, confirming that André Friedmann was very low on the scale of her admirers. How could Ruth have understood that behind those late flare-ups of acne there was a youth so attached to his teenage gang? Those kids from Budapest had remained true friends: someone took care of Csiki, Csiki took care of Bandi, and not even now that he was Robert Capa would Bandi have forgotten his childhood friend. And Gerda?

Gerda had walked out overnight, but enough of digging up the past. How can you still be angry with a dead woman, Ruth, with all you have to do and think about! Look ahead and consider yourself lucky. You've put aside some savings (not enough), you have a purpose, two older brothers ready to help you, a husband and a Swiss passport, and only a mother still trapped in Germany. Her mother, whose husband died of the Spanish flu when Ruth was five, would have chosen to perform outside the Neues Theater for a handout of a couple of marks, in a feather boa exhumed along with her theatrical repertoire, rather than send a child to the orphanage, and hadn't been too much of a lady to work in other people's houses.

And, as she's making her list, there is also the good fortune that she doesn't have to worry about that fine youth. Csiki can manage on his own, and she can remove him from her thoughts. She could even tell him the thing to say to Capa, just to be safe. Besides, isn't he the one who runs the show?

"Take your time looking at the magazine, Ruth, I've already seen it. I'll clean up."

And there he is with sponge and rag to clean the table and place the *Picture Post* on the tidy surface, following their ritual for opening the first copy that arrives in the studio. You just have to handle the envelopes of the magazines addressed to Mr. Capa carefully, while in the case of the dailies his assistant has perfected a precision technique to hide the fact that he's opened them: this consideration toward Bandi is typical of Csiki, while Capa, on the contrary, tears the wrapping off the mail completely unaware. Over time the eagerness to see the photos laid out on the page has diminished, but the beauty and truth of work destined to touch the eyes of the world survive in the heedless violence of the torn paper.

For this, too, Ruth would like to make amends, apologize to Capa for the bewilderment with which she listened to Gerda when, increasingly, she extolled the talent of André Friedmann.

"I can imagine what talent."

"No, you can't. And don't think that . . . "

"I don't want to know anything."

Ruth laughed, but Gerda insisted.

"If I tell you, that means it's true. All we do is wander around Paris, talk, go on talking in cafés when we're tired of taking pictures or freezing cold or something. I don't want it to be my fault if his Leica ends up in a pawnshop yet again. And also I've repeated to him in every language that all I can offer him is pure and simple friendship. Is that enough for you?"

"Let's hope so. You know what he has in mind, right?"

"All right. Just once. Maybe it was imprudent, but . . . "

The rest dissolved in the fizz of her trills, Gerda was radiant with each of her small childish faults, happy with every secretly stolen pleasure, and Ruth was swept away and overwhelmed by her. If it happened to her, if she remained seduced by her friend, and if in her case the seductive power wasn't the streaked irises or the heart-shaped mouth, even less the small breasts, the tawny pubis, the boyish thighs that Gerda scrubbed every morning with cold water and Marseille soap, how could she reproach her for Georg or Willy or André or any other man unable to let her go and forget her?

It was also Gerda who in every guise (lover, agent, friend) by herself compensated for the audience and the applause that Friedmann was always so in need of, all that anxiety for acclaim would never be limited to those halfhearted little rituals. But even now, when Capa receives so much praise, and so many firm pats on the back from Ernest Hemingway, so many bottles to celebrate their shared ventures, forget the defeats, and send the fascists to hell, the original head of the claque, Csiki Weisz, and she, Ruth Cerf, true child of the dramatic arts, are still there, preparing the little theater to say "Bravo!" Twelve pages in a magazine with a circulation of a million is proof of extraordinary success. And yet for Robert Capa success has become little more than the confirmation of a task performed according to expectations. So Ruth and Csiki exaggerate with adjectives and superlatives, even though he consumes them like water. Only Gerda would have given him a very different substance, she had ambition and conviction for both of them, and for defending free, red, Republican Spain.

Ruth has made up her mind to look at the *Picture Post*, to please Csiki, and then she can talk to him about her plans. She places the magazine in the middle of the table, ready to open it, when the girl on the cover catches her attention. She doesn't seem like a model: she's like a real girl, with a real smile ("The Girl with a Smile") and a nice short haircut, hair as white as a poodle's fur. *Life* would never do a cover like that, the *Life* cover girls are standard beauties. But the *Picture Post*, founded to tear the British Isles away from *Life*, though in an almost identical format, intends to be a progressive journal. The editor is one of ours, Csiki explained to her, someone from Budapest who brought the experience of Berlin journalism to London. And that experience, it seems, translates into a girl who rouses curiosity without disturbing the eye of the buyers. Spain is hidden inside, Spain will regain the headlines of the bourgeois press when it falls, that is to say soon. A bitterness rises in Ruth that brings her back to Capa, exhausted by the aftermath of Río Segre, with Csiki, Chim, and the others who take care of him like a sultan. And you, Gerda, would you manage to keep up his morale? Asking herself that she has to tighten her lips, because suddenly she hears her voice, clear and crisp: "Come on, let's not get demoralized."

Ruth had never seen Gerda reproach herself for a mistake, brood over a regret. The only time she had cried in her presence, for more than the blink of an eye, was in the autumn of '34, during a soirée organized by the Association des Écrivains et Artistes Révolutionnaires, which Gerda joined some years later as a photographer. But at that time they didn't have an invitation to sink into the velvet of the Théâtre Adyar, and Ruth had no desire to run down behind the Eiffel Tower. Only because, according to Gerda, seeing the last film of a director fighting with the censors, the producers, and the people who don't understand the avant-garde was a fitting tribute to Jean Vigo and his revolutionary cinema.

"It'll be as lively as a funeral . . . "

"We can see the film free, Ruth, what do you care."

When the protagonist of *L'Atalante* went up on the stage to recall the conditions in which *cet homme extraordinaire*, worn down by tuberculosis, had finished the filming, the room was electric with emotion, the people close to the dead man in tears.

You wouldn't have predicted that Gerda, with her serious, sober expression, halfway through the film would cough, which opened the way to a flood of sobs. But Juliette, who escapes from her Jean's barge toward the lights, attractions, and seductions of Paris, was truly the perfect heroine for Ruth's friend. Maybe sentimental tears would have flowed in front of another screen, if they hadn't been forced to count the change in their purses. In that period they had had to give up Garbo in the melodramatic *Painted Veil* and the grim Dietrich in *The Scarlet Empress*, but one rainy Sunday they had allowed themselves a second viewing of *The Paul Street Boys*, escorted by the Dachshund, who expected nothing else. But the few times they didn't skimp on an evening at the movies, they preferred comedies: as in the old days, when that extremely elegant girl from Stuttgart laughed like a lunatic at Laurel and Hardy, leaving her new companions in Leipzig incredulous. Except at the movies, in Gerda's eyes only minimal residues of rage appeared, veils of displeasure, and, more than anything, effusions of wounded pride. Tears of worry, suffering, or helplessness meant giving in to the extreme pessimism that, in those times, it was better to be free of.

Once, however, she had come home tired and sulky, taken off shoes and socks, massaged her ankles, and lain down on the bed with her clothes on, closing her eyes for a few seconds.

The next day Ruth couldn't keep herself from asking.

"Bad news? Work problems?"

"The usual," she said, "plus a stupid nausea that won't go away."

"Maybe you should go to the doctor."

"Right. I'll go tomorrow."

Ruth returned in the afternoon and found Gerda already home. Makeup removed, pale, eyes alight with a feverish vivacity.

"It's official: I'm pregnant. But Friday morning we'll resolve it. The doctor says a weekend of rest will be enough. She's a person who understands women's needs. And she charges so little that it's almost worth doing it again, almost . . . "

Gerda laughed at her joke, as if with that everything were half solved. But it had struck Ruth so wrong that she must have assumed a grim expression.

"Did I shock you? It's an accident, these things happen . . . "

"I know," she had retorted, with the graciousness of one whose feet are well over size thirty-nine.

Gerda was upset, too: by now Ruth knew her. And suddenly Ruth had felt their five-year ages difference and was frightened by it: not only because of what could go wrong, and then what the hell would they do there in Paris without money and without proper papers? Would they ask Willy for a loan? Send a telegram to Stuttgart? She was frightened by the very idea of a pregnancy. Yes, it really was strange to realize that she would make the same decision, claiming the freedom to choose. And it was even stranger to realize that her mother had spoken to her early, and in a clear way, about certain things, about how to avoid them or face them.

Ruth had been very tall and womanly for about a year. She had had a hopeless crush and some fleeting infatuations, returned by one or two schoolmates of the Kuritzkes brothers. She had rushed into a forgettable kiss and had absolutely not told her mother, while she had hinted at the disappointment about the boy she had the crush on. Sometimes she named names, gave opinions, and, provoked by her extremely handsome brothers, who had fun teasing her, elaborated on her own physical tastes ("blond, maybe light brown, at least a handbreadth taller than me, and in the upper grades of the *Gymnasium*").

Her brothers, however, were also coddled male children who thought of themselves first (and this, Ruth says to herself, is unfortunately still true: her mother lives in a neighborhood where hunting Jews is like shaking an apple tree in autumn. Kurt would like Hans to get the money so that she can leave, but Hans fled from Leipzig to Sweden after Kristallnacht without a cent. Background of her life that she'll have to tell Csiki and Capa about.)

In any case, that day Hans was traveling on business, Kurt had already landed in Manhattan—it must have been '29. Ruth had talked to Mutti about a boy, she doesn't remember which, let alone how they had ended up talking about him. But she remembers her mother's face in the circle of light from the kitchen lamp, the character of her charm, which resisted age and wear, her chin raised over the remains of the simple lunch she had prepared, waiting for her return from work: *Buttermilch*, boiled potatoes, strawberries for dessert.

"Promise me, Ruth: it's important. If you're afraid you have a problem, you must tell me at the first sign. We'll resolve any stupid mistake, you understand? But we can't afford others."

Was she fourteen at the time? Probably not, since she wanted to be swallowed up. She was about to give vent to the sense of insult that was rising in her throat, when her mother managed to anticipate her. *Mein Herz*, she had said, better to think than to be ashamed.

In their house not even that bit of secrecy that made you feel grown-up was allowed, Ruth had thought. But her classmates who had a living, prosperous father and a *real lady* for a mother, not a former actress, daughter of a street peddler, whose marriage had been talked of for months in the courtyards along the Brühl, would never have had the benefit of such intimacy.

Wasn't Gerda basically that type of girl? Ruth wonders, looking at the strange figure on the cover of the *Picture Post* that her friend would have liked. Yes, maybe at first, because later she'd resolutely gotten rid of that imprint, the same way she went to have the seed removed that would've swollen her belly. She was a hard nut, Gerda, regardless of her birth.

The mere idea of a pregnant daughter would have caused the tiny, meek Frau Pohorylle to die of fear and shame. Gerda had inherited her height, her white teeth, her alabaster skin in the bad season. But Gerda's mother looked somehow related, rather (perhaps she was?), to the young maid who had taken Ruth's raincoat when she arrived for the first time in Springerstrasse—even though the maid wore a mouse-brown *sheitel* and the mistress of the house was coiffed in the penultimate trend of the moment. But the two women must have had a stronger understanding than what Ruth had picked up in the hasty introductions in the doorway of the *Salon*, which they had entered with a certain embarrassment.

"May I offer you *a stikele* of my plumcake, Fräulein Cerf? I made it today and I think it came out well. Or are you watching your figure the way my daughter does and prefer fruit?"

"Thank you, Frau Pohorylle, I would love a taste of your plumcake."

"Nothing for me, Mutti, just water!"

Gerda had shouted as her mother left; she had already settled herself on the sofa, legs crossed, the first cigarette lighted, a nod to Ruth to sit in the other corner. Frau Pohorylle, on her return, was an elliptical, egglike form that advanced cautiously, cut in two by a silver rectangle: a plate for the cake, another plate with slices of apple and segments of orange, cake forks, a crystal carafe, two glasses, a gold-rimmed teapot with a matching sugar bowl and cup. Ruth wanted to get up but "Stay seated, *bleiben Sie do zitsn!*" she had been ordered, while Gerda restricted herself to moving the cigarettes and the ashtray to the side table. When she had performed the task of putting the tray down, Frau Pohorylle begged her to help her-self (*"Bitteschön"*) and then said to her daughter: "I'm in the kitchen with Rivka, if you need me."

Ruth took two slices of plumcake and left the fruit for Gerda. Finally, out of good manners and habit, and also because no one was taking care of it, she picked up the tray and went to find the kitchen. She opened the door of a large room, flooded with fresh air and light coming in from the bal-cony: walls, marble table, and newly painted white cupboards, all filled with a blaze of green and crimson jars. Gerda's mother and Rivka were "putting up" cucumbers and beets, in chunks and made into red *cren*, horseradish, and they handed each other jars and lids without noticing her.

"*Oj dos Fräulein hot gebracht di teler!*" exclaimed the girl, at which Frau Pohorylle murmured two incomprehensible little phrases that produced the rapid removal of the jars near the sink.

"There was no need to get up," she said, but wasn't in time to wipe her hands on the apron before Ruth had put down her burden and, with an "It's nothing," set off to return to the liv-ing room. Even with the door closed, she could hear that they had immediately resumed speaking in Yiddish. Rivka, just arrived from Galicia, is better off here than my mother at the Kaufmanns', she thought and she looked for a way to say so to Gerda.

"You're very liberal, in your house."

"Quite, yes. Why?"

"From the way your mother treats the maid."

"You know, she's not used to it. We're hardly like the Chardacks, what did you think?"

Ruth doesn't remember if it was a cousin of the Dachshund or of another of their rich friends, but certainly the girl ambas-sador sent to the Pohorylle house after that terrible March 18, 1933, when the brownshirts had turned the apartment upside down and taken Gerda away, came from a well-known family in the fur trade. Georg's siblings—he was in Berlin at that moment, studying medicine—had immediately called a meeting, past the first *Schrebergärten* of the Rosental, where they anticipated there would be only a few people, some dogs, babies in carriages, all brought out with a great desire to return to the warmth. In Friedrich-Karl-Strasse there had already been a visit from the brownshirts, useless from the point of view of a search and therefore intimidating. They had the right channels for getting information and wanted to inform the family that Gerda, detained in *Schutzhaft*, had been charged with belonging to an illegal union organization.

Were the Pohorylles, those small-time businesspeople who didn't understand how their daughter had gotten involved in certain milieus, aware that for the Nazis preventive detention was enough to detain anyone at will? That even without formal charges they could move Gerda to another prison or send her to a concentration camp? So someone had to inform them as soon as possible. It couldn't be Dina or her children, whose illegal affiliations were known. The least compromised of their group, starting with the Dachshund, had moved abroad. Thus, in spite of the union militancy at the Gaudig-Schule, Ruth went ahead, hypothesizing that going up there for ten minutes couldn't be so terrible.

"At least they've already seen me other times . . . "

In reality, she had goose bumps, not extreme but noticeable—the same fear that now, when she went to Berlin to bring information and aid to the families of detained comrades, suggested that she put her Swiss passport under her pillow. At times, waking at night, she made sure that it was still there, on the night table, before closing her eyes again.

That time, thanks to the expert instructions of Dina Gelbke, Ruth hadn't appeared the right candidate. Who else could they send to the Pohorylles'?

That was how they'd arrived at that Else, Ilse, or Inge. It seemed, on the spot, a very desperate thought, since she was thirteen at most, but Jenny, Georg's little sister, had played with her as a child and claimed she was a smart girl.

They could offer her something in exchange, a reward.

"So you think we buy a girl like that with a bag of candy for a few *Pfennig*? Come on!"

"Why not? It's not just candy, it's a prize," said Jenny.

"A medal for valor . . . "

"Exactly, Soma. You can spare me your sarcasm."

They decided they'd lose nothing by trying. During recess Jenny talked to this Else, Ilse, or Inge, who, very pragmatic, answered that she could drop by after school, but couldn't stay too long because her parents were already starting to make a fuss. Now she was escorted by the Aryan Fräulein to gymnastics and piano, and, when the lesson ended late, the driver for the store came to pick her up.

"I'll take you on the bike and wait for you at the corner," Jenny had reassured her. "But you have to be quick."

"Is it dangerous?" the girl had inquired.

"For you no."

"Because I look like a child?"

"Yes. And because you seem more interested in candy than anything else."

"No. If I can do something against *them* I'll do it free."

Jenny had recounted all this, laughing at a success that seemed taken from a children's book. Yes, their ambassador must certainly have read *Emil and the Detectives* and the other more recent novels of Erich Kästner. Novels or not, she had done what she had to do.

She had introduced herself with the proper formality (her good last name had had its effect) and, saying first that she was expected at lunch, hadn't wasted any time in delivering her message. All her friends, she had said, are close to Gerda and her family. The Pohorylles had looked at her in bewilderment, but hadn't asked anything, so, taking advantage of their disorientation, Else, Ilse, or Inge had launched the exploratory question.

"Can we help you in any way?"

At that point Gerda's father must have understood. "Thank you," he had said to her, as if speaking to an adult: "Our consul is taking care of it, the Polish consul. He is about to lodge a complaint with the Foreign Minister. Report that, miss."

The final note, the most grotesque, was that Frau Pohorylle didn't want to let the messenger leave without tangible proof of gratitude, but, given the terrible moment, she had nothing good to offer her. In the end she appeared with a package containing a carton of ten eggs.

"They're ours, Grade A, fresh today. They could be useful now that Easter's coming."

The eggs had ended up in Friedrich-Karl-Strasse, where they were served fried, on a stack of black bread and ham, at a hasty, hearty nonbelieving dinner.

Gerda was released in early April, a few days before the start of Passover. But the *Judenboykott* had stunned with incredulity and terror even the tradesmen and professionals who hadn't suffered physical violence or looting or vandalism, starting with broken windows. The wholesaler Heinrich Pohorylle had regained his daughter. He had thanked the Lord, restocked the goods he had lost, cleaned the egg warehouse. But the girls knew that nothing would be straightened out. They had to go.

Ruth had received the advice to leave soon from an admirer who had become a Nazi ("Good job, I didn't treat him badly!" she had said to herself) and hadn't wasted any time. Gerda, too, was aware that if she fell into the clutches of those gangsters again at the very least she would be expelled and sent to Poland: of that land she preserved a vague smell of warm milk and burned wood, the apparition of a fox that perhaps she had dreamed, and a fear of Cossacks that must have been equally imaginary. "You know, Ruth, I haven't been there since I was five years old. The only words I know are the ones written on the passport and I can't even pronounce them."

Later, in Paris, when André and Gerda exchanged their prison stories, it seemed to Ruth that she was present mainly at a conspiratorial challenge, a contest between lovers that required the presence of a competition judge.

"They gave me such a beating that when I got on the train for Vienna I still had broken bones and my backside burned so much that I stayed in the corridor smoking. I finished my entire supply of cigarettes before customs."

"We could hear the screams of the men being tortured by the brownshirts during the interrogations. Then I discovered that we could use the bell reserved for the police. It was like a school bell, a sound that shook the building."

"What did they do to you?"

"Nothing. Insults. I stopped ringing as soon as they started down the stairs. But the comrades heard us, and plus we really annoyed those bastards."

"Either you're not being straight with me or even there you conned them with your charms."

"Of course. And also I could tear up easily . . . "

Was it possible that Gerda had remained so lucid even in prison? That she had always been responsive and encouraging and, it goes without saying, surrounded by *chic* and *charme* like a creature from a different world?

"They arrested me when I was going dancing . . . "

"With whom?"

"Oh, I don't know, Georg was already in Italy."

"You're saying that just to provoke me, right?"

"Come on. I meant that it was quite an advantage, because the cops couldn't conceive that someone wearing shoes that matched her silk dress could be a rabid red."

Did Gerda really believe that her little smiles and her finery would serve as an impenetrable armor, and had that conviction been strong enough not to be damaged? Or was she truly impervious to fear, to anguish (in the torture chamber, good God!), and to the inexorable sense of defeat?

To live, but not with every compromise—they all wanted that. Georg and his siblings wanted it, she and Melchior and their comrades in the SAP wanted it. Chim and Kati Horna and Csiki Weisz and anyone who had gone to Spain, even just for a brief time, to support the Republican struggle with a camera, wanted it. How did Gerda manage to be infinitely better equipped than the others? Because there was no doubt that she was, she always had been. There was no need to open the *Pariser Tageszeitung* the day after her funeral to find confirmation in an article of how, already in the spring of '33, she had been an intrepid and worldly cell mate, how she had distributed cigarettes and sung American hits to the detainees, until from a dubious stranger (in jail, too, they must have thought of her as a "gussied-up featherbrain") she had become a leader.

Hard to believe that it had been like that, but the acts recounted by a prison comrade from Leipzig and by those who had known Gerda in Spain also confirmed it. Besides, going to Germany with Melchior as a clandestine courier, she herself had felt on her skin that no better stimulant for stage fever exists than crude, naked fear.

And then Fräulein Pohorylle, a Polish citizen born in Stuttgart, possessed the martial virtues that Hitler demanded from German youth: nimble as a hare, tenacious as a hide, and sometimes hard as steel. But Gerda's tenacity and hardness were modeled from different clay: not warrior, not mortuary. To live at all costs but not at any price: Gerda desired it more than all of them put together. And indeed she overcame the chains and obstacles placed in the way of that desire with an irresistible impulse, a force that only the steel mass of a tank had been able to crush.

On Friday Ruth had gone with her to the doctor's appointment. They awakened at dawn to get ready without hurrying and then cross half of Paris. On the metro they read the paper and commented on the news in a low voice so as not to bother the workers, who filled the early trains with the need for a little more sleep. They got out at Filles du Calvaire, entered a building at the start of Rue Oberkampf. "*Voilà*," Gerda said, as soon as they entered the front hall, similar to so many waiting rooms, except that at that hour of the morning it was completely empty.

The doctor came out almost immediately. From the little that Ruth was able to see, she liked her: middle-aged, medium-length hair, small pearl necklace under the white coat, fresh lipstick. She had noticed that in the pile of magazines on the table in the waiting room there were some copies of *Vu* and *Regards*, but she preferred the women's magazines. She distracted herself with the new styles suggested by *Le Petit Écho de la Mode* (the only idea worth copying was wearing big Scottish bows on the collar). She returned the "*Bonjour, madame*" of a young couple, seeing her stomach emerge like a coconut from under a pale wool shawl, and the boyfriend, still wearing his cap, said: "*Voyez, il-y en a deux, là-dedans*," there are two in there, and then had asked if he could look at the *Humanité* that Gerda had left on the chair next to her.

"*Bien sûr*," and they could keep the daily.

"*Merci, camarade!*"

"*De rien. Et beaucoup de félicitations, camarades.*"

"*Ce sera dur, putain, mais on va se débrouiller.*"

The girl gave him a hint of a nudge with her elbow and instinctively smoothed her belly.

They made an effort to laugh. They talked about extra

shifts, about how to accommodate the twins, and about the doctor, who saw them for nothing, because a worker, like any future mother, also had the right to give birth with minimum risk. Thus, when the first patient came out of the gynecological comrade's office, Ruth felt completely reassured.

"*On y va!*" Gerda had trilled, crossing the waiting room lightly, but in the elevator she had collapsed against the oily wood of the car.

Ruth wanted to look for a taxi, but Gerda insulted her. "Are you an idiot? Right here in front?" and insisted on the metro. A compromise came out of it, suggested by the first café that appeared along the sidewalk, where her suffering friend went in to get a glass of water.

"Stay there," Ruth said. "I'll come get you in a taxi."

On the way Gerda looked out the window. She went up the stairs ignoring Ruth's arm and even in the room didn't say a word.

"Shit, it burns. Next time I'm going to be born a man!"

She staunched it, changed the pad, folded up the old one, carried away the chamber pot full of red soup and brought it back to the room rinsed out. She went to do some errands and came back to see if everything was all right. Gerda was still curled up, unmoving, she couldn't tell if she was sleeping. Later, glancing at her from her half of the mattress, she had found her touching. A little ball of female limbs that breathed, snoring faintly, mouth slightly open. Sleep disarms even the most combative. The next day Gerda declared that she was fine, although she still felt disgusting ("like a fish cleaned before being boiled") and didn't need any more help.

"I just need some aspirin."

"I got it for you, it's there on the night table with a fresh cup of tea."

"You're an angel. Then see you around evening."

That was it.

No, not completely. Soon after the triumph of the Front

Populaire they met by chance at the Café Capoulade, and Gerda had told her, among various other news, that she'd been again to Rue Oberkampf to that kind doctor: no aftereffects, no problems, and there was even the positive side that the cops were occupied with the general strike, so she had allowed herself a taxi right away, not like the other time . . .

It was likely that the cause of the accident was André, but Ruth hadn't asked that question even the first time, when she was living with Gerda.

Poor Capa, she feels like sneering now, how happy he must have been to sneak in among the barricaded workers at Renault and photograph the salesgirls on strike at the Galleries Lafayette, rather than devote himself to female zones never touched from that point of view. But once he returned to Rue Vavin, he would have rushed to buy gauze and aspirin and cared for Gerda with cuddling and chocolate and maybe even fresh flowers. His lamed kitten and princess must have taken great pleasure basking in those attentions, while outside there was the whole country in ferment, along with the fine warm June sun. Until she whispered, "Leave me alone, André, I want to rest quietly for a while," and he, banished onto Boulevard Montparnasse, would have gone off in search of new kinds of comfort, and, to comfort himself, too, would drink up a good part of the advance for the exclusive report on Renault in Billancourt. The peacemaking bouquet, made by the florist near the Dôme, if it hadn't been forgotten at the café, would have ended up anywhere except in the pitcher of water on the desk. The next day, Gerda would have saved the salvageable or decreed that, too bad, the flowers had to be thrown away, but, apart from a scolding, because being drunk wasn't an excuse to collapse on the bed with your clothes on, she'd be in a splendid mood, as always. Splendid herself as well, regal and willing to give every intact part of herself and forget the tiff, the burning, the wilted flowers and all the rest.

*

Ruth is distracted by those somewhat entertaining conjectures, but the *Picture Post* brings her back to the reality that has to be looked in the face. "THIS IS WAR!" in block letters is the title of the report, followed by images with almost no text; one is printed on two pages, showing five soldiers, crowded beneath a natural gallery of rock, who observe, in the distance, a bare plain torn up by bombs. Except for that photomontage created in London, she's seen them all. She packed them and addressed them sitting at that table, and then found them again in the stacks of journals on display at the newsstand. Two weeks ago the back cover of *Regards* was devoted to the same men rushing into the attack.

Attaque sur le Sègre! Toutes les phases du combat. Photographies par CAPA.

She had grabbed *Regards* while she was running over to pick up the latest typed version of the script of *There's No Tomorrow* to bring back urgently to Max Ophüls. There was no time to stop at the Atelier, even less to visit the sick man. There were no seats on the metro, but, balanced precariously, she leafed through the pages of the magazine, and the photos had given her shivers again.

And now in the *Picture Post* she finds those men who, bent like dromedaries, advance sideways over the rocky ground. The man black as the rock, out of focus, completely alone in the world erased by the whitish smoke of the explosions. Three shadows: two hold up their companion at the center of the photo, in the middle of the nothing of the smokescreen that licks their steps. The man seriously wounded. The man who dies under the lens.

La victoire du Rio Sègre; un document unique et exclusif.

Victoire, victoire, victoire: at the top of every page.

The victory was heroic, but nothing changed. The final offensive is now in the air, you sniff the odor everywhere, even in Rome, where the Pope, confident of finding a listener in General Franco, has asked for a Christmas truce. It's the last unknown: will the Pope get what he's asked for? Melchior, when they talk about it at home, says, "Hypocritical bastards"; Csiki, "Well, let's hope." Chim considers it an insult to decency, since, when holidays are celebrated, *los moros* in the pay of the self-styled crusaders would be left free to slaughter civilians, as always. Capa wanted to return to Catalonia for Christmas at all costs. It was two weeks away.

Joyeux Noël! Joyeuses Fêtes! Joyeux Noël et Bonne Année 1939!

Ever since things in Germany have gone from bad to worse, for Ruth to pass from the silence of Rue Froidevaux and the winter darkness of the Montparnasse cemetery to the lighted boulevards, the decorated windows, the people loaded with bags or hugging Christmas packages is sometimes similar to being a city mouse who for a moment can't breathe and then darts away.

The reality that matters is elsewhere. The reality is worse than the crudest of Capa's pictures in the newspapers. And then Ruth allows herself a break, looks at the piece with the white-haired girl, and doesn't notice Csiki, standing behind her, who asks: "Seen it?"

"Magnificent!" she exclaims reflexively.

Csiki doesn't react. Not even when Ruth turns and looks him in the face, a Pierrot mask, drawn and pale.

"No," Csiki whispers, "look more carefully."

"What is it, what should I have seen? The photomontage, the photo of the dying soldier?"

"Another one."

Ruth, agitated, returns to the twelve pages of "THIS IS WAR!," scans them up to the page that escaped her, which contains only a portrait of the photographer. *The Greatest War-Photographer in the World: Robert Capa.*

And finally she understands. She understands his urgency to show her the *Picture Post*. She suspects that Csiki hasn't dared to deliver it to Capa, the reason he's now looking for advice from her.

The page with the portrait anointing *The Greatest War-Photographer in the World* is a peak never reached by a photographer, but if Capa should lose his balance, he could fall into the void from which he's just raised himself. The precipice is right before their eyes, right there on the table.

Gerda took that picture. On the front in Segovia, near the Navacerrada pass, when she was working with the Leica, he with the Eyemo provided by *Time-Life* for a feature that would inaugurate the great turning point. "*The March of Time* is a newsreel projected in more than a thousand theaters. We're entering Hollywood, comrade!" Robert Capa must have said something like that to her, because that was how Gerda Taro had portrayed him: focused, bold, his profile one with that of the movie camera that pokes out from the arch of his eyebrow like a metallic horn with the wings of a moth.

The greatest war-photographer without a still camera.

It's all so absurd that a perhaps incautious comment escapes Ruth: wouldn't Gerda, maybe so as not to appear too pleased with her success, have laughed at the incongruity?

"Maybe," Csiki sighs, "but at the time she wasn't at all amused." And, as usual, he was the one who'd had to report the bad news to Capa. "Explain, when you talk to him, that a film isn't a sequence of photographs," the guy from *Life* had told him, already about to hang up the phone.

"*D'accord, d'accord,*" Csiki had mumbled on the telephone, "*mais écoutez*, my boss is back in Spain *avec* the camera, he will do better, *il est en train d'apprendre . . .*"

"Well, keep on trying!"

The last to use the Eyemo, Csiki murmurs, was Gerda. The Leica, tossed away by the impact with the tank, had been recovered, the film still intact, but of the movie camera not a trace remained. *Time-Life* had called the studio to offer condolences, Capa was in Amsterdam, untraceable. Csiki feared that if Capa told them that the Eyemo had also disappeared in Brunete, the bill for the movie camera would not be long in arriving, and maybe even a warning, because only the person hired on the contract was supposed to handle it.

Ruth observes Csiki's Adam's apple, swallowing repeatedly, he looks like he's eaten a lightbulb, and she adds, icily, that Gerda loved to feel she was the better part of Robert Capa. She told everyone that she was better than he was at filming. But that detail about the Eyemo, no, that she didn't know . . .

The lightbulb in Csiki's throat is stopping. In the end, he says wearily, Capa called the editorial office.

"I'm very sorry, but your camera *c'est kaputt . . . perdue avec ma femme.*"

Ruth left the magazine on the table and grabbed Csiki again, who was ready to disappear into the lab (does he want to hide the fact that he's weeping?), to tell him that she'll go ahead with the jobs he's given her.

"Thanks. You know where to find the negatives. If there's no white paper, use the letterhead."

Outside it's started to rain again, the water descends in rivulets along the windows, exasperating. Maybe another coffee would help the cold feet, it won't hurt, anyway.

"I'm making another coffee, you want one?" she calls to her friend.

Csiki insists that he wants to make it, he invites her to sit comfortably and hurries to his *Wunderkammer* to get the water. Ruth relaxes into the rationalist armchair, undecided whether to take off her shoes.

Csiki brings her the coffee, impatient to turn into something positive the weight that's been removed with that confidence.

Gerda would have been proud to see her photograph in the *Picture Post*. "Capa should be, too, don't you think?"

Ruth nods and tastes a boiling-hot sip, while Csiki lets himself be carried away by memories, with the loquacity of taciturn men when, for once, they start talking.

"You can't imagine how thrilled Bandi was when *Time* gave him the Eyemo. He must have told you about the Navacerrada pass, how happy they were down there, camped in the middle of the woods and always working side by side."

Ruth doesn't have to do anything but give an affirmative nod and let him continue.

Two types of flashbulbs, an abundant supply of film, a store of coffee and chocolate: everything that Gerda had ordered via telegram from Valencia (Weisz had hunted down the photographic material, Capa had taken care of the refreshments) had had to make room in the knapsack for that precious compact object that was worth the sacrifice of the sugar cubes and the search for a space for every single pack of American cigarettes taken out of the carton.

But wasn't it a fabulous device? Bandi had exclaimed before wrapping the Eyemo in the sweater that was to protect it during the journey. Taken apart like that, didn't it resemble a little robot that looks at you sideways, yes, and it's female ("See, Csiki, it has tits!"), or a children's puppet invented by Picasso?

Bandi couldn't contain himself. He couldn't wait to arrive in Madrid and unwrap the surprise in front of Gerda. He couldn't bear to stay far from her and from Spain, so he had gone straight to Louis Aragon to say he was quitting. *Ce Soir*, with the exclusive contract for France, had given him an undeniable privilege, but now that the pathway to America was clear he didn't need it anymore. He wanted to tell Gerda and right away pull out the proof that he hadn't invented anything, placing the Eyemo in her beautiful, incredulous hands: all while embracing her, kissing her on the neck, until, entwined, they started staggering around the room like drunken polka dancers.

Yes, Ruth imagines all this. The rest she already knows, because Capa told her, more than once.

The next day they left Madrid, making a stop before reaching the Navacerrada pass. Gerda, seeing him filming in the dirt barnyard of a farmhouse, the camera around his neck and the movie camera on his shoulder, satisfied, happy, bursting up to the edges of that heavy turtleneck, had cried, "Look at me!" and in response got his most thuggish expression.

But she wasn't satisfied with the shot.

"Stupid, you're not supposed to be impressing girls, you're supposed to be showing the world you're a director: take the Eyemo, here, a little straighter, concentrate, you're Robert Capa, you're not afraid of anything, not even of that big German shepherd standing guard two steps from your backside," she provoked him.

"*Ça va*, now yes, you came out well, you can put it down."

Capa had approached Gerda quite slowly, turning only after he reached her. The German shepherd was there, free, in fact, but well trained, as if he knew exactly when and against whom he was supposed to move from defense to attack.

"He's one of ours! *Szép kutya, jó kutyus*, true that you're *ein braves Hundchen? Un perro alemán pero también un camarada valeroso. Te mandan a buscar minas fascistas, perrito guapo?* A German dog but still a brave comrade. Do they send you to look for fascist mines, you good dog? What language do you think you should talk to this dog in?"

It seems that at that very moment, when Capa moved toward the dog to give him a pat, a Belgian soldier from the Marseillaise battalion appeared, with an order from General Walter: they were to wait until he reached that *finca*, where he would host them and, the next day, take care of escorting them to the battlefields.

"*Ah, et ce chien maintenant c'est le chien personnel du commandant*—he's the general's dog," the Belgian comrade had said. "*Mais si le commandant lui parle en sa langue maternelle, le polonais, je ne sais pas*—But if the general talks to him in Polish, his mother tongue, I don't know . . . "

But Gerda knew, she knew how to talk to the German shepherd in Polish, and the dog was happy to trot behind her or stop at her commands. Gerda could talk to almost all the members of the International Brigades in their own language, and with a few phrases she won over battalions and generals, enchanted politicians and censors. Gerda was beloved by the correspondents of the foreign press and by poets and writers; Rafael Alberti and his wife welcomed her warmly whenever she stayed in Madrid at the Alianza. "And then, Ruth, I don't know how to describe to you the look on John Dos Passos's face when one night at the Hotel Florida she recited some passages from a novel of his. Hemingway hated her from then on, but he would have changed his mind if only he'd had another chance to meet her . . . "

When Capa began to inundate her with these rhapsodies, Ruth listened and nodded like someone drinking in every mouthful of a story, tasting the flowers and ripe fruits released by the *perlage* of pure gold, without knowing if that sharp note of acidity, that overdone fermentation, was a sign that he had passed off a cheap *spumante* as a Grande Cuvée Riserva.

The true from the false, how could you distinguish it with Capa? she wonders, while Csiki now speaks on the telephone with him, in Hungarian as usual.

And yet, Ruth recalls, there really was that book by Dos Passos that Gerda took to the pool at the Bar Kochba club one summer, a birthday present, and she pondered it between dives. At times she lost the thread, went back, muttering that, except for *Berlin Alexanderplatz*, she had never read such an

impenetrable modern novel. But she caught the beauty that
had been promised in the dedication:

For the greatest dancer on the planet
This great American novel
In which the orchestra of the revolution
Swings to the rhythms of the wildest hot jazz.
Your happy partner (in every dance)

Georg
Leipzig, August 1, 1932

To avoid getting the cover wet, Gerda had taken it off, and
the book looked like an edition of the works of Lenin designed
by a constructivist: a red bible with three close black stripes, at
the center the severe title, *Auf den Trümmern*, (*On the Ruins*).[3]
Those ruins of the Great War proclaimed nothing hot or jazzy
or wild, but Gerda was fascinated by that tome and got sun-
burned to finish it. She burned for everything that arrived from
Georg, before he left again for Berlin. She was at the peak of
being in love. Did she enjoy those moments aware that they
were coming to an end, or did the enjoyment intensify precisely
in view of the end? No, Gerda didn't like things that ended. She
had never let any of her men leave her radius. Not even in the
case of her damaged friendship with Ruth had she had the tact
to recalibrate the distances, something so shattering to Ruth
that she switched sidewalks; the only one who so much as
glanced at her sadly was the Dachshund. No, Gerda couldn't
conceive that something might break forever: only transitions,
phases, chapters, where the final period, which she herself
inscribed, anticipated the urgency of turning the page. Because
Gerda liked things that changed.

---

[3] Originally published in English as *Manhattan Transfer* (Harper & Brothers,
1925).

The Spanish turning point had been the most serious and the most thrilling. So it was believable that Gerda, hurled into the beau monde of Madrid under blackout, had had a ball with the world-famous writer who had accompanied her last summer in Leipzig. "The orchestra of the revolution swings to the rhythms of the wildest hot jazz: that's the effect of your novels!" Dos Passos was impressed, Capa by the impression that Gerda had made on Dos Passos, not knowing that her regard for Dos Passos had blossomed out of the German edition received from her beloved Georg Kuritzkes.

Maybe it hadn't happened exactly like that, but in this case Capa wasn't bragging randomly. When he ran into some scratch that blemished his splendid memories, he rustled up *d'emblée* the wizard of retouching. But he couldn't tolerate having others correct him, and as for souvenir photos forget it.

The one with the German shepherd, for example.

Csiki Weisz, knowing Bandi's attachment to the two photos that Gerda had taken of him, one day thought about cropping and retouching the one that showed his whole body. You saw who Robert Capa was, you saw the camera, and the photo ended there: a black half-length image on a white background, without the dirt stains on the trousers, without the squat heavy boots, the unpaved barnyard, the poor farmhouse guarded by an untrained German shepherd. But Bandi, rather annoyed, had said: "No, you don't touch a photo of Gerda's. The editors will do it, if they really want to."

Csiki was hurt. He muttered that it was foolish to send the newspapers one portrait with the movie camera and the other with a four-legged intruder. But he continued to reprint the photographs, as he'd been asked, and Ruth added the stamp "PHOTO TARO" on the envelopes she sent. What a well-fed German shepherd was doing in that sliver of rural Spain Ruth had never asked, until Capa suggested it to her.

The story didn't hold up. That the dog had been trained for

military purposes might be true. But it certainly wasn't General Walter's dog. The story of Gerda giving orders in Polish, a language she barely spoke, had crossed Capa's mind, and he couldn't let go of it. The commander admired her, adored her, according to Capa, to the point where he ordered her in person to withdraw from the battlefield immediately. And Gerda, paying no attention to General Walter, had continued to take photographs until it was too late.

For a second Ruth feels herself sinking into the rationalist armchair, her feet drop down in search of the support of her shoes.

Csiki is still on the telephone and Ruth doesn't understand anything, except *hotel, Bandi, Rue Froidevaux,* and other words that would be comprehensible even if they were spoken in Arabic.

She takes a sip of coffee and tries to reflect, annoyed by the rain.

Capa had at his disposal skills and strategies practiced on the streets of Budapest, which included telling tall tales, and it was an apprenticeship that had also taught him not to get too burned. On the other hand, Capa circled the fire with those Capa-style stories, exaggerated tales to laugh at like children at the Kasperltheater, laughing heartily when the impertinent puppet got hit on the head, and when the fabulous Gretel vanished through the trapdoor, astonishment protecting them from grief.

Ruth knows the picaresque resources of Bandi Friedmann very well, but she no longer has confidence in them. She's seen what happens if they fail, unfortunately, and she saw it up close the day she went with him to Toulouse to get Gerda, or what remained of Gerda.

For eight or nine hours, on the train to Toulouse, Capa had done nothing but weep and sigh, stopping every so often to repeat, "I shouldn't have, I shouldn't have, Ruth," swaying slightly forward and back on the second-class seat. Before going to the Gare d'Austerlitz, he had collapsed on a chair in her kitchen, hadn't taken even a sip of water while he waited for her to get ready, her trembling hands in a struggle not to ravel her stocking. "Tell the concierge something came up!" she had said to Melchior at the door, already less stunned by the peal of the bell at an improbable hour that, because of their contacts with the *Widerstand*, the resistance, had made her immediately think of Hans—that he'd been arrested, if not worse. It was worse, but didn't concern her brother.

As the hours and the kilometers passed, the sobs diminished, or got deeper, until they became subdued rattles. At times, turning toward the landscape outside the window, Capa murmured some violent phrase in Hungarian, but his eyes remained opaque, like the bituminous surface of the road that skirted the tracks. Ruth didn't know how to console him. She tried to take one of his hands, squeeze it hard. She tried holding both hands, resting them on her knees, but he pulled them away with a childish shake of his head, as if to say, "I don't deserve it." She had tried to tell him that it wasn't his fault. But the truth was that she couldn't do anything. She couldn't do anything but witness that suffering for eight or nine hours, hoping that Gerda, even in death, would have the power to calm him, to allow him to hold onto her coffin as if to a raft, as the only real support in the deep, swallowing sea. Maybe it would loosen some of that rock he had inside. Maybe he would weep for another eight or nine hours, but in a different way.

She hoped but didn't much count on it. She herself felt the same anxiety, or fear, of meeting Gerda, who in Madrid had been given a farewell with great ceremony (but in a city that had been under siege for almost a year how had they found the means to properly recompose a birdlike person dragged under a tank?) and honored by a great crowd in Valencia, too. The only way not to think about it was to pick up the thread of the conversation addressed to her, occasionally, by the man who at the Gare d'Austerlitz had introduced himself as comrade Paul Nizan, with tickets for the compartment reserved by *Ce Soir* and the task of bringing back to Paris *nôtre jolie camerade et chère amie.* A fragile thread. Ruth felt that suddenly every word in French emerged false, laborious. And then Paul Nizan withdrew again behind the ream of newspapers placed on the free seat between him and Capa, showing only the edge of big round eyeglasses.

"I was twenty. I won't let anyone say those are the best years of your life," he had written in a book of which Ruth knew only that famous beginning. A perfect phrase, given the circumstances, for those who were twenty-one, like her. Not to mention Capa, who was two years older. Ruth couldn't imagine the author of *Aden, Arabia,* with that Paris-intellectual look, at twenty, much less dictating an article in the Telefónica skyscraper in Madrid, which swayed and shook and rumbled (as did Gerda, imitating the dark rumble) when the bombs fell, that is, every single day. Nizan had also been overwhelmed by the news, and was visibly uneasy, having known Capa in other moments, with his insolent good-time guy's face.

Anyway, she and Nizan tried to pretend to have something to say to each other, and even ventured in Capa's direction. The longest of their attempts took place near Limoges.

"We're almost halfway," announcement from Nizan.

"*Ah bien,*" reply from Capa, who immediately huddled again between the armrests.

"Limoges," Ruth had said, "the city of the porcelain?"

Of course, the valuable porcelain, but since the times of the Grande Révolution those who produced it had given the owners a run for their money. Nizan, although he continued to discourse on the Limousin, and its praiseworthy working class, its kaolin resources, and so on, stared at her with the gravity of a plea for help.

"The people I worked for, when I'd just arrived in Paris, had a set of Haviland china. I nearly ended up on the street because of a broken plate, but they paid me on the black market, as with all us émigrés . . . "

Why, just to say something, had she told a story that had the vulgarity of a farce for the petit bourgeoisie in the mood for a stimulating evening? The Fräulein who, after taking the children to school, found the head of the family naked under the *robe de chambre*, cried, "*C'est dégoûtant!*," fled from the bedroom and the house, didn't know where to go, wept on a bench, looked for a telephone to call her mother, went back, packed her suitcases. And finally she discovered that they had informed on her at the police station as an illegal *étrangère*, which created endless problems for her. But then Gerda arrived and they had gone to live together . . .

The shock that passed through Capa's body was so violent that it made even Nizan jump. But the name of Gerda couldn't be taken back, and at that point she had to break the silence that had descended on the compartment at all costs.

"Are the owners of Haviland from the same family as Olivia de Havilland, do you know?" she asked Nizan.

Movie stars were not his field, he answered, staring at her through his round glasses, but he had read that the actress was related to the proprietors of an aircraft manufacturer: "In the realm *quand même* of the great capitalist dynasties, *n'est-ce pas, Madame?*"

In other circumstances, in spite of the ceremoniousness that France taught its children of every background and ideology, they would have let it go, out of a sense of the ridiculous and of decency. But the silence was too painful, and Paul Nizan unexpectedly went on talking about movies. When *Captain Blood* came out, he had immediately realized that Olivia de Havilland was destined for success; not to mention Errol Flynn, who, after his exploits as a noble rebel pirate, had gone to Spain to show solidarity with the right side . . .

"A total jerk, *ce Flynn-là*!" Capa burst out with a sepulchral disdain. A clown who used the Spanish cause and especially the Spanish women to do what he liked as a star, and he was really a disgusting chicken shit.

No one uttered another word.

Maybe Nizan was ignorant of the backstories that had made him stumble into that *faux pas*. Or maybe he knew that Errol Flynn had flirted with Gerda, too, but had given no importance to those rumors. The Capa of two days earlier would have buried his adversary in a flood of grotesque anecdotes, not with that spiteful phrase.

In the compartment an icy silence fell. Mountains, flocks, three travelers cocooned in their seats. They arrived like that at the station in Toulouse.

In Toulouse, Capa put on a veneer of restraint, until he found out that they didn't have a permit to repatriate the remains via airplane (but could this, Ruth thought, be called *repatriation?*). Gerda remained in Valencia, waiting to be put on a train car that was to stop at every checkpoint and tiny Catalan station. After some phone calls between Paul Nizan and Louis Aragon it was decided that the employee of *Ce Soir* would go to Port Bou to take care of the bureaucratic matters (did you need a *carte de séjour* even for a corpse?) and then travel on the special French railroad convoy along with the coffin. Capa, who had again become a dead weight, should be sent back without delay: both to avoid the incalculable wait at the border and because Madame Cerf was there, fortunately, who when she returned to Paris could provide support to Gerda's family arriving from Belgrade.

"*Il y arrive que des civils survécus à un bombardement plombent dans un état catatonique*," Ruth had written down during a first-aid lesson devoted to detecting internal lesions. *Civilians who survive a bombing may fall into a catatonic state.*

But she didn't know what to do with that *état catatonique*, except feel relieved that the Toulouse-Paris line didn't have many intermediate stops. "Let him sleep, he needs it," she said to herself, closing her eyes in turn. But at Cahors she had already reopened them. "At least rest," she repeated to herself, closing her eyes again in the useless attempt to silence the torture. "Why me?" she repeated to herself. Why not Chim, or Cartier-Bresson, or even the Steins, who were always close to the two of them? Yes, why not Lilo Stein, if Capa really had to hold on to a woman? We're not even friends, real friends, she said to herself, something that had recently, perhaps, also been true of Gerda. Don't you see what a wreck he is! she rebelled, squeezing her eyelids even tighter, speaking to Gerda, who could no longer hear her recriminations. And your family? You never mentioned that your mother was sick and now I have to take care of your father, with whom I've barely exchanged a hello in my whole life. What did you think, Gerda, that you were invulnerable?

Ruth had longed for a moment all to herself, but now that that moment extended from station to station, she continued to toss and turn in the hum of her thoughts, with waves of exhaustion roaring in her eardrums, as if underwater. Invulnerable, yes of course. Easy to feel invulnerable when you don't care much about others. Whereas we are here doing what we can, and I can't even collapse, because I have him across from me. You can't see him, you can't understand what a mess he is. He could jump off the train—no, now he wouldn't be able to, but better not to depend on it. Did you ever think of it? Did you ever think of those who remain?

There was no relief in those thoughts, in fact they made her feel even more miserable, trapped in the anguish that resentment stirred up: until a lump jammed in her throat emerged in a lament. Ruth felt it rising from her diaphragm, felt that it resembled the cry of a cat down in the courtyard, but having to push it down amplified the inner resonance, clear and tremendous. Her lips contracted, her jaw trembling, she began to cry with her eyes closed. Swallowing, erasing the threads of tears with her hands, she struggled to breathe normally, and that slowly led her to a brief sleep.

When the train stopped, André was looking at her.

"Where are we?"

"Orléans, a man with a lot of bags said."

"Then it's just over an hour. Someone from *Ce Soir* will be there to take you to the hotel. Unfortunately, as they explained, I can't."

André, indifferent to that news as to all the rest, kept looking at her. Did he realize that she had been crying? Her eyes remained reddened, a small companion to those swollen eyes that now sought contact. Instinctively she sniffed.

"*Entschuldige*, Ruth, I'm sorry."

"For what?"

"You must have had things to do, work . . . the cinema."

"No, they're all busy reassuring the director about the première of *Yoshiwara*. Ophüls had to resort to a Japanese garden in Porte de Saint-Cloud rather than film in Tokyo."

"What's the film like?"

"A consommé of *Madame Butterfly*, *La Bohème*, and *La Traviata*. I may be unfair, but, in view of the versions I've typed, I'd be more excited about a Soviet film about a Ukrainian collective of beekeepers."

Was it a smile, that grimace that appeared on André's face? Barely a reflex, but it denied the *état catatonique*. Ruth had learned that a physical response to external stimuli, if it lasted, dispelled the suspicion of permanent damage. They would resume living: even Capa, in some way.

She had to keep talking, tell him anything. What about that exotic garden outside Paris? An enchanting place, with a little bridge, lanterns, a pagoda, a *pavillon de thé*, other small houses with rice-paper walls, while the Seine ran nearby and bicycles jangled their bells on their way through the Bois de Boulogne . . .

"Seichi told me about it, maybe . . . "

"They only recently opened it to the public, almost no one knows about it."

And so, rather than the melodrama of the geisha and the Russian officer of *Yoshiwara*, Ruth told André the story of Albert Kahn, the son of a cattle dealer, who founded a bank in the Paris of the Belle Époque. With his enormous earnings he acquired a villa and land to create a park that would contain all the places he had loved. Forests, as in his native Vosges or distant Colorado, a French garden, an English garden, and a Japanese garden, which was the largest, because the stocks issued by the emperor had made him one of the richest men of the time. But those Jardins du Monde weren't enough for him. He felt he was a traveler, a philanthropist, a pacifist. He began to spend his fortune on encouraging direct knowledge of other peoples and cultures, and thus promoting universal understanding and brotherhood. When the summer of 1914 arrived, the idea turned out to have a cruel naïveté, but Albert Kahn didn't lose heart. He immediately created a rescue committee to provide food and shelter for refugees, as he himself had been as a child. And as soon as people could travel again on the continents, he relaunched his projects. The world had experienced the opposite of the civilizing progress that Monsieur Kahn believed in—irreparable ruin, hastened death—but he could still preserve its fragile variety and wonder in effigies. The idea dated back to a trip to Japan before the war, when he had taught his Paris driver how to use a camera and a movie camera.

"The driver? A photographer was too much for his pockets?"

"Wait. Kahn was used to going beyond the goals he'd

reached successfully. So he hired photographers and filmmakers, a dozen, and sent them to some fifty countries."

"Expenses, salary, and everything?"

"Salary I don't know, but provided with an unlimited amount of film and Lumière autochromes. He wanted to create an archive of human life, a planetary archive. They brought back around a hundred hours of film and more than seventy thousand color plates . . . "

"Color? Madness."

"If they hadn't gotten public funds the *Archives of the Planet* would have been lost. It's not a set of porcelain whose value everybody understands . . . "

"Including a pretty Fräulein who breaks it out of revenge . . . You should have thought about that."

Absolutely she had, she replied with a sharp laugh, surprised that he had been listening to her. But hearing her yelp, Capa began to cry again: not much, but as if startled out of the temporary suspension of pain.

The stories of life don't sort themselves out because you find a good one to tell. The story of the banker had a bad ending, too, and Ruth could only tell it the way it happened. Albert Kahn had feared wars, hatred, and prejudice, but not the network of interests he was part of, the network of global exchange that sees no substantial difference between war and peace. The French banks believed that they were safe from the tempest of Wall Street. Thus when, in 1931, they began to totter, the Banque Albert Kahn was too exposed to the markets and at the same time too small to merit an intervention by the Bank of France. Kahn mortgaged the properties along the Seine and the villa on the Côte d'Azur, but in the end he went under. The bank failed, all his goods were seized, he was granted the use under bailment of the Bois de Boulogne dwelling.

"And the plates, the films?"

"In a municipal warehouse, as I mentioned . . . "

Ruth realized that chance had inspired a story miraculously made to touch the residual curiosity of a photographer, but she could add only that when Ophüls learned that the banker knew the Tokyo of the time of *Yoshiwara* and possessed some images of it, he wanted to visit the villa at all costs. Kahn, a small man, still fit except that he used a cane, was happy to exchange a few words with Michiko, the young female protagonist, but he greeted the rest of the company with a slight bow and shut himself up in his home.

It was the truth, the truth had offered her an effective pause. And now Capa waited for the story to unfold.

"One day when I was there, Ophüls takes me aside and introduces me to Kahn. 'Madame Cerf, as you can easily understand, is of ancient rabbinical stock from Alsace—unlike me, who would be an Oppenheimer from Saarbrücken, like so many, if I hadn't taken a stage name.' 'I know very well,' Kahn answers, 'I went to the market with my father.' The intuition, Ophüls explained later, had come to him when his gaze met the tops of the firs, that linear perspective between the Rising Sun and the woods of his childhood. Anyway, from that day on, for Monsieur Kahn we were all compatriots, *Landsleut*, with whom to dust off even the curious *Jeddisschdaitsch*, the Yiddish German of his childhood. His preferred interlocutor was the cinematographer Eugen Schüfftan, who gets by with Yiddish because he's from Breslau. It was funny to hear them talk about technical aspects of cinema that fascinated Kahn, and in which Eugen Schüfftan is a real genius. He invented the special effects in *Metropolis*, and ever since Fritz Lang went to America, Ophüls has fought over him with all the German directors in Paris, and even the French."

Ruth was about to describe how Ophüls and Schüfftan had finally been invited to a projection of the amazing Autochromes, when Capa interrupted her vehemently. The disappointment of the first film Fritz Lang made in Hollywood! Spencer Tracy was very good, but certainly not at the level of Peter Lorre. *Fury* had nothing to do with *M*. The girl he had gone to see the film with had come out so frightened that he had to spend his last cents to take her home in a taxi. So he'd had to consume kilometers of dark Berlin neighborhoods, amid imaginary shadows of maniacal murderers, and the very real danger of being arrested for vagrancy.

He's calming down, Ruth thought. But it was as if he were speaking in the place of someone else.

"Months ago we were stuck in Paris," André continued, his voice flat. "I was supposed to cover a civil-defense exercise that seemed like a gas-mask costume ball, compared to Spain, where the fronts were at a standstill. Gerda wasn't working much and was getting impatient . . . "

"I can imagine."

"We were at the back of the hall, I was holding her tight, as always, until the lights go on and the audience gets up to leave. '*M* was something else,' I say to her, and I tell her about the Berlin experience, making her laugh. Gerda had seen it, right, with Kuritzkes?"

"I don't know," she answered, "it's likely . . . "

Was Capa listening to her?

"The credits were still playing," he resumed, "and Gerda announces to me that she's going to visit Georg. I felt like Spencer Tracy, furious, I felt like hitting her. When the first bombs fell on Madrid, she was still there, in Capri."

Capa burst into tears. After that, he shut himself up again in a protective silence, sending her back to her reflections.

That visit to Naples had lasted longer than expected: and Ruth knew Gerda, and knew Georg. The rudeness with Willy Chardack was water under the bridge, they were both focused now on the war in Spain. What did they have to lose except grabbing some glorious moments?

And on her return from Italy, Gerda had charged off to Spain, without hesitation. Poor friend, what did you get yourself into, Ruth thought with sudden, resigned lightness.

The train had slowed down and stopped outside Paris. Now that the lights, the buildings, the advertising billboards signaled that they had almost arrived, André looked at her anxiously.

"I'll call you at the hotel," she promised, "as soon as I can."

"*Macht nichts!*" André answered. "Forget it," with a gesture he had brought with him from Budapest, a gesture that was too vehement.

Because the opposite was true. It was clear to both that he would continue to seek her out, and Ruth would make herself available whenever she could, she would listen to him and see him weep, weep less and less, talk more and more. Talk about Gerda. The journey to Toulouse had bound them more closely than they had been when Gerda was there.

Weisz is still on the telephone with Capa, but Ruth can't stay in the chair forever, overwhelmed by thoughts that aren't helping her move on.

She gets up impulsively, moves the journal aside to make room on the table for paper and pen. She's looking for the negatives on the top shelves of the bookcase, when Csiki hangs up. Now she knows how to answer him: better not to show Capa anything until we're sure he's completely recovered, matter of a few days.

Csiki agrees thoughtfully, then shakes his head. But he's not doubting her advice.

"In Spain it's all falling apart. And we're getting lost in these stupid things."

"No, I understand."

"For him it's a catastrophe."

"I know and I'm really sorry, but I have other things to

think of now. Melchior found a job in Berne, and we're going to live there—that way my mother can get out of Leipzig, finally."

Csiki nods unemphatically, but then he asks if it was the Reichskristallnacht. His Hungarian singsong skids on those agglomerations of consonants.

"My brother Hans was supposed to get married two days later," Ruth answers with a sigh. "Instead he took his bride and escaped. He's just turned up in Stockholm, an enormous surprise. As long as he was in Germany, my mother wouldn't move a centimeter. Now the problem is money. The amount my brother left her after selling off the business and things of value in a hurry doesn't cover the expatriation tax. The Nazis are greedy. Your money or your life. It makes me furious."

"And the other brother, the one who came to visit you here?"

"I've written to him, but I don't expect much from the answer. Kurt was the first to leave and ask our mother to join him in America. Hans was supposed to pay for the journey, he was the businessman of the family, and it was the damn business of the fur market that kept him in Leipzig. But in '34 the capable Hans ends up detained in Sachsenburg and Kurt, ah Kurt, took it badly. Because our mother was hostage to Hans, and because in the end she went into debt to get him out of the concentration camp. Besides the Nazis, the old jealousies between brothers. Unbelievable."

Too much of an outburst, probably, but Csiki's attentive, melancholy silence doesn't do anything to restrain her. How many brothers does he have in Budapest? How many years since he saw them?

"Kurt will insist that Hans should have thought of her before saving his own skin. Couldn't he take her to Sweden? He'll repeat that life in New York is too expensive for an actor. Now Hans doesn't have a job, but, if I know him, he'll find one soon: I don't know what we would have done without him when Papa died. But Kurt couldn't bear Hans taking the attitude of head of the family because he was bringing home money, and Hans couldn't bear that Kurt did what he wanted just because he was younger. Meanwhile I'm writing the exact amount of my ridiculous savings to both. I'm trying to puncture their pride, which neither one lacks. We'll resolve it, somehow."

"Are you leaving right away?"

"No, no," Ruth replies.

There's no reason to hurry, since many questions are still far from resolved, but she wants to move forward. And she has to do it as a resident of Switzerland, married to a Swiss, in order to bring her mother to Switzerland, if everything goes as she hopes.

"I'd like to tell Capa before he rushes off again to Spain," Ruth continues. "In the next few days I'll try to come more often, so maybe I'll be here, too, when you decide to show him the magazine. Even if there's no need."

"Thanks."

"It's nothing."

Ruth, relieved, returns to the shelf of negatives, and Csiki, instead of getting sucked into the laboratory, follows her.

"Capa won't come today. Kati Horna's at the hotel. I told her not to move till he wakes up, so she's sure of finding him."

"I didn't know she was in Paris," Ruth says, and immediately notices how wrong that banal phrase sounds applied to the scene she is alluding to: the flight from Barcelona, weapons and baggage, the Republican exodus added to the arrival of Austrians and Germans, along with the propaganda about the Jews and the Bolsheviks invading France.

"She hasn't been here long. I told her to charge the calls she has to make to Bandi's room," Csiki answers.

They don't have money, work, lodging. Kati's husband

nearly caught pneumonia in the Pyrenees, where the French confined him to a camp, although, even as an anarchist, he put on the uniform to help the fleeing masses—those poor comrades who no longer have anything, or never did, and are now freezing in the mountains, who've never seen snow when they come from the coasts with no warm clothes.

We should be down there, Ruth says to herself. But it's a luxury she can no longer afford.

Csiki is talking about prefectures, procedures, and permissions, and she is distracted by her own business, the fear that the Swiss will revoke her citizenship, if they discover why she and Melchior are going to Berlin.

"Slowly things will settle down," Csiki concludes, and Ruth nods, but she doesn't really know in relation to what.

"Sorry, I'm lost."

"I said that the rest will settle down with Kati and José Horna here. And now I return to my burrow."

Ruth gets down the boxes she needs and that to and fro between the table and the shelves corresponds to the swing of her thoughts between Spain and Germany, makes her think of Georg. She's had no more news of him, but it's inevitable that he, too, has ended up in an internment camp: exhausted, exposed to illnesses, harassed by gendarmes and guards who hate them, people like them.

Georg seemed so radiantly handsome in the Paris winter ("As long as there's a ray of sun you're more comfortable outside: the houses aren't heated in Naples"), when she had seen him again in February of '37. His Italian comrades were thrilled to sit in a famous café on the Left Bank breathing that free and idle air after presenting themselves at the recruitment office of the International Brigades. "Maybe we'll meet again down there," Ruth had pointed out, "you as doctors, me as the nurse," explaining that she had enrolled in a course at the Red

Cross. At that point a brilliantined young man had made an observation, causing hilarity in the whole group, and Georg felt obliged to translate: "Forgive them, you can't understand people who've grown up in the Catholic patriarchy and fascism. My friend, who also met Gerda yesterday, wondered if you're all like that in Leipzig . . . A poor wounded fellow, he said, would faint as soon as he opens his eyes and sees someone like you."

The atmosphere was gay and hopeful, Madrid was resisting the atrocious bombings, Gerda had left again for the front in Jarama, where the new offensive on the capital would be repulsed yet again. "I'll be waiting for you," Georg had said, saying goodbye, embracing her.

Months had passed since that meeting, and Gerda hadn't been seen in Paris. One night Melchior returned from a Party meeting in a black mood. "Terrible signs: Georg Kuritzkes barely escaped execution. They were out to get him, charged him with being a Fascist spy, then an Italian doctor testified in his favor at the trial. Someone certainly informed on him. Here at the recruitment office they didn't recognize enrollment in the Kommunistischer Jugendverband, the Young Communist League, and accepted his application with reservations . . . "

"Are you joking? He was born a Communist!" Ruth exclaimed, almost burning herself with the match as she lighted a cigarette.

"Yes, everyone from Leipzig says so, convinced that the slander came from someone in the local Party."

In the kitchen, where he had gone to look for something to eat, Melchior told her the rest. They hadn't allowed Kuritzkes to serve as a doctor, giving him the choice of leaving immediately or fighting as a simple soldier, and he had been sent to the front.

"Maybe politics has nothing to do with it," Ruth said, sitting opposite Melchior to look at him. "Georg always had the girls at his feet. It was probably envy, or revenge by someone whose girl Georg stole. Consider that the thing goes back to February, when the air wasn't poisoned yet. Whoever is the author of that lie might have thought he was just getting him out of the way."

"I hope you're right," Melchior concluded.

After the terrible events in Barcelona, the SAP had negotiated with the Communists to allow its volunteers to join the International Brigades, since they were in agreement at least on the priority of winning the war. The climate had relaxed again, but Ruth couldn't free herself of the fear that, if she left for Spain, a rejected lover might inform on or blackmail her, too—that is, behave the opposite of the lover who, having joined the SS, had warned her to leave the country. The idea of being wary not of the Nazis but of her comrades was so intolerable to her that Melchior had taken time to convince her that their anti-fascist front had been their activities in Germany, period.

Ruth leans over the table to open the Taro and Capa notebooks—wounded young children, refugees sleeping piled up on the streets, straw-haired soldiers on horseback like peasants of distant eras—and goes on thinking about the last time she had news of Georg.

"*El doctor* Kuritzkes sends greetings."

Almost a year had passed since Capa, returning from Teruel, had surprised her with that opening.

"Gerda was right: wonderful fellow, wonderful person, a tiny bit rigid but—no offense—you are Germans after all . . . "

"Maybe he was startled that you went looking for him."

"Startled and therefore rigid: does that seem a valid objection to what I said?"

Ruth was astonished in turn, but not so much that she failed to ask the important question an instant before seeing him vanish after Csiki.

"You mean they finally accepted him as a doctor?"

It was wonderful news, but meanwhile Capa never explained how he had unearthed Georg. After all, he hadn't gone back to Spain, except in the last period, which had worn him out. Did he know what had happened to *el doctor* Kuritzkes?

She could ask him, Ruth says to herself, handling the negatives, in fact ask him to find out as soon as he arrives in Barcelona: it would be a good opening for warning him that he might not find her when he returns to Paris.

Then she has to get in touch with Soma, who went back to Naples, asking him to send his reply to the Atelier, otherwise the information that can help Georg is in danger of wandering from one country to another.

Now that he is back in Naples, Soma can share his worries with Jenny, but at the worst moment he was in Paris. They had met at the café and he had pulled out that letter from Georg, written from some remote Andalusian outpost, pointing to a phrase stuck in the middle: "Don't forget me." Soma was chilled by that imperative.

"Simply do what he asks: write to him," Ruth had said.

She, however, was so alarmed that she stopped in Rue Vavin to see how Capa was, at least. The concierge directed her to the small deserted lobby, where two men, sunk in armchairs, were in a daze induced by Billie Holiday:

A cigarette that bears a lipstick's traces,
An airline ticket to romantic places
And still my heart has wings
These foolish things remind me of you.

André kept putting the needle back on the record. Ted Allan, the youth who was with Gerda in Brunete, remained crumpled in the chair, his crutches lying between its arms, his cheeks streaked like those of a child whose favorite toy has been broken. Ruth thought that widowers' union was a *folie à deux* and that the crazier of the two was Capa. But then, discovering that he had gone to look for Georg, she had caught a method in the madness—an attempt to medicate himself by taking care of his old rivals, an idea of loyalty to Gerda as bizarre in its way as it was coherent.

Ruth understands that she can still do something before she packs her bags for Switzerland, something to feel less guilty toward those who fought for Spain. She has to finish cataloguing the images of that lost war. She has to do it just for that reason, and do it properly. Fascism won't last forever, no matter how many crimes and disasters it might still cause, so let's go on, she says resolutely to herself. A thought that merits a cigarette. They'll continue to act as they wish, the enlightened democracies, but they will not be able to come to us and say they couldn't predict what Hitler and his accomplices were preparing. We have here the evidence of the *hors d'oeuvre*: the evidence of popular resistance, the evidence of systematic destruction.

Février 1937: réfugiés de Málaga, après du bombardement fasciste de la ville d'Almería, she writes in one column of a blank page, determined to fill all the others.

She is so concentrated on the work that the door of the kitchenette makes her jump. Csiki has opened it suddenly and is now heading toward the entrance with leaps reminiscent of a waiter in a tourist café.

"I have to go make the deliveries. See you tomorrow?"

"Of course, and also the next days. I've finished '36 and I'm going on, I promise you that before I leave I will have finished. It's enough just to note the differences, right?"

"Only substantial ones: dates, places, circumstances."

"I was thinking I'd start with the notebooks, mark the printed copies in the adjacent column, then all the films that correspond to the period."

"Perfect. Like that, a little at a time, I'll arrange the negatives, which are the most important thing, and in the worst shape."

Csiki, muffled in a beret, scarf, collar raised over his ears, bag over his shoulder and bicycle keys in hand, gives her an affectionate goodbye.

"*À tout à l'heure*," she responds, and goes back to her task.

When she comes out of the Atelier there's not a living soul on Rue Froidevaux. The weather is so nasty that Ruth dreams of the metro sign from her first strides on the slippery, sleet-soaked path, while the heavy odor of wet earth invades her nostrils. Soon I won't be walking through a cemetery to get to work, she repeats to herself, and this, perhaps, comforts her. Now Csiki has been informed of the thing, she has only to talk to Capa about it. She can't wait to tell Melchior, and she does, in fact, even before she takes off her coat.

"Good. I'll warm some water to thaw out your feet?"

"I was thinking of it . . . "

"Take your time, change, we have a fresh baguette and leftover soup."

In flannel pajamas with a sweater over them, her feet in the basin stuck under the table, chewing a piece of bread ("I'm famished!"), Ruth listens to the news of the day. In Berne they've found him an apartment with two rooms, Melchior informs her, and he intends not to let it get away. Even if, after Berlin and Paris, Berne . . . really a small town. His heart weeps a little, but let it weep, he consoles himself, you have to adapt.

Ruth already imagines taking a cuckoo clock off the wall and hanging in its place a photo of Paris. But the Berlin accent with which Melchior muddles his concessions to sentimentalism reminds her that repatriation is just as difficult for him as being a foreigner everywhere now is for her.

"When do you begin at the printer? After the holidays?"

"Yes, first I'll make a couple of trips to get things ready. I'll go to Berlin around Christmas and return after New Year's. This time it's better if you stay here, so you can settle my last business. Meanwhile I'll report to the registry office. In case of arrest, Berne will be able to ask to expel me directly to Berne. How does that sound?"

She feels dangerously close to giggling, while she brings the spoon to her lips. There wouldn't be much to laugh at, in substance, and yet it's comic that a Swiss with ancient paternal roots reassesses his legal country as a waiting room, compared with the lost *Heimatstadt* Berlin.

"It sounds good. The reheated soup is, too. I'm glad to leave."

"Really?"

"I'm happy to finish what there is to finish. Not to stay beyond that. Then we'll see, with my mother, money, and all the rest."

Ruth is enjoying the warmth that radiates from two opposite directions to the center of her body, she relaxes. Meanwhile she talks about Capa and Gerda's pictures from 1936 till the last battles. Of how, listing them, she became aware of the volume as a whole, and its value. "When you look at those shots in a row," she says, with an excitement charged with rage that here can be let out, "you see very clearly how the Nazi-Fascist aggression becomes increasingly barbaric . . . the disgusting horror of total war . . . Madrid, Málaga, Almería, Guernica, Bilbao, Valencia . . . "

Melchior has taken the glasses to divide the rest of the wine, there's almost three fingers' worth for each, and he stops his glass in midair for a toast. He seems really happy.

"To the most loyal comrade of the loyalists!"

Happy to have her there before him, red from head to toe, determined and essentially allied, and Ruth feels encouraged.

The *vin de pays* has turned a little acid, it's not a sin to stretch it with water, and the pause to bring it to her lips dilutes her ardor and accelerates her mental leaps.

"Will you see Sas in Berlin?" she asks Melchior. "You could bring him something from me, a photo of Gerda. In the studio there are some very beautiful recent ones, I can't imagine why I didn't think of it before."

"Because you're a cautious girl."

"Are you teasing me? Maybe I just wanted to avoid making him sad. But Sas isn't one to let himself get depressed, just the opposite, and so . . . "

Melchior has interrupted her to say that if she's thinking of a photo taken by Gerda, not a chance, and anyway it should be chosen prudently.

"Sas and Gerda were made to understand each other," Ruth comments, rocking on the chair with the good back and the crooked leg, filled with a tension that's also good, as she leans forward, unlike the rickety chair she's sitting on which awaits only a more corpulent occupant to break. Imagining that it might happen soon cheers her.

Choose carefully, Melchior said, and so Ruth reviews the images she'd like to show the man with whom Gerda went off on a motorcycle to perform the first anti-fascist acts: two shots where she's sheltered behind a soldier, the one where she sleeps on a milestone with "PC" carved into it. Unfortunately the photo in which she holds a mule by the reins is impossible, because the *mono azul* would betray both the subject and the possessor, wouldn't it?

Melchior confirms, sighing.

"I know: I'll bring you a great portrait, and if necessary you'll say it's your fiancée."

"Wife," Melchior corrects her.

"Yes, wife, it's written on your passport."

Ruth feels a sudden embarrassment, and immediately tries

to get out of it. In the photograph she's thought of bringing Melchior, Gerda is buying lilies of the valley, which is the custom in France on the First of May. She was almost certainly going to Place de la Bastille with Capa. But to the Germans one can serve up a different story. You can say that she was choosing her wedding bouquet with her mother, who, in reality, is the florist. In that portrait Gerda is dressed informally, like a girl of the people, the way she usually dressed in Spain. But she always has style, with the matching scarf and hat, the luminous smile . . .

"Sas would be proud to see her like that," she concludes vehemently.

"All right," says Melchior, "unless a compromising detail has escaped you."

"No, it's perfect," Ruth replies, bursting into laughter. "Capa passes it off as their wedding photo!"

Yes, he had left for China with a supply of prints and handed them out the way missionaries do sacred images.

And then at the Atelier the apologetic and slightly morbid journalists would ask: "What about the beautiful wife he lost in Spain?" Indeed the story that they were husband and wife originated in Spain, a rumor fed to help Gerda, who went around with the soldiers by herself. And in the end Capa, the man most inclined to confuse reality and fiction, found in his hands the evidence: the white flowers, the smiling flower seller, Gerda wearing her suede jacket. "We were a single person, a single body," he'd mutter in the grip of a sad drinking binge. Oh, Gerda would have laughed in his face. But did this deny that she had gone out with him, that morning of May 1st, in her stained, beloved jacket?

"You know, seen from a distance, almost the same height, that is, short, they slightly resemble Charlot and Paulette Goddard on that country road?"

"You think?"

"You know them too well."

In fact, Ruth objects, the appearance is deceptive. He couldn't help capturing her in an infinite number of shots, in the crowd at a meeting, in a trench in Madrid: she devoted barely two portraits to him.

"Did he not like to have his picture taken or was it that she wasn't in love?" Melchior sneers.

"No, no, wait," Ruth replies, fired up, even though it's only as she goes on speaking that her thoughts take shape— thoughts that are not very reassuring, but that she feels she has to follow in the face of the immediate future and the man with whom she's preparing to begin it. So she tells Melchior about the portrait of Capa in the *Picture Post* and the Eyemo buried in Brunete. How much time (hours? minutes?) passed between the instant Gerda shot the photo of a burning vehicle and the instant in which the vehicle she was traveling in was hit? Were the soldiers burned alive in the tank in flames? Did Gerda hear them screaming? How many people did she see die before dying? A much greater number than those she photographed. The wounded soldiers in Sierra de Guadarrama, some in such bad shape that they had no hope . . . And the ones in the hospital in Valencia were already dead . . . Gerda made her way between tortured bodies, leaned over to shoot, she had photographed a body thrown onto the tiles with not even a rag for a shroud, a child, boy or girl, five or six, the face disfigured.

"I would have run away, or cried and vomited even my soul. Whereas she took pictures, three shots, then a different corpse, a dead man less obscene to the eyes, a dead man published in some newspapers. I ask you, since you're less involved: what did my friend become in Spain?"

"A very courageous woman," Melchior says hesitantly, uneasy.

Ruth, a horrible lump in her throat, shakes her head: "I've

never denied it. Courageous, capable of self-control, of focusing the lens."

"What upsets you, then?"

Ruth doesn't know how to answer, more confused than her husband, whose gaze reflects his bewilderment.

"She was carrying the camera, the movie camera, the tripod, for kilometers and kilometers. Ted Allan said that with her last words she asked if her rolls of film were safe. She blasted away in the midst of delirium, the little Leica above her head, as if it were protecting her from the bombers. The good soldier Gerda: I don't doubt it. But I don't understand it, no."

"What, Ruth?"

"I don't understand what she felt. Hardly any fear, O.K. And then?"

Her toes are wrinkled, the water in the basin is starting to get cold, and Melchior seems to have surrendered to her thinking out loud.

She returned to Madrid, Valencia, Barcelona, Ruth continues. She put on her heels again, lipstick, the smile. She returned to Paris and seemed the usual gay and enthusiastic Gerda, and she talked about Spain, yes, with some mention of the terrible things she had seen, in the heat of those adventurous reports: the bestialities committed by *los moros*, the weariness of the people, the surreal landscape created by the bombs. But they were all words expended for the cause, just like her photographs. International solidarity was supposed to make you feel, loud and clear, that nonintervention was a crime. That Gerda Taro said, and I understand it.

"I myself, how did I behave, all in all? The party at the Steins', in May of '35, do you remember it, Melchior? The colored bulbs created an atmosphere like a cave, the midnight soup served by the ladleful above the pot to gather the drunks. And did I tell anyone that Hans was in Sachsenburg again? Not Gerda, who was flirting with André Friedmann and other guests. I said it to no one, because it wasn't appropriate, right? Better to pretend that nothing was wrong. Months later, meeting on the street, we exchanged a few words. 'You look well, Ruth, what are you up to?' 'I'm getting married, and we've moved.' 'Congratulations! Seems things couldn't be better.' 'There's my brother in the concentration camp.' 'Kurt?' 'No, the older one, Hans, the one who stayed in Leipzig.' '*Ach so*, I confuse them. Terrible, but with Kurt in America certainly something will be done. Keep your head up.'"

"A normal exchange between friends who aren't as friendly as they used to be," Melchior comments, perhaps beginning to lose patience.

"Normal, yes. But you understand what I mean by 'pretend that nothing was wrong'? Talk about certain things as if they were normal, because they are, because there's no other way to treat them . . . "

"Because they've become normal."

"Right. Pass me the towel, that's enough."

In the time she takes to dry her feet, empty the basin, and put on a pair of socks fresh from the laundry, her husband has cleared the table and begun to wash the dishes.

"Don't stand there like a soul in pain," he says, seeing her poised in front of the door. "Sit down, finish your argument."

"Calling it that's maybe too much . . . " Ruth smiles, sitting down but not on the rickety chair. "On the other hand, what should we do if not pretend it's nothing? In the case of real danger, for example going to Berlin, or even here, where everything is peaceful in appearance. And the people arriving from Spain? Should they never stop recalling the horrors?"

Melchior listens in silence, bent over the sink.

"And yet Capa broke down the last time," Ruth continues. "He was always more fragile than Gerda. It's not a matter of courage, because he was always working under the bombs. It's a question of willpower and control. It was she who wore the pants . . . but no, what am I saying, the pants have nothing at all to do with it . . . "

Melchior interrupts his washing up and turns to look at his wife, tenderly.

"You know what the paradox is?" Ruth lights up. "The paradox is that for a woman it's easier. Certainly for a young woman like Gerda who excelled at preserving good manners, the façade. Smiles and jokes, you know your part, you've been practicing it for a lifetime. What man would be suspicious in the presence of a carefree girl? You just show up and pretend it's nothing. To resist is to pretend it's nothing, to resist is to play a part. Men think that they alone are capable of discipline: we women weren't admitted even as auxiliaries after the dissolution of the Republican militias. But Gerda was trained long before venturing onto a battlefield as a soldier. And in any case, under the worker's overalls, the tapered skirt, or the military uniform, isn't it always the human being who remains— *ein Mensch*?"

"Gerda was also daring by nature, at the time you would have said unconventional," Melchior replies, and the dirty water that he's dumped into the sink emits a gurgle of approval.

"Of course she was. Capa won't forgive himself for not being with her in Brunete. Even if you can't count the girls he's taken to bed in the meantime . . . For you it's simple."

"The man is a simple animal, everybody knows it."

"Maybe."

"Hasn't he been punished enough?" Melchior objects, and as he turns to look at her the cloth he's drying the dishes with sketches a swirl. "He even got a slap from Gerda's brother, a slap right in the face at the Gare d'Austerlitz, in front of the congregation of red journalists. Should he have let his beard grow and abstained me from the pleasures of the flesh like a Hasid?"

"You're unlucky, sweetheart. I'll leave the exhortations of

Martin Buber for your bar mitzvah and all those arcane religious activities to you . . . "

They laugh with the complicity of a couple who watch over
their own skirmishes as a rite: she who has never felt completely part of something, he brought up in Zionism and liber-
tarian utopias.

Melchior didn't talk about it much, which to Ruth had
seemed typical of a man who thought about doing, a man who
had chosen a trade he liked, and then a political party, and even
an emancipated woman like her. Above all he was a reliable
companion. "You thought you found a proper Swiss man," he
repeated to her, "instead you got a stateless and apostate Jew."

"The problem," Ruth resumes, less ironic than she would
like, "is that I am also a simple woman: I trust what I see. It's
true with you, true with Capa."

"Right," Melchior agrees, "but you just said Capa's an
incurable blowhard. You're a little naïve, yes, not gullible."

"You know, a few months after we buried Gerda, I saw him
at the Select with his dancer, the Arab panther, and I said to
myself that that was life, real life, while the memories he entertained me with were ghosts fated to fade away. 'People believe
what they want to believe,' Gerda used to say. Gullible in that
sense."

"I didn't mean that."

"Why don't you have a cigarette and I'll take care of the
rest?"

"Go on, I'm almost finished."

A little hoodlum like Bandi Friedmann had been weaned
on danger, it was impressed in his five senses. Not a girl like
Gerda: she was a beginner. She wasn't capable of protecting
herself, courage went to her head, like a *schnapps* tossed back
as a challenge. "Does it seem absurd to you?"

"Not at all." Melchior has sat down beside her and stares at
her with exasperated tenderness.

"But now this story is reaching its end. It was a good idea to think of the photo to give Sas. Our comrades who are supporting the *Widerstand* have more guts than your war photographers put together."

There's one last cigarette in the pack. After a couple of drags Ruth hands it to Melchior and nods: "I don't doubt it. But I also don't doubt that Gerda would still be alive if he had been there that day. There: here at home I can say it."

A long puff of smoke reaches her. "On Rue Froidevaux not even between the lines, I hope."

Ruth gestures no, discouraged. She gave Capa every means of absolution: bad luck, tragedy, the impossibility of keeping Gerda from acting without consulting anyone. But whenever she looks for him at the Select, she finds herself facing the tables of the Coupole, where one day in September of '34 she was accosted by a fellow in such bad shape she paid for his coffee out of the kindness of her heart. "*Mein wunderschönes Fräulein*, I really need someone like you, tall, natural blond. You will be the model, I the photographer, the client a Swiss insurance company, and with a Swiss insurance company, you can be sure, I will offer you more than a *petit café* in addition to the pay."

"That, however, is a Capa-style version," Melchior insinuates.

"Not at all: haven't I ever told you?"

"Not with this abundance of detail . . . "

"The fact is that Friedmann boasted with the flair that Capa continues to fuel. When I got home, I assailed Gerda with suspicions and the few reassuring excuses dissolved. 'Will you come with me,' I asked her, 'even if it's nine in the morning?' 'Will I come with you! In fact, let's go out early and get some fresh air: so you'll look even healthier at the moment he immortalizes you . . . ' 'If he immortalizes me . . . Maybe the only tool he has is between his legs.' 'Do you need money? Then start with the assumption that that photo spread exists and maybe the guy also wants to try it on with you, which is obvious. Worst case, Ruth, we blow raspberries at him all along the Left Bank.'"

Laughter at the expense of the presumed seducer of blond beauties and the certainty that Gerda would go with her had made her see the photographer in a more serene light. She couldn't understand, she had told her friend, where he got such arrogance, but he was amusing, and if you believed him he had photographed Trotsky in '32 in Copenhagen.

"Seriously? Trotsky never lets the press get close because he's afraid they'll infiltrate an assassin. I'd really like to know how he did it . . . "

Between Gerda and André Friedmann an understanding was established immediately, and the two inflicted overlapping commands: no, crossed is too much, bring them closer again, a little askew, we should show off my friend's kilometric legs, but with discretion and elegance, *natürlich, meine Liebe*, but yours aren't bad, either, if I may.

Ruth had been pleased with all that followed: Gerda, who thanks to Friedmann learned to take photographs, Friedmann, who thanks to Gerda gained a presentable look. And she hadn't been surprised when Gerda told her that she had gone to live with Friedmann, because there was no longer anything to be surprised by after the liaison with the Dachshund.

Now the time that André and Gerda spent together seems to her an enormity: two years exactly, one in Paris, the other in Spain, in large part under the same roof, even in the same sleeping bag.

Melchior, tired, says that every pot has its cover, or tries to find one that fits.

And if the pot can't stand the cover?

"Let's go to bed, Ruth."

"I'm the one who introduced them."

PART III
GEORG KURITZKES
Rome, 1960

War is no longer declared,
but rather continued. The outrageous
has become the everyday. The hero
is absent from the battle. The weak
are moved into the firing zone.
The uniform of the day is patience;
the order of merit is the wretched star
of hope over the heart.

It is awarded
when nothing more happens,
when the bombardment is silenced,
when the enemy has become invisible
and the shadow of eternal armament
covers the sky.

It is awarded
for deserting the flag,
for bravery before a friend,
for the betrayal of shameful secrets
and the disregard of every command.

Every Day
—INGEBORG BACHMANN
(translated by Peter Filkins)

Rome, September 18, 1960

My dear Ruth,
    Willy Chardack remains a rough-coated dachs-hund, but he appreciated my congratulations. As you predicted: so thank you for your help and advice.
    Here finally we can breathe. My Italian friends have returned, the ones with whom I, too, have launched an experiment—though its results won't be crucial for the health of humanity, it would simplify the job of showing our world in color. We're an improvised team, but we've got excellent skills; I cover the neuroscientific aspect, the technical is assigned to a much sought-after *directeur photo*, and it's being supervised by a professor at the University of Rome.
    It's good for me to get out of the *panem et circenses* routine (the FAO looks out on the Circus Maximus, where in the time of Julius Caesar the chariot races were held). To open a medical office you have to deal with byzantine bureaucracies or go around them through acquaintances, bribes, etc., and I find it so odious that I procrastinate.
    Meanwhile I've bought myself a Vespa. A deal, according to my mechanic.
    I'm sorry that school has already begun for you (here they start in October!), because it would be the ideal moment to visit Rome. Come when you want, with your

children, with your husband if he can allow himself a vacation. I would be happy to be your guide and offer you the
most up-to-date means for exploring the monuments and
the famous contemporary *dolce vita!*

Warmly

yours,

The racket of the typewriter, the only one disturbing the
quiet of the FAO building, is still echoing in the ears of Dr.
Kuritzkes when he adds his signature to the page pulled out of
the Olivetti: an energetic G, as disproportionate as the head of
a tadpole with its illegible tail, the familiar scribble that makes
him hesitate before typing his full name on the envelope.
Giorgio Kuritzkes, c/o PUTTI, Via della Purificazione 47,
Roma, ITALIA. For Ruth "Georg" would be more usual but
not for the neighbor who might respond if the letter was
returned, and for him it's the same: he's been changing his
name for a lifetime.

It's taken a while to write the letter, and now he has to hurry
to put it in the folder to show the guard whom he asked as a
favor ("an exception") to let him into the office on a Sunday.
It's a ceremonial performance ("Dotto', please, hurry"), and
the role-playing is preserved. And it doesn't matter that the
idea of telephoning came to him after he decided to stop at the
office to get some papers, and that he's never before used the
phone for personal communications, much less on a weekend.

It was a good idea to telephone Willy on a Sunday morning
in America, and a pleasure to find him at the first ring, to talk
to an old friend on another continent in the silence that rever-
berates with the rhythmic vibrations of the cicadas, so loud, in
this late summer, that they muffle the noise of cars passing on
Viale delle Terme di Caracalla. Spellbound by the compact
crowns of the pines, as if he'd never seen them, by the ruins, by
the paradisiacal gardens of the Aventine that he can't stop gazing

at. Hovering, privileged, extraterritorial. Enveloped by the eight-story marble building, which has a geometrical purity, and the marvelous quality of certain Fascist structures that seem designed to make you forget their origins. It was supposed to be the Ministry for Italian Africa and in 1952 opened its doors to the United Nations. An agreed-on retribution for the symbolic rent of a dollar a year.

Yes, he wasted too much time writing the letter, and the cigarettes left on the counter won't be enough for the guard, it will also take a present at Christmas. Carton, cigars, bottle? He'll have to inquire. Some of his colleagues will enjoy the fact that he's been corrupted by such customs, but never mind.

He comes out of the elevator satisfied. CONFERENCE EUROPE 10-15 OCTOBER, ROME says the folder under his arm that, in case of questions from the guard, is to be immediately delivered to the embassy of one of the countries invited at the last minute to balance the presence of the United States, which has asked to attend as an observer.

But Oreste is distracted by a boy who can't sit still yet doesn't dare move away from the bench. He must be about ten, still at an age that respects prohibitions, something that, in his way, he applies to the guard, who is peeling a peach, careful not to let it drip beyond the cloth on which his lunch is set out.

"The game starts at three, and, damn them, they won't wait for me. They'll let somebody else play if I don't get there!"

Oreste looks up. "Another bad word and you'll catch it," he mutters to the boy, and the patriarchal face and the uniform that pinches mid-chest suddenly stiffen.

There, he's seen me, thinks the doctor. The rhythm of his heels, the only sound that echoes in the long corridor, confirms how out of place his appearance is. Oreste's son wouldn't be able to hang around there; indeed, the guard gathers up the dishes in an instant, glancing in his direction, and now awaits him at the desk with an expression so serious that it reminds him of a story he heard recently. The town he left as a kid, years of labor on construction sites, the accident, the application for disability—feeling he'd been miraculously saved by the Madonna, since it could have been much worse—and, finally ("without connections!"), this job, which supports the whole family. But the doctor wouldn't dream of reporting that the sovereign space of the Food and Agriculture Organization was violated by the rite of pasta.

He and the guard know each other by name, and that's already something: a sign that Dr. Giorgio, as Oreste calls him, isn't among the bureaucrats who come and go and when they're transferred elsewhere haven't even learned Italian. No, when he arrived from Paris his Italian was already so fluent that almost no one settled for simply complimenting him, forcing him to explain that he had lived in Italy as a student. "Here in Rome?" even Oreste asked. The doctor, to cut it short, replied: "No, in Florence."

The guard doesn't know that Dr. Giorgio, having studied also in Milan and Turin and, finally, Naples, even learned to distinguish dialects. And if in Italy, at the time, learning was limited to the life of the neighborhoods, while the pomposity of the regime's Italian hovered in the universities, it wasn't like that in Spain, where the Italian volunteers, who came from all over, had brought their local speech.

Those volunteers knew how to read and write, and many—the majority as adults—had gathered secretly around a country hearth to learn. Having become militants partly out of pride in that Promethean undertaking, they listened to the political commissar with a seriousness that revealed that for them knowledge and Communism were synonyms. One day, when the radio was broadcasting a speech by Comrade Nicoletti, someone cried, "Peppino Di Vittorio!" and the diminutive of a man who had left as a laborer to incite the southern lands spread among the Italians a hopeful desire for redemption. Anyone, with a little training, could learn to shoot and follow orders, and that a Lombard mechanic could become a sapper, a Ligurian dock worker a tank man, and Sardinian miners gunners was only the first step on the way to the classless society of the International Brigades. The words, however, were distorted by accents, limited by dialects incomprehensible outside the radius of the fellow villagers with whom they arrived at the camp in Albacete. Georg Kuritzkes was well aware of having an advantage over those comrades. He had come with papers presumed false, he was stateless, but he had no difficulty understanding and being understood in various languages.

In the end he was assigned to the 86th Mixed Brigade under the command of Aldo Morandi, a Sicilian comrade whose military gifts had been rewarded by a rapid career rise, and then he had been transferred to the front in the Andalusian mining region. He had written to Gerda—just two lines on the bare beauty of Sierra Morena and a very affectionate greeting—but didn't consider how soon that letter, sent to the office of the censor in Madrid, would be delivered to her.

One day, returning from a reconnaissance, his head emptied by the mountain sun beating on his helmet, he made out a crowd from a distance and thought that the *campesino* who was surrounded was offering some rare goods, maybe even *jamón Serrano*. He calculated that it was pointless to hurry and went straight on at his pace until, light as a lynx in the typical Spanish cloth shoes, Gerda appeared before him. Tearing off her Basque beret and shaking her short sun-lightened hair, she exclaimed, "Do you recognize me?" and remained looking at him, exhilarated by the expression that must have appeared on his face.

She had arrived the day before, late. They had welcomed her in the *casita* that served as general headquarters and settled her on one of the two cots in the room reserved for the command. She had slept well, but was a little sorry that sharing her den, along with the officers and the ticks (the only defect of the hayloft), was the Spanish second in command, an authentic *hidalgo*. Morandi would have preferred to see her leave immediately, despite the credentials she had shown him and having decided himself that they would take turns giving her the cot.

The comrades in his group moved away, partly out of discipline, partly out of discretion, and very much, obviously, in order to comment on the sensational appearance of that *rubia* equipped with a camera in their marginal outpost. He and Gerda were alone on the path. It would have been the ideal moment to talk, since no one would have caught a syllable. He'd just have to tell her about the arrest and trial—"like Kafka"—with irony, naturally. But he had felt like a perfect K. and was still tremendously embarrassed about it. Gerda would have been dumbfounded thinking back to the last embrace in Paris ("I knew I could count on you") and was not to blame for what had happened. And also walking beside her in that dusty air, on that track of hard grass and crushed stone, had the unfathomable quality of a dream. He wished above all not to spoil the joy of that unexpected meeting (they were alive: wasn't that enough?), the pleasure of seeing her at ease in the harsh emptiness of those mountains mangled by war.

Slowly they had approached the comrades at the camp, while Gerda continued to vent against Morandi. Poor Georg, who had fallen in with that obtuse soldier for whom a woman at the front was more pernicious than the runs ("I sleep in this dirty overall, you know? and I don't even notice the stink anymore"), that severe father in uniform who concealed the instinct of a mother hen.

Georg, bursting into laughter (there was truth in what Gerda was saying, and all her energy), let slip an imprudent retort: "If we had more commanders like him, we'd be closer to victory."

He tried to mitigate it by saying: "Morandi's seen a lot, since the Great War . . . "

"Did he take you out of the lines? Does he use you as a doctor?" Gerda asked, suddenly softening.

Did she already know something and was she dawdling to avoid the subject? he wondered, with a relief that shifted the stone under his sternum.

"He can't. But he uses me as an interpreter, a messenger between divisions, help as a radio operator."

Gerda had found this very funny ("You'll get Berlitz as your nom de guerre"), probably so as not to have to show her gratitude toward the target of her derision.

"You can't imagine how much the lack of understanding among French, English, and Germans has cost us, as well as in coordinating with the Spanish. So many losses, even some defeats, I fear!"

Gerda, incredulous and irritated, retorted that none of the great generals with whom she had very friendly relations ("Unlike your hostile Morandi") had ever mentioned it, nor any of the soldiers whose trust and respect she'd earned.

"*Ein schlechter Witz*," she commented, spiteful, continuing to observe him with a questioning expression.

"It's true," Georg said, "even if it seems a joke."

"*Scheissdreck merde shit . . . mierda!*"

The spontaneous impulse to adapt to their spirit as an international barracks was irresistible. If there hadn't been comrades keeping an eye on what he was still doing there with the blonde ("a dear friend of mine," he was at pains to explain— an outrageous error), he would have kissed her immediately, not right on the mouth, to avoid making a mistake. Walking faster, he had longed for and feared a next occasion. But it was the only time he saw Gerda alone, for many days in a row.

*

In the FAO building, Dr. Kuritzkes never talked about
Spain or about the comrades he'd joined in the Haute Savoie,
while in Paris everyone knew he had been *maquisard*.

The aftermath of the war was protracted everywhere and in
a particular way on Avenue Kléber, site of the provisional headquarters of UNESCO. Parisians passing by the giant Hotel
Majestic, moving with their old nonchalance, had trouble per-
ceiving that the swastikas and the guns shouldered for protection of the Wehrmacht High Command had been replaced by
the flags of the winning nations. But those who entered the
lobby and headed for a suite stuffed with desks or the personnel department dug out of a *salle de bains* (with the folders in
the tub and the toilet lid like a side table) couldn't help feeling
that they were still an occupier. And an occupier at a disadvan-
tage, because a grand hotel was better suited to the brutal
requirements of a command than to housing the multiplicity of
projects devoted to education, science, and culture in the
repacified world.

Dr. Kuritzkes had gone to Rome before his colleagues could
move to the building on Place de Fontenoy, whose division
into three wings, conceived by three architects of different
nationalities and approved by a committee of great masters (Le
Corbusier, Gropius, Saarinen, Rogers, Markelius, Costa), was
the perfect realization of the universal mission for which the
Maison de l'UNESCO had been planned.

In Rome they knew his CV, but it was no longer the thing
to talk about the period that had given life to the new world
order, of which the United Nations was the precursor, like the
dove after the flood. The only one who did was a Yugoslav colleague, Dr. Modrić, a biologist with a degree from Trieste who
had specialized in ichthyology at the Lomonosova in Moscow.
He was a thin scholar whom Dr. Kuritzkes often worked with
on research aimed at improving fishing techniques. The

strange thing was that, face to face, Modrić never mentioned the war. He preferred to expound on the aquatic ecosystems that presented science with the continuous challenge of the unknown, and digress a little on private life when they'd finished the day's task. The complicated relationship with a Signora Carla who worked in a bank in Piazza Fiume. The worry about his children, who remained with his ex-wife in Zagreb and were enrolled full-time in school, as in the capitalist world they dreamed of, but just for that reason unreachable during working hours. It had been Dr. Modrić who suggested that for a modest baksheesh ("Here, dear Kuritzkes, we are not in Central Europe: you must have noticed") one could telephone from the office on the weekend, avoiding that annoyance of shutting oneself in a phone booth, with the smoke outside, the noise, the kids whose invented gestures became bolder the longer you stayed on.

Good person, Modrić. Basically a very discreet man. "Doctor, I know you're one of ours, but please allow me a question: wouldn't you, like so many, now prefer to cross the *atlantico*?" he had asked, while he was summarizing what neurophysiology had learned from the sophisticated intelligence of cephalopods.

"No," he answered, secure. "I, too, prefer to occupy myself with what is *in* the Atlantic. I find it more profitable and satisfying."

"*Ça va sans dire*," Dr. Modrić agreed.

That reply was so representative of his behavior that it was bizarre, in the cafeteria, to hear him assaulting his colleagues with stories of his partisan activities. He did it as a way to vent and out of spite, that was clear: the Yugoslavs should be treated with caution—irredentism and so on—much more than certain Germans with imaginable pasts ("Cordial with everyone, eh? Fascists inside!").

"You don't see all the rest, it doesn't concern you?" someone at the table tried to stop him.

The rest began with the cyclopic stake in the eye they ran up against every day. The UN had obtained an agreement for the restitution of Ethiopian plunder, but the stele of Axum remained in front of the FAO building, twenty-four meters of theft planted in the clear Roman sky.

"*Ils s'en fichent, les italiens!*" a colleague concluded. "They don't give a damn," another nodded; in fact, they were rubbing their hands at the fact that decolonization had fallen to the victors. Thus they landed on the subject that, outside their specialties, they knew better than any other.

In the cafeteria of the FAO, around the tables flooded with bright light, they'd been following the crisis in Congo for days, tense and passionate; in comparison, the Olympics just concluded had been a fleeting thrill. The dark news from Africa had swept away the triumph of Abebe Bikila, the Ethiopian marathoner who, rounding the stolen stele for the second time, had put wings on his bare feet and won the gold.

During the Suez crisis, the UN had helped avert a new world war, but now it was suffering a setback: two chiefs were sitting on the natural wealth of Congo, whetting the appetite of the superpowers and the Belgians. The UN, far from resembling a global government, wasn't able even to play the role of a referee who could suspend the match. A bitter observation, but, worst of all, the dispute had taken root in Rome as well. There were experts in forests and pastures, in *cultivar* and stockpiling goods, but the coup d'état in Congo had divided them. The crevasse that had opened in Viale delle Terme di Caracalla didn't even mirror the division into blocs, since the Soviet Union and its allies had left the FAO. The majority of the whites defended the impartial role that the UN had set for itself, a line that for their African colleagues, and also Turks, Indians, and so on, was turning out to be a farce of evading responsibility. In Congo Mobutu's soldiers had put under house arrest Lumumba, the prime minister who wanted the unity of his people, full democratic freedom, and fair allocation of resources, and the UN had done nothing but provide the ring of prison guards around the house.

"To protect him," some Swede or Canadian tried to say, causing an uproar.

Dr. Kuritzkes and Dr. Modrić found themselves among the white flies of the colored ranks. But those who knew the Titoist biologist better suspected that he felt closer to his beloved polyps than to the inhabitants of those unknown lands. Dr. Kuritzkes, however, unsheathed his old weapons of persuasion and rhetoric, although he would have preferred not to use them anymore, at least not there. He didn't want to feel doubts again about a choice, because political games now were poison to him. The emblem of the FAO was a stalk of grain, *Fiat panis*, Let there be bread, its motto. Was it asking so much to trust that he was doing an honest job under that motto?

In the past week Georg had started dreaming about Gerda again. He needed her optimism, her shameless pragmatism. Her brilliance at hiding uncertainties and disappointments, her ease in appearing realistic to the point of seeming cynical, so as not to give in. Even the derision that no other woman had shown him with such frequency.

What would you do, Gerda? It's not hard to imagine.

"Are you finished?" she'd say when, in Leipzig, she witnessed arguments so similar to the ones he carries on now in the cafeteria. "You promised we'd go dancing, or do I have to find somebody else?" she'd sing with a little smile.

"I'm not done, we're talking about important things," he retorted, hating her, and getting angry with the friends who, tapping their feet, indicated they understood that the discussion had been put off. *Ubi maior . . .*

But he was good then at not losing face. "All right," he said, "but let me finish this cigarette." And right away he offered one to Gerda, too, and while the match he'd lighted for her went out (how many fires had been extinguished by those gallant gestures?) returned to assessing the situation.

His friends didn't realize that he was agitated, nor did Gerda, maybe because she didn't care. It was enough for him to take her by the arm, shelter her with his jacket if it was starting to snow at the tram stop on Gohliser Strasse. And then they chatted until they arrived at the usual *Tanzlokal*, where the tension relaxed, and thoughts were silenced by the dancehall music.

He liked the low lights, the smoky, sweaty warmth, the swing that made you do crazy things with your shoulder blades, and he liked Gerda.

"I like you, too. I mean it."

She had assured him of it the first time he managed to embrace and then kiss her properly, finding himself stunned. How had she managed to free herself without a tug, only a phrase breathed a few inches from his mouth? No, probably she wouldn't be the right girl, she had then said to him, and besides in her life there's Pieter, whom she's very fond of.

Georg had immediately cooled off, but the foxtrot allowed him to hold her tight where the hooks stuck out under the silk dress, the route of the last tram to take her hand, the crowded platform to extinguish a laugh on her lips. His mind was obscured, the unconscious guided him.

Except that later, on those slow, overheated trams, steamed up by bad weather and the remains of agitation, he always got tangled up in analyses and questions of principle. It's not suitable to fix on such a bourgeois woman, he said to himself, the girlfriend of a capitalist whom she always defends ("Is it Pieter's fault if they're slave owners in America?"). And then Gerda Pohorylle never tired of appearing frivolous and superficial, maybe not exactly frivolous but impatient to return to her untouchable thoughtlessness. Don't let yourself be deceived by that lively and unpredictable little head, he warned himself, and continued to act the nice guy. Don't be flattered by her interest in your book recommendations, your critical opinions. Don't seriously believe that she cares anything about historical materialism or the emancipation of the oppressed. She's interested in not being bored, in your handsome face and entertainment, nothing else. So control yourself: have fun, yes, but don't delude yourself about the rest.

The rest had won. Attraction had followed its own course, chemistry flooded the synapses, prevailing over reason, which was natural, and just. Georg Kuritzkes was hopelessly in love with Gerda Pohorylle. The only question he ever posed to himself was how he had managed to win her, until what he feared was illusory turned out to be real.

Gerda had changed. She was transformed. Not like the girls who adapted to him with such obvious zeal that, in his mind, they ended up confused with one another: Hanni, Paula, Trudel, Marie-Luise . . . But the skirmishes with his mother hadn't changed, the times when he criticized her because she was crazy about Gerda and was always ready to take her side. "What is it?" he attacked her. "The horrible missionary instinct that's so much more interested in the sheep to convert? Or do you, too, aspire to the *dolce vita* . . . "

"Don't provoke me, Georg, you don't understand a thing."

"All right. I humbly ask you to enlighten me!"

His mother adjusted her reading glasses or picked up the dust cloth, while Georg pointed out that Hanni Paula Trudel and Marie-Luise had become comrades within a month, if they weren't already enrolled in the Young Communist League.

"Tell me, do I have time to waste with some little girls who won't last next to you?"

"And *this one* will last?"

"I hope so for your sake, *durak*. I do what I can, but you should make a bigger effort than usual."

Georg protested that he refused to play the lovesick suitor, that that was ruled out by the education he'd had, the ideas about equality between the sexes, and he pretended to misunderstand his mother, who had already turned to see what had become of his little brother, whom she'd had with Dr. Gelbke. In reality he just wanted to stay close enough to hear her repeat that Gerda was a woman of unusual insight, very likable, and, "pointless for me to tell you," attractive. Once he had extorted these confirmations, his mind was at rest.

The comfort that Georg got from his own dialectic was much more volatile than the tranquil routine that was being established between him and Gerda, his comrade-mother, and the other habitués of Friedrich-Karl-Strasse. The girl was the last to leave his attic, and sometimes she didn't go home. One morning his mother met Gerda in the kitchen, all neat and tidy, near the icebox, and heard herself asked: "May I take the milk bottle?"

"Go ahead, there's another for the baby," she answered. "Don't even ask."

Nights and breakfasts at the Gelbke house were repeated. Gerda approached the icebox, "May I?" she asked, and again his mother invited her to help herself, while Georg cut the bread, grinning, with his head down (it was ridiculous, yes, but he was happy). Then Dina read aloud the articles from the *Arbeiter Illustrierte Zeitung*, Gerda picked up the baby's pacifier and washed it under the faucet, while he pulled Fritzchen down from the chair he was trying to climb up . . .

In the morning they parted in the doorway, at night Georg stopped by Springerstrasse and waited for Gerda to come down. She was extremely punctual and that cheered him every time. One day he rang early, since he'd been loitering for a few minutes in front of No. 32. Gerda answered "I'll be right there," but then asked him to come in.

"Georg Kuritzkes, medical student," she introduced him to her parents. "We have to run, though, the movie starts in half an hour."

"Very pleased, do us the honor of a visit when you have more time."

"Thank you, Herr Pohorylle, and excuse the drop-in . . . "

"*Aber bitte*: you young people should have fun!"

The circumscribed episode in the hallway, where Gerda adjusted her hat in front of a mirror hanging above a rounded monstrosity of a secretary desk, helped to reassure him. *Spiessbürger*, he had said to himself, prosperous petit bourgeois. Courteous, the way tradesmen should be, but not excessively unctuous. Would they surrender to the idea that Gerda had given the goodbye to the great importer of coffee to go with someone like him? Still jobless, and an enemy of the class they boasted of belonging to?

The evening was cool but pleasant, and there was enough time to go on foot to the Capitol cinema. They walked in the shadow of the streetlamps that striped the surface of the residential streets with dirty yellow. Was it the rhythm of their pace, the darkness accentuated on the side of the street where the Rosental began, the clasp of their hands that relaxed and gripped with small syncopated impulses? The fact is that a question had arisen that, step by step, was trailing another behind it. Had Gerda told her parents what she had gone to Stuttgart to do? What had she told them instead? That she was going to visit her best friend from old times? And what did she say when she didn't come home? That she was staying at Ruth Cerf's? Or nothing?

"Let's walk a little faster, there's nothing here, it's boring."

Georg would have set aside those thoughts if Gerda hadn't started to hurry. He felt he was being tugged in a forward flight that speeded up his heartbeat, speeded up doubts, and suddenly linked them to the Pohorylles, whom he saw again in frozen images and details. Her father's swelling vest with the old-fashioned watch chain. The glasses askew in front of faded eyes that matched a faint beard. The mother very small, her pallor emphasized by the modesty of a mouse-colored dress. She hadn't opened her mouth except to agree in monosyllables with whatever her husband said.

Had Gerda kept him hidden from her parents? Did she want to hide from those tiny authorities not only him but all those whom, after a quarter of an hour along the Chaussée di Gohlis, she showered with admiration?

Georg hadn't even noticed if there was a mezuzah on the Pohorylles' door frame. But he was the son of a divorced woman remarried to a goy. And in the echo of the disgusting rotundity of that word, which seemed reckless to him, he stopped.

"Are you ashamed of me?"

"What?!"

"Are you ashamed of me and my family?"

The repetition had made him blush, embarrassed and furious that it was he who was ashamed of them. It couldn't be seen, luckily, under the jagged mass of shadows cast by the Rosental.

"Are you hiding from your parents the change in how we spend our time together lately?"

In response he had received a crystalline laugh: long and terrible, Gerda's hand detached from his and raised in a theatrical swirl.

"I don't give a damn about my parents: I've always done what I like."

With no other commentary in that regard, his hand had been clasped again: "We'll be late for the movie." But at a red light Gerda had declared that that nonsense was annoying, and her house a bore.

"I assumed you saw it the same way, but I'll invite you to dinner at our house, you can come to Shabbat, if you want . . . "

"Whatever you say."

The matter was closed, set aside before they rapidly reached the ticket window of the movie theater, which was always crowded on weekends. Why had he gotten involved in things that didn't concern him? Why had he given in to that petty moralism (only because he had seen the Pohorylles in person?), when Gerda was a grown woman, a liberated woman, and had all the right to manage her affairs as she believed best? He would get his degree, if necessary play the role of the well-brought-up youth, without hiding the fact that he didn't know how to say half a prayer in Hebrew, or softening his opinions, even regarding Gerda's parents. It wasn't right for him to do otherwise.

Then there had been exams, vacations, days spent all together in Dr. Gelbke's house on the Dübener Heide, and, finally, his departure for Berlin. No invitation to the Pohorylle house, no moment removed from the pleasure of their being together.

They had extended their happy routines to new territories. And if, unavoidably, these included Gerda's little sulks and the grand questions that assailed him, repetition dulled the analyses and blunted the questions of principle. There was a condition that decreed the suspension of time passing, and, without that, doubts didn't mature. Georg Kuritzkes had never been so happy, and would never be again.

The nostalgia he's allowed himself in the past days, thinking back to his years with Gerda, has had a comforting effect, and so he's reinforced it just outside the gates of the FAO. Feeling the breeze blowing against him as he rode home on his Vespa, he told himself that it was as natural as that warm air to have a language and city of origin, a great task, and a great love. If he hadn't had the capacity to live at the height of his dreams then, either, he would have become a survivor filled with bitter regrets or a traitor in a bubble of oblivion like one of those plastic globes where fake snow falls on the Coliseum and every other monument on the planet contained in that two-cent idyll.

All was not yet lost, at that point. They hadn't yet moved on to the need for the *Widerstand*, the resistance that was too weak for the winter of barbarism. If the pressure not to submit could have been multiplied, if that desire, as life-giving as his girl, could have gone farther, become insurrection, the lethal order would have tottered before its defeat amounted to a world of ashes and rubble.

In Leipzig and then in Berlin, the conflicts were extremely bitter, the divisions lacerating. The big cities were caught in the stranglehold of the petit-bourgeois substrate and in the mass resignations of the working class, which kindled a bipolar feeling even in those who didn't believe that revolution had to rise, like the Arab phoenix, from the ruins of the Weimar Republic. But the struggle was different as long as there was a possibility of winning it. And he organized, discussed, avoided the ambushes of the brownshirts and was always ready to fight— and beside him he had Gerda Pohorylle.

Gerda summarized the beauty and the difficulty of that period, rediscovered and renewed every day. At that moment the two of them were perfect: she took him out to have fun, and he put the tools for fighting in her hand. No one was to blame if that stupendous complementarity had fractured. It would have ended, probably, even if Hitler hadn't arrived to separate them.

Recognizing it doesn't sadden him, on the contrary it settles him in the proper place of a man of nearly fifty who accepts the limits, some limits, in order not to suffer them all.

Recently his mother launched a mission based on the conviction that "our Gerda" became a revolutionary saint thanks to the *éducation sentimentale* of Leipzig. Georg doesn't try to contradict her, even though he now prefers structures of thought that are examined through the cold, rigorous lens of the neurosciences. But if comrade Dina Gelbke manages to get a small street for comrade Gerda Taro, a concrete cube for the pigeons, who already foul every bronze head of our revered friend Lenin, she can only be rewarded for it. Mind and memory are a single thing, the integrity of memory establishes the integrity of every human being, even among the nomads (and wasn't he perhaps a nomad?); the preservation of memories is not a prerogative of the bourgeois inner life. Each remembers what serves, what helps him to get by. And Dr. Kuritzkes wants only to hold on to "his Gerda," even though he knows she doesn't exist.

Gerda the daring, the unpredictable, the *rubia* fox, who wouldn't give up a single bite of happiness that could be stolen from the present.

In Rome the temperature is still summery, and the first center-left government is working on reforms and attempts at détente abroad, but the thaw is distant, perhaps impossible. The fate of Congo angers him, but he wouldn't feel so cornered, and impatient with his odious clerical impatience, if he didn't spend every morning in the presence of the United Nations flag. Modrić isn't wrong when he complains that, on the outside, the UN is confused with NATO—it's all American stuff, from that point of view, and then "what does someone from the other side have to do with it—you know what I mean, doctor—a Communist?" A foreign Communist, and a non-aligned Communist at that, is considered a freak in this city that invented the circus.

Except that Dr. Modrić still has his socialist country and his familiarity with everything that lives in seas, lakes, rivers, and lagoons. Whereas Dr. Kuritzkes is an authentic fish out of water. He applies sarcasm to himself like a medical treatment. In the morning in the bath he sings *"lasciaaate ogni speraaanza . . . voi ch'entrate!"* imitating the heavy accent of Helmut Krebs, whose splendid interpretation of Monteverdi's *Orfeo* he came upon rummaging in the stalls of Porta Portese. Had it been left by a German? Or something much worse? On his dusty fingers he felt the irritation of those conjectures suggested purely by the Deutsche Grammophon label, before putting the record under his arm.

In the past week, however, it hasn't been enough for him to reproach himself, sing, discuss in the office, and then at home listen to *Orfeo* or J.S. Bach—the severe *Thomaskantor* who hovered over his youth—in a face to face between the wing chair and the record player. Now he has to sum up, and he does it best when he comes home sweaty and invigorated from a run in Villa Borghese, where in the morning he meets only other expatriate athletes and a few Roman dogs out walking with the maid.

He's never been under the illusion that the UN can remove itself from the great conflicts, and he is well aware that the neutrality of science doesn't exist. More than once, with his intellectual colleagues at UNESCO, he has eviscerated the interpretations of the famous phrase from Adorno's *Minima Moralia*: "There is no true life—or just life—within a false life." UNESCO offered him the best of compromises, a compromise that has, ultimately, remained acceptable. But he no longer accepts it. Driven by a need for truth, he could still reach a just choice, even if it resembles a false step. "I'm leaving, I'm quitting."

He was pondering those conclusions the other day after visiting his barber in Via Sicilia, when, coming down along Via

Veneto, he saw the German writers and academics who cus-
tomarily make the sidewalk tables of the Doney their
Stammtisch. Even though their voices were muffled by youths
on mopeds honking at friends sitting down for an *aperitivo*,
and the din of the Americans—who gravitate around the
movies or the embassy and hold court at the Café Doney—they
were utterly recognizable from the expressions and measured
gestures that lent a provincial aspect even to clothing bought
in the recommended tailor shops. Even the blond woman poet,
who was very famous in Germany, seemed a timid Carinthian
peasant in the bustle of that self-satisfied urbanity. But maybe
her Swiss companion intimidated her: no less famous as a nov-
elist, and attractive the way a rumpled frog speaking with a
pipe in his mouth might be. "You should also hold forth on
Adorno's maxim," he thought, putting out the cigarette butt
under his heel.

Suddenly a girl who was flying to a rendezvous made Gerda
flash into his mind. She would have been in tune with the setting, perfectly at ease with waiters and clientele of every sort:
she was at home in the bars of Montparnasse, while in Berlin
she always wanted to drag him to the Romanisches Café ("I'll
pay! I've spent almost nothing yet . . ."), where you met anyone who was anyone in the avant-garde. The young Italian
woman went by in the peasant shoes that Gerda wore in
Spain—espadrilles they're called, now that they're fashionable.
And, in a flash, he saw Gerda not as she was at the time but as
she would have been in those sinuous Capri pants, the sweater
over her shoulder, her hair weightless. The apparition cut off
his digressions, or, rather, intervened. That old story about the
true life and the false life, please, Georg, forget it . . .

Dr. Kuritzkes, however, admires Adorno, who returned
from exile to reclaim the chair in Frankfurt, while German
critical culture volunteers as an extra in *La Dolce Vita*.

Do you have a reason to reproach yourself for not going

back to remake Germany, beside those who have an iron cross in the closet? he said to himself, as he had before, but that day the thought is tinged with the clear and mocking intonation of Gerda Pohorylle. So he has descended the curves of Via Veneto in a state of amused wonder to the point where Piazza Barberini comes into view. He hurls himself into the traffic, as he learned to do in Naples, and, shortly after turning into the narrow street that intersects Via della Purificazione, he is persuaded that this time, too, it will turn out well. If the bristly Dachshund has managed to revolutionize medicine, he'll find space, too, modest perhaps, but free, to devote himself to his research—if not in Rome, then somewhere else. He just has to wait for the right moment, keep his eyes open.

As soon as he climbed the crooked stone stairs of his building Dr. Kuritzkes looked for Ruth's number to ask her for Willy Chardack's address.

He would send him a letter with the most heartfelt compliments. It was hugely encouraging, he would write, to see that Newton's apple continued to fall at random, and that, in spite of all the money that was spent to enslave it (that no, he shouldn't write), that random fall was still the prime mover of science. Randomness had helped him, too, when, studying the orientation of fish guided by filtered indirect light, he had discovered Edwin H. Land's theory of polarized light. Excited by that theory of color, which was so innovative compared to the classical theory, he had immediately talked about it with his friend Professor Somenzi, who had put him in contact with an experienced cinematographer. Having found a companion in adventure in Signor Mario Bernardo, he had redone the experiments described by Mr. Polaroid, but unfortunately the conditions had been too unstable to replicate his extraordinary results. Besides, their approach was novel in that they intended to reexamine the vision of color in relation to the new theory.

They had gotten out of it an article for a specialized journal, something that he had taken pains to let the inventor of the Polaroid know.

Maybe Willy would send him just a couple of lines of thanks. But that wasn't what mattered: the important thing was to reposition himself on the plane of possibility embodied by the Dachshund.

When Ruth advised him to telephone, he felt so relieved that he put on the Dave Brubeck record (gift from the neighbor for whom under the guise of friendship he looked after an epileptic granddaughter), tapping the rhythm of "Take Five" on the arms of his chair.

Now he's about to leave the FAO building, with an already worn-out sense of detachment and, having just used the office telephone to mention his plans to Willy Chardack, he's sure he's really on the point of turning his back on the Circus Maximus. All he has to do is offer, along with some cigarettes ("Have a couple for later, I've got a whole carton"), to take the boy, who it seems has to be in a certain place at three. That matter would be resolved, too, as long as the porter lets him ride on the Vespa.

"Damn, I got my bike!" the person in question objects, before the father can ponder a response adequate to the implicit meaning of the offer.

They stare at the pot, now wrapped up, on the reception desk, until Oreste puts an end to the embarrassment. "You'll come get the bike," he orders his son, "if Dr. Giorgio is so kind . . . "

Dr. Giorgio is so kind that heading toward the gate he asks the boy what his name is. "Claudio," he says, and then nothing else. However, he observes him very carefully as he hangs the bundle on the handlebar, adjusts the chain, starts it up.

"Where are we going?"

"Viale di Trastevere, you know how to get there? We gotta make a stop, then I'll explain."

"Good. Hold on tight."

At the end of Via San Francesco a Ripa the boy gestures to him to turn, so that suddenly they're going against the traffic, but luckily they're almost at the destination. The house is tall for a building in Trastevere, painted a muddy red, and affixed to it is a sign that seems inspired by a surrealist: VIA DELLA LUCE.

"I'll be quick."

The boy has left him to smoke a cigarette on the seat of the Vespa and guess the era of construction and the original use (lodging for the servants of some villa?). There are more cats around, not all of them mangy, than passersby or vehicles. Probably because it's Sunday and the city has just finished lunch. Domestic noises, radios sing and talk, a sign that the championship game hasn't yet begun.

A shutter opens, a woman with a considerable décolleté leans out. "You needn't bother," she shouts. "I wanted to come down and thank you, but Claudio's already gone."

The boy has just run down the stairs and emerges onto the street hot, his socks pulled up, a comb passed through his curls. "Mamma wants me to walk," he says with a glance upward, "it's nothing, just a few minutes to San Cosimato."

The doctor would like to intercede, but the bells are ringing, out of sync as usual. And when the echo is silent, the window on the third floor also closes.

"It's three, you'll be late."

"Don't worry, doctor, the others will be late, too."

The boy doesn't make a move to go.

"You're German, right?" he asks.

"You can tell from the accent?"

"It's that thing of being on time . . . otherwise it wouldn't seem like it," he comments, and runs off, saying goodbye with a wave of the hand.

It's three, time for Dr. Kuritzkes to head for Via Asiago. Mario Bernardo is waiting for him, he wants to show him some educational shorts made for television. They're thinking about a short film on the vision of color, but finding someone to produce it won't be easy. Is it possible that Mr. Polaroid suspects that he sought him out with the intention of asking for money? He wonders suddenly, stopping on the Tiber, along with troops of tourists and nuns lined up at the signal. He'd kick himself if so, if because of an absurd misunderstanding the correspondence with Land were to be cut off before it began. He has to talk to Mario about it and now not get lost, luckily in Prati it's not easy to get lost. He leaves the Vespa in front of the RAI, where they inform him that Signor Bernardo has left him a message.

> Georges,
> Excuse the hitch. The usual movie thing: they call and you have to run. The call comes from Fellini's producer, the place is much loved by the neorealists. Join me, if you feel like it. Otherwise see you tonight.
>
> Mario

Directions: Go to Termini, continue through Piazza Vittorio, after Piazza di Porta Maggiore take the Prenestina. At a certain point you'll see on the left an enormous cylinder, a Roman mausoleum. From there, follow my drawing.

Helped by the ancient monuments, Dr. Kuritzkes turns onto a side road that he hopes is the one drawn by his friend. Dubious, he brakes more than is required by the maze of densely inhabited narrow streets, sometimes to read the name of the street (Juvenal: they've relegated a poet like that to the middle of nowhere?), sometimes to stop someone, if necessary. He proceeds almost at a walking pace, his gaze attentive to everything he comes upon; the stagnant air between the houses envelops him in waves of heat, and even his breath slows to the drawn-out rhythm of bewilderment. Is he lost? Maybe. He's disoriented by the familiarity of the feeling of being a stranger, an epidermal reaction to an urban landscape that rekindles a vigilance practiced in Naples, dusted off in Marseille, much milder in Barcelona and Madrid, where he was also fighting for the freedom of the thieves. He doesn't recognize what he sees, he has no idea where to place it, but he seems to know it. Maybe it's the recollection of a film. No. Here the vision of color is important, the substance of the color, the yellowish dust rising from the street. The mellow eroded plaster on the low structures. The deep-set bricks, the rust on the tin roofs. The torpid or noisy indifference of the inhabitants. Poor and working-class humanity that for a few cents a day certainly doesn't scorn the tradition of the eternal Roman plebs, but asks for anything besides being crowded together in some *kolossal*. Forcibly urbanized, surrounded like the last fields, where the sheep are blackened by the traffic on the Prenestina. He's supposed to turn right at the first intersection, proceeding very slowly. He's not sure whether to turn then at the first side street or the second. A tree invades his line of vision, its roots raising the surface of the road: an oak. He could be on Sierra Morena, just as the entire inhabited area could belong to one of the abandoned villages where he went to work in the infirmary, strong word. Yes, Robert Capa had appeared, out of the blue, in a similar little house.

He was bundled up in a jumble of civilian and military clothes, so smoke-stained and dusty that Georg had immediately taken him for a soldier. The cold was tremendous in the first days of 1938, and the town behind the front lines was at an altitude of over a thousand meters. In the room where he was stitching up wounds, the bitter cold was diminished by only a few degrees: they couldn't stop up the window with paper and rags because they needed the light. He had sent him away with the sequence of phrases that he repeated automatically without even looking up from the table. *"Para buscar a unos compañeros heridos vaya a la cocina, si eres herido tu mismo, camarada, busca a una enfermera."* "If you're looking for wounded friends go to the kitchen, if you're injured yourself, comrade, look for a nurse." Someone else would take care of chasing him out, if he was only tired or in shock or looking for a little warmth. The man stayed in the doorway, but then left.

Usually darkness granted a respite during which the wounded were carried up there, the serious cases to be operated on in a circle of oil lamps reminiscent of a Caravaggio. Darkness also allowed a change of medical personnel, something not always possible, but that day Georg had been able to go off duty. At the entrance was the usual crowd of stretcher-bearers and soldiers who'd been treated, indistinguishable in the shadows. But the man from before had identified him: "Georg Kuritzkes!" He was frightened and turned reluctantly. There they called him only Jorge, *doctor*, or *camarada*, and he didn't want to believe that someone had been sent to make trouble. He wasn't the one who'd decided that the offensive was to take place without the International Brigades or that an exception had been established for medics.

"Was für eine wunderbare Überraschung! Und an einem solchen Tag!"

"Sind Sie Robert Capa?"—"Are you Robert Capa?" he had asked, with that form of courtesy that wasn't used here. He had recognized him in part by the hyperbole (absolutely "marvelous" the surprise of meeting him!), but the comrades had entered Teruel that day, and the news dispelled the suspicion that the emphasis was ironic.

"A day that restores our strength," he assented.

"You've done your job, I've done mine, now we can celebrate, no?"

"Naturally," he answered, "but after that news all the more reason I can't go far. In Teruel they'll be organizing relief, they'll come to get someone . . . "

"*Richtig*," Capa said. He had taken off his beret, stuck it in his pocket, and, without asking permission, gone back into the operating room.

Georg had imagined him bold ("Like those there," Gerda said, pointing to the urchins on the cliffs), but younger. The war aged you, at least when you were up to your neck in it.

"Doktor Kuritzkes," Capa resumed, unbuttoning the jacket under which he protected the camera. He apologized for stealing a few minutes of his time, even though the taking of Teruel was a joy to share with *todo el mundo*.

"But not this," he added, taking an envelope of photographs from a pocket and putting the entire bunch in his hand.

The faint light didn't help to look at them, but hid what it was better for Capa not to see: the cold burned his eyes as soon as they teared.

"Can I keep one?" he asked.

"All. We're photographers, reprinting costs nothing."

"We?"

He, Chim, and Gerda had rented an atelier: light, tranquil, spacious enough so that his friend and assistant lived there. Ruth Cerf came to help out, there was plenty of work, luckily.

Georg couldn't understand how he could go on like that: invite him to Paris, offer him a bed in the studio, insist that it was better than a hotel—Gerda had furnished it, with her consummate taste, her remarkable practical sense. He was annoyed to the point of wondering if Capa had a screw loose. He worked under fire and was continuously in danger of getting killed, even if a photographer could always retreat, but maybe his equilibrium had been affected by it.

"Is Ruth well?" he asked. "When you see her, give her warm greetings from me."

Among the photographs Georg had seen a posed portrait, illuminated by Gerda's unmistakable smile. Capa immediately noticed.

"Don't stand on ceremony, *bitte*," he said.

Did the photographer know how many times he had taken off that leather jacket?

And then there was another one, in which Gerda, pulling up a stocking, made one of her grimaces. You saw everything: the thigh displayed, the unmade bed, the flowers on the wallpaper of the rundown hotel, a bottle of Pastis, a kimono-style bathrobe hanging behind the sink.

He shouldn't have let him see that photo, but it was the other one that thrust his intimacy with Gerda under his nose.

When he gave back the bunch, Capa was weeping. He was weeping and nodding vehemently, approving his choice, while he struggled to put the rest of the photographs back in the envelope. Georg thought he had grown used to comrades who suddenly collapsed, gasping for breath or weeping in silence like broken faucets. But there was nothing to do about it: he began to cry, too.

"*Entschuldigung*, Georg, we don't have time to waste . . . "

"We should still have time for a cigarette," he'd said, looking for his last ration, consoled by the thought that, with the end of the siege, the tobacco shortage would end.

Capa offered him one of his American cigarettes, promising to leave him the pack. He would depart right away for Paris and then for China, where he was supposed to have gone with Gerda. He couldn't put it off any longer. But not to come to Teruel would have been a defection, a betrayal.

He talked with the butt in his mouth, sucking mechanically every time he breathed, then, fumbling inside his jacket, he pulled out a flask and offered him the first sip.

"You'll have to make do with this Aragonese *schnapps,* the brandy supply is gone."

From the way he continued to blather (about that home-made *aguardiente* which could melt rocks; about the great Ernest Hemingway, who drank like a sponge but was devoted to the cause with all his heart; about the infinite questions he would have liked to ask him if there had been time), he seemed to have recovered.

Whereas Georg, after the third round, felt dazed. He hadn't slept, had eaten only some of the usual beans. After swallowing a last drop (he felt like an ethnologist forced to fraternize with the object of his studies), he handed the flask back to Capa with a gesture that meant *enough*.

"To Gerda," he said softly. Not drunk, no, but perhaps thanks to that lethal *aguardiente* he'd swallowed he didn't give a damn about possible reactions.

With a wide, conspiratorial smile, made almost sinister by the effect of the only lighted lamp on the white of his bared teeth, Capa returned the toast, *auf unsere Gerda, lechaim*, to life, and to freedom!

He drank noisily and after wiping his chin and mouth started talking again: about the engagement that had kept him in Paris, about being slapped at the funeral (you know them, right, the Pohorylle brothers?), about the unforgivable foolishness of having left her down there.

"Imagine," he said to him. "I was convinced that if there was a decisive battle the entire militant press would rush to escort her! Hadn't I seen them? In Madrid or at the writers' congress in Valencia, like flies on prosciutto. The correspondent for the *Daily Worker*, the correspondent for *Pravda*, and I don't have to tell you the others. Did I like it? No. Did I have another choice? No. I assure you that I had even thought of relying on that Canadian journalist she liked more than the others. Big good-looking guy, the way a twenty-year-old can be who's been raised on beefsteak and milk, team sports, faith that good will triumph, poured all over Communism. I said to myself that he would die rather than abandon her, he had such a crush. You realize, Georg? *So ein Idiot! 'Teddie, please keep an eye on her.'* You know, like in a Hollywood film: he swears, turning all red, she smiles, all radiant, moving her eyes from one to the other. Gerda would have made him do what she wanted, and I, like an idiot, didn't realize the danger. So she stayed there. He pulled through, poor fellow. Ted Allan: maybe you met him?"

Yes, in fact the last time he saw Gerda there was that journalist. Their relations seemed perhaps too close, but he preferred to keep silent about that to Capa. He said he'd met him on leave in Madrid, you had to admit that Gerda was very fond of introducing her old friends to her new acquaintances.

Capa had scrutinized him at length, then asked a peculiar question compared with what one might have expected, for example what sort of impression Ted Allan had made.

Instead he asked: "And how did she introduce you?"

"The exact words?"

"If you remember . . . "

"Something like '*Voilà, je vous présente mon très cher ami, le docteur Kuritzkes.*'"

What, after a few seconds of silence, he had feared was a suffocated burst of tears, turned out to be a thin clucking laugh, held inside for the pleasure of nurturing it.

"You know what she told Teddie? She told him that she could no longer fall in love because Hitler had murdered her true love. Ah, how handsome and courageous, that great love, that doctor of Polish origin! *Docteur Kuritzkes, mon cher ami*, may you live as fit as a fiddle to the age of a hundred and twenty!"

Without leaving him time to react, Capa resumed talking nonstop. Better that way, since that confidence had shaken him.

Ted Allan had showed up in Paris, a wreck on crutches, and Capa looked after him, until he proposed that they go together to New York, and from there Teddie would return to

208 - HELENA JANECZEK

Montreal. On the ship he dragged himself from the cabin to the dining room like the hunchback of Notre-Dame, but with the rough sea he was glad to hold on to his arm. Looking at him, beaten and penitent, Teddie got lost in love stories. "What should I tell you, Georg? I didn't mind. Was it the proverbial effect of a trouble shared is a trouble halved? Maybe. I liked listening to how fantastic our Gerda was. I don't know about you, but I was jealous as a macaque, even though it complicated living together terribly. But since she's gone I don't care who she made eyes at."

Capa had offered him another cigarette, as if to encourage him to respond. "I wasn't jealous, almost never," he answered.

"Yes, Gerda said that, too."

The last confidence Capa made before they chased him out, before he embraced him on the threshold of the operating room, was that Teddie behaved properly during the day, while at night, when he drank ("There was nothing else to do on the ship!"), the music changed. He jabbered on about how he would have brought Gerda to America and cured her grief for the Polish doctor. There existed no obstacle to his dreams except death, and death, as at the end of a novel, could make everything possible after the fact.

"They're like that, the Americans. They dream of a house just like their neighbor's, with children and hearth, and maybe an enormous red star on the Christmas tree, and in their minds they've already as good as bought it."

On the ship Teddie boasted that Gerda had found his stories brilliant, had even encouraged him to send them to their friend Hemingway. And he would have proved his talent to her and, *sorry to say, my friend*, the reputation of a writer easily exceeded the success of a photographer.

"Those were not very pleasant moments, *mein lieber Georg*. But what was I supposed to do? Remind him of China and *adiós, my friend*? Or explain that Gerda wasn't too fussy in the moments of respite between a battle and a bombardment? She was considerate to offer him that lie, pity that Teddie, in his arrogant naïveté, decided to ignore the warning. She was enchanted by him, perhaps, but she also was by a lot of the youths she saw leave in the morning and not return again in the evening. In the end, the only thing that Gerda loved whole-heartedly wasn't you or me or anyone else but all those who committed their lives to fighting fascism, it was Spain and her work beside the Spanish people."

Georg had nodded.

There remained the question of whether she had started to get fed up with Capa, too, and he had to believe him on one point: in war the person closest to you is your comrade and the comrade of Gerda had been Capa, the only one she'd had beside her. Georg wasn't sorry to have to admit it, from the moment he saw him disappear, finally, around the bend in the road, knapsack on his back, collar raised, coarse wool cap pulled down to his neck. The pack of Lucky Strikes, unfortunately, he had forgotten to leave.

In the grip of his memories, Dr. Kuritzkes stopped on the street off Via Giovenale that should be the right one. He could set off again now, but he's just realized something odd: the encounter with Capa in Teruel is stamped more deeply in memory than the moment his comrades handed him a daily they'd brought back from a day's leave. Bad news, they said. The words of condolence, which also must have been offered, have disappeared. "*Enterrada en París la camarada Gerda Taro caída en Brunete.*" A hole. A hole that had a precise clinical name. There remained only the date on the newspaper clipping, kept in his pocket where a soldier keeps everything that is dearest to him: August 1st, which should have been a birthday.

Dr. Kuritzkes decides to look at Mario Bernardo's directions to make sure where he is, but it's clear that he's looking for a way out of these memories. I'm almost there, he confirms, as the engine simmers and vents, the soles of his feet still resting on the roadway.

The front in Cordoba was in a state of lethargy during that whole period, apart from a skirmish in mid-September that he'd taken part in. Letters arrived from Naples and Paris, and, by some tortuous clandestine means, even from his mother: grief-stricken, overflowing with rhetoric and advice. Pointless. Even Morandi came to offer condolences. Great courage requires great courage, he had said, shaking his hand. Thanking him, he returned the clasp. Only months later, when, absorbed in saving the lives of his comrades, he was regaining possession of his own, it occurred to him that maybe he owed his transfer to the old commander. Aldo Morandi was a man capable of saying that he would do without a soldier devoted to getting himself shot, when he could be useful for putting those still able-bodied back on their feet. Who knows if he had also explained that that soldier hadn't been marked by any collapse of morale, as long as he didn't know about the death of Gerda Taro. If only they'd learn to celebrate an imprudent person as an example of heroism and forget about the requirements of those who knew how to make war.

It's a new thought, the first that reassures Dr. Kuritzkes. Maybe he wouldn't be there, sheltering under an oak to let the cars pass, if he hadn't been guided by the cordial antipathy toward Gerda of an old-style officer and the long freeze of the Cordoba front, corresponding to the freeze in himself. Yes, yes he's reassured. Although he's still in another realm, he has realized that the cars he sees going by, among them one very shiny black one, can't belong to these miserable streets. The movie cars are leaving, he says to himself, so as soon as I find Mario we'll be free to work on our projects.

Then he sees a group of people gathered around a couple of mopeds and hears, in snatches, a clamor that seems too loud. Is it a fight? Maybe not, since in these areas people shout for no reason. But he doesn't want to pass through the middle of a fight, especially in a neighborhood where it could turn ugly, and so he turns off the Vespa and starts listening.

"Get out, there's nothing to interest you people here. Get it? You gotta go."

The response is a "Cool it," but then the voices are again indistinguishable. The only way to understand what's happening is to lean out from the tree.

Even though he sees half of the group from the back and the other keep disappearing and reappearing behind the branches, there is no margin of doubt. The clothes, the bodies, the physiognomy of those youths are middle class. At that point he plunges toward them with a strident screeching of brakes that silences the quarrel.

"Do you know where I can find Signor Bernardo?" he asks.

"He should still be at the café around the corner," they answer, without a hint of surprise.

In front of the café as well there are people deep in conversation, except for a young woman left alone with a notepad and a bottle of orange soda. At the top of the steps that divide the terrace from the street, Mario Bernardo is talking with the group whose jackets and purses are lying on the chairs of the other tables.

"Georges, what a pleasure," he exclaims, seeing him. "I hope you didn't have too much trouble finding us. May I offer you a coffee or a drink, since you've crossed the city in this heat?"

Dr. Kuritzkes pulls up, turns off the engine, follows his friend to the table where he's left his jacket, and the fact that he leans over to pick it up rather than inviting him to sit down lets him understand that Mario can't wait to go. But they have a coffee anyway, at the opaque marble bar, wiped off before the saucers are set down.

"They also do gelato, if you feel like it," his friend offers, as if to correct the too hurried hospitality. Then, in an undertone, he says movie people think that with money you can solve everything. He scowls, seems vexed.

"You don't want anything else?"

"Just some water. In Naples they would already have given it to you. But Italy is complicated, a continent."

His friend agrees, and finds it remarkable that he notices. Being in Rome, he observes, almost everyone starts to believe it's the navel of the world, beyond which there are only some negligible provinces. And this, he clarifies, when genuine Romans don't know much more than the few streets they're used to being on.

Serving the glass of water, the barman intervenes. "You're right, doctor, and your friend, too, and if you've been to Naples maybe you've also passed through my area. I was born here, but my uncles down in Ciociaria say that the Germans were gentlemen in comparison to what the others got up to! And then—we can say it, can't we?—there aren't many real Romans left, not the ones who had great-grandfathers in the time of Julius Caesar!"

Dr. Kuritzkes, by now used to those comments, answers that he was in Naples for reasons more pleasant than the last war and waits for Mario Bernardo to pocket the change.

"Lucky you came, Georges," he says as they leave the bar, "so I don't have to hear the same story again while they're taking me home. Who knows when this movie will be made . . . Meanwhile here is where they shot the greatest masterpiece in recent cinema, *Rome Open City*: the exact part where they kill Magnani and carry off the printer. Rossellini didn't make any of it up. This was really a subversive hideout, a fortress, if you prefer. One was shot in the Fosse Ardeatine, three deported to

Mauthausen and didn't return. But there were a lot of them, it was the whole neighborhood, it was all the working-class neighborhoods, and this one more than the others. Not like Piazza Barberini, with your Fascist countesses happy to have found the German doctor to treat their nerves . . . "

"Just one, Mario. And she," he reminds him, "stopped seeking my services when I filled in—how do you say *gründlich?*—there, when I exhaustively filled in her interest in my CV."

Mario Bernardo has only recently started hearing about such episodes, that is to say that the doctor no longer considers him a friend "Italian style" but a friend in the way he has always understood the word. Besides, Vittorio Somenzi had told him that he could trust him. He had known him in the war, in moments that bind, tragic but fortunately overcome. It was known that the professor had been an officer in the Air Force, but it was equally evident that he was a sincere progressive, not to mention a great gentleman. And Mario Bernardo himself had told him about their meeting, one evening when they had dined together after working on their experiment, enjoying the shade of the pergola at a good trattoria on the Janiculum hill.

Vittorio was in the aeronautic engineer corps, but he had never been in an airplane until September 8th, when he managed to make himself available to the Office of Strategic Services, which had parachuted him into the Bellunese Prealps to reach a Garibaldi brigade cut off by an overabundance of snow on the Cadore passes. Bernardo and his group of partisans were up there, on that farthest border of Italy subject to the Gauleiter of the Tyrol, short of munitions and provisions, and the man in the gray tweed suit who appeared on the ridge like the lost traveling salesman for whom they illegally sold false documents had seemed too handsome to be the person they were waiting for at the command.

"You should know," Mario explained to him, pouring some cool white, "that while the country was liberated we up there expected some hard times. The rumor was circulating that the Germans were preparing to resist indefinitely, gathering in the redoubt of the Alps plundered treasures, underground missile factories, and all the big shots, with the freshest and most loyal men. The American services believed it, we much less. We knew about the stockpiling of supplies, but we had never seen either deported slaves building fortifications or new forces. Vittorio had told that to his superiors, and yet we couldn't relax because we couldn't rule out that the Germans were organizing farther to the north. It's said that this was precisely the scenario that had driven Eisenhower to occupy Bavaria, leaving Berlin to the Soviets. On the other hand, it worried us that, although the Allies were apparently so convinced of this *Alpenfestung*, they avoided bombing the area, when they were masters of the sky. We knew that broad Anglo-American sectors wanted to keep the Italian contribution to the liberation at a minimum, especially in the case of us Communist partisans. There was a rumor that the northeastern regions would be joined to Austria, as a mugging of the red Italy that had emerged out of the insurrection, and as a barrier against Titoist Yugoslavia. So there we were, near the enemy, freezing, poorly armed, with the expectation of losing our lives there, and not even knowing if it would end up being useful.

"Things went smoothly afterward, but that didn't annul those fears. In fact, the last action that Vittorio and the youths from the Calvi Brigade were involved in confirmed them. Just after the 25th of April the services asked him to locate a group of hostages whom the SS had assembled in Dachau and transported to Val Pusteria, a working zone under our jurisdiction. Vittorio learned that the precious human cargo had reached Villabassa, and included prominent prisoners whom the supreme leaders of the SS intended to exchange, or would liquidate if they had nothing to lose. Vittorio was to some extent acquainted with the negotiations that the commander of the Wehrmacht was conducting in Italy, and even with the commander of the SS, but that I learned years later. Moral of the story: the hostage crisis had a good resolution, because the blond beast, or at least the two leaders of the pack, preferred to go belly up rather than carry out the orders with blind obedience. But it would have taken only a pair of concentration camp guards to act as usual, that is, throw the executed prisoners into the Lago di Braies, to put at risk nothing less than the end of the war in Italy."

Dr. Kuritzkes had devoted himself to his lamb and potatoes, but, as he listened to that story, he had an intuition. Was it by any chance the convoy that Léon Blum talks about in his little memoir? He had read it in Paris, and had been moved by the loyalty that the Blums maintained in Buchenwald and during the final transport, when the old socialist was so weak that he might not have reached the end of the journey.

"Yes, that one," Mario Bernardo exclaimed, and it was true that Léon Blum was in bad shape. And yet, after thanking the partisan command that had come to liberate him, he had wanted to wait for the Americans with his other companions in misfortune. They had respectfully said goodbye to him and returned to Cadore.

"The world really is small," Dr. Kuritzkes commented, and Mario listed the other prisoners. There was the old Austrian chancellor von Schuschnigg, with his wife and daughter; two of Churchill's grandsons; Badoglio's son; a grandson of Molotov; the entire Greek general staff; and other eminences of conquered Europe. A large number of Germans, mostly "von" whatevers—the families of von Stauffenberg and other conspirators in the plot against Hitler, a grandson of the last Kaiser, the prince of Hesse, who was the husband of Matilde di Savoia, many Wehrmacht officers who had fallen into disgrace, and a steel baron von Thyssen . . .

"Ah well, all anti-fascists from the start and committed democrats!" Dr. Kuritzkes interrupted him, reluctant to savor that list.

Mario laughed, but caught the too cutting thread of his sarcasm.

"No, you're wrong," he objected, mentioning Martin Niemöller, the courageous Lutheran pastor, and then a nephew of Garibaldi who had immediately joined the Calvi Brigade.

"Of course," he assented, irritated with himself. But he had little patience with the speeches of survivors, which were all so similar: and he couldn't stand the fact that even the old partisans' stories were full of a rigid nostalgia, the nostalgia of losers.

Maybe it was his fault if Mario gradually cooled as he described the turning point, which occurred thanks to a captain in the Wehrmacht, another of those unpronounceable Junkers, who managed to bring the hostages under his protection: something they were very happy about, especially when the SS obeyed the order to go home, where the Führer was about to kill himself. Thus at the Hotel Lago di Braies an idyll began among soldiers, South Tyrolese, and deportees, "only tea and waltzes were missing." In any case, before they could lead the Americans there, their visits to the hotel in a requisitioned Fiat Balilla were greeted with dismay: not only because all they had was a few submachine guns but because everything for their lordships was the stuff of small-time thieves. Only Molotov's grandson, poor Vassily, who had seen Stalin's son killed in Sachsenhausen, remained deaf to entreaties to stay at the hotel, on pain of some misfortune or other. He had gone with them, had been welcomed in Belluno, delivered to the Soviets in Bologna, and finally thanked his liberators via Radio Moscow. Garibaldi's grandson, on the other hand, they had to deal with as self-proclaimed general of Val Pusteria, and with him a certain Ferrero, Davide, a partisan captain in the Langhe captured and deported by the Germans. In those frenzied days they were focused on free Italy, Italy to be rebuilt, but they learned that Ferrero had sold himself to the SS, lending his own men as guards for the Rice Factory of San Sabba, hardly the second-in-command of a Garibaldi!

Suddenly the roles were reversed: Mario asking to change the subject, he replying of course, forget it, I understand.

"Let me add just this, Georges," Mario concluded. "They accuse us of having carried out summary justice, but was a just justice ever seen, later, in Italy?"

"Comrade," Georg answered, "I would skip dessert and coffee. Let's move on to a grappa or an amaro?"

"Whatever you have, I'll have, too."

That night, after taking Mario Bernardo home, Dr. Kuritzkes felt like walking a little, and he pushed the bike along the winding curves of the Janiculum. Maybe other times he hadn't turned onto Via Garibaldi, but the fact is that he had never noticed the spectral white of the ossuary with which the Fascists—ROMA O MORTE (ROME OR DIE)—had appropriated the dead of the Roman Republic. It was only a particularly brazen example of something he encountered everywhere, a continuous absorption of customs, traditions, and historical events into one another, which placed him in a suspension of time and judgment, ruptured as soon as love for the Duce erupted from the breast of a noble Roman caryatid, or, contrarily, Bernardo and Somenzi came out into the open. Suddenly he understood what it meant that Vittorio had never been in an airplane before he was parachuted by the Americans, as Mario had just told him. He wasn't flying any of the Savoy-Marchettis sent to bomb the Spanish cities or the Fiat BR.20s of the legionnaire squadrons that, firing at low alti-

218 · HELENA JANECZEK

tude, had caused the collision in which Gerda died. And from the moment the shadow was dissolved (wasn't it Somenzi's superiors in the meteorological engineer corps who decided that conditions were favorable for the attack on Brunete?), shouldn't he have left the mausoleum behind and rushed down to Ponte Sisto, enjoying the splendor of the Eternal City, like everyone else? Wouldn't Gerda have managed it wonderfully? Wouldn't she have traded the parades of the Fascist decades for a press pass for the Emilio Schuberth fashion show, ready to shoot away when the bride came out? Chim and Capa had done it, and they understood less about high fashion than about the trajectory of a bullet; and why not, if it was the most desirable work for a photographer, after the war . . .

He couldn't reproach Gerda's capacity to adapt; it had always seemed enviable to him. But Capa's carefree attitude when they met after the liberation of Paris had disappointed him, and it was the other who had sought him out and embraced him. Capa had promised that he would stop by Springerstrasse if he happened to be in Leipzig, and would bring Georg's mother food and medicine. Then the May '45 issue of *Life* came out, with that small impudent G.I., the American soldier par excellence, making the rude gesture of a "Sieg Heil!" at the Nuremburg trial: an image of such triumphant irreverence that only one photographer could have come up with it. He had been excited to recognize in him the author of the photograph, as if that cover, which showed the entire world the triumph of small men, Capa style, were a tribute to the spirit of Gerda, the right way to dedicate the victory to her. He had opened the magazine on the Champs-Élysées and, as he walked, discovered the last Americans on a balcony in Leipzig, operating a machine gun, and then the photos of one of them killed by a sniper ("*maybe the last man to die in WWII*"), the blood spreading over the parquet of a bourgeois interior. On receiving his message of congratulations,

Capa had called him almost immediately. Too many dead fools until the end, a big mess with a girl, he hadn't had the time or a mind to stop at his mother's: *c'est dommage, Entschuldigung.* But he'd had a mind to photograph a man just killed, and probably also to decide that it wasn't worth visiting an old Bolshevik, even though Dina would have repaid him with amazing stories about Gerda, even without the offering of some K-rations, which would have really helped her out.

Photography is a job that rewards opportunists, favors skaters on the surface. A doctor, on the contrary, finds himself implicated in the lives of patients, lives that even with the help of X-rays often don't offer an unambiguous image. Some are born to steer a middle course and some do it anyway, for better or for worse. Gerda would have had the *Souveränität* not to turn back and at the same time not to deny anything.

Nor had Capa, he had to admit, been an absolute weathercock: that trip to the USSR with Steinbeck hadn't been a good idea even in 1947. Even less so in the succeeding years, when Paris and Rome were full of his American friends who had ended up on the blacklists, and who, certainly not penniless exiles, as they had been, didn't move from their comfortable lodgings beyond Montmartre or Trastevere . . .

Georg recalls and ponders all this, while Mario, outside the bar in Pigneto, has been summoned by some very long-winded guy from the production. He waits patiently, smoking a cigarette and fantasizing about this bar, so similar to a village *taberna*, saying to himself that for Capa it would have stirred a chord more secret than the *caffés* of Via Veneto did, and for Gerda, too.

He'd better go out to the terrace and liberate his friend, Georg says to himself, and finally they manage to get on the Vespa and leave. At the intersection with Via Prenestina, Mario

220 · HELENA JANECZEK

proposes a quick side trip to where most of the scenes of *Rome Open City* were filmed, if it would interest him.

"Let's go."

Via Montecuccoli is on the other side of the consular road, Via Prenestina. New construction has cleaned up the ruins and the rubble that you see in the famous scenes of the film, and buildings are going up no higher than the prewar structure in front of which Mario signals him to stop. It's the added floors and, especially, the expansion of the apartment blocks that has drastically changed the face of the neighborhood: it's still the periphery, since the street ends near the railway tracks, but unmistakably working class.

"On this side of Via Prenestina is the city of workers, on the other the semblance of an ancestral habitat, where the visitor feels a generous frisson in the face of a population of thugs and beggars—you get the same thing right in the center in Naples," Georg observes to his friend, who nods thoughtfully.

No one pays attention to the two men who, leaning on the Vespa in front of No. 17, discuss abstract things, neorealist poets and directors, while around them people come and go serenely on this day of rest.

"It won't be the cinema that changes things—whatever they are," Georg reflects. "It will be the people who live in these apartment blocks, the new worker conscripts, the girls who bring home a salary. For them it's easier to stand up to the boss than to win at home and between the sheets, but once they've started, you can't stop them. Believe me, I saw it: in Spain, which was no less backward than Italy, not to mention Leipzig and Berlin in the early thirties. You know, sometimes the female students seemed almost envious of their proletarian peers? Because the freedom to wear their hair short or go have a beer—and they even went by themselves, our workers—wasn't granted by a father or a boyfriend but won with their own hands. These are slow gains, not well suited to *épater la bour-*

geoisie or, still less, to attract it, because they reflect its hypocritical petty-mindedness."

"I hope you're right," Mario replies, and, already back on
the Vespa, objects that when they were fighting for freedom
even the reactionary Veneto was stirred up, but now it's
returned to the way it was before.

"You never go back completely," Georg says, before starting up again.

Did the optimism of the moment pull the cliché out of him?
And yet those neighborhood streets and, ultimately, the whole
of Italy feed a certain faith in progress, while the comparison
with Germany is distressing.

Georg sometimes gets letters from the International
Brigade members who went up into the mountains with him or
enlisted in the Foreign Legion, less frequently from those who
were in Buchenwald, Mauthausen, and so on. They returned to
their native cities, to replace fathers and brothers killed in battle or destroyed by prison, or following the call of what, in spite
of everything, was *Heimat*. They write that they are distant
from politics, "because if you let all those old Nazis get too
close you can't breathe." A gunner who had returned to the
lathe of a steelworks in Mannheim wrote that "everywhere you
breathe a *Mief* and a *Spiessigkeit* that you can escape only by
going into the *Kneipe*." The translations suggested by the
Sansoni dictionary aren't really equivalent: "moldy, spoiled,
stagnant air," and "respectability, smugness" isn't right, either.
"We have gone back a hundred years," a doctor comrade
echoes, a baptized *Halbjude*, retaking possession of his villa in
Frankfurt but not the goods accumulated by generations of
Kommerzienrat. "The country has been washed with Persil in
one of those washing machines that everybody dreams about
now: it came out white and very starched."

They cautiously describe their state of disquiet. They appeal to him as a specialist, "because my doctor says nothing is wrong, but at my insistence he has prescribed these pills." What advice can he give, by letter, when he doesn't know the name of a colleague in the entire *Bundesrepublik* to recommend?

It's different in the DDR, where the veterans of the Spanish Civil War are celebrated as heroes, covered with medals, given advantages at work. They write seldom and don't complain, but let a flash of nostalgic impatience surface.

When he thinks of his sister, though, something jars. She's still a considerable beauty, that is to say that in the monochrome streets of Leipzig her slender figure, the scarves he sends her from Italy, her scaffolding of teased hair stand out.

The receptions that Jenny organizes when he returns to Leipzig reveal how eagerly awaited these visits are. "Let's toast my brother who works for the United Nations." She fills the Bohemian glasses with *šampanskoe*, hands around the tray of tarts ("Taste the caviar, Georg, they give it to us but we don't have many occasions to eat it"). A perfect hostess, the enchanting wife in whom her companion Professor Doktor should consider himself fortunate. But he has only to look at his mother, already settled comfortably with her glass or intent on conversing in her powerful voice, to notice a divide not reducible to character, the divide of an era. "She's happy like this. During the war she had the higher education of an American diplomat," Dina says curtly, and he has no rejoinder.

Dina would never have agreed to appear beside Prof. Dr. Karl Gelbke the way Jenny does. As far back as he can remember, he's always seen his mother send her children to get drinks and food, while she sits talking to the others. Dina would never have dreamed of washing the glasses because you were going from a dry wine to a sweet one. She can ignore it now, strong in the license of age and a venerable history, she can fail to remember what her daughter was like as a girl: a good savage,

more good but no less savage than her brothers. And so, recalling "our Gerda," she can superimpose a nonexistent heroine
on the girl with bare feet, blouse unbuttoned over the slip, who
worked beside her in the garden, pulling up weeds, hoeing,
planting roses and salad greens.

Dina had an outfit more suitable for gardening, a faded
green smock, a pair of old sandals, a colorful kerchief on her
head, knotted in the manner of a peasant woman, from which
a few gray-black locks escaped. The two women were so
absorbed in the rhythm of the work, marked by a very Russian,
very danceable tune, that they didn't notice his arrival.

They weren't expecting him, and Georg wasn't expecting to
find Gerda. He had told her that the trains from Berlin were
packed, and had advised her to go in the evening with Dr.
Gelbke. He wouldn't leave early, in order not to travel standing
up with his heavy suitcases (shoes, sheets and towels, school-
books), and had no idea when the bus went to the station.
Then a truck driver comrade had given him a ride and, despite
stops at Luckenwalde, Wittenberg, and Dessau, where he had
helped unload OSRAM bulbs, he had arrived in the late morning. He had been dropped off at the intersection at the bottom
of the hill, walked up, dragging his bags (the suitcase with the
books weighed a ton), and dropped them in front of the door,
a sore on his right palm and breathing so hard he could barely
recover.

They were singing loud enough to silence the birds of the
Dübener Heide, his mother and Gerda, and they weren't
expecting him. Nor did he, stopping to look at them from the
porch of the vacation cottage, expect to see them together, and
so in tune with a melody that belonged to his deepest childhood memories. He would have liked to announce his presence by joining in their *tumbala tumbala tumbalalaika!* But the
inner voice that anticipated the refrain sounded invasive, out

of place. They repeated the refrain, going faster. And Georg, still mute and unmoving, no longer felt like the uncomfortable third but like the protagonist of a dream scene, where the strange and the familiar are confused, the closest things appear unreachable, and then are suddenly yours, before you've even touched them.

"Tumbalaaaika, spiel Balalaika, tumbalaika, fröhlich soll sein!"

Or was it Gerda, proceeding from verse to verse without any hesitation, who wasn't supposed to be woken from the spell?

Anyway it had all become clear, as in dreams: what Gerda saw in his mother and vice versa, despite appearances and real differences. The two resembled each other. That's why his pretty young lady was so liked by the eleventh child of a weaver who arrived in the city of Łódź from a Lithuanian shtetl driven by hunger: a daughter who ran away from home to follow the revolution, at sixteen was wanted by the czarist police, fled Russia at eighteen, became a mother at twenty, was divorced at twenty-seven with three children to take care of . . .

And then? Then there was a final repetition of the refrain, so fast that his mother stopped with the hoe in her hand and, straightening up, finally saw him. Not Gerda, who had ended on a drawn-out, wavering high note. She hurled a sharp little cry at him: "Oh Lord, have you been here long? I think I was terribly out of tune!"

"Not at all, you were wonderful! It's centuries since I've heard 'Tumbalalaika.'"

"Really? Come on, I'll help you with the suitcases . . . Did you put rocks in them?"

"Books, Gerda. You take the other one, if you really insist."

After the first swim in the lake with his siblings, they returned to the house. His body only slightly tan (he had never been so pale at that time of year, whereas Gerda went to the pool often), the beating of the other heart still rapid, the smell of lake water and sweaty skin enveloping both. He had stretched out on the bed and fallen asleep. Gerda was snoring beside him, one foot sticking out past the mattress. She pulled it back only after he got up. For a moment she opened her eyes, turning onto her back with a *mmmhm* that unnerved him, a sigh that was unusual for dozing. She had stayed like that, one hand on her stomach, legs spread.

Leave her alone, it's not the time.

He had covered her and gone to unpack the suitcases. That day had ended without questions.

Stopping at the signals in Piazza Esedra, Georg hears buzzing in his head the stupid adjective "exceptional" that Gerda evoked in him thinking of those orgasms snatched from the vacation habits of his family. Soma and Jenny who came home late, Dina who read in the shade of a tree waiting for Dr. Gelbke, while Fritzchen, tired out by the games and dives with his older brothers, slept next to her in the stroller.

He had grown up in a milieu that gave him some advantages. He had been spared the anxieties and desires of a double morality, the poisoned apples in paradise, that original lie on which the domination of man over woman and the exploitation of man by man is based, and which he has to atone for with the sweat of his brow. He was given the example of certain monkeys that coupled in a playful way, shared the care of their offspring, formed in practice a communal tribe. "We, however, do not yet live in Communism and are not monkeys," Dina concluded, "but you should go slowly and be careful, you understand me? That way you satisfy the girl, too." All that had made him more confident than his high-school classmates; even those at the top of the hierarchies resorted to their wallets to relieve themselves. And every time they boasted about their couplings, they confirmed his contempt for the hypocritical vulgarity of the wealthy classes. Toward his friends, no, he was tolerant: after all it wasn't anyone's fault or merit that they had obstacles and difficulties unfamiliar to him.

Gerda could have been his nemesis, but she wasn't. The first time, Georg was so excited to discover that it was mutual that he hadn't let himself be diverted by any anxiety. Only afterward he had wondered if the fait accompli had established victory over Pieter. His mind had been on the alert until Gerda returned from Stuttgart, his body trusted in that stupendous body that spoke to him unmistakably. Gerda was Gerda: a worldly woman who in the small hitches of intimacy burst out laughing like a girl, a lover with the grace of a princess and the self-possession of a housemaid, a natural talent that resembled neither bourgeois nor working girls, and certainly not his mother's Edenic monkeys, who maybe weren't even real.

It was joie de vivre. Something that existed, was renewed, happened everywhere, first in Leipzig and then in Berlin: in the *Pension* not far from his dormitory, in the room rented near Alexanderplatz from the war widow Hedwig Fischer, and finally on the cot belonging to Max and Pauline, called Pauli, in the middle of Wedding.

Frau Fischer had no problem with the *Frollein*, as long as he paid a supplement, calculated on the basis of the elegant young woman's appearance, and yet less than the cost of the hotel that had weighed on his student finances. He had been afraid of an increase, but the crisis had become so dark that it was best to hold on to the lodgers who paid. Georg was grateful for Gerda's flexibility: who had learned to get to Berolinastrasse when he couldn't come to meet her at the station. Who hadn't commented on the abrupt transition from a street crossing Unter den Linden to an area where there was an abundance of stalls selling cheap goods and the *Kneipen* were open until late at night. Gerda was curious, not at all put off by the sinister faces and the unequivocal female presences. Did she realize, rather, when she no longer saw that streetwalker, the one so voluptuous, what had become of her? Had she caught the flu, had she had some problems with the vice squad, or some more serious trouble?

And if those observations were due in part to the slightly artificial attraction of the garish, disreputable metropolis, her feline eye was trained to see the rest as well. The increase in sleepers, men and women, in every building entrance they managed not to be kicked out of. The lines for the distribution of a charity *Suppe* inversely proportional to the assortment of foods in the store downstairs. The solid façades built in the time of Kaiser Wilhelm that turned black because the chimney sweep cost too much, the sewers that stank more, like the people crowded in the U-Bahn. Gerda noticed everything. She called things by their names, precise and angry. She even noticed—and reported to him with supreme enjoyment—that people stared at her as at an apparition, sometimes they whistled at her, rushed to ask her: "Are you lost, *Frollein*, can I give you a hand with your suitcase?" Of course she let them give her a hand: "Thank you, truly, very kind." If Georg urged her to be prudent, "because, listen to me, you don't know what sort of effect you have around here," she answered with a smile.

"I can distinguish a poor unfortunate fellow from a creep: why should you worry if a worker or a jobless man follows me—wouldn't that make you a bit of a classist?"

"What do you mean classist: only brute physical force counts here, if you get in trouble."

"I can get in trouble even when I'm sunbathing in the Tiergarten."

She must have been right, to continue, as always, to do things her own way.

One day he had watched her arrive in the company of a youth with the build of a dockworker. He was walking bent over, muttering under his mustache words that you could imagine were in a coarse *Berliner Schnauze*, while Gerda amazed him with conversation, along with some questions, in her impeccable salon German. Georg, moving away from the window, had shaken his head and, from that moment, stopped worrying. Gerda wasn't an intruder in those places, but a celestial creature whose lack of bad faith meant that you wouldn't dare to graze her with a finger. He felt proud of his girlfriend, but also inadequate: the two things together kept him from scenting that, deep down, the matter was a little more complicated.

It was a question of scent, literally, an event that started with a package containing a bottle of Aqua Velva that Gerda had given him months earlier. That beribboned acquisition, he understood, was similar to other gifts he had learned to appreciate, he who in the big department stores would have been unable to choose the perfect wallet to replace a worn-out one, the scarf of a particular blue. Sometimes they were birthday presents, sometimes she dragged him to the famous sales, when the temples of commerce filled up with all those who otherwise wouldn't venture in, and the salespeople displayed the impassive endurance of notables forced to receive homage from the plebeian rabble. But he had to admit that watching her try on a dozen hats or parade in evening gowns, which she then abandoned, saying she was looking for something simpler, entertained him, even excited him a little, like a forbidden game.

One afternoon, leaving Tietz, they came upon a picket line turning its grim gaze toward the *Polizeipräsidium*. No Berlin square had been as caught up in protest movements as Alexanderplatz, none had seen so many dead, wounded, barricades, mass arrests: since the Spartacist insurrection of May 1, 1929, the last bloody proof of the treatment that the Social Democrats reserved for the opposition on the left. Holding him under the arm as couples out shopping do, Gerda had immediately pulled him toward those accusatory faces, raising her fist. In the gesture, the half-empty Ka-de-We bag, used for the role of the client accustomed to the best, had slid to her elbow, and he had whispered in her ear: "Ka-de-We for all, comrades: we won't be satisfied with Tietz or Wertheim!"

"Stop it, stupid."

That weak answer had confirmed that, for Gerda, a world cured of inequality would also have to accept the universal right to excess. Watching her raise her fist with the bag on her elbow, he desired her very much, the promise of an earthly paradise that he had the privilege of tasting in advance.

But he couldn't learn to like the aftershave she'd brought him from the Kaufhaus des Westens. He thought he had weighed the words in which he'd told her that for him it was an unjustified waste, but she could exchange it for some nice little thing for herself. All hell broke loose. Gerda really insisted on the antiseptic properties of her gift, as if that were the reason that she was mortally offended. The fact is that in the blink of an eye they had arrived at accusations that skirted insult: you want me to be something else, forget it, I'll never be what your schemes require. You know what I say? Go back to your Pieter. And get yourself someone who marches like a dragoon, preferably with a mustache, since that's what you deserve. Gerda turned fierce to the point of trying out all the amateur endowments of the virago, only then the exaggeration made her laugh, change her tone, repeat in the most persuasive way how happy she would be if he kept that fresh-smelling American lotion. Keep it? He had kept it, used it almost never. The perfume on his face disturbed him—not bad, in fact, but useless and alien. To preserve the peace, he sprinkled it on when she came to Berlin, waiting for the parvenu-like odor to evaporate. For that reason it disconcerted him how in the world it could bother him again at the end of the day, when it was the last thing he wanted to be invaded by: sinking his hands in Gerda's hair, directing his tongue to her small nipples, sniffing the secret stuck to his fingers in a perfumed secretion so rich that the trail of Aqua Velva arrived like sabotage, an olfactory hallucination. So he had suspended the morning applications: if Gerda had to rebuke him, he would say that he preferred her in her natural state to the chemical.

But there were no explanations that time or the next. Having spent a glorious weekend, Georg resumed his classes and the training at the Charité, but those commitments weren't the reason that Gerda didn't prolong her visits to Berlin. She no longer went around like a tourist, even if she still loved to sit in the fashionable cafés, go to the movies when the weather was bad, walk on the sumptuous boulevards of officialdom. But walking in the morning past Alexanderplatz she often stopped at the tobacco shop in the Karl-Liebknecht-Haus, and went on to the Communist stronghold where Georg occasionally sent her: to make a contribution to Rote Hilfe, to leave leaflets in the right places, to meet someone in a shop-office-print shop or a union headquarters. She luxuriated in the welcome she found everywhere, ignoring the initials and symbols that changed from one red sign to the next. Following Georg's directions, Gerda, heedless by nature, hopeful by principle, traced a possible route for a united front on the left. She never described a moment of fear, except once, when she ran into a Nazi scumbag who, complete with paramilitary equipment, was advancing on Grenadierstrasse, the most distinctly Jewish street in the *Scheunenviertel*. She didn't seem too worried by the clashes between reds and browns that were the order of the day. She was confident that he wouldn't send her near the hot spots, and, in any case, they followed the news of expected outbreaks of violence like a weather bulletin. It was an illusion to think you could foresee all the disturbances, anyway: another young lady from the provinces would never have ventured into the capital, perhaps not even to visit. Gerda instead had an expression of satisfaction when she repeated to him that she had learned to skirt the dangers like a genuine Berlin girl.

Georg, finding her on the bed reading as if nothing had happened, hugged her hard. And one day he smelled the unmistakable scent of Aqua Velva.

"I'm using your aftershave, since you don't. Do you mind?"

"No, no, go ahead," he had replied, incredulous, "but I was wondering . . . "

"You know, I find it really good, otherwise I wouldn't have got it for you. Who cares if it's not very feminine . . . "

"Well, that scent . . . what do you need it for? You don't seem to have a beard growing."

"I should use up my *eau de toilette* when I go out in that foul air?"

The question had evaporated: Gerda didn't fail to find her solutions, and she would never go along with anyone's schemes.

Then things changed, suddenly came to a head. Dr. Kuritzkes would prefer not to think about it, but the long circuit around Piazza Venezia, the incubator and stage of Fascism, makes it impossible to avoid those memories. He wasn't in time to tell Gerda he'd been arrested. No evidence had been found, but after his room in Berlin was searched, which happened while he was still in prison under investigation, the widow Fischer had barely let him in. "Take your stuff and go: here everything is all right, but I will not tolerate the enemy in my house. Fine young man, sent to the university to learn how to stab Germany in the back!"

All this he had told her later, when he went to pick her up at the station, as they had agreed earlier. To force her to listen to him he had put down her suitcase. It was better for her to return to Leipzig on the last train. The witch didn't want traitors to the country, but she wanted her money on the nail. So he had moved to Max and Pauli's, in Wedding, where he shared the kitchen with a tram worker. That is to say he was sleeping there, and would stay and live there.

"Let's go to the old *Pension*, I'll pay" had been Gerda's immediate and generous offer.

"I don't know if they'd take us. I'll go to trial, there could be reports."

"Now don't exaggerate, having a girl isn't a crime yet. Or you want to have every movement dictated?"

During the week when he had adapted to the stagnation of reboiled coffee and the Maggi bouillon, to the springs of the cot and the sleep of his tram-worker companion, Georg had prepared himself. Just as he had reckoned with arrest, he had thought about Gerda's reactions, calculating which would come next. Not a shadow of fear crossed her face, a hint of bewilderment, a spasm of vexation.

"No. It's not a good idea to go to that hotel. Believe me," he replied.

"O.K., but there are others, *much worse*, where they won't make such a fuss. Maybe you killed someone? It happens, these days, but I'd like to know . . . "

Was she provoking him out of persistence or had she become annoyed? Right there, in the middle of the Anhalter Bahnhof, teeming with uniforms regular and irregular, maybe even more abundant than the pickpockets, the beggars, and the homeless? And he, rather than saying come on, I'll explain everything, but let's get out of here, had in a choked voice yelled how out of place her sarcasm was. Didn't she know that *murder* was never at the top of the list of crimes in a state crippled in war, or blinded in the right eye? Hadn't he dragged her to the cemetery of Friedrichsfelde, where she had been so moved before that wall of oxidized brick, the enormous star that reminded her of a Christmas *Zimstern*, the pile of roses offered to their Rosa? What punishment had the murderers of

Luxemburg and Liebknecht received, and then what about Leo Jogiches, killed in custody in Moabit by a cop whose first name, last name, and even rank were known? Or the killers of the minister who signed the surrender, that Erzberger, further guilty of having taxed the landowners, how many years had they served? And the students who had murdered with a shot to the head fifteen workers detained for who knows what seditious act near Marburg? Zero. Not to mention the little Austrian corporal who for a beer-hall putsch had gotten away with eight months and not even expulsion, for love of country! No, such a sincere lover of Germany could aspire to the chancellorship. Ludendorff: absolved. Hindenburg, the murderer of millions of soldiers: president of the Republic! Whereas the Rote Hilfe lawyers had told him that, if any evidence emerged that he was close to the revolutionary left, a charge of High Treason couldn't be ruled out. Why? Because he hadn't run away in the face of yet another fascist terrorist assault. Because the entire papier-mâché republic built in the Ufa film studios in Babelsberg was coming down . . .

"Yes, better," Gerda had whispered to him, and then, taking him under the arm, aloud: "Don't be angry, dear: if you already bought the tickets for the operetta we'll go to the movies another time!"

The operetta?

Of course, people were looking at them. As they quickly crossed the waiting room with Gerda's suitcase, which seemed a serious hindrance, and his anguish, which, however, was easing, he let out: "How will it end?"

"They lost more than four percent compared to July . . . "

"But they have Hindenburg and his cabal on a tight rein."

Outside, a Siberian wind was blowing, and the rain came down obliquely; Gerda was freezing in her short jacket. They had gone into the first cinema, one of those which showed old silent films without interruption and served as a shelter for people like them. Gerda huddled up as close as possible, her feet on the suitcase. He kissed her for a long time in the wavery darkness that was like an underwater background, a shiver of two merged temperatures that melted in the mouth. Nervous, aroused, stuck on the hard narrow seat, he suggested that they go to Wedding, since at that hour there was no one home.

Walking from the bus stop they passed by the most notorious apartment building in Berlin. There was still no visible sign of the rent strike that the tenants had just joined, only the aspect of a wretched fortress, of a musty prison. "Meyers Hof, right?" Gerda commented, and he, nodding, pulled her past, when before he would have taken her from one courtyard to another, to show her how the proletariat was reduced to living.

Georg recalls the cot pulled down, the damp cold (lighting the stove was ruled out), the neutral gaze with which Gerda observed the room, hesitating over which garments to take off. Dress, shoes and stockings no, leather jacket put on again over the slip. The underpants ended up on a clothespin attached to the line where the baby's diapers were hanging. He recalls the constant noise on the stairs. The framing of the bucket of potatoes, the bucket of coal, the child's beloved ball (what was it doing there, or had that always been its place?), the ironing board that leaped to the edges of the view in his plunger-like movements. He recalls that Gerda came suddenly, prodigiously, came with her hand over her mouth, biting it, and, with just time to pull out, he, too.

And then? Then who knows. They had composed themselves, probably, tidied up, exchanged some words, some kisses. Held hands returning to the bus stop? Feeling good? Yes, that yes.

There were two seats at the back on the upper deck of the bus. There was a rolling motion, a stable-like warmth that made them sleepy. Gerda's bare head on his shoulder, her rain-soaked hat on her lap. Was she dreaming? Not necessarily.

There was a lot of traffic, because of the bad weather, or because it was near Christmas, but that jerky progress met the euphoric daze in which every tension melted.

Without changing position, Gerda opened her eyes again, whispering something in his ear: a proposal to be better organized whose details he no longer remembers. He recalls that she asked him to find out about hotels by the hour and to buy Fromms again: a pack cost nothing. A certain desire must have been revived in him, an animal hope that had been gradually fading as she concentrated on the economic aspects of their next Berlin meetings. Money wasn't a new theme, so Gerda's talk was reduced to an enveloping hum.

The Pohorylles had let go the maid, and then an errand or shop boy. With her brothers settled at the big Ury department stores, Gerda had to apply herself to balancing the accounts of her father's business. Herr Heinrich seemed among the most hopeless of Galician Jews at running a business, having asked for loans not only from relatives but even, through his daughter, from the former boyfriend in Stuttgart. And yet what Gerda claimed was undeniable, that is, that the times were difficult, much more difficult for those who sold eggs than for those in the fur business, no matter whether they did a modest trade, like Georg's father compared to the Chardacks, for example.

"The rich are always rich, as you teach me, while those who aren't start saving even on eggs. The egg is a perishable good, the supreme fragile merchandise. Now they want to let them rot; using the ideology of race, the competition takes advantage of it until it's up to us to lower the prices again. But then we become the incarnation of the disloyal Jew, and in the end the Aryan earns twice as much with the same eggs that come out of the same filthy asses. What to do? Let's hope for salmonella, in any case let's not get discouraged. Anyway that's enough: I didn't come to Berlin to complain."

Gerda's outbursts were like that, as evanescent as they were energetic. Often they weren't even outbursts, but the summary of what had happened to her since they parted, poured out on some mode of transport or an unattractive stretch of street. But there, at the rear of that bus that was taking them back to the center, the usual outburst had broken off: with a sigh, no, an uncontrollable inhalation of air, a disconsolate sob.

"What's wrong? Why are you crying?"

"Nothing. Leave me alone, it'll pass."

"No, tell me, please: maybe we shouldn't have, I don't understand . . . "

She didn't answer, looked for a handkerchief, and when she opened the purse the hat fell off her lap. Georg made an awkward move to pick it up from under the seat, while Gerda sat with the handkerchief balled up in her fist, tears coming down again, a frightening look he'd never seen before.

She was unable to speak. He embraced her again, caressed her, putting a lock of hair in place.

"I can't do it anymore."

She seemed of parchment, suddenly old. And her voice, when she managed to find it, was a squeak that became hoarse as soon as she calmed down a little.

Righting herself after every blow, she whimpered, always finding a remedy. Since she was a girl, thanks to her aunt, who had means but no children, she'd always dressed fashionably. And so she had sworn never again to bring home the classmates who'd sneer at their strange German, the strange candelabra, the house in the courtyard, the untidiness, her mother. Never mind, they didn't deserve it. And then, moving from elementary to *Realschule*, running off at the first bell, running to get the piece of paper showing the exact quantity of eggs transmitted to the uncle's business, Vereinigte Eierimporte, where Papa was a traveling salesman with a commission on the sales: half in currency (and in that half lay their salvation), half in wastepaper. The number of cartons sold diminished, the zeroes of the exchange rate exploded, the calculations had to be made before New York woke up, eggs and commission estimated, each egg was worth a hundred and more billion, up to three hundred and twenty billion Reichsmark, which after the reform became thirty-two *Pfennig*, nothing. And her brothers hurried off on bicycles with suitcases full of bills to get in line at the baker and the butcher, she at the dry goods store because it was the most important shopping. At the age of thirteen she established priorities and strategies, running to Karl and Oskar to know what they could buy and how much they had to pay, if they were still in line. If her father couldn't call in time, if the line was long, if the American stock exchange had reopened before their turn came, all the plans had to be remade. Not even the cash was enough. To possess nothing but the provisions bought up on the good days or traded for with the eggs to be discarded, and she was always the one who had to deal with it. Not being able to count on anyone. Hearing the math teacher say that she didn't deserve a better grade "because you already have calculation in your blood, but you lack the geometric spirit of the ancient Greeks." Hearing her mother, frightened by the volatility of the numbers that forced Papa to move around between illegal Switzerland and anti-Semitic Poland, repeat that, thank God, people there couldn't do without eggs: for breakfast, for cakes, and for the *Spätzle* that were a meal in themselves. Hearing the same old story again today, without the *Spätzle* and with much more fear. Hearing again that her parents were talking about leaving, returning to Lviv for a while, moving to Yugoslavia, looking for contacts in Argentina, as in '23 and '29, when there had been the bankruptcy and the move to Leipzig. A life sitting not on suitcases, Gerda said, pointing to the one in front of the seat, but on cartons of eggs. "That's why I wanted to be much better off, or, to tell the truth, really rich."

"And now?"

"Now, too, but it doesn't matter . . . "

"What do you mean?"

"That I don't really know what I've chosen . . . you, for example."

"Ah, magnificent! Come on, get ready, we have to get off."

How luminous it all seems now, with that broad view over the Tiber at the point where it embraces the Tiber Island, flowing past the unharmed synagogue (if only they had destroyed it, like the German ones, and spared the congregation), the sun in front reflected by the water for a more dazzling effect. Even memories that aren't altogether good become so at a distance. They are restored the way the frescoes of saints and Madonnas and angels in heaven are for the Olympic Games: and if in Berlin little remained to restore, it's not a problem that has anything to do with him.

He stopped meeting Gerda in Berlin. He saw her in Leipzig, but he can't remember if it was before the catastrophic Reichstag fire, when he had hidden in various *Schrebergärten* in the Rosental, waiting for the customs stamps for white fox with which business friends of his father would smuggle him to Italy.

Now he returns to Leipzig to see his family, but, walking along Gohlis or, worse, happening onto the Brühl, he has to keep both feet in the present. He almost never sees a known face. Most of those who didn't die in a concentration camp stayed in the city where they spent the years of exile. Some comrades who fled to the USSR were swallowed up by the great white Arctic from which the skinned foxes came, the most valuable of the goods his father dealt in. His father, suicide. The families in Łódź and Odessa, discovered through searches set in motion by some surviving relative to whom the Jewish organizations announced their death at the same time.

What's worse is to have to admit that in the city where he was brought up, along with the barbarism, life and death had also been a matter of class. Where did you go, a Jew with a small egg warehouse, a small fur business, or an unemployed worker and small militant Communist? The thieves took your life when you had nothing else to steal: with calculation, however, a calculation without precedents in the history of exterminating invaders and bloodsucking tyrants. Licensed thieves, exploiters, and opportunists, under the cover of the fanatical obscurity that glorified the need for murder. No, he has nothing to reproach himself for, since he could have stayed in Naples rather than leave for Spain, and then it was the extremely taut thread of fortune that enabled him to arrive in one piece at the moment of Nazi Fascism's surrender. But sometimes it weighs on him, the simple injustice of being alive.

That's how it is, but he can't do anything about it, except enjoy the injustice, which isn't too difficult on a September day like this. Wasn't it in fact Gerda, the last time in Madrid, who said that it was almost a sin to be entertained again by Charlie Chaplin, when so many boys she had met the day before no longer could? And hadn't she laughed just the same at the most memorable scenes in *Modern Times*, although the film, which had been shown so often, crackled in a scary way? Even Ted Allan had discarded his artificial cocky expression and relaxed into high-pitched trills. And he? He had appreciated everything: there was really nothing else you could do in wartime.

He wouldn't mind telling Mario about the projectionist who thundered from above like Zeus, "Quiet down there," and rightly, because it took a superhuman calm to put on shows in a city that had been under siege for years. But meanwhile he's stopped to wait for him, just beyond Piazza Belli, where a cigarette vender has appeared; Mario has concluded negotiations, and is about to return with a carton of Murattis.

Once they were something else, a luxury item. Gerda's preferred brand, as long as she could afford them, which later coincided more or less with the discovery that they weren't *as Smoked by Royalty and the Nobility* but, rather, produced in a factory in Kreuzberg, where Pauli worked. Oh really? They could keep them: basically, except for the stupendous box, their aroma wasn't much different from the others.

The problem with Gerda, Georg thinks as his friend gets back on the Vespa, was that her readiness for change made her seem always the same to herself. Of course it produced astonishing things, but they passed over the surface and, deep down, fed the conviction that she was undamageable. The war, yes, changed Gerda, just as it changed everyone, civilians and, much more, the men at the front. And why shouldn't a woman who went to the front almost every day resemble a soldier?

Georg, to tell the truth, had seen her at work when she was based near his brigade, then a few other times in Madrid. He had been fascinated by the casual way she could choose her subjects, had admired the rapid, instinctive shots, but had never seen her photographing during a battle or a bombing. That is to say that, then, he knew that part of Gerda only through reflected images: the photos that she herself showed him, spreading open her notebooks at every one of their meetings; and then the figure evoked by the comrade-like tone with which men of every rank greeted her, the reputation for outstanding courage, the familiarity with which they called her *pequeña rubia*, little blonde. There was an echo of extraordinary respect around her, a flattering echo in which talents and characteristics that Georg knew well reverberated but were amplified into a fabulous aura. Was it true that she appeared on the barricades in silk stockings and high heels? That she was welcomed as a sort of talisman, a pilgrim Madonna who gave protection to the fighters?

"Come on! Where'd you hear that garbage?" Gerda shied

away, amused, and maybe not too much. The idea that someone venerated her seemed incredible, nonsense intended to diminish her work and her commitment. Yes, it was true that a couple of times she'd gone to the university neighborhood in nice clothes, seeing that one arrived directly by tram at the first defensive lines. But it was only a cheerful way of saying to those youths that, thanks to them, Madrid was managing to live, a way of encouraging them, and "you can be sure they appreciated it."

In those reactions Georg found the confirmation that Gerda, even in war, had remained essentially the same. She loved to be admired, of course she did, but there was no fire, smoke, or flaming skies that could go to her head—her head was attached to her shoulders, especially at critical moments. Not even the photographs of the fronts in Segovia, Jarama, and Guadalajara, and she said much less about the circumstances in which they had been shot (Why should she have to? They both knew the outcome of the battles and what it meant to be in the midst of them) and much more about the newspapers that had published them—not even those photos had roused in him the suspicion that she'd gotten reckless.

Georg feels a retroactive pang as that word surfaces, and he nearly skids on the curves of Via Dandolo, and then recalls the only time he had the sensation that Spain was modifying Gerda: not under the blackout in Madrid or in the Sierra Morena but as early as November of '36, when she came to see him in Naples.

It had all been familiar, deliciously familiar, after more than a year apart that coincided with the time needed to absorb the affair with Willy and then the inevitable separation: the wait at the station, Gerda's appearance on the platform, recognizing her at a distance by the astrakhan jacket, the sporty cap, the quick pace. Hearing her cry out his name, seeing her wave her free hand. The euphoric embrace as she handed him the suit-case, then they walked side by side, enveloped in Gerda's chatter. The only variation was that he led her to the bus stop on the Rettifilo without asking if she would prefer, as usual, to walk. "Is it so far, where you live?" she in fact asked. "I've been sitting for days, I need to walk a little." "No, in fact it's close. But it's not a nice walk." "Only not nice? Or not nice where they'll cut your throat?" Georg laughed. But waiting for the tram that was late in arriving, he began to push away the circle of kids who emerged rapidly from the alleys. They talked one on top of the other, in collusion or elbowing one another. They asked for change, cigarettes, candy, they offered tours and *bell'otelle*, ancient finds, corals, miraculous prayers, "Pretty lady, won't you give us an offering for your health . . . "

"As you see, this is the main problem. And if it goes badly, stealing or pickpocketing."

Gerda brightened, uttering an answer incomprehensible to a little *Schnorrer* and, perhaps, thief who would never guess that *Strumpfband* and *Büstenhalter*, those nasty, martial words, indicated respectively girdle and bra. To be safe she had thought of the money before getting off the train, and "Sorry, Georg, can't we skip the tram, which will be very full, and get one of these kids to carry the suitcase? If we give him a tip, he won't steal it, I suppose, and he could also keep his friends away . . . "

Amazement that she had had this idea after ten minutes in Naples made him hesitate just enough so that Gerda, misunderstanding it as assent, spoke to one of the bigger ones, who had a more pleasing appearance.

"You, what's your name?"

Leaving Georg the job of making a deal with the chosen one, she wonderfully disguised the fact that she hadn't grasped anything but Mimì ("Isn't that a girl's name?" she asked him later). In order to be recognized as a resident and not a tourist, Georg had taken care not simply to give the address but to indicate the route that seemed shortest to him, since the lady had traveled for many hours and was tired: cut through Forcella, cross Via Duomo, and turn onto Via dei Tribunali until he reached the little square with the seventeenth-century church and the noble palazzo where he had found lodgings with two other students. He warned Gerda that her little *ganef* with the big eyes might still disappear with the suitcase, "but don't worry, they've explained to me how to get it back."

"Good," she replied, already distracted.

On the way, Georg had realized that Naples was not only the cheapest city to live in and the most protected, because the Duce was in control there, up to a certain point: it was also the best suited for slipping out of the coordinates you belonged to. The writings BELIEVE OBEY FIGHT were concentrated in the larger squares, along the avenues hollowed out by earlier rulers. They stopped at the façades, where they crumbled along with the stucco corroded by the dampness of the soil and the stagnation of rains going back to who knows when. The first fifteen years of the new era in Naples had been reabsorbed by baroque fatalism. HE WHO STOPS IS LOST. Not him. As they proceeded, he offered the boy a cigarette, and he sucked it with a childish greed, happy, walking slightly lopsided. He had come to live there among the lost people, he was the comrade of that barefoot *criaturo* more than their antithetical prospects might lead them to imagine. Gerda also had to do with it, the fact that she had remained in Paris, the fact that he had lost her following a choice that he couldn't object to. And yet seeing her walk through those alleys frozen in a millennial poverty, with the drawn-out cries that bonded men and strays in the stench of pee and remains of fish thrown from the peddlers' carts; seeing her notice everything with impassive curiosity, the votive altars, the filth, the new growth of Mimì's hair compared with the other boys, shaved and deloused, the children hanging onto the balconies to pull themselves up, bottoms sticking out and noses snotty ("Not as many as you see in summer." "*Ach so!*"). Seeing her like that had made him perceive something unusual that he didn't know how to define. What was different in that fluid way of moving and looking? And then what should he have expected, outrage, frightened disgust, squeamish pity? From Gerda?

That night they had gone to dinner with a group of friends, both foreigners and Neapolitans, and she had satisfied her curiosities in an adventurous Italian in which she mocked both the fear that the *scugnizzo* ("That's how it's pronounced?") might steal her suitcase and her own recklessness, which she justified as a blinding effect of the photographic gaze. When she arrived in Barcelona for the first time, she recounted, the whole world had told her about a German woman who had settled in Barrio Chino, a very bad neighborhood, and who fit in so well that thieves and gypsies not only didn't try to touch her anymore but came running to her lens. That example hadn't made for an *agréable* welcome: she had been sent as a war photographer and left to others the task of capturing the intolerable conditions of the poor.

The sentence roused an admiring dismay, which Gerda picked up immediately, returning to her first confrontation with Naples and calling herself stupid because she had left the Leica to her companion. But after all she was on vacation, and would take advantage of it to learn again to see beautiful things above all. Which of them would offer to help her?

Spurred by that request, they had taken her to the terrace of the Grand Hotel Excelsior for coffee (spending little less than in the trattoria of Borgo Marinai frequented by tourists and the middle class) and then to walk along the sea, where the low season and the western wind had swept away other presences. Enough that Gerda, attached to his arm, could describe without hesitation the grand Republican struggle and, in the pauses, sigh: "Look at the stars, feel the air and how peaceful it is!"

Georg was relieved. They had spent the first week in visits to Gambrinus, panoramic walks on the Posillipo, returns to Via Toledo on a wave of second thoughts about a pair of suede shoes ("They're very pretty, but in Spain what use would they be?"), increasingly extended forays into the working-class neighborhoods. A day of bad weather, when he had suggested a brief itinerary of churches, museums, and catacombs, had been enough to understand that Gerda's patience for beautiful things, or at least beautiful and old, was rather limited. She had never been particularly attracted by them, but now her gaze seemed oriented by a journalistic instinct even when she was admiring the scenes of life on the frescoes and mosaics of Pompeii.

She had become a photojournalist. But that was only the end point of an evolution that Georg had encouraged in his letters, and Gerda had never hidden anything from him. Maybe, after the liaison with Willy and all that talk about the laboratory at the Steins', the didactic flâneries with the Leica belonging to her Hungarian friend, and then—hurray!—the first photograph sold to a newspaper, a fashion photo, Gerda wanted to regain her faith in what seemed to her more necessary: to photograph the things that needed to be shown.

But even Georg was tired of being a guide. His life in Naples was a promised land, but a promised land for the wretched. He wanted to go home, look again at the photographs pulled out of a voluminous *Baedekers Italien*, find out how to enlist in the International Brigades.

*

Had Gerda written to him about that photo she sold before they saw each other in Turin in April of '35? There they had talked about the preparations for war, which weren't being taken seriously enough abroad; about Italy, which, pursuing its vocation as a warmonger, could only pull Germany along behind. The conversation resumed under the porticoes had the pleasure of a conspiratorial tone. There was little time for talking alone, which was also by his choice. How should he introduce the schoolmate he was seeing? As a sweetheart, the word that was used there (but he wouldn't have said it like that)? Friend was sufficient, partly so as not to seem subtly vindictive, hence inadequate and a little ridiculous.

"Don't dig up anything" had been the advice of Sas, the man who had watched him grow up, and whose liking for Gerda was unquestioned. Sas had come to Turin to spend some time with him and his brother, and also—as he later discovered—to get information from Gerda to bring to Berlin. He'd been engaged for some piano performances by a Prussian widow who wintered in Portofino and had arrived after that comfortable but exhausting interlude. Gerda was happy to see him again, happy with everything. Perfect in the frame of elegant Savoyard aristocracy, which she savored with splashes of irony along with the Punt e Mes, friendly with his girl, unsuspicious as a clandestine courier. The courage of his musician friend and all those who were resisting in the brown sewer provided a subject of sincere empathy until, after accompanying Sas to the station of Porta Nuova, Gerda had left, too.

Georg had continued to see the Turinese girl but had also answered the letters in which Gerda told him of her prohibitive desire for a Reflex-Korelle. Then there had been the gap of the vacations, the stab of pain on hearing that she would go to the Côte d'Azur with the Dachshund (but with Willy it had been terrible, Gerda confessed to him, and that was easy to believe). Finally the predictable news, relegated to the back of his mind for so long that, at that moment, he had managed to take it lightly. Have fun with your photographer until you get your camera, he would have liked to write. Instead he hadn't answered her. So Gerda had tracked him down on the telephone. "I'm calling you from the agency where André found me a job, it's important for me," she had said, "but I don't want to lose you." He answered "I'm here" and "cordial good wishes," sarcastic, distant, and yet emotional. Afterward he started writing a redundant letter of concepts like "respect," "truth," "need for clarity," but hadn't sent it. Meanwhile, Mussolini had declared war and in three days conquered Adwa, in the repugnant revanchist jubilation of the *Stampa* and the *Corriere della Sera*. The League of Nations had met and announced punitive measures. The postal services, overwhelmed by patriotic communications, threatened to swallow up the correspondence between Turin and Paris. A letter that arrived while Italy was denouncing the sanctions with authentic populist fury (he could count on his fingers the acquaintances who remained cool, or rather anti-fascist) had been buried somewhere or other for around a month. Gerda urged him to stay calm: "Listen to me, our paths at the moment are proceeding separately but they always run parallel . . . " He had sent a short answer. He never knew if that letter reached the Paris address where she had gone to live with Friedmann or, with the help of the post office, had continued to travel on those parallel paths. Anyway, he had had his moment of clarity. At the university as well, where the Fascist students had begun to target foreigners, that is to say refugees, managing to expel those who were already working in research institutes. So he had moved to Naples, unhappy to lose a barely established circle of friends and the girl he realized he was fond of just as he said he had no idea about the future. But he felt in some way refreshed by a disillusionment that embraced everything, forcing him to turn the page.

He and Gerda had exchanged some letters that, because politics couldn't be discussed, reinforced the confines of pure friendship. Then came the war in Spain, and finally the chance to meet in Naples and tell each other a thousand things, as she had written prudently. Eager to listen to her, Georg had found himself chasing a woman who, after smuggling a collection of militiamen, peasants with fists raised over collectivized lands, and children in anarchist berets, was now running up and down the *salitelle*, the steep alleys, with that hungry look in her eyes. It was all so interesting, she said, all so comparable with Spain—even if the Spanish people were liberating themselves. The kids sitting on the pavement playing cards, the bars crowded for the magic rite of lotto, the old women in black in the doorways, the Arab-influenced music. And Capa who would sneak in everywhere, like the mouse in the cheese. Yes, Capa seemed just like those people, as dark and wrinkled as he'd emerged from his Eastern cradle: a skillful operator, a sympathetic blowhard, a heavy-duty Casanova. No, not really a Casanova but with the itch to impress girls and an impudent face that helped. Great. You're free, I'm free, we're all free. But as soon as she went freely with someone else, he went bananas . . .

Had she come to Naples for that? For an amorous insult? Or to give him a signal that the love was cooling? But why cite Capa at every step, why always call him by the name she boasted she'd given him, as if it were a title that invested her, too, with some unknown greatness? She considered him a colleague, a teacher, in short a photographer she couldn't find fault with, except to complain that he had returned to Madrid while she at the moment was out walking around. Therefore did the interesting things she noted really not interest her at all?

At home they listened to the Fascist radio for what it didn't communicate. The "valiant progress to free the capital from Bolshevism" meant that Madrid hadn't fallen at the first assault. The city must have put up a frenzied resistance, since, according to the booming voice, the offensive enjoyed the moral, physical, and military support of the great pact of friendship between Rome and Berlin, now extended to embrace General Franco. At that news Gerda stiffened, jumped up from the chair. "If they weren't convinced that no one will lift a finger, those two criminals would never have announced the end of formal neutrality." They would let all hell loose on Spain, from now on, considering that they had never tried too hard to hide their interventions. She was tense as a rat, her jaw trembled. Georg had taken her to Villa Floridiana in the funicular, but the park was a nice park, like so many ("Nothing like Gaudí's garden of wonders in Barcelona!"), the bay was obscured, and Naples, with its reminders of Spain, its noisy indifference, was beginning to get on her nerves a bit.

They decided to go to Capri.

In the farmhouse where Soma had found a compromise between country idyll and saving on the rent, you had to get water from a well and there was no electric light. But Gerda was enthusiastic. She liked the host family of winemakers, the community of students who took the ferry to the university, the villa sheer over the cliffs where Gorky had received Lenin, and the other famous dwellings, with those paradisiacal gardens that protected what elsewhere was persecuted in the name of the law. A paradise for devils, according to the respectable, and you didn't have to be a Krupp or anyway rich and homosexual (she learned from the locals) to live there! She fantasized about it, flushed by the fresh air and the homemade wine, getting in Georg's bed with the simple explanation that a thin body would take forever to get the very damp covers warm: her feet, by experience, would unthaw around dawn. She no longer spoke of Capa, of Spain rarely, except when there was an audience to persuade about the cause.

Georg preserved a threshold of vigilance, even if sleeping next to Gerda, kissing her two or three times, was anything but unpleasant. Until, one Sunday, his sister Jenny came to visit them, who in the house of the United States vice consul, where she had found a job as a *Fräulein*, could read the American newspapers. The New York *Times* reported massive bombings of Madrid, whose purpose was not military but to cause the civilian population to surrender. Even the Prado had been damaged. And if the capitalist press wrote it, the devastation must be unimaginable. "*No pasarán!*" they uttered, throwing Anurka apple cores into the pot that had been cleaned after the poached mackerel, with a rage as solid as it was futile. And then a last time, in a whisper, saying goodbye to Jenny at the wharf where she was getting on the five-o'clock ferry. It was urgent to go to Spain, the rest was foolishness. Gerda would leave in a few days, certain she could get an assignment and join Capa, who in the meantime had managed to capture an untold number of images of that heroic and criminal war.

"Are you worried?" Georg had asked her.

"For him? He can always get out of it, he'll manage. But the Madrileños?"

He hadn't answered, only kicked a stone with the tip of his shoe. The path out of the town was barely visible, the rapidly fading light of the sun, which had already disappeared, seemed to bring the dance music behind them closer, along with the sounds of the boats in the Marina Grande.

"Give me time to put together a group and I'll join you."

"I knew it."

I also know something, he had said to himself: that you're more attached to that man than you want to admit. I don't know why, I don't know if he deserves you. But here at least we can both surrender to circumstances, and everything will be as it should.

They've arrived at Mario's, and he's gone to change his shirt, inviting Georg to get some water in the kitchen. Georg goes to the window, lights a cigarette, and looks down in the direction of the sea, metallic with reflections, dark, almost flat . . .

Soma and Gerda are growing distant along the path, he puts away the matches and continues walking, without lengthening his stride, feeling that he has nothing to lose and that he would never lose Gerda . . .

He takes a deep breath, blows the air out like a patient, tries to recover that boundless feeling that had the kindness to re-emerge and not suffocate him with dismay and tenderness. Then he returns to the table, where Mario is waiting for him, adjusts the chair, and concentrates.

Together they go over the proofs of the article, reading aloud when necessary. By now there are only a few typos, and some lexical questions that he proposes directly to his friend the native speaker are quickly resolved. They finish in half an hour, and only because they've begun to reconsider some of the hitches in the experiment: the Wratten filters that couldn't be found, the photostat machine in place of the single-lens camera with the image doubled by a prism, filtered in two different ways so the scene could be photographed twice at the same instant. Too bad, but they couldn't do better, they don't have the means of Polaroid.

Georg remembers to get the letter to Mr. Land out of the folder retrieved from his office.

"*Avec Monsieur Mario Bernardo nous avons l'intention de réaliser un film publicitaire de vulgarisation scientifique sur la vision des couleurs en présentant vos expériences. Nous serions très honorés de connaître votre avis et d'avoir vos conseils en ce sujet,*" he reads, marking the sentences with a finger and wondering again if the letter might be misunderstood as a discreet way of asking for money.

"Georges, I see you've written four pages—are you sure our genius self-taught in French will manage it?" Mario inquires.

"It's just about the subject of his theories and his studies . . . "

"He's a businessman, I've seen a lot of them at Cinecittà over the years when I was working my way up. It's not the same as speaking to a member of the scientific community. Let's wait for a couple of lines in response, or, since *time is money*, not even that."

They can put away the papers, freeing the dining table, and stick them in the envelope that Mario has ready. A messenger sent by the editorial office of *Filmtecnica* will come to pick up the proofs of *Colore bidimensionale*.

"Anyway, look, we've shown that it just takes the right light to give color to black-and-white images," says Mario, to console him in advance for a possible disappointment, and heads toward the balcony, where it's pleasant to sit and talk, especially on an evening like this.

His friend has said nothing new, and yet Georg is surprised. This is vision: to see the same thing again and project something different. Reconfirming that outside the circuit between the eye and the brain there's nothing, and that the brain, charged with the activity of selection and transmission of impulses, sometimes plays strange tricks. It's the side of the research that interests him, the impetus that originally led him to embark on this experiment. But to carry it out they used film, projectors, camera, and photographic images. Reproductions of abstract geometric paintings, it's true, nothing that recalls the revolutionary photographs hidden in the pages of a German tourist guide, or the last shots taken in the trenches of Madrid, when Gerda showed him the movie camera she got from *Life*, claiming that she'd become better at using it than Capa.

"Do you know Robert Capa?" he asks Mario.

"You mean did I meet him in person? I did, when they were shooting *The Barefoot Contessa* with Ava Gardner and he came to Rome to photograph the shoot. I knew in passing his friend David (Chim) Seymour, I met him in Trastevere, at Checco er Carrettiere. He always stayed at the Hotel d'Inghilterra. He had the requirements of a gourmet, bizarre for a foreigner—they can't usually even distinguish an overcooked pasta—and he cultivated an incongruous elegance, with the well-fed look of a teacher: the antithesis of a paparazzo, so discreet that you could understand how he was the preferred portraitist of divas—Loren, Lollo, Bergman, who at the time of the scandal gave him the exclusive—but so blind that he seemed improbable as a war photographer. Capa, on the other hand, was appealing because of his romantic fame, and rumors about a tormented liaison after which Bergman consoled herself with Rossellini. Did you know him in Spain? Maybe your face appears in those extraordinary photos of the farewell to the International Brigades?"

"I was wary of him. It irritated me to see him perched like a bird of ill omen, arriving just in time, while we were ragged, desperate, forced to clench our fists and our teeth to hold back the tears in front of those who were looking at us, or, in fact, photographing. You can't understand how much we who'd been disbanded detested not him but his Hemingway-style friends, who'd go on a heroism binge in Spain and then, as soon as they crossed the frontier, it was oysters and champagne, and they moved around as they liked with a driver or a plane. But it's true, those images express exactly what we felt, Capa with his camera was really great: a stateless man like us in the International Brigades, a Hungarian who'd tasted the joys of fascism as a boy. Chim I didn't know at the time, we were introduced later, in Paris, I don't remember the year."

"It must have been terrible, not even the Italian comrades I know want to talk about it."

"We've seen, no?, how it ended. But at least you got them out of Italy . . . "

The chairs on the terrace of Mario Bernardo's house let you sink back, one shoe against the railing, to face a courtyard too steep for billiards or marbles, but the children of this part of Monteverde, almost without space to make a course, meet there just the same. The roofs one on top of the other, the last cranes and cement mixers, the women coming out to get the laundry or shout down into the courtyard, the neighbors opposite who are doing what they're doing: chatting, sending curls of smoke up toward the faded green screen of the awning. Being up high, in the life of a neighborhood—he likes it so much it makes him wish to get away from the chaos of Via Veneto, but he still considers himself too temporary to think seriously of moving.

"We got them out, yes, but it wasn't easy or pretty. What should I tell you, Georges? You know what civil war means. And lucky that today they remember again what we did, that to someone it matters . . . "

In July, with their friendship already consolidated by Sundays spent correcting the article at the table in Via Dezza, they had met in the crowd of demonstrators pouring toward Porta San Paolo. Right there, on that balcony, they'd discussed the events of Genoa, following the meeting of the sixth congress of the neo-fascist MSI, but they hadn't yet had a chance to comment on the expansion of the revolt as far as Sicily, where the day before the police had used machine guns against the striking laborers and workers of Montecatini in Licata, killing a youth of twenty-five.

Dr. Kuritzkes was entering the office, where he was supposed to collaborate on a project with Modrić, but, at the sight of the groups with flags walking along Viale Aventino, he had chained his bicycle to the gate and set off to follow the march.

That the marchers were already appearing at the Circus Maximus wasn't a good sign: maybe, after the prohibition of what was supposed to be only a ritual laying of wreaths, the metro stop at Piramide had been closed and access to the train station was blocked. Mario Bernardo therefore might also not be there. What gave him hope was that the demonstration had been called by the Council of the Resistance. On the other hand, an ex-partisan but current cinematographer, with various contracts signed, might not be disposed to risk arrest or a blow to the head. The atmosphere was unmistakable: like a planned clash, latent war, a popular movement that erupts on the surface, competing with a potentially opposite movement, underground and coup-like. It was that familiar feeling, so toxic and intoxicating, even before the tear gas, that impelled him to advance past the cordon, where his friend, behind the row of deputies from all the left-wing parties, had waved enough to be recognized. If he hadn't arrived so soon, if Mario, surprised to see him, hadn't found a way of getting out to greet him, a few minutes later they would have been caught in full by the horse charge launched against the deputies who were trying to get to the plaque at the Martyrs of the Resistance, near the Pyramid of Cestius. It wasn't clear how they had managed to avoid the worst, to escape to the side, join a line of youths who, dragging away a companion who'd been kicked by a horse before a riot cop could pick him up, led them to the barricades of Testaccio. "I'm a doctor," he announced, at which they'd taken them to a garage serving as an improvised infirmary. Outside the sounds of the fight and the incessant shouts continued: "Fascists, fascists, murderers!" A youth in skinny American jeans asked him what he was doing there with that nice cream-colored jacket and that Kraut accent. He heard the reply, in a Venetian singsong accentuated by agitation, that his companion Georges had been in the Resistance in France and the Spanish Civil War on the right side.

"I don't believe it! That guy is younger than my father: and all he kills off is a bottle of wine at dinner."

The boy just bandaged had started laughing, too, and Dr. Kuritzkes, stupidly flattered, stated the year of his birth and sang "Ay Carmela!," "Los cuatro generales," and "El quinto regimiento."

"Damn, that's really Spanish, but we like our music better!"

Later someone thought to get the partisan comrades out of the shambles, escorting them to the foot of Ponte Testaccio. On the Trastevere side they walked to Piazza San Callisto to have a glass.

"Using horses against elected deputies I wouldn't have expected," Mario said, "but thank heaven we're in a democracy . . . a Christian democracy!"

"Let's hope it's not *aperitivo* time. Otherwise we'll have to put the T-shirt and blue jeans uniform on over our tired limbs and resume the fight . . . "

"I see you're worried."

"A little. Less than this morning."

People at the other tables were commenting on the news. Many wounded, many arrests, deaths avoided by a miracle. Georg claimed he'd seen a throng of all ages, true, which couldn't be contained. The slogans, the Roman-style insults, the posters "WHAT ITALIAN MIRACLE? ROME ISN'T LA DOLCE VITA" proved it. They could close down the factories, bring everything to a halt: either the Christian Democrats really were ready for civil war, which wasn't a good idea for them or the Americans, or the Tambroni government would have to pack its bags in a hurry. But, Mario said, those youths didn't have a political conscience, much less any discipline. They would soon go back to letting loose in their wild dances after the week at work.

"We were like that, too," he objected. "Agreed, we didn't dance to such hysterical songs, but it was *Katzenmusik* for a good number of our adult comrades. Between one clash and the next we partied like lunatics. We were wild, I assure you."

The children in the courtyard have stopped playing hopscotch, which is a pity. The acrobatic jumps of some of the little girls, curls flying out from their hairbands, were a true delight. Now they've moved on to hide and seek, and have scattered to their hiding places, except for the boy who now and then runs at breakneck speed toward home base, in a garage that you can't see from the balcony.

They're taking it easy up there, relaxed, too lazy even to get a drink from the refrigerator. They're still talking about old acquaintances and the double life, between battlefields and returns to five-star hotels. A life that seemed increasingly odd as the reconstruction advanced and others found a job, a wife, a two-room apartment with hot water. In Paris Capa stayed at the Lancaster, which had provided the suite for Dietrich's gilded exile before she went to Hollywood, and those ancient splendors had been resurrected after the war. The bill for the room burned up even the future earnings of the Magnum agency, but he insisted that otherwise he couldn't get jobs worthy of his photographs. You met him at lunchtime on the Champs-Élysées, you with the baguette under your arm to nibble on in the street: sometimes he barely exchanged a greeting, others there was no way to avoid being taken to Le Fouquet's, where he'd refresh you with everything you could wish for, while he, barely awake, ordered for himself and the ethereal mannequin or whore, not always of the highest quality, first a coffee, then an omelette, and finally a second bottle of champagne, after the one that had been uncorked to toast a friend of the glorious old days.

Chim was a character of a very different type, they agree. Mario recalled that, according to the gossip of the circle, he was among the many international homosexuals for whom

Rome was turning out to be a party. And if they looked for clues in his cared-for clothes, his reputation as a gourmet, and the exquisite politeness toward changing female presences, the aura of secrecy seemed the most crushing proof. It was easy to observe that he kept his acquaintances carefully separate—the fashionable world, for example, from the circle around Carlo Levi, with whom he made those trips to southern villages that were to be dragged out of illiteracy. Maybe his motives were political and not private, and anyway it was his business.

Georg began to laugh, a dry laugh, commenting that people here think they've been clever for centuries, *caput mundi*, but they have the mentality of a provincial bigot, only more arrogant and vulgar.

"You're telling me. But it's comfortable in Rome."

"Up here at your house certainly."

In the courtyard a boy has stumbled and been grabbed by the pursuer—who is smaller, besides—amid loud complaints, because to have that kind of bad luck isn't fair, and he limps willfully in the direction of home base.

"Did you ever see the series Chim did for UNICEF?" Georg asks. "It was the first time we'd commissioned that type of project—*Children of Europe*. Scarcely more than a brochure with a limited circulation, but the photos were published everywhere. If I bring you the book, perhaps you'll remember some of them."

"What year?"

"Around the end of '48, the book came out in '49."

"It could be. I was writing for the newspapers at the time, I was still struggling to support myself in the cinema. I did a lot of jobs, I even worked in a blast furnace in Marghera—a little of everything. I came to Rome in 1950, the year after."

Georg describes the material that was delivered to UNESCO when Chim returned from his trips, anxious to submit it to him, because they had in common Capa and many other things: Leipzig, where the photographer had studied at the Academy of Graphic and Editorial Arts, Spain, obviously, and even Polish origins. Discovering that Russian was the language Georg had heard as a child, Chim occasionally threw out a phrase, but mostly they spoke in German. It was the natural choice and guaranteed a certain reserve. They worked at four desks, one behind the other, like school desks. UNESCO was established in a provisional way in what had been one of the most sumptuous of the Belle Époque hotels, the Majestic. And since it was a quarter of an hour from the Lancaster, Chim suggested that he go with him when he went to see Bob, as he was calling him by that point. Capa, on the other hand, hadn't gotten used to calling him David, even though it was the only genuine name between the two of them.

"He was from Warsaw, right? A Jew from Warsaw?"

"Yes, a Jew from Warsaw."

The countries Chim visited for UNICEF were the ones where the condition of children was most desperate: Italy, Greece, Hungary, which was very important to Capa, Austria, which was overflowing with refugee camps, and inevitably Poland. A series of images showed a line of students crossing the rubble of the Warsaw ghetto—low damp mounds of earth, scattered with the last smashed bricks—to reach the area that had been rebuilt with the first socialist apartment blocks. Chim noted that his father's publishing house, which brought out books in Yiddish and Hebrew, had been behind the big church that represented the only building not razed to the ground by the Germans. The most direct testimony that his parents were no longer alive, he had murmured as he turned the contact sheet, he had received not in Warsaw but in a city where, as luck would have it, he had shot many rolls of film. In that vacation town spared from the destruction, schools, orphanages, homes for disturbed children had been set up. Thanks to a Jewish organization, the *pensione* run by an aunt had also been turned into a sanatorium, where his father and mother had moved when war broke out. "It was this," he said, showing him a couple of photographs. In one you saw a tubercular patient who, propped against her companions' mattresses, displayed a rigid corset. Chim didn't remember what he had done to get that smile and that comical expression in the dark eyes. Timid and radiant, a little in love maybe, Georg had observed. Chim made a sign of denial, and he had ventured a prognosis for how long it would take the spinal column to heal, something he knew about, having fought against TB when he was a partisan in Haute Savoie.

"Really?" Mario asks.

"The people in the villages were almost as afraid of TB infection as of the Germans, especially for their children. Dealing with it meant earning their gratitude and sincere collaboration."

"I understand. So up there you didn't fight?"

Georg gives an absentminded yes of confirmation, distracted by the cry "I'm coming!" down in the courtyard, which turns out to be the unlucky boy, or maybe not too unlucky, given his speed.

Mario is probably more curious about the Résistance in the mountains than about the genesis of a publication by means of which UNICEF, newly hatched and in search of support, wanted to publicize the state of need of millions of minors forced to do anything just to survive—steal, beg, prostitute themselves, pick up cigarette butts and resell them—and at the same time highlight the efforts to help them grow, study, and heal, so that Europe, too, might grow and heal. But the commitment to defeating the evil of ignorance is something they share, otherwise they wouldn't have come up with that didactic film that explains how we perceive colors.

Then Georg takes as a starting point the children in the courtyard, emerging here and there from their hiding places, sometimes in time to touch home, sometimes grabbed in the last stretch, where, crushed behind the corner, "it" has found a system for capturing them.

"In theory the youngest children playing down there could be the offspring of the oldest kids photographed by Chim back then. Let's say the most fortunate or obstinate or endowed with talent, and let's say also a talent for life—I don't know how that can be taught, and maybe it's better not to know."

Mario laughs, comments that he appears to be optimistic, and all in all he's not wrong: yes, what they lived through seems truly far from these children of the miracle, even if stating that means supporting a certain kind of propaganda, and peace will never be a certainty.

"Anyway, they can run, catch each other, play . . . "

Georg recalls some images taken in the park of a Roman villa to explain more clearly—not an ordinary villa but the one where Mussolini was arrested in '43. Ironically, right on the burned grass of Villa Ada, Chim photographed some barefoot children, stripped down to the comical bloomers provided by the pious institution that had brought them to the outdoors and had them playing volleyball. Some without a leg, some without an arm, one, with prostheses on his lower limbs, even had a crutch to compensate for the rigidity of his movements: the child in the foreground, the only one wearing a shirt and long pants. Chim pointed out to him that the only two players whose faces were looking toward the camera, though at a distance, were blind, blinded by the impact of a bomb. Maybe not completely, but enough so that the effort of taking part in the game was enormous.

"He was able to capture the energy along with the incurable injuries. His art owed a lot to that refined consonance, a quality that caused his partner to say that, of the two, Chim was the better photographer. I think he was also alluding to the human material, because certainly Capa would never have made the pilgrimages to refugee camps and orphanages, the dive into the void of his own childhood: not for six months and a laughable fee, maybe not even for all the gold in the world."

Mario wants to know what year Seymour and Capa died, and it's a question so easy that Georg continues to follow the echo of the squabbles in the courtyard that accuse the tall boy of cheating. In the meantime he thinks of the invisible damage, the alterations of the nervous system spilling onto the perceptual-sensorial apparatus caused by certain experiences, not as a combatant but as a photographer. Not shell shock, as the Americans called it, only a vague imbalance that amplifies the attraction of danger, as if it were a sporting challenge, a game in appearance more like the one down in the courtyard than like the volleyball match at Villa Ada.

Chim was aware of it. At the time, Georg was confident that UNESCO would take on a task more significant than the works of reparation, as Chim had defined them. He was sorry that that sensitive man, evidently afflicted by melancholy, intensified by his experiences, had said he was content with the children portrayed on his journeys (he had even noted their names: Tadzio, Tereska, Elefteria, Angela . . .), since he was unable to bring any of his own into the world. Chim's speech seemed unacceptable, since most of those who had lost their families were trying to create one of their own. So one day, while they were looking at the photographs, he had allowed himself to object that the war was over. Chim, embarrassed, had changed the subject to Capa and said that in other circumstances their friend would have wanted ten kids, like a rabbi with a long beard.

"Too bad that *other circumstances* had a different idea," Georg replied delicately.

"Maybe I shouldn't say it to you, doctor, but I saw those two more happy than not . . . But things, *natürlich*, can always change, as long as there's time."

There's no more time now, there hasn't been for a while. But there's always something left to repair, for example with a phone call to the Dachshund and, when he's about to confide it, Mario asks him the question he was expecting from the start.

No, he answers, he didn't know Robert Capa well. They were friends, it's true, even if he had to be taken in moderate doses. But he was infinitely grateful to him. The free world would have preferred not to see the dirty life that la Grande République reserved for the Republican refugees: and the great photographer, who came to Argelès-sur-Mer to capture all the prophetic shame of it, had discovered that he was in one of those camps. If Capa hadn't been able to obtain his release, he probably could have expected the fate of his companions who went from democratic-French barbed wire to Nazi German barbed wire.

"How is it that Capa came to mind today?" Mario asks.

The silence that follows delivers them to the last cries of the children excited by the game that has ended happily, radios broadcasting the news, horns and engines noisy down in the street. Then Georg, washed by those sounds, answers, lighting up.

"We had a friend in common who died in Spain. Today no one knows who Gerda Taro was. Even the traces of her photographs are lost, because Gerda was a comrade, a woman, a brave and free woman, very beautiful and very free, let's say free in every respect."

Mario must have understood: he asks no more questions. The children in the courtyard have decided to stop playing hide and seek. Sometimes, to follow an example, it's enough to say a name.

L ook at them, finally, sitting outside at the Café du Dôme, with those smiles that speak to each other, gaiety unleashed by some sweetness or stupidity, the merest trifle is enough. You see it at a glance, looking at this photograph, the light uniform over André's profile, the sun that lets him keep his jacket open, a spring day so mild that Gerda has taken off hers, or maybe she went out in short sleeves, since Rue Vavin is nearby.

They don't realize they're being photographed. The photographer has placed himself on the sidewalk opposite, focused with the wide-angle lens and shot in a second. Someone, however, has noticed that shot: the man at the table behind has interrupted his reading of the paper and, having lowered the page, now peers at the couple's moves, as the direction of his gaze and the little smile emerging on his lips indicate. On the other side of the scene, and of the time that the photograph straddles, there's a man of the past century who, like you, observes. If you look at him more closely, you note that his friendly smile seems almost a comment on the radiant smile of the protagonist: *ah ils sont beaux, les jeunes*, when they can make the girl they're in love with laugh . . .

But how does he know? After all he has before him only the photographer, who has left the third glass half full of a milky drink. Maybe he happened to observe that lively liaison and it amuses him that someone has taken the trouble to capture it. Behind them, the busy *garçon* avoids the concert of smiles, and shines instead in the whiteness of his jacket, enlivened by the play of folds around the elbow, perfect center of the frame.

The waiter, well, he knows the habitués, you can be sure of it. Starting with that Friedmann, who has given himself a decorous look, thanks to Mademoiselle Gerda, always *très chic* and friendly to everyone. But the waiter wouldn't measure up to that well-known haunt if he didn't also know the clientele that doesn't sit out on the sidewalk every damn day. Like the man who arrived from Montmartre and sometimes exchanges his photos at the tables: portraits of people more important than that couple, who are famous mainly at the Dôme, and some pictures that make those who work amid artists think that Monsieur Stein has a talent for capturing the *flair* of Paris.

In 1934, Fred Stein, who had arrived less than a year earlier, had caught a nocturnal winter love, a secret covered by the hair and coats of the two lovers, bodies fused in the shadow imprinted on the snow by the light of the streetlamp.

That snapshot perhaps carries within it the living memory of a flight disguised as a honeymoon, the quickest and most unsuspicious way of getting passports, when Fred's arrest had become just a matter of time. The Steins were married in Dresden in the town hall—outside people applauded, shouting Heil Hitler!—and then gave themselves a present, because Fred loved taking photographs and according to Lilo was talented: a Leica.

You imagine that Fred rose quietly, going out to capture images of Paris, and that he left without making any noise, so as not to wake Lilo, exhausted from the off-the-books jobs—cook, dishwasher—that allowed him to become a photographer. Later, after the move to the address that on the visiting

cards appeared as "Studio Stein," she, too, learned to photograph weddings and baptisms, replacing her husband when he
had other engagements. And it was Lilo who kept the accounts
and the ménage of sublet rooms in the house that was always
open to any friend or Party comrade who rang at the door. The
daughter of a great doctor, she managed a life that was the
polar opposite of her childhood, with servants and garden, but
that life was also far from the solitude *à deux* captured by Fred
in his nighttime wanderings: noisy and—even though the
apartment looked out on the cemetery of Montmartre—rich in
luminous moments. In '35, when they celebrated the arrival of
Gerda and Lotte with bulbs hooded by red and green shades,
Lilo was immediately won over by the exaggerated bow with
which André Friedmann introduced himself. She liked the
disheveled look, the comical way of showing off, the boyish
bluster. Fred and Lilo were a few years older, they were twenty-five, but had become a support for those who were less dis-
ciplined with money, lodging, and feelings.

That day in April of '36, Fred Stein arrives at the Dôme and
stops to have a drink with friends. Paris is no longer the nighttime theater of disorientation, love no longer needs to bundle
up in the anonymity of figures that draw a dual self-portrait of
exile. Now it requires the close-up, belongs to those who man-
ifest it: to Gerda Pohorylle and André Friedmann, on the sidewalk of the café where everyone knows them.

André has just begun to call himself Robert Capa, Gerda
has just got her first press pass, the Steins live in a more comfortable apartment near Porte de Saint-Cloud, where Lilo
manages the lab without having to take on countless other
duties. Fred has developed a good clientele, and a name as a
portraitist. The next year, included for the second time in a
group show at the Galerie de la Pléiade, he will show some of
his portraits of writers beside Man Ray and Philippe Halsman

(who in those years chooses Ruth Cerf as a model). He's not the only one who embarked on that career out of necessity, but in Dresden he didn't do any apprenticeship, unlike Chim at the academy in Leipzig or Capa through Eva Besnyö and Kati Horna, who during high school were taught by a master of the Hungarian avant-garde. Fred Stein learned by himself, thanks to the wedding gift of a Leica and to Lilo, who helps him. It's the Leica, he says, that taught him to photograph, he always carries it around his neck, treats it as an extension of his body. He can't help it if that symbiosis clashes with the distrust of clients who, used to grandiose hocus-pocus, doubt that an acceptable portrait can emerge from a device scarcely bigger than a wallet. Things were so hard at the start that he had to insert *"Promotion gratuite photo portrait"* among the small ads in the newspaper.

Adversities, the good fairy, the magic gift: the story of Fred Stein seems a fable that is heading toward a happy ending, and maybe not even he, emphasizing the role of the Leica, told it exactly right. Camera, trust, perseverance, and a bold spirit wouldn't have been sufficient for him to emerge among the hundreds of photographers who poured into Paris. The same goes for Capa and Gerda, even though they had thought up their millionaire fable with the ambition of establishing themselves as photojournalists. Creating art didn't enter into their job, but they knew what the quality of a photo depended on: they had absorbed the aesthetic ideas of the time along with the political and social ones, and were aware that right there, in art, a revolution had taken place. Fred Stein, involved in politics since he was a high-school student, active member of a small socialist party, brilliant law graduate, hadn't brought only an easy-to-use camera in his luggage. In Dresden he would have liked to be a lawyer for the weakest and, once in Paris, he photographed workers, peddlers, beggars—the poor in general. Yet that says nothing about how he did it: with respect joined to the ironic gaze, with the modernist rigor of the frames, with the particular aesthetic sense that coincided with his sense of justice.

And then Paris took care of shaping his photographs. You had only to go to the café and you'd meet Cartier-Bresson or André Kertesz, with whom the younger André had excellent relations. Walter Benjamin also loved the Dôme, when he was a Berliner in love with Paris and not yet a refugee avoiding the jumble of German émigrés. But still he headed there as soon as he left his den on Rue Bédard, as might have happened the day Fred Stein took the photo of André and Gerda. Besides, the editorial office that in the spring of '36 is waiting for a proof that has been much discussed is in Saint-Germain, and maybe on returning Benjamin needs to stop outside and have a glass.

In June, when *The Work of Art in the Age of Mechanical Reproduction* begins to be on the lips of the Paris intellectuals, the author holds two meetings in German circles, one at the Deutscher Klub, the other at Café Mephisto. Gerda, who often takes advantage of these free opportunities for culture, is occupied by commitments to the Alliance agency and by the efforts to sell her first photograph. But how did Fred Stein, who has already taken portraits of Ernst Bloch and Bertold Brecht, to name two close friends of Benjamin's, allow those occasions to get away? Or was it Benjamin who wouldn't agree to be photographed? And when in New York Fred hears talk about him from Hannah Arendt—whose friendship is demonstrated by the photographs he takes of her over the years—surely that lapse must have weighed on him?

It's likely that Stein had read Benjamin's essay, having grown up in a house full of books and precepts. His father a reform rabbi, his mother, left a widow, a teacher of Hebrew and religion. With the Torah closed so that he could open himself to socialism, for Stein all the faces had taken the place of He who had created him in his own image and likeness. In an article of '34, he writes that a portraitist must capture "the story and the character that every model possesses," an ideal task for the Leica, whose small size makes it so "disarming." The consistency with which he translates that thought into method is remarkable: not only does he choose subjects whom he respects and likes but before meeting them he takes the time to study their works and then to talk in such a way that they forget it's a session.

The most exemplary episode dates to 1946, when Einstein allows him ten minutes and ends up talking to him for two hours. The result is barely twenty-five stills. In the portrait, which becomes one of the most famous, Albert Einstein has a gentle, sorrowful gaze, and isn't smiling. An image that aims at capturing a man's story and character has to be able not to reduce him to a mirror or an object, even if he is the most attractive of icons.

The friend who that day finds André and Gerda so absorbed that he captures them at once is one who pours those aspirations into the portrait. If Stein didn't believe he'd caught a moment of truth on their faces, the photo at the Dôme would perhaps have sunk into the limbo of negatives that do not rise as images, but instead now you, too, can look at it, as if the time that has passed since that moment didn't exist.

So you imagine that Fred and Lilo withdraw to develop the rolls. There's some work done on commission, photos to offer the newspapers, and the portrait of André and Gerda. Fred observes the negative under the magnifying glass and finds confirmation of the sensation that he's hit the bull's-eye: the composition balanced, no detail too out of focus. "You see here?" he says to Lilo pointing to the waiter in the right place. "And look at the man smiling . . . Marvels of the Leica that captures what you don't have time to notice." Then he adds: "Lilo, you're sensitive to the subject, how would you define this face? Arrogant? Scoundrelly?"

It's no longer the Montmartre house, but the darkroom is still the apartment's small bathroom. The light is minimal, the space, too, the wait for the images to appear in the trays on the sink always magical.

Fred touches Lilo's arm and she responds that it's really true: "André came out just the way he is. Power of love and the photographer who caught him on the spot."

"Let's make a print right away, so I can bring it to him."

Lilo, waiting to take it out, looks at it more carefully. "And Gerda?"

"Gerda, why?"

"She didn't come out well."

"The photo yes," Fred replies. "And then I've taken so many where she's stupendous, spirited, in other words Gerda . . ."

"Exactly."

Fred now reconsiders the portrait from that inevitable female perspective. The beret that covers her hair cuts across her forehead, shortening it, and accentuates the protuberance of her straight nose. And those hamster-like cheeks. Eyes closed, the shadow of the visor that almost creates the effect of a double chin—and she cares so much about her profile, Gerda, who as soon as she woke up did gymnastic exercises in their living room, torture and delight of the other tenants.

"She won't be very happy," he grumbles.

Now it's Lilo who insists that the photograph should be delivered. It's beautiful, a beautiful memory, a beautiful gesture of friendship, something that a person who is vain but not at all stupid can certainly recognize.

And then?

Then Fred returns home and says that it went as predicted. Gerda who sees herself as ugly, André who snatches the envelope off the table at the Dôme ("This, *mein Schatz*, I'll take"). Anyway she's the one who thanks him when he gets ready to leave: "Dear Fred, you were thoughtful, as always."

Was she sincere? Or did she just want to make her companion believe he'd had it his way, so that he would forget the photograph and never mind if it disappeared in the next move?

"It doesn't matter," says Lilo, "you did what you had to. And then with André things get lost anyway. For a future memory, we have it."

This is a first conjecture, but it's equally possible that the photo remained with the Steins waiting for an occasion to be delivered to André and Gerda. They're all absorbed by the campaign of the Front Populaire, and then by the electoral victory. In May, Fred takes a picture of Prime Minister Léon Blum and sells it to *Life* for a thousand dollars, which they can live on for a month. In June a mass of work arrives with the wave of strikes and, in the blink of an eye, they're into the great celebration of *Quatorze Juillet*, suddenly remembering the portrait still in the delivery drawer.

"I'll leave the envelope with the concierge if I don't find them, I'll do it this week," Fred promises.

But then a mere three days pass and July 18th arrives, when the euphoria of the 14th is upended into shock that a fascist coup is under way in Spain. Fred runs out, finds his friends at the café, excited by imminent departure, and, with the warmest wishes, finally takes out that envelope. They're happy with their portrait, they find it auspicious, but they're already elsewhere, André and Gerda.

Then there's a story that that photograph can't tell, because it begins on September 3, 1939, when France declares war on Germany. *Drôle de guerre*, the French call it, since for eight months nothing happens to them, but that's not the case for men whose nationality is that of the enemy, even if it's to escape the Nazis that they came to France. On September 5, 1939, Fred Stein is transported to the stadium of Colombes, which is overflowing with German and Austrian refugees, and sent from there to the first of various internment camps. He paves French roads until, in June of 1940, the strange war becomes a debacle for the nation that hosts him as a prisoner. In the shame of the imminent surrender, an officer solves the problem of their *boches*, whom the Germans are just waiting to knock off: "*Les allemands sont là, débrouillez-vous.*" Fred gets the order to fend for himself, escapes through the countryside, shelters in abandoned farmhouses, covers six hundred kilometers to reach Toulouse. He has no news of Lilo, who's in Paris with a child of less than a year. Marion was born so close to the fateful September 3rd that the process begun with the help of the Salzburgs, relatives of Lilo's who emigrated to America after Kristallnacht, is useless. The most tormenting thing is that the one who organized the mother and daughter's return to the city, raising hell to get a license, was him. In Normandy stateless people were not accepted among the evacuees. The orphanage that eventually took them in keeps Lilo in the cellars, allowing her minimal contact with her daughter. The child is wasting away, without the care and mother's milk that would soften the privations of the religious institution.

Now that he has no idea of where they are hiding, he tries the most unsuspicious way of communicating that he's alive. He lines up at the window for advertisements, where he dictates only names that pass for French: even Stein is associated with the flight of the Alsatians, who swell the columns of the newspapers with the search for relatives. "*Alfred Stein, demobilisée a Toulouse, cherche sa femme Lilo e sa fille Marion.*"

His wife doesn't see that advertisement. But one of two postcards that Fred has sent to his most trusted contacts she receives on a date that she will remember for the rest of her

274 - HELENA JANECZEK

life: July 9, 1940. She has to move quickly, she can't wait to get there, only it's so difficult. There's the child, there's the indispensable baggage, a suitcase full of negatives and prints that contains too many heads sought by the Nazis. How can she carry both through the occupied zone and then the "free zone" that, for someone like Lilo, isn't free at all?

Ever since Maréchal Pétain established the seat of government in a Grand Hotel at a spa to offer his services to the occupiers like a maître d', his gendarmes and private citizens have been divided into those who are eager waiters, carrying plates to the Gestapo, and those who secretly spit on them. It means you can't trust anyone you don't know well, and Lilo Stein doesn't know anyone outside of Paris. So she rushes into a game in which she gambles everything. She carries the child in her arms and, with the help of Marion, who threatens to wail, like a hungry nursing baby, she skips the line at the *Kommandantur*. The father of the *petite gosse* is demobilized in Toulouse, S-T-E-I-N she pronounces with an élan so Parisian that the official doesn't even ask for her documents. Rewarded with a pass bearing the Nazi cross for a courage that surpasses the imagination of the German, Liselotte Stein née Salzburg gets on the train with Marion. And when, finally, she can put down the suitcase and be held tight by Fred, in that embrace there is a kind of spark, a jolt of almost criminal pleasure. Now they are reunited, yes, but stuck in Toulouse. To get out of the bottleneck of France requires endless visas, which governments are increasingly stingy with, or which have to be paid for at a very high price, and the Leica that might have been used to pick up some money was requisitioned while Fred was in prison. If Vichy hadn't implemented a "delivery on request" to the Gestapo and Fred hadn't appeared on the lists of those sought, they could ask for an exit visa, reach Portugal, get in contact again with Lilo's family in the United States. Time presses, Marion has acquired her first words, which could betray them, but it's torture to keep her in the chicken coop where they've found lodging. Finally a glimmer of hope reaches them, a rumor that seems reliable. Fred has to go to Marseille and track down the American Emergency Rescue Committee, where a certain Monsieur Fry is expanding a list received in Manhattan: two hundred great names in art, literature, and science that America, selective, as is suitable for the highest bidder, wants to grab in the liquidation sales of the old continent. "SAVE CULTURE EUROPE STOP," a telegram from Varian Fry repeats with the peremptoriness of a cry that doesn't stop at the desideratum. The excess of zeal (what is a Harvard classics graduate doing mixed up in current affairs?) risks damaging relations between France and America. And this to bring to the Land of the Free and the Brave an anomalous wave of Jews and extremists, whom no one feels any need of—not the State Department, and the American people even less. Varian Fry ignores the calls that are increasingly indistinguishable from threats, spends discreetly the dollars intended for saving chosen persons, procures false documents, considers clandestine paths and dilapidated boats that have become more expensive than a transatlantic liner. He doesn't have the ability to prevent what can still go wrong, producing sometimes irreparable results, as when, annihilated by the non-validity of his transit visa, Walter Benjamin kills himself. The *passeurs* will have to leave him in Port Bou, given that the next day the Spanish will let the other refugees continue. Fry can't even help all those who line up at his office, the lawyers and doctors who appear, imploring him with the terror of middle-class men reduced to the last family jewels. Fred Stein instead finds help because of what he has become: a photographer, an artist of the Leica. He can return to Toulouse and report to Lilo, not too loud but with the erotic warmth of a promise, the word that the American emissary has given him.

Lilo carries the baby, Fred the suitcase. Or vice versa. Maybe Marion prefers to be in Papa's arms, while her mother drags the anthology of photographic work thanks to which they now have American visas and passage on a boat direct to Martinique. Safety, fingers crossed. Varian Fry, on the pier at the port of Marseille, signals the vigilance of a great nation, in case the authorities venture to pull out one of his protected. In the group on the boat are other photographers, like the famous Josef Breitenbach, much tested by prison, and their friends Ilse Bing and Ylla. But they meet many people they know, among whom Willy Chardack turns up. They're as packed in as prisoners, but in compensation the Winnipeg has the reputation of a "ship of hope": it carried to Chile two thousand Spanish refugees extracted from the camps of the Midi. That's why the hold of the old cargo ship is crammed with bunk beds, a golden opportunity for the French steamship company that in '39 refitted it in order to crowd in the Republican refugees.

Pablo Neruda will extoll that voyage on the Winnipeg, which he organized to evacuate the two thousand exiled Spaniards from the French camps, as the only one of his poems that no one would ever be able to erase, but in recent years a stain has marked that indelible work. In his capacity as special consul for immigration in Chile, Neruda chose to put on board mostly Communists. Fred Stein photographs the poet in '66, mindful of the ship and hope, but on May 6, 1941, he sees nothing of what will happen behind him or beyond the horizon of sky and water that opens the future. The numbered months of Varian Fry, who, under United States pressure, will be expelled from France in early August. The fact that the Winnipeg is one of the last ships to leave a French port. It doesn't land on Martinique, because the British reroute it to Trinidad, where Fred again ends up in a camp for "enemy aliens," separated from Lilo and Marion. But on June 6th the S.S. Evangeline, a ship on which one travels as comfortably as

if it were a normal thing to go on a journey, delivers them finally to Ellis Island.

If Capa had been in New York in that period, maybe the
Steins would have discovered that the person who issued his
visa for America was, coincidentally, Pablo Neruda. They
could have exchanged stories of their mishaps, relieved by having had to choose only the contents of a suitcase, a choice
much less thorny than that of Varian Fry, Neruda, and whoever
applied a selective criterion to those who had to flee and, even
so, can never be thanked enough. But the archive in
Amsterdam where Lilo managed to send Fred's more political
work will be burned by the bombs with which the Allies recon-
quer Holland, and many of Robert Capa's negatives will never
reappear. But the photo at the Café du Dôme, arriving at the
port of New York, is safe.

The *drôle de guerre* exposes Capa to a tragicomic reversal.
From early September of '39 he offers himself to the French
military authorities, but they will not accept the services of
someone who has worked for the Communist press. Ever since
Hitler and Stalin made the Molotov-Ribbentrop pact (sending
the Spanish to despair and the International Brigades to the
refugee camps and their German comrades sheltering in the
USSR directly to the Nazis), in France the Communists—the
Party, the newspapers, etc.—have been outlawed. At that point
he is not only an "undesirable foreigner" but a rather visible
foreigner. They could, overnight, deport him to one of the
camps reserved for politicals, the best guarded and harshest. In
a frantic search for a way out, Capa spends his time making
phone calls and running around Paris. His contacts at *Paris-
Soir* and *Match* say they are *très désolés*, but there is absolutely
no way to get him a visa. Even at *Life* all they do is fill him with
compliments ("*today you're the number one war photographer*") and promise him assignments, if he can get around the

United States immigration quotas. Given that the bourgeois press can do nothing for him, Capa remembers Pablo Neruda. They met during the siege of Madrid and maybe again after the defeat, on a joint visit to the tent cities held together by barbed wire, where the photographer no longer sees only a subject for an exposé but the looming image of his future. To help a comrade who had done so much for the Spanish cause was a small gesture for the Chilean consul, still full of emotion for his "great poem" docked in Valparaiso. From September 19, 1939, *André Friedmann, Profesión: fotógrafo; Nacionalidad: húngaro; Estado Civil: soltero; Religión: no tiene*, can therefore go *en viaje comercial*—on a business trip—to the Republic of Chile. Time, Inc., the colossus of capitalist information, will take care of the rest, reserving one of the last cabins on the Manhattan, departing from Le Havre. Capa reaches New York with a tourist visa for the USA, but he'll have time to invent something when the expiration date approaches. Meanwhile he can toast his twenty-seven years just completed and collapse where Julia, his mother, or his brother, Cornell, direct him.

You can imagine the things to do before leaving for Le Havre. Pay the hotel, get in touch with the Americans for confirmations, send a telegram to Julia. A rapid goodbye to the relatives in Paris, a last glass with friends. The embrace of Cartier-Bresson, like the plasticine model for a Giacometti bronze, when he lowers himself toward Capa, who's sweating anxiety and alcohol. The fraternal recommendation to Chim (*"Mon vieux*, follow my example, quickly!"), the first to sign a contract with a Communist newspaper. A last night with a daughter of Paris, parting with little French kisses on the side of the cheeks, love corresponding to banknotes, too many, *c'est bien, chérie*, have fun, you're O.K.

No flowers for Gerda. Not even a pebble to place on the tombstone watched over by a Horus commissioned from Alberto

Giacometti by the Party. Père Lachaise is out of the way, the dead take care of themselves, the Hebrew prayers learned carelessly at thirteen for one who is "*soltero*" and "*religión: no tiene*," single and has no religion, threaten tremendous outbursts.

But he takes the photos of Gerda. They're in the room, on the untidy desk or in the drawer of the night table. Ready for two years, returned from China, brought safe from the Republican lines, sliding always upward, toward the border, toward defeat. Gerda sleeping, Gerda putting on her stockings, Gerda collapsed on an Iberian mile marker. Gerda choosing lilies of the valley to celebrate May 1st, stuck in his suede jacket, the one he's wearing in the picture at the Dôme, when it was still almost new.

Did he take only the photos he had at the hotel and was Fred's double portrait among them? Or in view of that conclusive crossing did he add some, when the last rolls were delivered to Csiki, the accounts still open, the instructions for the period when he would be unreachable? Instructions of barely a few sentences, sentences based on the understanding that his comrade in thefts and fishing frauds, the friend who escaped with him from Budapest to Berlin and from Berlin to Paris, would take care of business, as he had the other times Capa was traveling.

While he wanders through the only place he possesses where everything responds to his name (Atélier Robert Capa, 37 Rue Froidevaux, Paris (XIV), Tél: Danton 75-21) and the time until his departure for Le Havre expands, perhaps the classic demand crossed his mind: "What have I forgotten?" And, dumped on Csiki, maybe it was translated into "Will you find that photo of me and Gerda?" Then enough, a fleeting exchange of farewells ("Take care." "You, too.") and the relief, as soon as he gets in the taxi for the station, of having done everything, at last.

Anyway, if he's forgotten anything, Csiki is still there, the assistant there's no reason to worry about. He isn't profiled as a Communist sympathizer and isn't yet a citizen of an enemy country, even if Hitler and Horthy are in fact allies on the eastern fronts. With the money that Cornell sends from New York, and the various contacts, apart from the friends who have been interned, evacuated, or have left, like Ruth, for a more secure country, Csiki Weisz doesn't live badly.

Things change suddenly with the blitzkrieg. The Germans, arriving in Paris, will cancel out any distinction between Jews of whatever provenance. Lilo Stein doesn't even attempt another evacuation. In the rays of a flashlight she looks again at the negatives, while Marion turns over in her sleep, kicking a little foot at her. Having to prepare for everything, perhaps she confides to a trustworthy person the photographic hiding place. In any case—so you imagine—she starts packing the suitcase long before closing it for the last time.

Thus, as the Nazis advance, Csiki, too, chooses the material that should be kept safe from their clutches at all costs. He builds three flat rectangular boxes, covers them with different colors (red, green, ochre), installs cardboard dividers. They resemble the packages of a *maître chocolatier*, too large for the means of someone who has a small stipend sent from America. But in place of the handmade pralines he places in the grid the most crushing evidence of what happened in Spain—a selection of Capa, Chim, and Taro's negatives—labeling the frames on the inside cover in very clear handwriting in pencil. When the work is done, he puts the boxes in a knapsack and, loading it on his back, gets on the bicycle. On wheels weighted by his minimal personal possessions, he makes his way along the *routes nationales* clogged by Parisians in flight, pedaling to Bordeaux or Marseille. Maybe he pedals to Bordeaux and continues without the bike to Marseille, but it's a fact that he's also pedaling for his life, the life of a Jew from Budapest burdened by baggage that would betray him as an accomplice of those who fought, with photography, the first Nazi-Fascist war on the continent.

Why did Csiki flee so late? So as not to make trouble for his friend, who when it was still calm in Paris was beginning to fear extradition to Budapest? Robert Capa walked the promised land of the United States without a visa, so in March of 1940 he was condemned to six months of expulsion. *Life* could send him far from the prison countries, but to be able to return to the USA he had to act on his own initiative. The first available New Yorker ("Can you do me a big favor, honey?"), a honeymoon shared with a couple of photographer friends in the same situation. A doctor testifies to two fake pregnancies, a minister of God celebrates the Christian bond of marriage paid for by the brides. The return from Elkton, Maryland, in the rain, in a stunned nervous silence. The next day the men would be sent to Latin America.

As the Germans march toward the Atelier Robert Capa, the owner is serving his six months of expulsion in Mexico City. He is following the presidential campaigns of two generals, one with a mustache, the other with a double chin, who at rallies puff up the bellies and the rhetoric of those who fought beside Zapata. He wanted to become an American photographer, so he practices playing Robert Capa. He goes out with colleagues "for drinks and chicks," and swallows, along with swigs of bad whiskey, the bitter pills of the way *Life* uses his images ("Nazi Fifth Column and Communist Allies Active in Mexico")— photographs he was able to get thanks to the Spanish Civil War veterans, who greeted him with open arms. Sometimes he disappears, takes a leave from himself, goes to the friend who is comfortable in that absurd country. Kati, who already in Spain was calling him a sellout, picks up on his disgust, although she doesn't believe the outbursts when he says he'd like to give it all up. But those Hungarian friends were inseparable, and while Kati and André recall their youth in Budapest, the last of the trio is pedaling on his bicycle in search of safety for himself and the photographs.

Csiki, too, went to Spain as a photographer, although for a shorter period than his friends. So as soon as he arrives in Bordeaux he looks for a Spaniard leaving for Mexico, which welcomes the Republican refugees much more generously than any other country in the world. Finally, unable to get around too much while the Germans are advancing, he contents himself with a Chilean comrade, entrusting him with the three boxes to be carried to the safety of a consulate. From there the traces of Csiki Weisz are lost until, probably in Marseille, he is arrested by the collaborationist gendarmes and deported to Morocco.

It must have been in that period that his close friend receives a letter from a concentration camp full of Republican veterans who enlisted in the Foreign Legion and a good number of Jews who'd taken refuge in Casablanca. The visa, the documents, the place on a ship: getting them is a task that requires the levers of Robert Capa. Disappointed that the wait for permission to stay in the United States made him miss the Battle of Britain, Capa is living at the Dorchester in London, which functions as an anteroom (with a view over Hyde Park), waiting for someone to have the courage to send him to the war that he wants to cover at all costs. Ever since Hungary entered the conflict, even The Greatest War Photographer in the World has become an "enemy alien." So he goes to the Mexican Embassy, where he appeals to his acquaintanceship with the former president Lázaro Cárdenas and his commitment to anyone who contributed to the Republican struggle. Once the visa is obtained, the problem of the ship remains.

The boat that emerges, the Serpa Pinto, was acquired by

the Companhia Colonial de Navegação to increase the transoceanic crossings that in the forties only Portugal's neutrality could still guarantee. Returning from Rio de Janeiro, it carried a few German colonists eager to fight for the Führer, but the inexhaustible demand was in the other direction. In its twenty crossings, the Serpa Pinto transports Marcel Duchamp, Simone Weil, a stunted Berlin child who becomes the manager of the Grateful Dead, even the Lubavitcher Rebbe, who, arriving in Brooklyn, was supposed to reveal himself as the messiah—a jumble of saints and iconoclasts with the addition of a sort of scarecrow who gets on in September of '42.

Csiki Weisz boards the Serpa Pinto without a suitcase. He has only an overcoat, a toothbrush, and the false passport (Hungarians are not accepted even in Mexico) that Capa managed to get him, along with the necessary money. When he disembarks at Veracruz he doesn't have enough to pay for the train, but one of the Spaniards he hung out with on the ship gives him a ticket. He arrives in Mexico City, Kati Horna opens the door to him, feeds him in order to reconnect him to the clothes that are falling off him, helps him find a job. Csiki Weisz photographs for the press, hangs around Kati's artist friends cautiously, even though he's already met many of them. Nazi-Fascism has created a boundless refugee camp that a monstrous current of air transports from one country to another. In Mexico, however, that community of exiles is transformed. Impotence, which is the reverse side of safety, measures thousands of kilometers, and the discussions sink into the ancient myths of the new world. Now Kati, too, produces surrealist photographs that, according to her, are truer than the ones taken by Csiki.

Before the end of the war brings him the news that his mother and siblings have gone up in smoke, something happens to the orphan of Budapest that is as fantastic as the place where he has found asylum. He meets a woman: married, enveloped in a legendary fame (she was the companion of Max Ernst), beautiful, like the heroine of a fairy tale escaped from a lugubrious mansion in England into the boundless world that she paints. Csiki has nothing to offer her, and he doesn't know how to act with women, he reminds Kati, who, however, shakes her head: Leonora Carrington isn't wrong about what she sees and what she's seen in Csiki isn't a whim. Maybe she also said to him that when they marry ("You'll see, you'll get married") they won't have to look for a photographer. Kati Horna in fact will photograph them on their wedding day as if they were a couple suspended in time and space. Csiki with that enormous beret that is like an homage to Leonora's art, not to mention an expedient to lend grace to the protrusion of his nose. But not enough to hide how happy he is at that moment.

They have two children, who grow up with the daughter of Kati and José Horna in houses very near each other, full of cats and furniture created by the artist-mothers. They won't live happily and contented forever, but they'll die at a very old age.

Csiki at ninety-five, in 2007. Leonora almost at the same age, in 2011, having spent the preceding years with a man who was losing sight, mobility, and, finally, speech.

Leonora Carrington was, on the other hand, perfectly lucid accepting, with her upper-class-rebel sense of humor, a coup de théâtre equal to her surrealist imagination: the reappearance of the three boxes of negatives in the attic of a general, the former Mexican ambassador to Vichy, that her husband would have been able to walk to when, to let her paint in peace, he took the children to the Parque México. Or when, with the general dead and in '95 the general's heir dead, the artifacts are passed down to a grandson who finally understands what he has inherited, but puts the boxes back in a closet whose doors he keeps closed for twelve more years: years of negotiations with the International Center of Photography and Cornell Capa, who, anxious to bring the "Mexican suitcase" to New York, somehow or other achieves, the exact opposite.

In the documentary *The Mexican Suitcase*, by Trisha Ziff, Leonora Carrington sits next to her son like a maternal divinity to be placated with cups of tea and cigarettes, rummages in her purse, and doesn't say a word. The excitement about the forty-five hundred negatives brought to light after Csiki's death doesn't concern her. She has already told her story: a shark-zeppelin that, avoiding a tornado, ferries in its belly a chosen few, among them a small man with a beret—bent over the page of a newspaper, alone.

Tiburón is a drawing auctioned by Sotheby's in 2008. Comparing the date attributed by the auction house (ca. 1942) to the dates reported in an obituary for the husband of the artist (*"En 1944, en una reunión en casa de José y Kati Horna, Chiki conoció a Leonora Carrington"*), imagination crashes head-on into the chronological order. But then one trusts in Leonora and tries to invent a fantastic leap.

In 1944 Leonora Carrington had the feeling that she had already seen Kati's timid friend, who was beginning to interest her. In Montparnasse, probably, when she was with Max Ernst, but how many people do we meet who aren't worth remembering. It was she who had seen him, she alone. The "*hasard objectif*" that André Breton spoke of had inspired her when drawing a gift for a friend ("Remedios, I told you I made you a charm—last night I had a fever of 38, autosuggestion, perhaps . . . ") who also had an escape from death in her bones. Remedios Varo, a Spanish Republican and surrealist painter, had fled from Barcelona to Paris, from Paris to Marseille, to sail from Casablanca in late 1941 on the Serpa Pinto. That is to say that while Leonora inserted her future husband into the belly of the apotropaic shark, he was waiting to get on the ship that had brought her friend to safety—proving that the truer reality travels in leaps, spirals, anticipations, halts invisible to the empirical eye. But Csiki, too, who never went out into the Mexican sun without his beret, had included a gift in his boxes.

When the "Mexican suitcase" is officially opened, seventy-four negatives come out that have nothing to do with the Spanish Civil War, among them the one of the photo at the Café du Dôme and the series of Gerda at the typewriter, which reveals another game of mirrors. The model is having fun acting like a diva being fought over by two photographers. Fred Stein captured the other photographer from behind, one shoe on the table, and in profile, while he was shooting. His dark hair is pulled back, he has an imposing nose. Csiki saved Fred Stein's stills, and Fred saved the image of Csiki Weisz photographing Gerda. Of that rescue Gerda was the moving force—like the shark with the rosy propellers that cuts through the turbine of death, because love is a propellant drawn from the past and you don't know where it will carry you.

What's left to imagine is the moment when Fred Stein

decided to separate the negatives of every image—posed, casual, even blurred and out of focus—in which Gerda appears.

The Steins had seen André during the days of the funeral march: drained of the strength to hold himself upright, spectral, unrecognizable. They had gone home, run the water ("Will you pour me a glass?"), taken off their shoes, lain down on the bed, perhaps embraced, perhaps not. It wasn't then that the idea of the gift surfaced but later, when he happened to ask "How's Capa?" and the acquaintance met at the café didn't know what to say. Fred mentions this exchange, Lilo looks at him: "What can we do?" Shrug.

You imagine that after the funeral they offered André their support, you always hypothesize backward, starting with the negatives that have reappeared. But they didn't see one another as much as they used to, and the fact that they had been friends of Gerda and then friends of a couple that was broken in that unspeakable way made that sincere offer a sequence of words without result.

Fred isn't resigned. At the time he had given Capa the photo at the Dôme and the best photographs of Gerda, but now they had another value. And it was now that Capa had to have them, have them all.

At that point Fred and Lilo get to work in the laboratory. But the closed door brings back the time when André and Gerda worked in their bathroom, the wait for the photos to surface duplicates the sensation of sinking, the alchemy that's good only for extracting the past that returns but doesn't come back to life.

"Enough, Fred. I don't think it'll do him any good if we're already upset."

There's a silence in which—maybe—Fred's eyes redden more than his wife's, but in the darkness of the laboratory you can't see. They don't move, they don't touch, for an instant they wait for a signal that arrives like a faint sigh from one of them.

"Let's give him all the negatives. We just have to find the

ones with 'Gerda' written on them. He doesn't have to look at them now."

"Sure?"

"What's the difference if they're here or in Rue Froidevaux?"

"Not much," says Lilo. "Csiki Weisz is a reliable fellow." And they take care of it very quickly.

It's true that Stein gave Capa a certain number of prints as well, because some reappear in 1979, just after the death of Franco. The new Spanish foreign minister receives from the Swedish ambassador a Louis Vuitton trunk found in Sweden that contains documents and letters belonging to Juan Negrín, the head of the Spanish government in exile, along with a hundred or so photographs by Capa, Chim, and Taro, plus some portraits of Taro at her typewriter. A journalist reaches Csiki on the phone, who confirms that he gave them to Negrín, begging him to deliver them to the Republican archives in Mexico. Where? In Bordeaux, shortly before the politician boarded a boat direct to London.

Bordeaux was the refuge of the last elected French government, a place of negotiations and diplomatic meetings, and this throws a new light on Csiki Weisz's bicycle trajectory. He wasn't looking for just any Spanish comrade; he was aiming at someone high enough to assure him that he would be leaving right away.

Arriving in the center, Csiki goes directly in search of people who count, Hôtel Splendid, they tell him, the lobby and the Grand Café are so crowded with politicians and other prominent types that his dusty figure passes unobserved. But when, in that throng, he finds the prime minister of the Spanish Republic, why does he leave him only the prints and not the boxes? Did Negrín tell him he didn't have room? Or did Csiki fear that he would be among the first to be arrested in the unfortunate event of a mishap and didn't want to entrust him with the negatives?

And so more pedaling, more trips: to the port, to the ticket offices of the steamship companies, screening all the public parks overcrowded with refugees, more and more exhausted. In the meantime, in a building he'd passed too many times, France had signed the armistice. He heard it on the radios turned up high, saturating the Atlantic air with an odor of the end of the world. There wasn't time to find someone with a place on a ship, he had to be content with that Chilean, and then out, away, hurry to Marseille.

The treasures that Csiki Weisz loaded onto his back truly had a surreal landing place, despite his obstinate prudence: the prints meant for Mexico ended up in Sweden, the negatives to be carried to the Chilean consulate in the diplomatic luggage were sent to Mexico City—discoveries confirming after the fact that it would have been impossible to get them back by following their traces.

But there is an element that raises some more questions, and it is, again, Csiki.

In a 1998 photo that shows him with Leonora at the age of

eighty-seven he's dressed as if he's about to go out. And if his memory, not his body, had begun to betray him, it would almost certainly have erased more recent memories rather than those tied to the negatives that reappeared in the city where he has spent a large part of his life. How is it that no one thought to get in touch with him? Why didn't anyone try to take him to see his boxes again, something that, perhaps, could have put pressure on those who had inherited them? Or was it Csiki who no longer wanted anything to do with the whole business? It's possible, certainly, that he was tired.

More than twenty years had passed since his friend's most famous photograph—the *Falling Soldier*—was accused of being inauthentic. At that time Csiki had been quick to send Cornell Capa a testimonial, in English, ready to be taken up in the debate.

In 1939, when the Germans approached Paris, I put all Bob's negatives in a rucksack and bicycled it to Bordeaux to try to get it on a ship to Mexico. I met a Chilean in the street and asked him to take my film packages to his consulate for safekeeping. He agreed.

The letter of '75 reechoes in an advertisement that Cornell sends to the French magazine *Photo*, when the Louis Vuitton trunk rekindles hopes of finding the negatives, which have now become crucial as evidence to clear his brother.

In 1940, before the German advance, my brother gave a friend a suitcase full of documents and negatives. On the way to Marseille, this man entrusted the suitcase to a former soldier from the Spanish Civil War who was supposed to hide it in the cellar of a Latin American consulate. The story ends here. The suitcase, despite much searching, has never been found. Naturally a miracle is possible. If anyone has information regarding it contact me and you will be blessed in advance.

Someone shows up. A team from the International Center for Photography departs to dig holes in the countryside of southern France and returns to New York empty-handed. Seen in hindsight, the undertaking couldn't have had a better outcome—and yet the advertisement, although correcting the mistake about the year in Csiki's letter, diverges from it with details that make it more imprecise. It doesn't matter that Cornell placed his brother in Paris when he was stuck in Mexico City—by another twist of fate later revealed to be salvific for the one who had loaded the negatives on his back. But why does a rucksack become a suitcase and Bordeaux disappear in favor of Marseille? And why, above all, does the consulate of Chile become a generic "Latin American consulate"? Why didn't Cornell realize that, if you want to reestablish a truth or recover a treasure, the precision of the footholds is essential?

Suddenly you think you can guess. A faint laugh cancels out every laborious reflection, a laugh that you imagine reached the inner ear of Cornell Capa when, before trying the ad in *Photo*, he began to plan an expedition to Chile.

"Forget it, you hear me? Let sleeping dogs lie."

It may be that the negatives were in Chile, but no one would turn up. They had become dangerous again, as when Csiki was pedaling in order not to be captured by the Germans. With luck, they would have ended up somewhere else, taking yet again the path of exile: in Mexico or Paris, wherever Chileans fleeing the country that had been very hospitable toward the Spanish refugees were welcomed.

"When one coup dies, another emerges. In Spain freedom is returning, magnificent, in Chile they haven't yet finished the dirty work. You want someone to get in trouble based on a

suspicion that they have something to do with some old photos? 'And what's the difference, anyway,' for Chim and Gerda
and me?"

Cornell names his brother numerous times a day, he still
often dreams about him, and sometimes those intense dreams
wake him in the night. It's Bandi who causes him worries, worries that fill his life, and if now he has the sensation that he can
almost hear him, it's not unusual for him to summon him to ask
for some advice. Who better to give it than the older brother
who has gone through wars and flights, threats of expulsion
and regimes? The great Robert Capa, however, wouldn't
understand that today not only politics can ruin him, and so
don't say *what's the difference, anyway,* Bob. Not when I'm
the one who's losing sleep over your negatives and who will go
on looking for them as long as I live . . . "

In the heat of driving out ingratitude, Cornell Capa no
longer hears his brother's voice. He says to himself, "I'll think
it over tomorrow," adjusts the covers, and goes back to sleep.

Rinvenire, to discover, and *inventare,* to invent, descendants
of the same verb, remind us that to recover something you have
to draw on memory, which is a form of imagination. And yet,
setting out on the search, you make some unpredictable discoveries. So the nocturnal dialogue between Cornell and Robert
Capa has brought to light a new clue. It was already there, black
on white, but you didn't see it. Cornell Capa didn't know that
the negative of the *Falling Soldier* wasn't in one of the three
boxes, and it was also impossible for the man who made them
to remember. But Csiki hadn't forgotten Bandi, who had
obtained false papers to get him out of a concentration camp.
The occasion had arrived to pay him back, even if he could do
nothing but add a tiny adjective: all. Yes, it was all.

But maybe "I put all Bob's negatives in a rucksack" didn't
ultimately satisfy Cornell Capa. So he could have called Csiki

to press him with a question: was that particular negative in the baggage left in Marseille?

"In Bordeaux."

"Who cares: was it there or not?"

"I think so . . . "

"But if you wrote that you took them all, it means it was there."

Silence falls in the receiver, or the meowing of a cat that takes advantage of the immobility of the man on the phone to seek attention.

"The photograph was among the ones I gave Juan Negrín, the negative must have been there, too."

Cornell understands that he isn't getting anything. Annoyed, he counters that Csiki could at least tell him in writing that the *Falling Soldier* was authentic, since in Paris he was the one who did the lab work.

"What do you want from me: a death certificate? Haven't you got enough? I wrote you that I tried to save *all* your brother's photographs, I can't do more than that: please, Cornell, leave me in peace."

Cornell, resigned, sends his greetings to Leonora and, at the end of the useless phone call, delivers the letter to his secretary.

Meanwhile Csiki, a little agitated, makes an effort to remember in spite of himself. In the green box Chim's work, in the ochre the clippings. So maybe among those? Or in the red box along with the battles of Madrid, Brunete, Teruel . . .

Then he remembers that he took a break to arrange Fred Stein's negatives and see how much space remained. He remembers the strips of Gerda at the typewriter, he remembers that even his portraits hadn't come out badly—she was so photogenic!—and it doesn't really matter that he had to leave them in Paris, along with most of his own work. The images that Bandi wanted to have—he had taken all of those, starting with the only shot where they're together, he at the height of happiness next to Gerda.

Maybe Csiki, having reprinted it more than once over the years at the Atelier Robert Capa, wondered how in the world, just at that precious instant, Gerda had a smile so far outside the range that illumines every other portrait of her. And then, you venture to imagine, he gave in to the curiosity to see the entire series blown up.

There she is, usual story, usual scene. Gerda at the table with a handsome youth who laughs, jokes, flirts. Suddenly, when he gets up to call the *garçon* or goes somewhere or other, Bandi appears and positions himself on the chair that has just become free. He smiles, smiles at Gerda, after saying something that, to a guy from Budapest, comes out as a joke ("I can't leave you alone for even an instant!"), but in fact comes out of absolute love of that girl, even though she likes to joke and flirt with others. The girl laughs, and in the picture she has a slightly artificial smile, but she's not an artificial girl, at all, and in fact she reprimands him: "Cut it out, O.K.?"

And Bandi immediately lowers his gaze, he's sixteen again and Julia is scolding him, only then he did it mostly for show, while with Gerda he's sincerely hurt. Then Fred photographed a wall of electoral propaganda and finally went back to the

Dôme, where Gerda has resumed talking to that other guy and Bandi must have left with his tail between his legs.

The audience for the second act is the same as before: Fred, who's shooting (but then is careful not to bring a print to his friends), and the man at the table behind, who's no longer smiling but, rather, seems a bit dismayed. Maybe he, too, was an émigré who could catch Gerda's growl word for word, or the tone of voice and the shake of the head were enough: *Mon dieu,* what a temper! These modern girls, but really . . .

Finally, there's you who wonder if the snapshot that comes out of the "Mexican suitcase" in some way changes what you imagined, or only contradicts the effect of the preceding shot, where the lovers are smiling at each other against the background of one of the most legendary spots in Paris. You realize, then, that it's more frequently the spectator who falsifies a photograph than the subject: and in the case of the snapshot at the Café du Dôme this is proved by the sequence of rediscovered negatives that reveal André's intrusion into Gerda's flirtation. Those snapshots, or *clichés,* as they're called in French, narrate a different story from the romantic cliché projected onto the famous portrait of the couple, but that view doesn't originate with a diffusion of the image that not even Benjamin could have foreseen. Maybe it begins when Capa brings the photo to New York, or even at the moment when Fred offers him that gift fated to send into oblivion everything that it doesn't frame: because souvenir photographs, and memories themselves, serve to forget.

Forget what? That she didn't feel the same rapture toward him that both snapshots capture on his face? That squabbles were the order of the day, because Gerda couldn't bear his jealousy of the boys she never stopped attracting? That if a tank hadn't crushed her he would probably have been an episode for Gerda, and she his great youthful love, who would take on the coloring of a beloved old photograph?

Capa couldn't have seen her with detachment during a time that, with Gerda's death, seems to have accelerated the flow of the sand in the hourglass. So you try again, now that you can interpret what the two images together narrate. There's the evidence that, although glowing with triumph at having stolen a rival's place, he immediately appears so contrite, as if admitting that he shouldn't behave as if Gerda were his. And finally it explains why, at that moment, she doesn't seem happy and in love. And yet she's laughing at some foolish thing that André has said to her, first she laughs and then she gets angry.

Couples break up or stay together for inscrutable reasons, maybe partly because the same man who so often exasperates you can still make you laugh. And if that wasn't enough—maybe because in the long term everything can become boring, maybe because there would be little to laugh about in the years to come—maybe need would have prevailed, or convenience, compelling them to confront those years together, if Gerda had returned to Paris. Fleeing with Chilean visas, starting again, thanks to *Life*, resuming the experiment of the agency on a grand scale and baptizing it Magnum . . .

Many couples that formed before or during or soon after the catastrophe that destroyed the world of their youth (Gerda's brothers and parents who had taken refuge in Yugoslavia were shot; Capa's father and older brother escaped, because they died in Budapest before the war) remain together all their lives: joined in the memory and the oblivion that they embody, living like a gift of good fortune any affinity that existed before that endless void. Lilo and Fred, Leonora and Csiki, and, finally a couple that forces the narrator to use the first person. My parents became engaged in the ghetto, found each other again after the war, loved each other and, at times, hated, amused, and supported each other, until death parted them. My mother, who had the stubborn coquetry of Gerda, could have been a cousin of hers. My father, like Capa a great storyteller, a younger brother. No, I have no trouble imagining Robert Capa and Gerda Taro on a bench in Central Park, she's telling him to straighten his shirt, he's grumbling *mein General, jawohl*, mocking her indelible accent, and she is irritated that he again has to play the clown, showoff. And while they continue to squabble, a kid passes on a skateboard in shorts and T-shirt so big that, as they flatten and swell in the wind, he looks like a giant, gaudy neon-colored bat and, since he's speeding just a foot or so from the noses of the two old people, they are silenced for a moment.

"That would have been something to photograph."

"*Ach!* Now where has he got to . . . "

Acknowledgments and Notes

First of all, I'd like to thank Irme Schaber.

I met *The Girl with the Leica* at a show organized by Schaber, and my book is based on her biography. (Unfortunately, the most up-to-date edition, of 2013, is available only in German.) Above all, she was truly generous in giving me access to the materials she had collected in the course of the work that brought out of oblivion the life and photographic oeuvre of Gerda Taro.

Warm thanks to Mario Bernardo[4] for his responses and to Zenone Sovilla for restoring the podcast in which Bernardo describes his time in the Resistance.

Thanks to Professor Giovanni Battimelli, of La Sapienza University, and to Nicoletta Valente, who opened to me the Vittorio Somenzi archive—which had never been examined before—and found the right volumes.

I'd like to thank Professor Peter Huber, of the University of Basel, and Harald Wittstock, the president of the Kämpfer und Freunde der Spanischen Republik 1936-1939 association, for information about Georg Kuritzkes. Thanks to Professor Paul Mendes-Flohr for information about Ina Britschgi-Schimmer.

[4] Mario Bernardo died in February 2019.

Thanks to Roberta Gado, who drove me around Leipzig and helped me consult the Staatsarchiv Sachsen.

Thanks to Giacomo Lunghini and Sabrina Ragucci for explaining how a Leica and an analogue reflex camera work.

Thanks to those who tried to rein in my mania for documentation, reminding me that I was writing a novel. It's true: although I've stayed close to the sources, the soul of the book is, necessarily, the product of my imagination.

I took the liberty of calling my protagonist Gerda, although her name was Gerta Pohorylle, because she herself preferred the softer and more common version of her name.

Thanks to all the friends, who listened to me, encouraged me, and supported me. They know who they are.

PHOTO CREDITS

ABOUT THE AUTHOR

Born in Munich to a Polish Jewish family, Helena Janeczek has been living in Italy for over thirty years. With *The Girl with the Leica* she won the Strega Prize, Italy's most prestigious literary award, and was a finalist for the Campiello Prize. She lives in Milan, Italy.